A Story for Mates

A.G.R

Published by ZANI

7P's, copyright © 2020 by A.G.R. Electronic compilation/ paperback edition copyright © 2020 by A.G.R.

All rights reserved. No part of this book may be reproduced, scanned, or transmitted in any form or by any means, electronic or mechanical, including photocopying, recording, or any information storage and retrieval system, without permission in writing from the publisher. Please do not participate in or encourage piracy of copyrighted materials in violation of the author's rights. Purchase only authorised eBook editions.

While the author has made every effort to provide accurate information at the time of publication, neither the publisher nor the author assumes any responsibility for errors, or for changes that occur after publication. Further, the publisher does not have any control over and does not assume any responsibility for author or third-party websites or their contents. How the eBook displays on a given reader is beyond the publisher's control.

For information contact:
info@zani.co.uk
ISBN: 978-1-5272-5836-5 (paperback)

This book has been printed and spaced

In such a way so as to ease its understanding

for people with reading difficulties.

Acknowledgements

I would like to thank the inventor(s) of Microsoft Word. It took me almost seventeen years to write my books and this was only achievable by using the technology you created which helped me to overcome my dyslexia and word blindness, thus enabling me to realise a yearning goal that for the whole of my frustrating younger years was beyond my reach. Whilst having a voice and telling a joke never evaded me, any literary acumen was always beyond my capabilities, but you gave me the 'pen' to cement my thoughts and I am truly grateful for your life-changing gift. I cannot believe that the word 'author' will now, hopefully, accompany my name, and not that of 'remedial', a tag that I was cruelly blighted with by short-sighted teachers that spread to the schoolyard, sending me on an angry, retaliatory and defensive path that forged my rebellious beginnings in life.

I feel at this point that I should point out that all

teachers were not short sighted: RIP Mr Alec 'Pop' Allan, a brilliant boxing coach, fund raiser for charities and mentor to many who should have received the OBE, and Mr Ron Hanson; whose voluntary work with the youth club kept a local generation on the straight and narrow, most of the time.

Also, to all my readers, numerous in number and you know who you are: not professionals but prolific readers, some friends and others I met along the way, usually after spotting you with a book in your hand.

Without your kind advice and stern critiques, I would never have been able to iron out and enhance my work. Learning how to write was difficult, but if not for you and Microsoft Word, learning how to write a book would have been, I think, impossible.

And you, 'EP', my inspiration, comrade, back-watcher, friend and cuz. We live in life as we do in these pages – together. Cheers arkid.

Introduction

Ireland—its mere mention for me brings forth many mixed emotions, none of which I shirk from or dislike. Even the fear and trepidation I once felt while treading its paths as a young soldier only serve to this day to continue to intrigue and excite. A bow-fiddling, whistle-piping, drum-beating, vibrant country, which in truth, despite its many troubles is simply a beautiful and inspiring place that delivers everything from its bustling cities to its picture-postcard villages set in backdrops of lush undulating fields and rolling hills. Hills, lots of them—calf-aching, back-breaking hills, many of them carpeting the base of tall mountains, which in turn give life to the lowlands through their numerous rivers and streams while guarding them like a well-kept secret. When the sun shines, its beauty overwhelms the beholder, as its many shades of green are pronounced as though oiled on a canvas, and when the rain falls, those oils mingle to create an arc of many colours that span the ranges and disappear beyond sight, possibly hinting at the location of that fabled pot of gold.

    On this day in 1985, the conditions were of the latter, providing a cold and damp scene for my books to begin, and although at its roots the story may sound political, the events that unfold are not. For this is a tale of the friendship and camaraderie that exists between lifelong mates, told as it happened, and I have attempted to pen it with no leniency to either side, colour, creed or cause. From its outset in the '80s through to the present day it continues, and always will do, so long as the people that were, and are still involved in it keep their hand in the game. How it all began will reveal itself in these pages, but one thing is for sure—that the future from that point would never be the same again, because this is a hand in a deadly game that cannot be stacked or walked away from. This is a game of life, which you play for the whole of your life.

    What have I learnt? That's a good question. Well, I'm still alive and still growing older, which is more than I can say for a lot of acquaintances and foes from my past, and I'm a bit wiser, so I like to think. But if I have learnt anything from my experiences, it is to never let your guard down. Never think that the past is in the past and what's done is done because it simply isn't. There's always someone with a long memory. Someone who thinks they have a score to settle and believes in an eye for an eye at any cost, a mentality that few people comprehend or understand. Stay alert, stay fit and keep one eye on the door because the day you are caught napping may just be the day your old friend 'the past' comes to pay you a visit.

Chapter One

The Killing of Finbar Flynn

South Armagh, Northern Ireland, 1985

A dark blue Transit van skipped along the narrow country lanes, splashing water on the hedges and drystone walls as it parted the numerous puddles in its path. Approaching a secluded crossroads, the vehicle was dropped through the gears, causing its engine to groan noisily as it was slowed and eventually brought to a halt close to the centre of the deserted road. The driver applied the handbrake, dragging the lever through the ratchets before looking over at his map, which was spread across the passenger seat beside him. A large circle had been drawn around a road junction and from that circle a line led to some writing that outlined his directions (Dromintee and Newry crossroads at the red TB). By his estimation, he was where he was supposed to be, confirmed in fact by the two-directional, white wooden sign that stood on the corner bearing both those names; and, on the right-hand side of the junction stood the TB the map had indicated, a bright red telephone box. The driver, happy with his location, released the handbrake and continued forward and to the right, crossing the white line entirely and bringing his vehicle to a halt alongside the red marker. Immediately, and with some disgruntled force, he switched off the windscreen wipers, silencing the annoying squeak that had accompanied him for the whole of his two-hour journey from Belfast, a journey that he had been in no mood for making.

"Fucking shitty rain," he mumbled to himself as the noise of its impact on the van grew louder. The dark, miserable and overcast weather that had shadowed the country for two days with intermittent showers was finally beginning to worsen into the storm that the weatherman had predicted for just as long.

Winding the window down, the driver stuck his head and an upturned hand out to check how heavy it was becoming, as though the amount of water falling on the roof and the windscreen was not a good enough indication of its force. With a contemplative sigh and wishes of being elsewhere, he took a long hard drag on the cigarette that hung from the corner of his mouth.

"Fucker," he further sighed as he removed the tab, which quickly became sodden from his rain-soaked fingers causing him with another sigh to eject it half-smoked into the hedge before winding the window back up and releasing his seat belt. Leaning forward, he used the back of his hand to clear the windscreen, as though a different view may change the conditions, but alas, whichever way he looked at it he was going to get wet.

"Mother fucker," further and more intense he cursed; he really didn't want to be there but he couldn't afford to be there too long either, so it was time to move his arse. Raising the collars of his jacket in preparation to get out, he was about to reach for the keys but thought twice about switching the engine off, deciding instead to turn the heater up and leave the vehicle running to ensure a warm and mist-free return. As he slid out of the door into the downpour, he turned and reached back for the map, which was about to turn dual-purpose. After serving its use in a directional capacity, it would now make a good umbrella. With it squared on top of his head like some oversized floppy hat, he took time to check his surroundings, looking as far into the quiet countryside as the weather permitted. The roads were empty, and apart from a single herd of cows, so were the fields that surrounded him. Some distance beyond the crossroads, though, he could make out the shape of a roadside tavern, and after wiping his brow and eyes, followed by a couple of squints, he was able to focus on its name. "The Three Steps Inn," he read and spoke quietly. The thought of a nice wet pint in a nice dry pub was a tempting pull, even at this early hour, but alas, once again he remembered that time was crucial and he had other duties to perform. He looked back at the beasts in the field, obliviously chewing the grass.

One of them raised its tail, and with quite some force, propelled its waste some distance across the ground behind it.

"I couldn't have put it better myself," the man mumbled while raising his gaze to the falling rain and muttering some more meteorological defamatory words before moving towards the phone in a tiptoed movement, attempting to search out the driest areas.

The man's name was Davy Mactazner. He was a large, ginger-haired, heavily built chap of portly stature, and once he had squeezed himself into the box, there wasn't much room left for manoeuvre. In a search for comfort he vigorously moved his large mass around, accompanied by the sound effects created by the crumpling and squeaking of his leather jacket, until eventually finding an acceptable position, his only use of the phone being as a shelf to rest his big arm in the limited space. The map now found yet another use, as it was crumpled up like chamois leather and used to wipe one of the small Perspex windows, giving him a limited view of the outside through the droplets that rolled down the exterior. He leaned his forehead against the window and began to hum a tune before stopping to curse the weather once again.

"Fucking rain. Will it never let up?" he moaned, while wiping the moisture of his words from the rectangular glass. Frustration and impatience niggled the big man. He was tired and his face showed signs of stress and lack of sleep, which probably accounted for his shortness of enthusiasm and bitter mood. His accent, which could only be derived thus far from his string of four-lettered fornicating words, was a mixture of New York and Belfast Irish, having spent nearly all his youth in the USA.

He was sixteen when he left the Big Apple to come to the Emerald Isle, but his colonial heritage could still be recognised in his husky tones and Yankee mispronunciations. Mactazner's early years were hard and unsettled. While other young men of his age were leaving Ireland to find their fortune in America, Davy was coming the other way in a move of self-preservation—he was fleeing the vengeance of an Italian mobster who had ordered his head on a platter and his balls as a keepsake. Back in the mid-sixties, it was still the Italians and the Irish that ran New York, long before the black gangs came along and got in on the act by taking charge of their own neighbourhoods. Mactazner's story was that one night he got into a knife fight over a turf war with a rival Italian gang member, except the Italian, not fancying the one-on-one confrontation, brought a gun as back-up. He shot Davy, shattering his shoulder, but Mactazner, even at that age, was a big powerful lad—probably the reason his opponent brought the gun—and he managed to get to the Italian several times with his blade and fists. The aftermath was that the young Italian bled to death from his wounds, which didn't go down well with his father, who turned out to be a top man in the Cosa-Nostra (Mafia). As soon as he was healed, Davy was shipped out of America to Ireland for his own safety, and being of a working age and built like a pack mule, he was put straight to work in the employment of the local coal merchant, delivering the heavy bags. But given his past and his attitude towards all things non-Celtic, he was always destined for other duties. A few years later, at the age of twenty in 1969, when the Troubles re-kindled, Davy was recruited straight into the ranks of the IRA, and the rest is history.

From his snug-fitting viewpoint looking back down the road a few yards beyond his van, Davy eventually saw his reason for being in the remote area on such a dreary morning. A man appeared from beneath a drain culvert, popping his head out like a shy rabbit leaving its burrow. Immediately, he began to scamper up the slippery rain-soaked walls of the roadside ditch, grabbing at the saturated earth for leverage. Once clear, he paused to check the roads were empty while trying to flick the sticky mud from his fingers and hands. Satisfied there was nobody in the area, he began a dash for the vehicle, keeping his back bent and head low as he moved. Reaching the van, he opened the side door, pausing for a moment to look at the telephone box to see who had driven to his rescue. A look of disgust replaced the one of appreciation as he recognised his cork-in-a-bottle saviour as Mactazner. The pair gave each other equally hate-filled looks before the man jumped inside the vehicle and slammed the door shut behind him. This was Davy's queue for departure. He eased himself out of the tight-fitting box and back into the rain. Again, he lifted the collars of his jacket before reaching into his pocket and taking out his cigarettes and lighter. Cupping his large hands, he shielded the flame from the weather, at the same time using the movement as a guise to check that his surroundings were still clear. The now-redundant map met its end. Screwing it up, he tossed the makeshift football into the air, which was met on the way down by his boot, volleying it over the hedge into the field of cows beside him. This wasn't a movement of play by Mactazner; it was more one of frustration and anger. Less than twenty-four hours earlier and only a few miles from where he was now, his best friend had been killed by the security forces. The loss, obviously the cause of his disgruntlement, was hitting him hard and he was blaming himself because he hadn't been there to help. In addition, his new passenger *had* been there and had survived the confrontation, which twisted Mactazner's gut in knots. He would gladly cut off both arms for the situation to be reversed and his friend to have survived and the man in the van to be in his place.

He returned to the vehicle at a lot slower pace, no longer caring about the weather as his thoughts became more solemn. His heart wanted to stay, as though the closer he was to where his friend had met his end, the closer they were together. He wanted to go to the place where his friend had fallen and look upon the ground with a prayer on his lips but that was impossible—the area would undoubtedly still be crawling with police and army personnel, and now he had picked up his passenger, he needed to leave, not hang around. After lingering at the van door for a moment of remembrance, he eventually opened it and climbed back inside, but not before looking skyward into the falling rain and saying the words, "See ye later, Finbar—Bronx is gonna miss ye." Bronx was his nickname, used only by one man—his best friend and comrade, the man who had been killed, Finbar Flynn.

Settling back into his driving seat, he once again lowered the window, but this time only a couple of inches—just enough to allow the cigarette smoke to escape—before switching the wipers back on, lowering the heater, selecting first gear and releasing the handbrake. Pulling away, he manoeuvred the vehicle into the crossroads, using the large area to do a U-turn before stopping and once again applying the handbrake. Looking in his mirror, he had noticed mud smeared on the side of his vehicle on the door where his passenger had entered. He climbed back out and gazed upon the tell-tale smudge that had obviously been made by a hand and would attract the attention of any Police or soldier that they passed.

"Fucking prick," he growled, as he wiped away the damning splodge with the sleeve of his leather jacket, wishing he had retained the map for yet another use. He thought about opening the door and delivering a bollocking, but common sense prevailed and he decided that the quicker he got back, the quicker he could get rid.

After he had travelled a few miles, the man in the back began to shout.

"Stop and pass me a cigarette, will ye?"

Mactazner could hear his passenger's request through the thin plywood that separated the cab from the rear, but he made no movement towards complying. A distance more was travelled before the request, which now sounded more like a demand, was reiterated.

"Stop the fucking van and pass me a cigarette back. Did you not hear me?"

Again, Mactazner had heard the repeated request but instead of pulling over, he reached to the dashboard where a number of cassette tapes lay. Picking up the first to hand, he read the label.

"That will do," he mumbled to himself through a self-satisfied grin before slotting it into the player. Frankie Goes to Hollywood began to boom out, and as if it wasn't loud enough, Mactazner increased the volume. The word 'relax' filled the cab, accompanied by Mactazner as he sang along with his baritone accompaniment. He wasn't normally a fan—Foster and Allen were more to his taste—but he wasn't bothered what he listened to so long as it drowned out his passenger's calls. The man in the back knew what Mactazner was up to and angrily banged his fist hard against the boarding.

"Fucking wanker," he shouted, but his curse only served to bring an even broader grin to Mactazner's face that lifted him slightly from his sadness, making the return journey a bit more bearable.

Back in their home town of Belfast, Mactazner drove the van into a warehouse, leaving the rain and the wind that now accompanied it behind. The vehicle was quickly sealed in by the actions of another man already inside pulling down the roller-shutter door and turning on the lights. For a few seconds, the room was in darkness before the strip lights began to flash, bringing illumination to the unit. Mactazner climbed out and walked around the vehicle, acknowledging the man at the shutter as he did.

"Do you have him?" asked the man.

"He's in the back," replied Mactazner as he slid open the side door.

Inside were some old carpet offcuts and cardboard, which began to move as from underneath emerged the mysterious passenger, who had been doing his best to keep warm on the journey.

"Come on, Maguire," beckoned Mactazner with a sarcastic tone. "You're safe now."

In the back, Maguire shuffled himself forward on his backside, grumpily throwing the rubbish out of his way as he hung his legs out of the side door.

"Fuck you, Mactazner," he retaliated while holding his head in his hands. He was cold, wet and in no mood for sarcasm after his night sleeping rough under a hedge, and the cold and bumpy journey back hadn't helped. "Do ye have a fucking cigarette or don't ye?" he asked, raising his eyes, knowing that Mactazner had heard him the first time nearly two hours before.

Mactazner took his cigs from his pocket, removed one, leaving the packet half full, and placed it in his mouth. He lit it and blew the smoke high into the air before replying with a smirk.

"No."

Maguire sighed, his patience stretched after his ordeal.

"I've been out all night in the rain freezing my fucking nuts off without a smoke. Now will ye give me a fucking fag?"

Mactazner didn't care how long Maguire had gone without a cigarette or how cold and wet he was—in fact, the colder the better as far as he was concerned. There was no love lost between the pair and he wasn't giving him anything. Instead, he just smoked his own, exaggerating his enjoyment in an attempt to wind up the situation.

"Will you two give it a fucking rest?"

The man who had pulled down the shutters cut short the confrontation before it went too far. It was common knowledge that they didn't like each other, but this was neither the time nor the place for their petty bickering.

"Mactazner," called the man as he approached the pair, "fuck off over there, ye big Yankee fucker."

He pointed towards a workbench, which stood a few metres away against the wall. Davy did as he was told and leant against it, still glaring at Maguire.

The third man was called Stanton. He was higher up in the organisation than Maguire and Mactazner, who between them formed two parts of a three-man team known as an ASU (Active Service Unit), and now it was time for Maguire to explain what had happened to their third member. Stanton took out his own cigarettes, placed one in his mouth and then Maguire's. He was a big, powerful man with a chest and arms to match his booming voice, which was now turned on to Maguire as he leant over him to give him a light.

"Right, Benny boy," he said firmly, calling Maguire by his first name but not with the tone of a friend. "Start from when Flynn picked you up yesterday morning and don't miss anything out. I want to know everything. What the fuck happened?"

Maguire pulled hard on his cigarette, as though trying to replenish the nicotine intake that he had missed out on overnight. At the same time, he ran his left hand over the top of his hair and down the back, where it was gathered together in a ponytail. He blew out the smoke and glanced at both men. Stanton waited impatiently for answers as to how he had lost his ASU leader and best man, while Mactazner stared with contempt, deep into Maguire's eyes, wanting to know what had happened to his best friend. Maguire gathered his thoughts and took another drag, before beginning to relate the happenings of the previous day.

"Flynn picked me up about eight thirty yesterday morning and the first thing I noticed was that *he* wasn't in the car." Maguire pointed at Mactazner with the two fingers he was using to hold his cigarette. The movement was more like a stab, which perhaps held a hidden urge.

"What was the reason for that? Where were you?" interrupted Stanton, questioning Mactazner.

"Flynn came to see me in O'Reilly's Bar the night before," he explained in a defensive manner. "He said it didn't need the three of us to pick up the weapons and from the directions he had been given, they were hidden in a hide that we had used before."

Stanton paused, thinking over the information, his interlude adding to Davy's guilt for not being there the previous morning.

"Fair enough," he accepted, before instructing Maguire to continue.

Maguire took another drag before resuming.

"By the time we arrived in Dromintee, it was nearly twelve. Like Mactazner said, Flynn seemed to know where he was going. I was bursting for a piss and had been asking him to pull over for the last ten miles. When he finally did pull over, he said we were about three hundred yards from the weapons and pointed at a crooked tree further down the road, which was the marker for the hide. Flynn told me to get out and piss where we were. You know what he was like—he said he didn't want me doing anything near the hide and leaving a scent that might attract any army dogs in the future. I thought he was going to wait for me, so I left my fags and lighter on the dashboard, but instead he told me to keep a watch out for any vehicles coming from my direction before continuing the rest of the way himself."

Maguire paused once more to smoke, but was egged on by an impatient Stanton.

"Go on, keep talking."

Maguire quickly exhaled to resume.

"He was already out of the car and entering the tree line to retrieve the weapons before I had even put my dick away. I checked behind me down the lane, which was clear, so I started to walk towards him. He was soon coming back out of the woods and only yards from the car. I could see he was carrying a bag, which obviously contained the weapons. The next thing I heard was shots. Flynn fell to the ground and, within seconds, there were soldiers everywhere."

"So it was an ambush, but how did they know? You're sure they weren't just regular army on patrol that stumbled across you?" Stanton needed answers; when he had finished debriefing Maguire he had to go and explain to the people above him what had happened. And if it was an ambush, it could mean that there was a leak in the organisation.

"I don't know," continued Maguire. "I was too far away. I couldn't tell if they were regular army or SAS."

"And you didn't stick around long enough to find out," interrupted Mactazner, whose gut was twisting hearing the details of his friend's demise, continuing to blame himself because he hadn't been there to help.

"Fuck off, Mactazner, I was unarmed. What was I supposed to do?" Maguire reacted angrily to Mactazner's insinuation of cowardice. Again he pulled on his cigarette, his hand shaking with the cold from the wet clothes he was wearing as he raised it to his mouth.

"You can get changed in a moment," said Stanton, noticing his discomfort. At the same time, he gave Mactazner a look that told him to keep his mouth shut and stop butting in. "Carry on—what happened next?" he asked looking back towards Maguire.

"I froze," he replied, while raising his eyes to look at the pair. "For a second, as any man would with the shock," again he defended himself. "I didn't know whether to run or put my hands in the air, but the decision was made for me when two shots went over my head. That was when I realised that they probably were SAS, because they were shooting to kill. I wasn't going to stick around while they got their aim right, so I jumped over the wall I had just pissed against and rolled down the hill at the other side. I picked myself up at the bottom and headed for the woods. Luckily, I had a few hundred yards' head start. I ran through as much water and as many farmyards as I could, just in case they called in the dogs. I kept on the move for the rest of the day and when night fell, I used the safety of its cover to take shelter under a hedge. If I heard any helicopters, I mingled with the cows in the field just in case they were using infra-red. When morning broke, I moved to the drain culvert near the phone box from where I rang you to pick me up."

After finishing his story Maguire pulled on the last of his cigarette, before dropping what remained onto the floor and extinguishing it beneath the sole of his boot. With a sigh while releasing the smoke, he raised his head to look at Stanton and then Mactazner.

"I couldn't do anything to help Flynn," he added. "I swear it."

Stanton nodded his head, accepting Maguire's words, but Mactazner was having none of it and voiced his reluctance with a mumbled curse.

"Fucker."

The man who had been killed was called Finbar Flynn. His wife had been visited by the RUC (Royal Ulster Constabulary) the previous evening to inform her that her husband had been shot dead by the security forces, so Stanton, without hearing Maguire's version of the events, already knew the worst of it. Flynn, Mactazner and Maguire had worked together as a team for years and Flynn had spent most of that time stopping his two partners from killing each other. He had been one of the Belfast IRA's most respected members, watched closely by the higher echelon of the organisation and tipped one day to become one of its leaders, although by that time it would probably be under the banner of their political wing, Sinn Féin. It was all about the cause for Flynn. He had no aspirations of notoriety or personal gain, as there were for a lot of their members. He had a job to do and that was it. He believed in what he was fighting for and his vision was clear. Finbar didn't hate the British people; he hated the British Army being in

Northern Ireland. Get the British Army out, and the reunification of the north with the south were his goals. He was also a man of high morals and a stickler for professionalism, who expected all the men who worked with him to conduct themselves and behave in the same way, a code that most could not adhere, or live up to.

Sadly, he had left behind a wife and teenage son, the situation worsened by the fact that she was heavily pregnant and in no fit state to be burying a husband.

Stanton paced around the unit, deep in thought as to his next move. He knew there was nothing more to be done right now, except for him to report back to his superiors what Maguire had told him. But first, the main thing was to get the pair of them out of the way. Finishing his own cigarette, he brought the meeting to a close, looking towards Maguire with his final orders.

"Right, there are some clean clothes in the bag over there. Get out of those wet things and as soon as you are ready, the pair of you need to move your arses over the border to County Laois for a few days. John

Flanagan, who owns a guest house in Mountmellick, has entered you in the books for the last three days and he has several good witnesses who will swear that they have been pissed with you every night, so for anyone checking, it looks like that's where you've been, doing a spot of fishing. Put your personal dislikes aside for once and use the time you have together to strengthen your alibi. Make sure your stories tally exactly. And you, Maguire," Stanton's tone strengthened, "Make sure you have an answer ready for the reason why your fags and lighter with your fingerprints all over them were in Flynn's car yesterday morning. Stay there until we call and tell you it's safe to come back. We'll keep an eye on what the police get up to at this end and ring you as soon as possible. When you return, the bastards are bound to pull you in for questioning. Army intelligence will have photographed the three of you together enough times to know that you were part of the same team, but don't worry, when you return, we'll have our solicitors ready, so they'll have you out in time for the funeral. If you keep your stories straight and your mouths shut, that is."

Both Mactazner and Maguire's heads fell into their hands. The thought of spending another second in each other's company, let alone maybe another week, didn't appeal to either of them. And without Flynn there to keep the peace, it would probably end up in a lot of blood and snot. But orders were orders, so begrudgingly they both acknowledged agreement.

Mactazner, with a request of his own, turned to Stanton.

"Will you tell Catherine and young Michael why I can't visit? But tell them I will be at the funeral—there's nothing and no man that will keep me from that." He felt bad not being able to comfort his friend's wife and son but again, orders were orders.

"I'll pass the message on," confirmed Stanton. "Don't worry yourself, Catherine will understand."

Mactazner gave a nod. He knew Catherine would understand, because she had to. The visit she had received from the police the night before, telling her of her husband's death, was one she had been expecting to receive every time Finbar went out of the house. For the whole of their eighteen-year marriage he had fought for the cause, which made it as much a part of her life as it was of his. Like it or not, she had learned to take it in her stride, accepting his antics along with every other duty she performed every day as a wife, such as making the beds, washing the pots or putting the tea on the table, a thankless task with the only recognition coming from the odd loving pat on the back from Finbar.

He was seventeen, the same age as his son Michael was now, when he started, and he always knew that some day he may have to give his life for his beliefs. Well, that day had come, but it was Catherine who had truly made the sacrifice. She was the one left to pick up the pieces and it was her who would have to live with the loss of her husband and bring up their family alone. The next few years were going to be hard for her and she would undoubtedly call in to question whether the cause had been worth it, but right now she was certain it wasn't; nothing was worth the pain, no belief or cause.

Chapter Two

Milltown Cemetery

It was two weeks before the body of Finbar Flynn was released by the authorities so that he could be laid to rest. The papers had made his shooting front-page news every day since it happened, the main headline being the disagreement as to the circumstances of his death. Sinn Féin's argument was that Flynn was unarmed at the time of his shooting and called his killing an execution, alleging that the SAS had a secret shoot-to-kill policy, whereas the police, to rebut their claims, showed off the weapons that were inside the bag that he was carrying as proof and evidence that he was. Maguire's renditions of the happenings that day were basically confirmed by the press releases of the police, and although he and Mactazner were arrested upon their return from the south, no charges were brought and they were both released, as Stanton had predicted.

Combined with the publicity and the fact that Finbar Flynn was so widely respected, his funeral was going to be one of the biggest that Belfast had ever seen. But that wasn't the way Catherine his wife would have wanted it; she would have preferred a quiet ceremony without the fuss. Not just because she was pregnant and wanted to say her private goodbyes to a husband she loved, but also because she was worried about what effect the whole thing may have on their seventeen-year-old son, Michael. But the IRA and Sinn Féin weren't going to allow that. It would mean missing out on an opportunity to gain massive amounts of sympathy and funding for their cause. The burying of a man such as Finbar with full military honours was worth its weight in gold, both for the media coverage and in the collection boxes of their biggest backer, the American sympathy group NORAID. It wasn't as though the organisations were using Flynn's death—if he weren't the man in the box, Finbar would be burying one of his fallen comrades with exactly the same regalia. It had been done that way before and no doubt it would be done that way again.

It was a cold, damp morning when Catherine and her son Michael stood at the centre of the numerous mourners that had gathered in Belfast's Milltown cemetery for the funeral. The coffin, draped illegally with the Irish tricolour flag as a sign of resistance, lay on two trestles next to a large hole in the ground, which was to be the final resting place of Finbar Flynn. Behind the tearful pair, with his steadying hands on their shoulders, stood Davy Mactazner, trying to give as much comfort and support as he could while desperately fighting back his own overwhelming urge to join them in their sobbing. On the outskirts of the funeral looking in were tens of reporters representing the different television stations that were covering the high-interest ceremony and above, high in the sky, so high that the rotor blades could not be heard, an army helicopter hovered, videoing every move of the crowd below. This was a normal occurrence at high-profile funerals and gatherings such as this, not only as a security measure but also as an effective way for the police and army to identify sympathisers to the cause and gather as much intelligence as possible.

One after another, the political heads of the organisation climbed on their soapboxes to call for justice, not only for Finbar but for all the Northern Irish Catholic people. Rising calls of freedom and support for the cause filled the air, stirring the crowds of mourners into rapturous applause and cheers of support. The service, which now more resembled a rally, started to draw to a close when the coffin was gently lowered by straps deep into the snug-fitting hole while the priest, with a hand full of soil, began to recite the famous last words of, "earth to earth, ashes to ashes, and dust to dust." As he scattered the damp mud over Finbar's casket, suddenly and swiftly from out of the crowd, three men emerged wearing paramilitary-type uniforms and balaclavas to hide their identities, prepared to deliver the second sign of resistance. They lined up alongside the grave and together, under the orders of a fourth man, raised the handguns they carried and fired a volley of three shots into the air. Finbar's son, young Michael, held his grieving mother tightly, his embrace growing stronger as each deafening volley was released, causing the pair to flinch as though every shot represented another nail being hammered into Finbar's coffin. Their job done, the honour guard, while being applauded by the mourners, disappeared back into the safety and cover of the crowd. The military salute they had provided hadn't exactly been up to the standard of the Royal Marines, but it had served its purpose. The IRA had turned the loss of one of their premier members into a successful final show of defiance. But for a grieving mother and son, there was no success, no rising hope or upliftment. For the pair of them there was only emptiness and loss.

The widow, still propped by her young son and flanked by Mactazner, stood firm at the graveside long after the mass of mourners and onlookers had dispersed.

In fact, they were still stood there over an hour later, as the machine approached to backfill the soil. Davy beckoned the cemetery workers, holding them back with a word and obtaining two shovels. Handing one to young Michael, he assured him with a wink that it was the right and proper thing to do, as together they began to bury their friend and father watched proudly by his widow. As Michael cut into the earth, his tears mingled with every shovelled load that he gently cast upon his father's casket, which, when disappearing under the falling earth, brought home to him the reality that he would never see him again. A husband, a father and a friend had gone, leaving a void that could never again be filled. From this day forward, when Finbar was talked about, the stories that were told would always be preceded with the words, "Do ye remember?" and ended with: "Bless his memory."

With the coffin shallowly covered, Davy managed to prise the pair away, leaving the rest of the duties to the gravediggers. They had done enough; it was a final mark of respect that they would remember for the rest of their lives. They left the grave and made their way slowly to the cemetery gates, resisting the temptation to look back, keeping instead their fondest memories as their last, and not that of a JCB over a hole.

Stood waiting at the entrance from where he had been watching was Stanton, who made eye contact with Mactazner as he neared. Davy made his excuses to Catherine and Michael, then broke away for the quiet word he knew Stanton obviously wanted. They waited a moment before speaking, allowing the mother and son time to climb into the waiting hearse. Stanton gestured his respects with a raise of his hand and the lowering of his head. The movement seen by young Michael was acknowledged with a return nod, followed by a smile of thanks towards Davy. Stanton watched the chauffeur close the car door behind them and the vehicle pull away before starting his conversation with Mactazner.

"It will be you now that I contact when there's work to be done. You and Maguire will stay together and

I'll bring in another man, maybe two, to make up your numbers."

"NO," was Mactazner's quick and stern reply to Stanton's proposal.

"What do you mean 'no'?" This was a word that Stanton seldom heard following any of his requests. "Look, Davy, I know you're upset about Finbar, but there have been other good men that have gone before him and no doubt there will be more in the future."

Mactazner knew that but it didn't make any difference. Finbar was his only friend and his only reason for sticking around. Doing his duty wasn't a problem, but doing it in Belfast without him was. He pulled out his cigarettes and gave one to Stanton, followed by a light and his reasons.

"Look, I'll carry on doing my bit but not here and not with that fucking dickhead Maguire. I'm getting out of Ireland and not just for a while—for good."

"Ye're not thinking of going back to America, are ye?"

"I shouldn't think that would be a good idea," replied Davy with a smirk. "The old mob boss may be dead but there's plenty of his Italian family that would love to hear that I was back walking the West Side streets of New York. No, I'm going to London and taking my daughter Demelza with me. I have distant family there that she has never met. Maybe Flynn's death has left me feeling a bit vulnerable, but either way, just in case the same fate befalls me, I think it's about time she did meet them so she isn't left fending for herself. When you've something for me to do, let me know and I'll do it, but keep Maguire away from me and mine."

Mactazner made his intentions clear. It was obviously something he had already considered, knowing this conversation would arise. Maybe it was the tone in his voice or the delivery of his refusal, but he received no argument from Stanton, who seemed to accept that there would be no talking him round.

"Okay, I'm not sure how it will go down, but I'll sort it and give the move my blessing. Give me a call when you get there and we'll sort you out something steady so you're earning a wage."

"What do you have in mind?" asked Davy.

"There's a pub in Kilburn we need taking over quickly. The previous man we had running it died suddenly of a heart attack yesterday morning. How would you feel about becoming a landlord?"

Mactazner, with a pout of his lips, gave the suggestion a little thought.

"Well, I know my way around a pint," he admitted with a gentle tap of his belly. "The rest should come easy enough."

"There will obviously be other things involved. You'll be taking over the duties of Q.M. (Quartermaster). But we'll discuss that later. Anyway, if ye fancy the job, I think I can swing it for ye."

"Fair play," replied Mactazner, holding out his hand appreciatively. Stanton shook it, while voicing his regrets.

"I can't say I'm happy about losing you. It's my second big hit within a month." Stanton glanced back towards Finbar's grave. "But I can sympathise with your reasons. I feel the same way about Maguire myself. I may even have to promote the fucker so I can get rid of him."

"Do what the fuck you want with him; just don't send him to London."

Stanton and Davy shared an agreeing smile before the two men parted, leaving the cemetery empty apart from the JCB and its driver, who was putting the finishing touches to the grave of Finbar Flynn.

Chapter Three

The Deed

<u>Twelve years later – December 31st 1997</u>

Beeeeeeeep! The horn sounded on the car as it screeched to a halt to avoid hitting the group of lads crossing the road. A few choice words formed on the lips of the driver, who quickly calmed down as the pedestrians raised their hands apologetically while hurrying to the curb. They weren't bad lads, just a group of off-duty homesick squaddies trying to let off some steam while out for a New Year's Eve drink.

Bangor is a beautiful seaside town in County Down on the northeast coast of Northern Ireland. It was a favourite haunt for soldiers stationed at camps within a few hours' drive: Ballykinler Barracks an hour along the coast and Palace Barracks, Belfast, to name but two of the many. It was a great place, with plenty of bars and women, and being a largely Protestant area made it a reasonably safe place for off-duty soldiers to enjoy a drink. But even though Northern Ireland was in the midst of a ceasefire and its troubles were supposedly coming to an end, it was still advisable to keep your guard up at all times.

The group of men carried on fooling around as they made their way towards the booming disco music echoing through the doors of the next bar on their route. Beyond, a few hundred yards further up the street, a blue Ford Escort with four occupants was parked. A cigarette end flew out of the passenger-side window, followed by a puff of exhaled smoke.

"Would you look at those fucking idiots? They walk our streets all day with their guns in their hands playing soldiers and then come out at night like some do-gooder called a ceasefire and we're all the best of pals."

The passenger doing the talking was a now mature

Michael Flynn. He was the leader of the four men in the car and just like his father, Mactazner and Maguire, they also formed an ASU—basically the business end of the IRA.

    Michael had grown up to be the double of his father, even sharing his differently coloured green and blue eyes, along with his chiselled features and reasonable good looks. He wasn't a pretty boy, nor did he try to be, and he would have never been chosen as a member of a boy band, but he wasn't un-pleasing to the eye either, his looks were more rugged, again like his father and that suited him fine. Even his mannerisms were the same, right down to his gait and stance—so much so that he often caused the locals in his home town who were old enough to remember his father to look twice in a double-take movement. His colouring, though, was all from his mother. From his freckled skin to her light brown, almost blonde hair, his shading was all hers. He was about 6'2 in height with a strong pair of shoulders and a lean muscular frame which he tried to keep in shape but his training regime often fell fowl to days out with his mates and too many Guinness.

Next to him in the driver's seat was Sean Keenan, but everybody called him Fatty. He never stopped eating, drinking or smoking, and was a walking advert for a coronary, but he could drive anything, car or machinery, and was afraid of nothing and no man. You had to be careful what you said and did around Sean because if he could make a joke or take the piss out of a situation, he would do, repeatedly and excessively, and he didn't care how close to the bone he got. This part of his character often earned him another nickname—'toothache'—because he was that annoying.

The large man behind him in the back seat was Danny. He and Sean were brothers, but you would never have guessed it. Danny was six foot four and eighteen stone, good-looking and loved to exercise, whereas his brother Sean was five foot nine and 19 stone. The only part of his body that got exercised was his right arm while lifting a pork pie, or a pint, or both. There were always plenty of jokes about the milkman when the two brothers were together, but not in Danny's earshot—not if you wanted to keep your teeth and the rest of your facial features intact. It hadn't always been that way though. Up until their teenage years they had looked similar, but after that, Danny grew, up whereas Sean grew out. The brothers moved to Belfast when Danny was twelve and Sean was eleven, after their father took work on the shipyards. Leaving the tranquillity of the Wicklow Mountains in the south for the Troubles of Belfast was a bit of a culture shock, to say the least, but they were eased into their unfamiliar surroundings by their newfound friend on the school-yard, Michael Flynn. You didn't get much change out of Danny. He was tight-lipped about everything and the conversations he did have were mostly kept between himself and Michael. He had three passions in life: his mates, which amounted to a grand total of three, one of whom was his own brother; horse-racing; and women. But while finding a woman was never a problem for the big man, finding a winner on the nags more often than not eluded him.

The last of the group was Dermot (the worrier) Barry, a bit of a gormless-looking lad who always had the world on his shoulders, or so he thought. You could count on Dermot to see the downside of any situation and his worrying often made him a prime target for most of Sean's jokes and piss-taking. In fact, to him, Sean wasn't just toothache, he was also earache and a pain in the arse all rolled into one. Dermot would seem to be the odd one out of the quartet, looking more like a public schoolboy than a member of a hardened gang, but looks can be deceiving because he was no fool. His specialities didn't just stop at weapons; he was also a bit of a whizz-kid with explosives and, when it came to the crunch, he would never leave his mates. Like the other three he brought something different to the table, which, along with their loyalty to each other, was what made them such a formidable force.

Michael had always been the leader of the four; he wasn't chosen or elected, it just happened that way. Even when they were kids on the streets of Belfast, throwing stones at the security forces, he had always taken charge. He wasn't the biggest or the oldest, but he was the brightest and the quickest and he had a way about him that everyone liked. He had been brought up to be a gentleman but he could turn into a ruthless bastard at the blink of an eye and then back again as though nothing had happened. He had an eagerness to seek out new challenges, almost as though he had something to prove or was carrying a grudge, which would reveal itself from time to time, often involving an elaborate plan, which in turn would involve his mates, which in turn would mean trouble. He had come a long way since the day of his father's funeral, but the direction he had taken was not of his mother's choosing. Despite all her numerous pleadings, he had followed the well-trodden path of his father's footsteps and joined the IRA. In a way, she knew nothing could stop that from happening, not after what had happened to Finbar, but nobody blamed her for her protests. She was a mother, and a real mother's loyalty will always be with her children before any cause or belief. Catherine had lost enough to the troubles of Northern Ireland and now every day she was in fear of losing more—a fear heightened because Michael's younger brother Peter was now approaching his teens. But the cause was something that Michael, like his father, believed in; and like his father, he was prepared to die for that belief. This was a sickening knowledge that sat deep in his mother's stomach and she had to live with it every day.

He was recruited into the ranks by one of his father's old partners, Benny Maguire, who was now the equivalent of a captain in the organisation. Maguire was in charge of Michael and the ASU that he and his friends formed, but the relationship was a strained one, and in the past it had seen its fair share of problems. The lads received all their orders through Maguire, but there were plenty above him. It went all the way up to majors and generals, just like the structure of any army.

Before the mid-1970s, the IRA was one large organisation, covering the whole of Northern Ireland and stretching into the safety of the south. All this changed though, when one man who was caught decided to turn Queen's evidence and brought down nearly half of its members in what came to be known as the supergrass trials. Now each of the six counties took charge of its own force, with only one leader. This man would meet with the other division commanders to discuss and make plans, but the trust was gone. These men were not just chosen as leaders because they had risen through the ranks; they were also chosen because they had large families and a lot to lose. In other words, it made it impossible to take everyone you loved into witness protection. It was a good safeguard to make sure that members who were caught kept their mouths shut, but even with these safeguards in place, it was still run on a need-to-know basis. You only met the people you needed to meet, so if you were caught and did decide to cut a deal, the damage was kept to a minimum.

From the car, the four continued to watch the group of off-duty soldiers as the last of them filed into the bar.

"I suppose in some ways a ceasefire has been called," remarked Dermot from the back seat. "Maguire will be none too happy if we go killing anyone while the talks are going on; we've been warned off once already."

"Fuck Maguire and his fucking peace talks," ranted Sean, while puffing disagreeably on a tab. "It's been ten years since they signed the Anglo-Irish Agreement and since then, it's been one bollocks peace talks and ceasefire after another."

"I'm only saying," continued Dermot, while wafting Sean's cigarette smoke away from his face. "We've had our orders."

"Calm down, boys," interrupted Michael. "No one's killing anybody; we're just going to have some fun. I just want to let these fuckers know that they can't be doing as they please, just because Sinn Féin and Paisley are sat around a table with the British Government at Stormont Castle."

"I wish I was sat around that table with a loaded gun. There would be a few less for dinner, I can tell ye."

Michael smiled at Sean's input: even when he was talking about killing people, he still managed to get in a reference to food. He lit another cigarette and passed one to Danny and then Sean, who lit his with the end of the one he was just finishing.

"Lower your window, ye chain-smoking fat fucker,"

protested Dermot, being the only one of the group who received his nicotine intake passively.

"There are three of us in the car smoking. How come you're picking on me?"

"Because their windows are down and they're blowing the smoke out."

Sean reached for the window-winder, muttering abuse at Dermot's moaning.

"Don't bother," interrupted Michael stopping him from going any further. "You're getting out now, the pair of ye. Make your way into the bar to do the business while Danny and me get into position outside." Michael raised his arm and pulled his sleeve back from the face of his watch. "It's nine thirty now. Try to get one out to us as close to ten o'clock as you can. Have ye got that?"

"Okay, ten o'clock," Sean repeated, as he and Dermot got out of the car and made their way down the street towards their objective.

Things were in full swing as the pair entered the premises. Sean pushed his way through the crowd towards the bar to order some drinks, while Dermot followed in the void that was conveniently created behind him.

"Two bottles of Pils, please," he shouted to the barman over the music, mouthing his order prominently and holding up two fingers. The barman took the drinks from the cooler, removed the tops and placed them on the bar, holding up five fingers, indicating the cost.

"Fuck me," said Sean, shocked at the price as he begrudgingly passed over a five-pound note. "Keep the change!" he said with a sarcastic grin, then turned and passed one back.

"I wanted a pint, not a bottle," complained Dermot upon receipt of the beverage and examining the label. Sean lowered his drink from his lips in disbelief.

"You could have had Dom fucking Perignon for what they just cost me. Now shut the fuck up and drink it, you ungrateful shit." With a sigh and a shake of the head he took a large drink from the bottleneck while surveying the room. "Besides," he continued, "the doctors told me it's good for me as part of my diet."

Dermot stopped mid-drink and looked at Sean.

"That's some fucking doctor you have there. They don't often recommend that you drink Pils as part of your diet."

"Well, I wasn't going give up the drink altogether so we came to a compromise, the doctor and me: we agreed that I would stick to the Pils. When it's brewed, all the sugar is turned to alcohol. Haven't you seen the fucking advert with that little fella, Donald Pleasance, wearing the glasses?"

Dermot still wasn't convinced.

"I've seen the advert, but I don't see much weight-loss!"

"Give it time, will ye? I've only been on the diet a week. In a month or so my doctor has assured me that the weight will be dropping off me."

Dermot shook his head, smiling, while gazing down at Sean's gut and the rest of his mass.

"I think you have more chance of being hit by a surf-board in Belfast than you have of losing any weight off that fat arse."

"What are you talking about?" replied Sean, with

a confused expression. "There aren't any surfers in Belfast."

"Exactly, ye fat fucker."

Sean gave Dermot a dirty look, not appreciating the jokes coming the other way.

"Would you not give a man a bit of encouragement, instead of pulling him to pieces all the time?

"Me pulling you to bits?" exclaimed Dermot. "That's rich, coming from you."

Sean ignored his reply. They both took another drink in a momentary pause, like two lovers taking a break from a tiff.

"Look, here we go." Sean nudged Dermot with his elbow and used his bottle to point across the room towards the toilets. "There's a queue forming at the bogs. What time do you have?"

"Nine fifty," replied Dermot, checking his watch.

"Right, I'll go off and do the business. You wait by the door where you can see me and I'll give you a nod when I have a bite."

Sean made his way towards the toilets, taking

a shortcut across the dance floor. In an attempt to blend in with the people using it, he shuffled his feet and gave the odd wiggle of his large hips in time to the music. He was surprisingly light on his feet for a big man, but a few of his fellow boppers still fell fowl of his swaying mass. He joined the queue, timing it perfectly, and positioned himself in front of what looked like and he presumed to be one of the off-duty soldiers. He paused for a moment, waiting for the right time to strike up a conversation, which he eventually and clumsily initiated by standing accidentally on the man's foot.

"Sorry, fella," apologised Sean, pulling back his leg. "We're a bit short of space. It's like this every week in here. They cram you in like fucking sardines and people are always queuing for the bog. I didn't break your toes did I? This bit of excess I'm carrying weighs on a bit." Sean tapped his belly with a smile, trying to draw the man into a conversation.

"Don't worry about it, mate," replied the man, latching on and confirming to Sean with his accent that he had the right target. "No harm done. You're right about these toilets, though. I'm dying for a piss."

"Piss, is it?" answered Sean, quick as a flash. "I wish it was only a piss that I wanted. I'd nip outside down the passage but it's a shite I'm waiting on. Last night's curry's giving me the old ring-sting. My arse is twitching like a rabbit's nose."

The man laughed at his joke as the two of them were forced even closer by the pushing clubbers.

"Which passage is that?" asked the soldier, falling into Sean's web.

"Like I said, it's just outside. It's where they take the deliveries. All the locals use it. There's a gate, but it's never locked. Just give it a kick."

The man took a moment to study the length of the queue as to how long he could hold his bladder. He literally was bursting and Sean's makeshift urinal was sounding like a good idea.

"Just outside, you said?"

"Say again, fella," replied Sean, trying to sound uninterested.

"There's a passage, you said. Is it to the right or to the left?"

"To the right. Everyone uses it. I'd let you go before me but I'm touching cloth now. I have a bad case of the old Raj's revenge. Hopefully, the other crapper will become free first, which will save you having to follow me because I wouldn't advise it."

To add more weight to his off-putting description, Sean, who from being a young boy in the schoolyard playing party tricks had always been able to expel his hoarded gases on request, let go a ripper of a fart, which spat from the rear of his trousers like a Harley Davison motorbike being forced outwards through the cheeks of his big fat arse. At the same time he waved his hand behind his back from side to side to help aid circulation of the ejected sewage and cause as much odourised discomfort as possible.

"Phoo," he said, accompanying the comment with a look of disgust to hide his pride. "I don't want that one back. You could strip paint with that. Close your eyes, ladies," he added in a raised giggling voice. "That one's gonna sting."

The smell reached the man's nose and most of the noses of the other customers. It didn't seem possible in such crowded surroundings, but a space quickly formed around Sean, who stood with a look of approval on his face as though he had created a work of art. In fact, if you could hang a fart on the walls of the Tate gallery, Sean would be banging the nail in to mount this one right now. The escaping inhalers, most of them women who hadn't heeded his joked call, wrenched from their stomachs almost to convulsion, but the pungent release had done its job. The foul, almost throat-burning smell gave the man a good indication of the rest of the impending stench that was going to be emerging from that region and what would undoubtedly be waiting for him in the toilet after Sean had finished. Convinced that the passage was now his best option, with sealed lips and his nose pinched between two fingers, he exited towards the door in search of some much needed relief and fresh air. With his job done, Sean, from his raised position, looked over the heads of the people in the bar and gave Dermot the nod that their man was on his way. Dermot, when eyeing their approaching target immediately left through the door before turning to his right to pass the gate that Sean had spoken about, rapping hard on it twice when he did as a signal to get ready.

The passage was dark, damp and smelly. Old urine and stale beer accounted for the smell and a leaky gutter that ran along the side of the pub supplied the other. The soldier, who was coming to the end of relieving himself, moved from side to side whilst looking upwards, in an attempt to anticipate where the next drop may land, hoping to step out of its way. As he shook off the last drops that were falling from his manhood, his concentration was captured by a noise from deeper inside the passage. He zipped himself up and turned into the darkness, trying to give his eyes time to focus. Immediately, a realisation came over him that he was alone and that he had broken the golden rule of serving in Northern Ireland—never leave your mates. He turned hastily towards the gate in an attempt to get back to the security of the crowded bar, but instead ran straight into a brick wall in the shape of Big Danny, who let rip with a huge right hand, sending the man crashing to the ground. The unconscious soldier now lay rigid in his own urine which had rolled down the wall and pooled on the floor. Michael, the maker of the distracting noise, emerged from the shadows.

"Jesus, Danny. You nearly took his fucking head off."

"Well, now we have the fucker, what are we going do with him?"

"Like I said, Danny Boy, we're going to have some fun and give these soldier boys something to think about—a bit of a belated Christmas present for them."

"I hate to admit it, Michael, but Dermot was right. We can't kill him." Danny, while being the voice of caution, turned to secure the gate.

"We're not going to kill him. We're going to cut his fucking balls off."

"Castrate him?" Danny with a cringing face, winced at the thought. "Fuck me. That seems a bit harsh. Can we not just give him a good kicking and maybe jump on a few limbs?"

"Don't go getting squeamish on me big man. If we're going to make a statement without killing anyone, it will have to be something a little bit more frightening than a good slap and a few broken bones—now grab his legs."

Michael took the man's arms and Danny secured the other end as they carried him down the passage to the rear of the building. Danny, as he undid the soldier's trousers and pulled them down around his ankles, thought he had remembered something Michael hadn't.

"It's a good plan you have, but did you think on to bring a knife with ye."

"Fuck me, Danny. Use your loaf. We're at the back of a pub and surrounded by beer crates. Just take a bottle and break it."

Danny, realising his oversight, reached into one of the crates. He pulled out a bottle and read the label under the dim light, as though what beverage it had previously contained would make a difference as to its use as a cutting implement.

"Holsten Pils," he said, relating to Michael what was written. "Do ye know that silly fat fucking brother of mine has started drinking these things? He thinks they're going to help him lose some fucking weight off his fat arse." Michael made no reply, he simply smirked, believing the task to be as impossible as Danny obviously did. Breaking the bottle on the ground, the big man selected a suitable large shard from the many pieces, before returning to the soldier's crotch. Reaching out, he paused, having another cringing moment at the thought of touching another man's parts, before grabbing a handful of flesh and making an incision in the base of the sack.

"Hang on a minute, Danny Boy. Perhaps you're right," halted Michael after a rethink. "Maybe cutting both his balls off is a bit harsh. But he and his mates have to know how lucky he was."

"So, we give him a good kicking then?"

"No, we just take the one."

Michael's change of heart still seemed a little rough, but it was a compromise. Danny let go a quiet giggle.

"What's funny?"

"I was just thinking that his mates will probably nickname him 'economy' from now on."

"Why?" asked Michael, with a feeling of what was coming.

"Because he will only be shooting half a load in the future." Michael smiled. Playing the comedian wasn't Danny's forte, but that one was nearly funny. "Well, at least something is better than nothing," Danny added, as he slid one of the man's balls out of the opening before another pause. "Or they may call him Hitler. That could be another name that will suit him."

"Go on, then. Why would all his mates call him Hitler?" asked Michael, continuing to humour the big man.

"He only had one ball."

Michael looked at Danny with a shake of his head. He knew it wouldn't take long for the jokes to return to their usual crappy standard.

"Danny, Hitler did not only have one ball."

"He did so. They even wrote a song about it." Danny started to recite the jingle to prove a point. "Hitler has only got one ball. The other is in the Albert Hall."

"Danny, leave the jokes to your brother and get on

with the job in hand." Michael, with a sarcastic tilt of the head, looked down at what *was* in Danny's hand. "Are you enjoying that?" he added with a grin.

"Fuck you," replied Danny with a smile, followed by a quick movement of the shard, slicing the tube that connected the man's testicle to his scrotum, and 'the deed' was done.

"You look like you have done that before," remarked Michael, impressed by the skill and speed at which Danny had performed the procedure.

"If you are talking about the castration," Danny replied with a return tilt of his head, "I have, but the last time, I was fifteen and it was my horse I was gelding. You never know, it might make soldier boy here a better jumper. It did wonders for the horse."

Danny and Michael laughed at the gruesome joke as he placed the piece of gristle in the soldier's shirt pocket, before wiping his bloodied gloves down the front of it.

"So long as he doesn't try to do an Adolf and jump all over Europe," added Michael.

Again, the pair laughed as Danny looked at their victim, who was showing signs of coming around.

"Come on, let's get the fuck out of here. This place stinks and if he wakes up screaming, I'll have to knock the poor fucker out again."

Michael took a hold of their victim and leaned him up against the crates as though trying to make him comfortable. An odd thing to do, Danny thought to himself, after just separating him from his left nut!

"Stay there and we'll call you a taxi," he said talking to the unconscious man and gently tapping him on the cheek, before the two of them slid back down the alley. Danny, as they removed their gloves, let go another little chuckle.

"Go on," said Michael, expecting another crappy joke.

"I was just thinking that when they find your man minus one ball, there won't be a soldier in these Prod bars for months."

"Well, that was the whole point of it, Danny Boy. It's funny, when you think about it," he continued, almost explaining his reasoning for the macabre act they had just committed. "If we had just kneecapped the fucker or broke his legs, then all his soldier mates would be back down here drinking next week, in a show of defiance like nothing had happened. But if you castrate some fucker, it scares the shite out of every man."

Danny agreed. The thought of a good tear-up or receiving a good hiding had never bothered him, but if his nuts were on the line in place of a broken jaw, that would certainly make him think twice about getting involved.

Beyond the gate, the street was getting busy with drunken revellers all getting into the party spirit as the midnight hour and the New Year approached. The rowdy celebrations were going to provide the pair with good cover, allowing them to slip back into the street unnoticed. Michael slid off the bolt from the gate in preparation for their exit.

"Walk down to the phone box, Danny, and ring ye man an ambulance. We don't want him bleeding to death. I'll go back to the car to meet the lads and then we'll pick you up at the other end of town."

Danny gave Michael a pat on the back in acknowledgement before they both slid out of the gate and headed off in separate directions.

Chapter Four

Benny for Breakfast

"Michael, you've got ten minutes and your breakfast will be on the table. And wake yer brother, will ye."

It was Saturday morning now and Michael's mother was shouting at him from the foot of the stairs to get up. He rolled over to look at the clock on the bedside table just in time to see it change to 10.30 on the digital readout. The alarm was triggered and the radio came on. The Christmas number one, *Too Much* by the Spice Girls, annoyingly began to blare out, causing Michael's finger to come crashing down on the off switch. His hands now fell to his face, rubbing his cheeks and eyes. He contemplated turning over and having another hour in the comfort of his bed, but he had things to do and Catherine wouldn't be happy if he let her breakfast go to waste. Sitting up, he spun on his backside, putting his feet on the floor. The customary male morning ritual now followed, as he rubbed his eyes, soon accompanied by a vigorous scratch of his crotch before letting out a morning yawn and a stretch of his arms. At his feet were the underpants he had disregarded the previous night, which he picked up and placed under his nose, sniffing out the possibility that they may endure another wear.

"They'll do for an hour until I get a shower," he thought to himself, before sliding into them and moving across to the window, with the stretch now working its way down his legs to his feet. Pulling on the curtains, he scowled as light flooded the room and he looked down on the street below. It was a bright, crisp morning but obviously cold given the time of the year, confirmed by the people walking below in their thick coats and gloves. He reached down and touched the radiator under the window, which was on but wasn't exactly throwing out heat. Grabbing a T-shirt and some shorts from the drawer, he made his way out of the bedroom and down the hallway towards the bathroom, knocking on his brother's door as he passed.

"Come on, Peewee, you heard Ma!"

Peewee was Michael's nickname for his little brother Peter. He was twelve now and at that cheeky age just before his teens when he was about to be startled by puberty and discover that girls weren't just there to have their pig-tails pulled, both of which were fuelling his transition into a grumpy sack of tired hormones. He was also the reason why Michael still lived at home.

He wouldn't leave his mother and brother alone, not before Peewee left school and was working for himself. Michael didn't mind, though, and luckily neither did his girlfriend, Roisin. She understood his reasons for being there and gave him no grief.

He had done a good job stepping up to the plate and becoming the man of the house in the thirteen years since the death of his father. It had put an end to the larking about of his teenage years and it had built a part of his character that made him the man he was today.

One thing was for sure—his mother's predicament had been eased because of him.

Coming out of the bathroom, Peewee's door was still closed tightly. Michael opened it and switched on the light to reveal a room full of Celtic, Manchester United and George Best posters. Another mark to the footballer's greatness—even the Catholics loved him. Inside the bed, two skinny legs protruded from beneath a quilt patterned with the Celtic football club emblem.

"Come on, ye wee shite. Your breakfast is ready."

The two legs began to move, along with a few groans from the area of the pillows. Michael left the light on and the door open before making his way down the stairs while slipping his T-shirt over his head.

"And brush your teeth," he shouted as he reached the bottom and turned for the kitchen. Inside, his mother was hard at work in front of the oven, multi-tasking while making the breakfast.

"Morning, Ma," Michael greeted while taking a seat at the table.

"Morning, son. Is your brother up?"

"Nah, give him another ten minutes. By the way, Ma, give Pat the plumber a ring later—I think the heating is on the blink again."

Catherine, half-turning from her food-preparation, looked back at Michael with a knowing, smug, almost cheeky smile.

"There's nothing wrong with the heating. I turned the thermostat down, that's all."

"Why did you do that? It's freezing outside!"

"You're not outside, you're inside, so if you're cold, put some clothes on. What do you expect when you're walking around in the middle of winter in your shorts and a T-shirt?"

"That's my point, Ma. It is the middle of winter, so turn the heating back up."

"It costs too much money."

"I give you the money for the bills, Ma. If you need some more, just let me know."

"Don't be silly. I have more than enough for the bills." Michael looked blankly at his mother, confused at her reply.

"So, what's your problem? Turn it back up."

"If I turn it back up, then that will cut into the change I have after paying the bills." Michael was still none the wiser.

"So?" he prompted.

"So, I use the change to pay for my bingo."

Michael shook his head, happy that they had finally got to the bottom of the heating mystery.

"Ma, turn the heating back up and I'll put an extra twenty in your jock for the bingo."

"Okay," agreed his mother with a returning smug smile, as though the whole thing had been part of a cunning plan. "Were you with Roisin last night?" she asked, quickly changing the subject.

"Nah, just out with the boys." Trying to avert the new subject, Michael grabbed the newspaper and began to flick through the pages, quickly getting to the horse-racing section.

"What did you get up to? Did Roisin not mind that you didn't see the New Year in with her?" Michael gave a sigh, followed by the lowering of his paper and an incomplete answer.

"Mm."

"Mm? That's no answer. What does 'mmm' mean?"

"It means Roisin was fine, Ma. We're not joined at the hip. She was out with a few of the girls from the hairdressers, and me and the lads just had a few drinks that's all. Nothing special."

Ma placed his breakfast down in front of him with a large mug of tea, before returning to the side to butter some toast. Call it mother's intuition, but she couldn't help wondering what all the secrecy was about.

"What's up with Peewee? Why's he so knackered?" Michael asked.

"I let him stay up with me to see the New Year in. It was past one when he went to bed."

"Well, if he doesn't get up to eat his breakfast, he can have it warmed up for his tea. We can't afford to be throwing good food away with the price of the heating in this place." Michael gave his mother a sarcastic look to go with his jibe, but it was ignored as she stayed facing the cooker, pretending the comment had gone over her head. A knock came at the front door, causing them both to look up. Ma looked at the clock on the wall to see the hour approaching eleven.

"Are you expecting your friends?"

"No," replied Michael. "I'm meeting them down O'Reilly's bar later. It might be young Paddy Fahy for Peewee."

"Well, I can't think of who else it would be at this time on a Saturday morning."

"Well, if you pass the toast and answer the door, Ma, you'll find out sure."

Catherine put down the freshly buttered toast while giving her son a dirty look for his second piece of sarcasm. She wiped her hands on a tea towel before leaving the kitchen to find out who the caller was. While opening the door, she paused once more to shout up to young Peter, just in case it was his friend, but was cut short by the sight of who was there. To her, anyway, it was an unexpected blast from the past.

7P's

"It's Benny Maguire!" she called—or exclaimed would be more precise. She was shocked to see him to say the least. He hadn't been near the flat since before Finbar was killed. Michael said nothing on hearing his mother's shout. He expected a comeback concerning last night, but not this quick and not at home.

"Hello, Catherine. Is Michael in?"

"Well, I didn't think it was me you had come to see, Benny. Do you want tea?"

"No thanks. Just a bit of time with the lad."

Maguire had aged in the thirteen years since he and Catherine had last met, and she couldn't help giving him the once-over. When he removed his hat, she noticed that his hair and ponytail had gone, bringing a smile to her face as she remembered the jokes Finbar used to tell about it. He had also quit the cigarettes in exchange for a pipe, which he removed from his mouth.

"He's in the kitchen. Go through. I'll go get his lazy little brother up and make the beds, giving you time to talk. You can smoke your pipe if you please."

Catherine pointed at the kitchen door then took Maguire's hat and hung it on the rack.

"Thank you," he said, replacing the pipe back in his mouth as he watched her disappear up the stairs before entering the kitchen. Michael picked up his mug of tea and took a large drink, staring at Maguire over the rim as he entered. Maguire stared back through the smoke rising from his pipe as he made himself comfortable by leaning back against the kitchen units. The two were locked in a glare while Michael chewed on the food in his mouth. Deliberately, he took his time, eventually swallowing it before taking another drink and looking back at his visitor.

"Well, mister?" Maguire said, instigating the conversation with a tone that left Michael in no doubt that this wasn't a social call.

"Well what?"

"Did you do it?"

"Do what?"

"Come on, mister. Did you cut the knackers off that fucker in Bangor last night?"

"What makes you think I was in Bangor last night?"

"Because they got a description of your fat fucking mate Sean Keenan and that dopey twat Dermot Barry. That's what."

"Well, if you already know, then why are you asking?"

"Because I didn't think you would be that fucking stupid. You were told to leave things alone."

"You said no killing. We only took the one ball and we rang him an ambulance. He was never in any danger. Sure it was just a bit of fun to keep the Brits on their toes."

"Fun is it, mister? Well, fun isn't what I got at seven o' clock this fucking morning. It might as well have been me you cut the fucking balls off last night because I had them ripped off this morning."

"What's up? Are the boys down at the Sinn Féin office scared we might upset their peace talks?"

"You know they are. Orders are orders, Michael. I get mine and you get yours. You four have been good soldiers doing great things for the cause, the same as me and your father did, but Sinn Féin will get a seat in Parliament if these talks go right and they won't allow you and your mates to fuck that up."

"And while you and the boys from Sinn Féin are all becoming members of Parliament, what do we do, Maguire? First thing Monday morning, do me and the lads get our arses down the job centre with our P45,s and fill out some application forms? Let me see, how would the old CV read?

"Previous employer: IRA.

"Job description: freedom fighter.

"Tools of the trade: Armalite rifle and fertilizer explosives.

"Reason for leaving last employer: shafted up the arse and sold down the fucking river by wannabe politicians. Do you think we'll get many takers, Benny? And by the way, just what is the going rate the IRA are paying for redundancy these days?"

"You'll be looked after. There'll be other earners."

Michael's anger reached boiling point as he threw the cutlery in his hands onto the plate in front of him, reacting to Maguire's offer, which went against all his principles and everything he believed in.

"Other earners doing what, Maguire?" he repeated, disgusted at the thought at what he knew was being implied. "Demanding protection money from my own friends and breaking my neighbours' legs if they don't pay the going rate? Or should I stand outside Peter's school gates getting all his mates hooked on drugs so they turn into good customers? The young girls will be value for money though, eh, Benny? If they can't pay their smack or cocaine bill, I could always put them on the street corners, selling their arses for a fiver a time to cover their dues, which should delight all the dirty old fuckers and paedophiles in the area. By the time they are eighteen, they will be seasoned prostitutes and top-rate earners, if they haven't overdosed on heroin by then that is. No thanks, Maguire. That side of the business doesn't interest me. I'm no East European bully-boy mobster. I'm an Irish freedom fighter."

"If you're suddenly developing a conscience, Flynn, that's your problem, but you've been warned from the top to leave things alone. And remember this—shit rolls downhill and you and your mates are at the bottom."

"We know all about shit, Maguire. We've been listening to yours for the past ten years and I didn't need a conscience when we were fighting for what was right. It's what my father fought for and I was proud to follow in his footsteps."

Maguire stayed quiet for a moment, silenced at the mention of Finbar. Then, trying to reinstate his grip, he moved his pipe from one corner of his mouth to the other and intensified his stare.

"I've given you the message," he growled. "You know where you stand."

Michael laughed.

"Yeah, up to our necks in it, by the sounds of things," he replied, dismissing the glare and having none of the intended reprimand Maguire had turned up to give him.

Maguire reiterated his cutting look while puffing angrily on his pipe, causing the tobacco to glow bright orange as he sucked and bit hard on the end, trying to control his temper. He didn't like the answers he was getting but this was a confrontation that had been a long time coming. Now, with the peace agreement being signed and Sinn Féin soon to get their seat, the situation had only worsened.

There was going to be peace in Northern Ireland but a lot of people saw it as a sell-out. Just a way for the top boys to bow out safely with their pockets full while making sure that they didn't wake up one morning with their brains on their pillow next to them. A lot of Paisley's mob on the Protestant side felt the same. Peace is always good, but at whose cost, and whose gain?

Michael picked his knife and fork back up from his plate and returned to his food.

"If we're done here, Benny, my breakfast is getting cold."

"We're done, mister," replied Maguire, taking a firm grip on the kitchen door handle, still with his stare fixed on Michael. "There'll be no more warnings," were his final words on the matter.

Michael said nothing. He didn't even look at Maguire again. Instead, he just continued eating his breakfast, almost cutting through the plate in anger as he dissected his last sausage. Maguire closed the kitchen door behind him and came face-to-face with Catherine, who was between the bottom of the stairs and his way out. She had obviously heard most of what was said and was supporting a stare of her own, which wasn't going to go away without some answers. Once again, Maguire removed the pipe from his mouth, followed by a slightly nervous cough as though caught on his back foot.

"Catherine, would you have a word with the lad, make sure he does the right thing?" Michael's mother turned slightly and reached up to the stand to retrieve Maguire's hat. Passing it to him, she showed her displeasure, as only a woman can do, with a knowing and disappointing look.

"So you want him to do the right thing, Benny? The right thing for who? That boy has done everything you have asked so you can't blame him for being angry. I wanted him to have no part of it all but he's Finbar's son, you of all people should know that. I for one will be happy to see this agreement signed. Not because

I think it will be good for Ireland but at least it will be an end to the Troubles, although that's debatable. And if that means that I get to keep my sons away from danger then it gets my vote. I'm not on my own either. There's many the mother that thinks the same as I do. So I'll be having no words with the lad, Benny, at least not the ones you would have me say. Now take your hat and don't darken my door again because I've been coping just fine with the two of them these past years since Finbar was killed, just in case you or any of your mates down the Sinn Féin office were wondering."

Maguire turned but was stopped by one last thing Catherine had to get off her chest.

"Not one penny piece was I offered after Finbar was killed," she stressed with a pointed finger that jabbed into Maguire's chest. "Not one bag of shopping or even a few nappies when Peter was born. That's what I got from you and your cause, Benny. That was the thanks I got for losing my husband."

Silence was Maguire's answer, accompanied by a gob-smacked look, which was about as much use to

Catherine as the help she had already received. Angrily she bustled him out of the door and no time was wasted before it was closed sharply behind him. Maguire paused on the flat steps to replace his hat and refill his pipe, which gave him time to realise that his intentions when coming to the flat that morning were to give Michael a bollocking, but in her own little diplomatic way, Catherine had just given *him* one.

"Have you got an old pound, mister?"

Maguire looked up to the next flight of steps, where a young boy was sat with his hand outstretched in anticipation that his request would be fulfilled.

"Now why the fuck would I be wanting to give you a pound?" replied Maguire while lighting the fresh tobacco in his pipe.

"Because I've been looking after your car, the nice shiny silver one outside with the four wheels and no scratches."

"Of course it has four fucking wheels—it's a car, ye little scrag."

"Not if you don't give me a pound because you can't get down those stairs quicker than I can get to the window and shout to my mates that you're a tight-fisted old bastard that wouldn't pay."

Maguire, reacting to the threat, began to move up the stairs towards the young entrepreneur.

"Come here, ye cheeky wee bastard. I'll knock the living shite out of ye."

"Then it will cost you a fiver," replied the boy while standing his ground defiantly. "The price has already gone up to two quid."

Once again, for the second time that day, Maguire's pipe glowed bright orange as his anger over-spilled. It had been a shitty morning already and now he found himself in a standoff with a scruffy young waif. With a sigh of disbelief that he was being hustled, he began to shuffle through the change in his pocket, making sure that he brought nothing more out than the two pounds he was being mugged for.

"There, ye little fucker." Maguire threw the coins onto the stairs in front of the apprentice gangster. "And I won't forget your face."

"And I won't forget your car," replied the young boy with a smile and a 'two can play at that game' tone in his voice.

Maguire, powerless, frustrated and a little lighter in the pocket, continued his descent with the pipe smoke rising behind him and the young boy collecting the coins from the floor.

Ma returned to the kitchen and took the now cleared plate from in front of Michael and placed it in the sink. The air could have been cut with a knife. Michael knew she and Maguire had talked in the hall. How much she had heard he didn't know, but he was under no doubt that he was about to find out.

"'Nothing special.'"

There was a pause while Michael, with a puzzled look, turned his head from his paper.

"What, Ma?" he asked sheepishly, knowing that the onslaught had just begun.

"'Nothing special.' That's what you said when I asked you what you did last night."

"Ah, Ma. Leave it, will ye? Did I not just have all this with Maguire?" Michael thrashed about, showing his discomfort by discarding his paper to the table, but he knew he had been caught out.

"Come on, son. It's not Maguire that I'm worried about. He's only the messenger boy. It's the ones that pull his strings that bother me." Michael hung and shook his head, cursing Maguire's visit. The least his mother knew about what he got up to, the better, especially when it was put on his toes on a Saturday morning while still eating his breakfast. He cursed the man, wondering how his father ever stood him in his presence.

Young Peter finally emerged into the kitchen for his breakfast, causing an interlude in the conversation. He slumped in one of the chairs, placed his arms on the table and rested his head in an attempt to return to his slumber. Michael used his brother's sleepy entrance as a means of escape. Picking up his tea and the paper, he made his way into the living room, but had barely time to switch the television on before his mother was at him again. As she closed the door behind herself, Michael made himself comfortable for the continuation of the nagging.

"Look, son, I don't care what you and your mates got up to last night. I was used to all that with your father, but these are dangerous times and if Maguire is at our door for the first time in over a decade this early on a Saturday morning, it means that someone has rattled his cage. And that could mean trouble."

Catherine moved away from the door and sat down on the arm of the sofa. She stretched across to Michael's chair and placed her hand on his. The tone in her voice softened as she tried to explain her worries.

"Michael, I've been watching the politics of Ireland since I was a young girl. Not that my opinion ever mattered or counted for much, nor has the opinion of any woman for that matter. But I haven't been walking around with my eyes closed, just because I'm a woman. Now, I saw it with your father and I'm seeing it again with you, so don't brush me off as a nagging mother." Again, she stroked his hand and gave him a smile. "Ye know, sometimes, when you were young and in bed, your father and I would stay up until the early hours of the morning discussing his problems, and do you know why son?"

Michael shook his head slightly and looked at his mother for an answer to her question.

"Because I was the only one he could trust. Don't get me wrong, he trusted Davy Mactazner, but there were some things even he couldn't know. That's why I know that you have to be at your most careful when there's a prize on the table, because it will bring all the back-stabbers and wannabes out of the woodwork. And when the money or the prize on the table is big enough, people will sell their own mothers for a piece of it, so they won't give a second's thought about getting rid of the likes of you and your mates."

"I presume by 'the prize' you're referring to the agreement and the seat Sinn Féin will get in Parliament."

"Exactly, son, but don't think that that's the only perk they will be getting for convincing the IRA to accept the terms. There'll be pieces of that cake flying all over Ireland to both Protestants and Catholics." A simple look of agreement came from Michael while pondering her words and taking a drink of his tea. "Now then." His mother shuffled her position, readying to change the subject. "How much money do you have saved in that box you have hidden in your wardrobe?" Michael, caught off-guard by the switch in conversation, sat up paying attention, shocked that his mother even knew about the box in his room.

"How do you know about the box and how do you know I have money in it? Have you been picking the lock, Ma?"

"Don't be silly. I'm not a safebreaker in my spare time. Besides, what else would you be keeping in there? I didn't raise no idiot to be hoarding anything illegal in the house. So, come on, how much have ye?"

Michael looked at his mother, realising that she very rarely asked a question she didn't already know the answer to, so honesty, in this occasion was probably the best policy.

"About ten grand," he admitted, before raising his cup to his mouth to finish the last of his tea.

7P's

"TEN FFF GRAND!" Ma, with a stutter and almost an out of character curse was shocked. She obviously didn't know that one. "And what would you be wanting all that for, and me struggling to get to the blinking bingo?"

"It's a deposit."

"A deposit? A deposit for what, a Ferrari?"

"No Ma," he chuckled at her sarcasm, "For a house. Well, a bungalow. I want to get you out of this place. We've been living in this flat since I was Peewee's age."

Catherine gazed around her well-groomed living room, paying special attention to Finbar's pictures on the mantelpiece. It was all she knew and everything she wanted.

"What's up with this place? It's fine when the lifts aren't broken and don't I keep it spotlessly clean and tidy. Plus I have all my friends about me, and it's only a short walk to the shops and the bingo hall. Now what would I want to be moving for?"

"You keep the place beautiful. Ma. But I just wanted something better for you, that's all."

This time it was Catherine's turn to pause, warmed by her son's love.

"I know you do, but better isn't always something you can go out and buy. Ye see, I have all I want right here with you and Peter, and if you marry Roisin, well then, maybe I'll have some more."

Michael did a double-take and looked across at his mother.

"You're not talking about grandkids again, are ye?"

"And why not? You have to go your own way eventually. Ye can't look after me and your brother forever. And Roisin, she won't wait around much longer, especially when you're out with your mates doing God knows what on old year's night when you should be out with her. She's in her thirties, the same as you, and her body clock is ticking. She won't stay ripe forever."

Michael looked up, smiling at his mother's description.

"She's not a piece of fruit, Ma."

"No, she's a woman and women want kids. Anyway, forget that for now. That's not what I want to speak to you about. There's something else I want from ye."

"Anything, Ma," Michael said, noticing a change in her voice while the grip on his hand tightened.

"Would you go away, son, just for a while until things quieten down? Take the money you have saved and use it to take a trip. It doesn't matter where you go. Just get away from here while these talks are on. I'd rather have that than a bungalow."

Michael smiled at his mother's unselfishness. Going away wasn't something he had thought about doing, but after what had gone on with Maguire, he could see the sense in it.

"I'll tell you what, Ma. I'll think about it today while I'm out with the lads, then I'll talk it over with Roisin tonight. But I'm making no promises." Catherine released her son's hand and immediately tapped it, followed by a gentle and loving rub.

"Okay, son. Would you like a refill?" she asked, pointing at his mug.

"That'll be grand," Michael accepted, passing her the empty vessel.

His mother left the conversation there; she didn't

want to push it too much. She had planted the seed and given time; she knew her son would come around. Michael had never refused her any request in his adult life, but maybe that was because she knew how to ask.

His going away wasn't an idea she had suddenly hatched because of Maguire's visit though. Times were changing, and the town was full of talk about the agreement, and how, when, or if it happened, not everybody was going to get what they wanted. That would mean trouble, not just between the Catholics and Protestants but between the IRA and the INLA, two organisations supposedly fighting for the same cause that would now be fighting each other to become the voice of the Catholic people. Catherine wasn't alone in her predicament either. She wasn't the only mother with sons doing what Michael and the lads did. There could be another two or three ASUs in the same area, but you wouldn't know, not since the supergrass trials. The mothers knew though—there wasn't much got past them. There was more information passed in the supermarkets and bingo halls of Belfast than in the corridors of Whitehall. It was a network that any secret service organisation would have been proud of.

An hour or so later and it was time for Michael to go and meet the lads. He came down the stairs and took his jacket from the rack, slipping it on while reaching for the door.

"Ma, I'll be staying at Roisin's tonight, so don't wait up," he shouted from the hallway.

"Will you be bringing her for dinner tomorrow?" his mother shouted back from the living room chair where she was now fast at work knitting Peewee another jumper, a relentless task at the rate he was growing.

"I will, but don't be going on to her about grandkids." His mother smiled.

"Okay, I'll expect you about three then, and think on about what we discussed, will ye?"

"I will, Ma. Peewee, be sure you're in before Ma goes to the bingo tonight and don't be giving her any trouble or lip." Michael gave young Peter his usual orders as he opened the door to leave the flat. "And Ma," he added halfway out.

"Yes, son."

"Turn up the heating."

Catherine, again smiled at Michael's last words before the door shut behind him. The thermostat had already been returned to its original higher setting the moment he went upstairs to get ready, her little ruse being a success now she was in receipt of an extra twenty each week for the bingo.

"Peter, come here while I see if this fits."

Young Peewee, engrossed in his Saturday morning cartoons, stood up from his position in front of the television and reversed back to his mum without even taking his eyes off the screen. Catherine held up the half-made sweater to his back, estimating the amount of work still left.

"Ma," young Peter said, with a question on his lips.

"Quiet and stand still, will ye, or you'll end up looking like an octopus in this jumper."

"But Ma."

"Quiet."

"But Ma."

"Oh what is it, Peter?" she mumbled after gripping one of the knitting needles between her teeth whilst balancing the incomplete garment across his shoulders. "Can it not wait?"

"Is Roisin up the duff, Ma?" he blurted. He had obviously been earwigging on his mother's and brother's conversation.

"No, she is not!" she replied, losing the implement from her mouth as she turned to land a swift one on his ear. "And who's been teaching you to talk like that?"

Chapter Five

Old Bobby Tomes

As Michael got to the bottom of the third flight of stairs, he was forced to move to one side to make room for Peewee's friend, young Paddy Fahy, who lived on the fourth floor. He was a dishevelled young lad with hair that needed a wash and a nit comb running through it. The clothes on his back needed similar treatment and a needle and cotton running through them. A scrappy little waif of so slight a build should not have taken up so much room that it caused Michael to have to step to one side, but the horse he was leading may have accounted for that.

"What have I told you about bringing your gallower

up the stairs, Paddy?" Michael, often included his brother's friends in his bollockings for the way they behaved around the flats.

"I've got to, Michael," he answered, reckoning to misunderstand his meaning. He won't go in the lift. I think he's got that clausta-whatsit."

"It's called claustrophobia and I didn't mean that, ye little gobshite. I meant that the horse belongs outside. No wonder the lifts are always broken."

"No, Michael, don't make me take him outside," young Paddy pleaded. "It's fucking freezing. I worry about him."

"Then throw a blanket on him," Michael shouted, while pointing at the horse, offering the usual cure for the cold.

"I can't. Ma has it on our bed since the lecci company cut the power off."

"For fuck's sake," muttered Michael under his breath. Not because of the horse but because Mrs Fahy was obviously struggling on her own with her five kids and he hadn't realised it. From past experience he knew that having no electricity in winter was no laughing matter.

"How long has it been off for?"

"Three weeks now," answered young Paddy.

"You mean the bastards cut you off before Christmas?" The boy nodded, as his face changed, showing that the Christmas period hadn't been very festive in his house.

Michael sighed, beginning to feel a bit guilty for the good time he and his family had experienced.

"Tell your Ma that I'll sort the power out first thing Monday morning. But right now, here's twenty quid." Michael pulled the note from his pocket and passed it to young Paddy. "Give her that and tell her to get you and your brothers and sisters fish and chips for your tea, and, with the change, to get herself to the bingo tonight with my Ma."

"I will, Michael."

"Oh, and by the way, how much did you hustle the fella for this morning that came out of our flat?"

"What fella?" replied young Fahy, denying all knowledge.

"You know what fella. Pipeface in the hat."

Young Paddy couldn't help the giveaway smile forming on his face.

"Two quid," he admitted with a giggle.

"Well, there's another two," Michael doubled Paddy's take. "The next time you see his car, give it the works, and I mean a right good going over."

"Thanks, Michael I will. And thanks for the twenty for my Ma." Young Paddy, with wide eyes, stuffed the note into his pocket. "We'll probably go to the Chinese, though," he added. "Their curry sauce is better than the chippy, it's a lot thicker. Plus they give you a free bag of prawn knackers."

"Crackers," corrected Michael.

"Crackers," repeated young Paddy, with a smirk forming. "You can say that again. It's fucking stupid if you ask me to be giving good food away." The lad, with his grin now covering his face, continued to lead his horse up the stairs.

"Cheeky little fucker," Michael said to himself with a laugh and a shake of his head. "And, Paddy," he shouted, looking up between the flights, "when the power's back on, get the blanket back on the horse and the horse tethered back outside."

Michael heard no answer back from the young boy over the clip-clopping of the shoes on the steps. But it didn't matter—he would make sure Peter gave him the message later.

Michael didn't complain too much. Horses are a part of an Irish boy's upbringing, it's in their culture, whatever the religion. It's no accident that he best jockeys in the world come out of Ireland, and that it's not just because of their size, it's because of their understanding of the animal. It doesn't stop with just the equine family, either—canines are as much a part of their lives and, like their horses, they work for a living. A good lurcher or whippet can keep a family fed with rabbits from the surrounding fields when times are hard, and if they are a bit speedy, they can also win a few quid hare coursing at the weekend. It is an Irish way of life that goes back to the Normans and one that will never change.

Leaving his flat, which was one of a block of three, he looked at all the other horses that were tethered on the grass between them. Feeling the cold in the air, he could sympathise with where young Paddy was coming from—the other horses looked like they also needed stabling, and Paddy's old nag had a good eight years more on the clock than any of them.

He had been given it by an old tatter rag-and-bone man who was trying to worm his way into his mother's good books, amongst other things. It had become too old to pull his cart and he probably thought that it was worth more as leverage to sweeten up Paddy's mum than he would get for it at the knacker's yard.

Michael was soon on the high street, which was as busy as always, with the bars all advertising the different sports they were showing that day in the hope of dragging in the men to do their drinking, and the women with their shopping bags rushed from store to store in search of the best bargains and a joint for the next day's Sunday dinner. In fact, if it wasn't for catching sight of the odd army patrol, you could mistake it for any other town in Britain. But this was Belfast; it wasn't like any other town. Life went on here because its residents knew the unwritten rules of where and where not to go. There were a few barriers of segregation but it was the painted murals on the walls and the gable ends of houses that mainly separated the two warring communities. If you saw a picture of a freedom fighter wearing a balaclava, with an orange, white and green tricolour behind him, you knew you were in a Catholic area, whereas the Protestants, although they had a few murals of their own, much preferred to paint the curb stones red, white and blue to prove their allegiance to the Crown. It didn't take much working out.

This area was definitely Catholic; this was 'Michael's Town', or at least his part of it. He knew every nook and cranny, every face and new-born child. He knew the postman, the milkman and what time they delivered. He had to—not only his life but the lives of his family and friends depended on it. In fact, if either of the delivery men were ill and had to take the day off, they would ring Michael to let him know before they rang the company they worked for. That way, it saved the stranger standing in that day from being mistaken as an enemy in disguise and shot. The threats to Michael were numerous, top of the list being the Protestant paramilitary organisations such as the UDA (Ulster Defence Association) and their offshoot the UVF (Ulster Volunteer Force). Then came the police, the RUC (Royal Ulster Constabulary). Of its thousands of members, none of them were Catholic, but that was a choice of both parties. If the IRA found out that a Catholic man had joined the ranks of the RUC, he would be looked upon as a traitor and a collaborator. He would have about as much chance of survival as a grouse on the 12th August. It truly would have been open season. Last but not least were the security forces, the British Army, back on the streets of Northern Ireland since 1969, when, ironically, they returned to protect the Catholics from the Protestants. The army posed the biggest threat to Michael, with their information and intelligence-gathering units and, of course, the undercover forces, their business end, the SAS.

The IRA had been infiltrated many times by the SAS, and since Margaret Thatcher had come to power and South Armagh had been nicknamed 'bandit country' by Airey Neave, the regiment had been given virtually a free hand in the province. Its members were inserted everywhere. They could be in uniform, hiding in the roof space of some abandoned house, or factory-watching and logging the day-to-day comings and goings of the streets below, or out of uniform in civilian clothing, passing themselves off as part of the community. They might even be the pretend drunk at the bar, listening to the conversations of the pub-going locals; information falls freely from drink-loosened lips. For these reasons and many others, Michael had to be constantly on his guard, watching for them both in uniform and out. In fact, if you came across the SAS in uniform, chances are you were dead. As a safeguard, none of Michael's movements were ever the same as the day or week before. He was careful never to set patterns or be a man of repetition. He didn't even own a car because it would be too easy to target. Besides, that was Sean's job. This was life for Michael and many others like him on both sides of the fence. He had to know everything and everyone around him so that what didn't belong would stand out a mile. In Michael's world, there were no rehearsals, you didn't get a second chance. Laziness and stupidity were paid for by the highest price. The soldier in Bangor the night before had been guilty of both those sins. He broke the Army's golden rule while serving in Northern Ireland of never being caught anywhere on your own. The ceasefire had saved his life, but it wasn't an agreement that all the organisations were adhering to. If it had been members of the INLA (Irish National Liberation Army) that had caught him down that passage, he would without doubt have been killed or, worse, kidnapped, tortured for information and then killed.

Today, Michael's head was full of the problems caused by Maguire's visit. He felt guilty for putting his mother under stress but knew Maguire was out of order for coming to the flat, especially when he hadn't been near since his father had died. Michael kicked himself; he didn't really know why he had rocked the boat, doing what he had done the night before. In hindsight, it was out of order and possibly a step too far. If he had wanted to rebel, he should have done it alone and not dragged the lads along with him.

"Ah, fuck it," he thought to himself. "Ma's right—maybe it is time for a change." A few months away and some distance between himself and Maguire wouldn't hurt. It wasn't a cop-out by Michael, but all things being equal, it was probably the right thing to do. But it would only work if the lads went with him. They were a team and if one of them stayed behind and fucked up, it would come back on all of them. The threat from Maguire wasn't a deadly one, yet, but if there were any repeats of last night's performance that could soon change. He didn't foresee a problem convincing the lads to come away with him, but what about Roisin? How would she react?

"I'll go see her first," he thought to himself. "Before

I go to the pub and meet the lads for a drink. Maybe I should even stop at the florists and get her a bunch of flowers. Nah, fuck that for an idea. I haven't done that in the ten years I've known her. If I do it now, she will know I'm up to something. I'm better off just turning up at the salon and coming clean."

"What about ye, Michael? How are ye, son?"

Michael's thoughts were broken by the appearance of a man in front of him. It was old Bobby Tomes. Bobby had been a fixture about the town for as long as Michael could remember, and probably longer, being that Bobby had a good twenty years on him. He looked like an old sea dog and was partial to the odd tipple, but he was well liked, especially by Michael. He had a soft spot for old Bobby, not for any particular reason, but he would usually drop him a few quid at the weekend for a pint and a bet; it was just his way.

"Not bad, Bobby. How's ye self?"

"Ah, I'm grand lad." Bobby, proving that his wellbeing surpassed his looks, gave Michael a soft jab on the top of his arm but made the movement look as though he was sparring in the boxing gym.

"Steady on there, Bobby. That's a sweet left hook ye have there. Ye going to damage my drinking arm."

"Ah, sure I wouldn't do that. It's only a few pounds in my pocket for a warming meal that I'm trying to beat out of ye."

A frown formed on Michael's face as he decided to have a bit of fun for the old boy's cheek.

"A meal is it, Bobby? I think if I was to be giving you a few quid, you would be in O'Reilly's Bar before I was. You wouldn't even have fifty pence down in a packet of crisps, never mind a meal, you old goat."

"Ah, not at all. Sure, I've cut right down on the drink these days." Sensing a bit of reluctance on Michael's part, Bobby decided to change his tactics. "How's your mother anyway? Is she well?"

"Don't give me all that bollocks." Michael immediately dismissed Bobby's enquiry, not falling for the old tapper's softening tactics.

"Bollocks. What bollocks. I was only enquiring."

"I know what you were doing, and it won't wash. You're like a glass door, Bobby Tomes."

"A glass door. What does that mean?"

"I can see straight through ye. Now follow me or ye get nothing,"

Michael continued down the high street, with old Bobby behind him, doing his best to keep up. Bobby knew that Michael would soften eventually but today, it looked like he was going to have to work for it.

"Where are we going, son? Sure, I only want an old fiver."

"Well, stay with me, Bobby, and I might see me way to making it a tenner."

Bobby rubbed his hands in anticipation of a few quid, at the same time blowing warm air from between the stained whiskers that surrounded his mouth onto his equally tobacco-stained fingertips that protruded from his fingerless gloves. His dreams were soon dashed, though, when Michael stopped outside the local café.

"Here you go, Bobby boy: Mary's Pantry."

Old Bobby stared at the café, panting for breath after his slight jog, his eyes wide with fear, knowing that eating only meant one thing: heartburn!

"Mary's Pantry, my arse," Bobby blurted. "You mean Greasy Deasy's." Bobby gave the café its more common name as it was known by the locals after the owner, Mary Deasy. "You won't find any Michelin fucking stars in that old 'slop shop'. Ah, what the fuck are we doing here, Michael son? Just buy me a whiskey and we'll call it quits—er, a double."

"You said you were hungry. Now do you want the money or don't ye?"

Michael pulled a crispy ten-pound note from his pocket to increase the temptation.

"Of course I do," Bobby replied, all puppy-eyed, while rubbing his whiskers anxiously.

"Then get your arse in there and sit down, ye conniving old git."

Old Bobby begrudgingly did as he was told and took the first available seat. Michael followed him inside, smiling broadly as he approached the counter.

"Mary Deasy, where are you, ye gorgeous woman?" he called in search of the café-owner.

A middle-aged, well-groomed lady appeared from the kitchen at Michael's beckoning, while adjusting her multi coloured beehive-style hairdo and wearing a welcoming smile.

"Michael Flynn, how are ye, mi darling?"

"I'm all the better for seeing you, Mary girl. Do you have a special on today?"

Mary turned to look at the large menu board on the wall behind her.

"I do indeed," she replied. "Steak and kidney pie with colcannon potatoes and veg, all with thick onion gravy, and for an extra pound, there's apple crumble and custard for afters. Is it for yourself?" Mary asked, turning back to Michael, at the same time leaning over the counter towards him and revealing her other special—an ample-sized cleavage.

"Ah no, Mary girl, it's not for me," Michael answered with a hint of a stammer. "It looks, I mean it sounds grand, but mi Ma's already fed me to the hilt this morning.

No, I'm afraid that your less than enthusiastic diner today is old Bobby over there." Michael dragged his stare away from what was on offer, and the menu, and glanced back at the disgruntled old tapper, who sat looking like a condemned man about to receive his last meal.

"Do you not see anything you fancy yourself?" hinted Mary, looking down towards her half-opened blouse and seductively nibbling on the end of her pencil. Michael couldn't resist having another look at Mary's assets. The words 'chicken fillets' and 'Wonderbra' came to mind, but Michael dismissed them both, having a clear view all the way to her navel and beyond to Brazil!

"I think I'll have to take a rain check on that one, Mary. I'm in enough trouble today as it is. Now, there's a tenner. When ye man's finished everything—and I mean everything—give him the change."

"Ah, don't do it to me, Michael," Bobby pleaded after overhearing the instructions. "I could live for a week on that lot."

Michael again averted his eyes from Mary's chest and turned back to answer Bobby.

"Good. Then you'll be all right till next Saturday when you'll probably be putting the nip on me again. I'm already fifty two quid down this morning and I haven't even had a drink or a bet yet."

Happy that old Bobby was going to put some packing between his liver and his next session on the booze, Michael said his goodbyes.

"See you later, Mary."

"See you later, darling. Come back soon and get something warm inside ye."

Michael looked at Mary, unable to hide his smile. By the way she was looking at him, he could tell she was more interested in him putting something warm inside her.

"Remember me to your Ma, will ye?" she added, while picking the note up from the counter and slipping it between her breasts, out of old Bobby's reach.

Michael, leaving the café, turned at the door.

"Enjoy your lunch, you old bollocks, and I'll see you in O'Reilly's Bar later."

He gave Bobby the thumbs up, with a large cheeky

grin. Bobby, wearing a face of discontent, unappreciatively gave him two fingers back.

Once again, Michael set off down the street, giggling to himself at the thought of old Bobby wading through all that food. The crack was well worth the tenner if only to take his mind off the morning's troubles with Maguire. He continued on his way, taking in the comings and goings of the main street while nodding and waving at all the passers-by that knew him, which was just about everyone. His spirits began to rise; it was still the beautiful, crisp day that he had viewed from his bedroom window and the fresh air, combined with Ma's big breakfast, had put him right in the mood for sinking a few pints of the black stuff. First, though, he had to see Roisin and break the news of his intended departure.

Five more minutes and a few hundred yards further down the high street, he reached the hairdressers Roisin had owned and run for the past five years. Michael was a silent partner in the salon, after putting up the money to buy the lease, but the closest he got to the business was a free haircut once a month. He stopped to peer through the corner of the window, from where he watched Roisin, who was standing behind a customer, advising her on a style. The shop wasn't exactly at the cutting edge of the trade—her customers were mostly old girls wanting their weekly shampoo and set, pushing the boat out now and then for a purple or blue rinse, but she was busy enough and enjoyed being her own boss.

She was a tall, blonde-haired girl with a beautiful face and shape, which Michael studied lovingly from his viewpoint at the window. At that moment, it occurred to him just how much he did love her and that leaving Belfast was going to be just as hard for him as it would be for her. He consoled himself by thinking that it would only be for a few months and that he had been away for longer periods in the past, but still he was going to miss her.

They had been together for over ten years now, after meeting when Michael was out with the lads for his twenty-first birthday. Back then they were both just a skinny couple of kids, long before Roisin bloomed into the woman she was now and Michael grew some shoulders. There were no rings or ties, but they had an understanding and a trust they both respected. She was pretty much an orphan, after losing both her parents when she was a teenager, and being an only child must have made the few years she was on her own until she met Michael a very lonely time. But the minute he took her home to meet his mother, Catherine had accepted her as part of the family and treated her more like a daughter than a prospective daughter in-law. Even though Michael was only twenty-one, she could see with her mother's intuition that her son had set his cap on Roisin, and Catherine agreed she was a keeper.

Michael tapped on the window, grabbing her attention, and gave her a wink, accompanied by one of his cheeky smiles that he knew she couldn't resist. A mirrored look beamed across her face, as she turned and made her way to the door to greet him. They kissed and squeezed each other tightly, giving the ladies in the salon something other than their glossies to look at.

"Happy New Year, gorgeous," Michael said, while grabbing himself a handful of Roisin's firm buttock.

"Behave yourself, will ye?" she said, slapping her hand on his shoulder. "Think of mi customers."

"Ah, they don't mind, DO YE LADIES?" said Michael, raising his voice so the shampoo and set brigade could hear.

"Don't mind us," answered one of the three old dears sat beneath the dryers. "When my arse was as firm as that, it would get grabbed all the time, and not always by my husband."

The rest of the ladies laughed, all remembering their younger years.

"I don't normally see you until later, so to what do I owe the pleasure?" she asked, while running her fingers through Michael's hair appreciating her own work.

"Does a man need a reason to come and see the woman he loves?"

"And saying the 'L' word? What have you been up

to? Do you have a guilty conscience, Michael Flynn? I hope you weren't chasing any tarts last night with that womaniser Danny Keenan."

"Give it a rest woman, will ye? I came to tell you to meet me at six in the bar and pick up a couple of bottles of wine on the way. We'll order a takeaway and have a night in front of the telly."

"So, you came to tell me that we will be doing exactly the same as we do every week on a Saturday night."

"I came to remind you to get the wine."

"Are you trying to get me drunk, Michael Flynn, so you can have ye wicked way with me?"

"Sure, if I wanted that, all I would have to do is lick my eyebrows and you'd be all over me, woman."

Roisin gave Michael another slap on the shoulder.

"Have ye no shame?" she said, turning red-faced to look at her customers, who looked back at their magazines, pretending not to be listening.

"None at all," he answered. "Now don't forget the wine and I'll see you later."

"Sounds grand," she whispered in his ear, while planting another smacker on his cheek. "I'll see you at six."

"See you later, ladies," shouted Michael while giving Roisin's bottom another slap for good luck before setting off on the last leg of his journey to O'Reilly's Bar.

He hadn't had the intended conversation he wanted—the salon was too busy for that—but at least he would have another chance that evening.

Roisin returned to her customers with the evidence of her blushes still glowing on her face. The ladies in the salon were full of smiles, while pretending they hadn't enjoyed the spectacle of Michael's visit.

"Don't be embarrassed, love," said the lady in the chair. "If I were twenty years younger and he licked his eyebrows in front of me, I'd have my knickers around my ankles in no time!"

Roisin smiled, joining in with the laughter of her customers and staff.

Chapter Six

O'Reilly's Bar

O'Reilly's had been Michael's local since the lads and he were old enough to drink. His father had drunk there, along with Mactazner and occasionally Maguire. It was a safe haven in a troubled area. Michael had experienced the taste of his first pint of Guinness there on his sixteenth birthday when his father took him in there to test the ground. He had to drink the pint in front of all his dad's mates, then they all gave him a cheer and a quid before he was then told to 'fuck off' and come back when he was eighteen. It was a kind of ritual with the locals; all his mates had gone through the same thing. Now, whenever Michael entered the bar, he would always look at the space where his father stood that night. They never made it back together for his eighteenth.

The bar itself was split into two rooms: one very large, one very small, called the taproom or vault. The large front room had that olde-worlde feeling of spit and sawdust to it, a mixture of young and old. The floorboards were stripped back to the wood with neither polish nor stain. It was as though they had been intentionally left bare, knowing that future years of spilt beer and customers' working boots and shoes would scuff them into an almost furry look, giving the premises the character it now so beautifully held. The rest of the timber that made up the seating, tables and bar were a different matter. That was dark and deep in colour, giving the room a feel of strength and structure. Finally, the bar-back was the centrepiece of the establishment, with lavish, carved wood and newel posts surrounding large mirrors etched with the name 'O'Reilly's Bar'. Hidden source-lighting picked out the mirrors and the neatly stacked bottles on its shelves made the bar-back jump out and shine back at you, as though inviting the punters to sit admiringly whilst drinking to their hearts content. The fittings on the bar also held their own sparkling intrigue. They were made of brass that was highly polished, which included the hand and foot rails that ran along its length. It was indeed a tempting oasis where a man could get drunk, and many of the locals regularly fell under its allure.

"The usual?" the barman asked, automatically putting a pint glass under the Guinness pump.

"How's things, Jimmy?

"Not bad, Michael. I won a million on the pools this week but thought I would still come in to do my Saturday shift out of loyalty to my customers." The barman smiled with an if-only look on his face.

"Ah, yer a good man, Jimmy, and I wouldn't put it past ye, being the tight-fisted bastard that you are. Are any of the boys in yet?" Jimmy continued smiling at Michael's returned comment.

"There's no sign of Sean or Dermot, but the big

fella's in the other bar with his head in the paper, writing his bets."

"Well, make that two pints then, and have one yourself. Pass them through if ye don't mind, and there's a tenner. Or will you be needing that now that you're a millionaire."

"I'll have a drink, Michael, cheers. And I'll take the money, just to make sure that the till is balanced, you understand."

Michael, shaking his head, passed through the dividing door that split the taproom from the main bar. This was the point where the premises lost its lustre. This room looked as though a hundred quid had been invested in its refurbishment, and Jimmy the Landlord was still waiting for his ninety quid change. In the middle of the room, with hardly enough space to bend down with a cue, a pool table stood complete with torn cloth and enough beer stains that if you rung it out you could fill your pint back up. A decent-sized television set sat on a raised shelf in the far corner and an empty void took up the area where the dartboard should have been. That had been stolen a few months earlier and

Jimmy, who was widely known for his tightness, had refused to replace it on principle. That was all well and good, of course—a man should stick to his guns—but the lads in the games league that played twice a week were getting a bit sick of bringing in their own.

"How's it going, big man? Do you have all the winners?" Michael asked Danny as he entered the room.

"Ah, they're in here somewhere. It's just finding the buggers," Danny replied while studying the racing page that was spread across the table in front of him.

Danny loved his horse racing, especially his flutter on a Saturday afternoon. He wasn't a heavy gambler, which was just as well because he very seldom backed a winner. It was just that when it was being shown on the television, if he didn't have a bet, he thought he was missing out.

"Well, double me up on what you do find," added Michael, collecting the drinks from the bar. "My head's too full of shite to be picking horses today."

"What's up with you now? You were in fine form when we left you last night. Has Roisin been at ye?"

"Nah, Roisin's grand, the same as always. What's on my mind is a bit more serious."

Danny looked up from the racing page, his attention grabbed by the word 'serious'.

"Come on then, spit it out. What's the crack?"

Michael took a good drink before answering, with Danny following suit after clinking their glasses together. "Cheers. Now, come on, what's the crack?" Danny repeated.

"I had a visit from Maguire this morning, over the fun and games we had in Bangor last night."

"Fuck me, that was quick. Who lit the rocket under his arse? Was he pissed with ye?"

"He wasn't best pleased. Never mind the rocket—he'd had a new arse ripped for him and was trying to pass the bollocking on to us. Well, me."

"I hope you told him where to go."

"I told him to shove it, along with Sinn Féin and the fucking peace talks."

"He won't have liked that. I bet the sparks were flying out of the old fucker's pipe."

"You're not wrong. I thought for a moment he was going to explode. It was like Guy Fawkes Night had come early, but I think I may have gone too far."

Danny could see from Michael's face that the visit from Maguire had left him with some worries.

"Fuck him, Michael. We haven't had any work from that lot for nearly a year now. I'm sick and tired of robbing post offices so I can afford a drink and a bet. Then, to rub salt into the wounds, they expect a percentage of the loot as well. It's all one-way traffic with those fuckers."

"I know what you mean, Danny Boy. I said as much myself this morning. But I've no right to be risking your lives by running off at the mouth."

"You have my permission to be saying what the fuck you want to that wanker. It's a free country. Well, almost."

"I know that, big fella," Michael said, proudly patting Danny on the shoulder. "But last night Dermot wanted no part of it and I didn't listen. Thinking about it, things could have been a lot worse than Maguire at my door this morning and yours as well, for that matter."

"Ah, Dermot worries. Sure, he always does, but if he didn't want any part of last night, he would have said so."

"Just the same, Danny, when the lads arrive we need to talk. I've something to discuss with the three of ye. Where are they anyway?"

"Dermot rang the house this morning for Fatty to pick him up. I think he's got some woman trouble he needs to sort out."

"Dermot with woman trouble? That's a new one. I didn't even know that he had a woman. I thought he was still seeing Pam and her five sisters, the little wanker."

"That's because he's been keeping it a secret on account of whom this certain woman is."

"Why, it's not my mother, is it?" joked Michael.

"No, but nearly as old. That's why he's a bit embarrassed about it. He doesn't give a crap what me and Sean think, but for some reason he respects your opinion, the poor deluded fucker."

Michael carried on looking at Danny, waiting for the rest of the information, but Danny wasn't forthcoming.

"Well, who is it then?" he urged. "Spill the beans. Don't leave me in suspense all day."

"I can't. I promised I wouldn't. And you know that once I've given my word that my lips are sealed, so leave it alone."

"Come on, big fella. I won't say a word," Michael assured. "Dermot will never know it was you who told me, I swear it."

Danny continued to shake his head, determined to stick to his vow of silence.

"If he wants you to know, he will tell you himself when he gets here. I'm sure you'll be asking him what the pair of them got up to this morning."

"Come on, man. You owe me one for not telling Jimmy behind the bar that it was you that nicked his dartboard."

Danny turned his head at Michael's grassing threat.

"I only did that because I had forgotten about young Peter's birthday and needed a present, quick."

"I know that and he plays on it every night. He has a picture of Paisley stuck to it for target practice—he's becoming quite the dart-thrower. But you still owe me one."

7P's

Danny didn't want to break his promise, but he knew Michael wouldn't let it go until he had revealed the name of the woman in Dermot's life. Plus, the time was knocking on and the racing was about to start.

"It's Mary Deasy," he whispered as though the whole world was listening.

Michael couldn't believe his ears, while nearly choking on his Guinness.

"What? Mary from the café with the six kids and the big jugs?" he exclaimed in amazement.

"The same," confirmed Danny, with a lowering of his hand indicating to Michael to quieten his voice. "You'd have big jugs as well if you'd breastfed six kids," he added in her defence.

"Fuck me." Michael was gobsmacked with disbelief. "Talk about chalk and fucking cheese."

"As I said, I think he's a little embarrassed about the age difference and doesn't want you to know. But she's not a bad-looking woman and she's a fine old frame on her."

"I know all about that, sure," agreed Michael. "I'm

only after looking at most of it not half an hour ago. I'd say Dermot has his hands full there, in more ways than one. Why didn't you tell me before?"

"Because, Dermot asked me and Fatty to keep it to ourselves, plus I was being the soul of discretion, as I was throwing a length up her myself this time last year." Danny lowered his voice even further. "Dermot doesn't know that by the way, so don't go opening your gob."

"Fuck me, Danny. Who haven't you thrown a length up? Make sure you stay away from my Roisin, by the way," Michael warned with a pointed finger and taking a large drink of his pint.

"Ah, don't worry about that. Sure, she only has eyes for you. Besides, she already turned me down." Danny's answer was accompanied by a cheeky smirk, which fell quickly into the brim of his glass.

"Go away, ye fucker. If you spent as much time studying the horses as ye do studying the women, you might pick us some winners one of these Saturdays. Then we wouldn't have to go robbing post offices, would we?"

"You'd rob post offices anyway, Flynn, even if we picked all the winners that ran. It's the only thing that keeps you from getting bored."

"Probably," agreed Michael. "So, what problems does Dermot have with Mary, anyway, apart from an obvious lack of stamina that is?"

"He wasn't saying, and he wasn't telling where he was getting Sean to drive him either."

"Well, no doubt we'll find out when they eventually arrive."

"Don't forget now," reminded Danny. "You said you wouldn't say anything about what I told you—about Mary and me, I mean, and the rest."

"Don't worry, big fella. Unlike Mary's legs, my lips are sealed."

"Yeah, well, so were mine until you prised it out of me, so keep your gob shut."

"Don't worry, Danny Boy. I will take the information to my grave, cross my heart and hope to die." Michael, while making the sign on his chest to go with the childish promise, stood up from the table and finished the last of his Guinness, before placing the empty glass down in front of Danny. "Now, write down what you have picked, and I'll go to the bookies and put our bet on while you get the drinks in."

Danny passed Michael the slip of hopeful selections, which Michael looked upon with little expectation.

"I'm surprised Fatty never said anything," Michael added, still talking about Dermot's secret. "I'd have thought he would be the first to blab and take the piss."

"He's enjoying having Dermot by the short and curlies. He keeps dropping hints every time he wants him to get a round in," explained Danny. "He's been doing it for weeks, it's just that you haven't cottoned on."

"Things don't usually go over my head. I'm not normally that stupid, but saying that, I am on my way to the bookies to have good money down on your horse selections."

Danny pointed his finger.

"Just keep your mouth shut about what I told you, and nobody's forcing you to go halves on the bet." He didn't bite at Michael's parting statement. He got the same every week, but it never put him off gambling.

A few hours and a few pints later, Michael and Danny were still sitting at the table, which was now littered with numerous screwed-up betting slips about to be joined by yet another as their last horse came over the line in a disappointing fifth place. Michael, although not really bothered, couldn't resist having another dig at his mate.

"Well, Danny Boy, you were bang on form as usual. We didn't even get a nag in the first three. It would be nice, one of these Saturdays, to at least come second in a photo finish."

Danny, well aware that his run of bad luck was with him for yet another week, didn't appreciate Michael reminding him of it and this time had a little chew.

"Well, choose the fucking horses yourself next week, if ye think you can do any better."

Michael got up to go to the bar to get another couple of drinks, smiling at the big fella's outburst. It was only friendly banter between the pair, which played every week like a broken record. As Michael got the beer in to show him that there were no hard feelings, the other two arrived through the taproom door. Sean entered first, still indulging in his favourite pastime besides smoking and drinking—eating.

"Get me one," he spouted, seeing Michael at the bar. "I've a terrible thirst." His words were accompanied by sprays of half-eaten pork pie, most of which went in the direction of his brother.

"Close your mouth, you fat horrible fucker," a disgusted Danny shouted as he shielded himself from the flying meat and pastry.

Sean shrugged off the insults about his eating habits and leant forward to retrieve one of the larger pieces that had fallen on Danny's racing page. He picked up the morsel, which left a grease stain over the number six horse in the five thirty at Kempton, and popped it in his mouth.

"I'd back that one, if I was you—it could be an omen," Sean predicted while picking another bit he'd nearly missed from between his teeth.

Danny looked at his brother, still disgusted, wondering if he really could be the milkman's.

"If I had have known that a pork pie could tip horses better than your brother, I would have bought one from the butcher's in the high street," Michael added, laughing as he paid for the drinks. Danny, still not appreciating his wit, said nothing, but he couldn't resist reading the stained name of the horse in the later race at Kempton.

"Where the fuck have you been?" questioned Michael, turning from the bar with two pints in his hands.

"We were..."

"We were taking care of a bit of business," Dermot interrupted, butting in over Sean's answer before he let anything slip.

"Important business, was it?" Michael again questioned knowingly, while at the same time giving Danny a wink.

"Important enough," replied Dermot, not giving any details.

"Important enough to make you four hours late?" Michael pushed it once more.

"Important enough to take all fucking day if needed. Now leave it alone." Dermot was getting tired of the questions, but his reluctance to talk was only egging Michael on more.

"Have you picked any winners yet, big fella?" Dermot asked in an attempt to divert the conversation away from himself and towards Danny.

"Not yet, but I've been close," Danny replied, immediately receiving a dirty look from his partner, who was shaking his head.

"Here," said Michael passing the drinks. "Sit down, because now we're all here, I want to have a talk with ye."

Danny removed the paper from the table so the four of them could sit round it, as Michael collected the last two pints and joined them in the huddle.

"Maguire came to see me this morning," he said starting the chat.

"Do we have a job on?" interrupted Sean.

"No, it was over the crack last night in Bangor."

"Fuck me, I knew we shouldn't have done it. I said

7P's

Maguire wouldn't like it," shouted Dermot, immediately springing into his favourite place, the worry zone.

"Calm down, ye worrying fuck. Listen to what Michael has to say."

"It's okay, Danny. Dermot's right but it's spilt milk now. Listen, there's no problem with Maguire. We'd harsh words and I don't think we'll get another warning, but as long as we keep our noses clean, there'll be no more said about it."

"Fuck me. What are we, bound over to keep the peace or something?"

"I don't like being told what to do, the same as you, Sean. But the fact is we've no choice. Maguire made it quite clear that they're not going to allow anybody to do anything that might interfere with these talks."

"So, what do we do now?" asked Dermot.

Michael took the head off his fresh pint before revealing to the lads his plan to leave Belfast.

"I've decided to get out of it for a while and go to the mainland for a few months—London or Leeds, maybe."

"What? You're going on holiday with Roisin?"

"No, Sean, not with Roisin. With us. The four of us, and it's not a holiday. We'll go find some work on the building sites, like we always do. Not for long—just a few months while things calm down. There's no work here, anyway, and I for one am sick of sitting on my arse."

A moment's silence came over the group while they each gathered their personal thoughts on Michael's proposal.

"Well, I'm in," replied Sean without hesitation.

"And you know I am," confirmed Danny, leaving the three of them looking at Dermot for his decision.

"Well, I'm not. I mean I can't. I've got things to do."

Danny and Michael looked at each other and then at Sean, who seemed to know a little bit more about Dermot's reluctance but wasn't declaring.

"Are these some more of those important things you have to do, like the ones this morning?"

Dermot looked at Michael, letting him know he was tired of him pumping the subject. Whatever it was holding him back, he obviously thought it was important enough to stay in Belfast alone. Michael and Danny smiled at each other, thinking they knew his secret, both wondering what all the fuss was about. Okay, she was a good few years older than him and she had been around the block a few times, but who hadn't?

"You three go. I'll be okay here. Like you said, it's only for a few months."

"Come on, Dermot. We can't leave you here. We're a team. We come as a package. There's no point us going if you stay. It's all or none."

"Things have changed, Michael. You don't understand."

"I understand more than you think."

"No, you don't. Not this time." Dermot was stern with his answer, trying to put an end to the conversation and believing that Michael had no knowledge of his secret. Michael paused before his return comment. He didn't want to repeat what Danny had told him, but he had to keep the lads together.

"I know all about Mary Deasy from the greasy spoon, if that's what you mean."

Dermot looked at the two brothers, wondering which one of them had done the blabbing. Danny gave Michael a 'shut ye gob' look, hoping he wasn't going to say anything else, but it was nothing compared to Sean's next statement.

"Yeah, but what you don't know is that she's in the club!"

"Button it, ye fat fucker," cursed Dermot at the sound of his business being made public knowledge. "Jesus, can't anybody around here keep a fucking secret?"

Michael and Danny looked at each other, before breaking into fits of laughter, with Sean soon joining in. Dermot sat in silence, looking like he really did have the world on his shoulders, as the other three enjoyed a laugh at his expense.

"Sorry, sorry, Dermot, but without stating the obvious, are you sure it's yours?"

Michael had to say what was on everybody's mind, knowing Mary's past, and having been subjected to a few of her advances earlier in the day told him that she wasn't exactly a one-man-woman.

7P's

"I knew you'd say that. We've been together for five months and she's only three gone. We had it confirmed earlier at the doctor's."

"Fuck me, Dermot. I'm not calling the woman loose, but she has been known to flatten a bit of grass in her time."

"Who's been saying that? I'll break their fucking jaw," Dermot shouted, holding up a clenched fist.

"Isn't she a bit old to be getting pregnant?" added Sean, fuelling the fire. He had been dying to say something all the drive back from the doctors. "She has six already, all of them to different fathers, and every one of them from a different country. It must be like the League of fucking Nations around at her house. I don't know why she's wasting her time in that café; she could be earning a fortune working at the tourist board. She's already like Belfast's own one-woman welcoming committee."

"Watch your mouth, Fatty. I'll not have her talked about like that. Besides she's only forty-four and she's a good mother."

"Forty-four, my arse. She might be a forty-four

double-D in the bristols, but she's more like fifty-four in the age department. Fuck me, they should put her in the medical journal for conceiving at her age."

"Shut it, toothache," interrupted Michael, cutting Sean short in the tracks of his piss-taking. "We don't doubt that she's a good mother, Dermot." Once again, Michael tried his best to be diplomatic. "But if you're going to go knocking out all the men she's known in the past, you'll be fighting half the town, including Danny here!"

Again there was silence, but not for long, as a shocked Danny, who couldn't believe that his best mate had thrown him in, began to shout.

"You grassing bastard," he cursed. "You gave me your word you wouldn't say anything."

"Well, you told me Dermot's secrets," replied Michael, defending his reasoning. "What sort of a friend would I be if I didn't tell him yours? It's only fair."

Michael laughed, which was enough to push Dermot over the edge, as he lunged forward, trying to reach up to land a punch on Danny's chin.

"Hold on there, Dermot," Danny shouted. "Don't go

getting your ambitions mixed up with your capabilities, lad. Besides, it's been a year since I had the pleasure with Mary, so the child's got nothing to do with me, and that also means that I haven't been near her while you've been seeing her." Danny explained his innocence quickly, while holding Dermot at arm's length, who was swinging away like a windmill.

Jimmy the landlord came to the taproom side of the bar to see what the shouting and commotion was all about, but quickly walked away when he saw that Big Danny was involved.

"Well, seeing as how we're all getting our past indiscretions off our chests, you better give me a punch as well," added Sean, who was sat back in his chair, supping his Guinness and watching the proceedings. "I was having a tamper with her about the same time as Danny. She has nothing against doing Kane and Abel, I can tell ye."

The other three stopped their laughing and fighting to look at Sean in disbelief. "What?" he exclaimed, seeing their faces. "Don't let this portly stature fool ye.

I can fire a mix in just as good as the next man, and probably better," he proudly boasted. "I may have a fat arse, but everybody knows you need a big hammer to bang a big nail in."

Dermot sank back from Big Danny's defending hand and slumped into his stool.

"Fuck me. The mother of my future child is a slag," he declared, while taking a long drink from his pint in an attempt to drown his sorrows.

"Don't be a fool, Dermot," consoled Michael. "Roisin must have known other fellas before me but that's none of my business, nor is my past hers. Besides, at Mary's age, she's bound to have had a few more men in her bed than the younger women you've known."

"Fuck me, you can say that again."

"Shut it, Fatty, you're not helping," snapped Michael at another of Sean's ad-libbed interruptions. "Listen, Dermot, if Mary thinks anything of you then she'll wait, and if she doesn't then good riddance. It will be another six months until the baby is born and, either way, you'll want a blood test. So unless you're going to sit around every day in that café of hers, watching her belly get bigger, there's nothing to keep you here."

Dermot had a few more drinks from his pint while giving Michael's words time to sink in. He gave Sean a dirty look for his last comment, but quickly looked away when visions of him and Mary going at it started to slip into his head. It had been a long day in Dermot's world. He had done ten times as much worrying as he normally would and the pressure was beginning to show. Danny stuck out his hand for a shake, trying to calm the situation. He hadn't done anything wrong apart from telling Michael his own and Dermot's secrets, which he knew now was a mistake.

"Come on, Dermot. Don't break up the team," he said with his right hand on offer. "If you think about it, it's me that should be pissed with you. After all, it's you that's got my ex-bird pregnant."

"I didn't know she was your ex."

"I know you didn't, so what are we arguing about?"

Dermot was still a bit reluctant for a second, but

when Danny pushed his hand even closer, he gave in and took the big man's gesture.

"Ah, fuck it," he said, coming to his senses. "But I don't want to hear no more jokes about either of you two and Mary. The thought that I've been stirring the Keenan brothers' porridge for the last six months turns my gut." His words were mostly directed towards Sean, who was sat with an 'I don't know what you mean. What's all the fuss about, whose round is it and is it time for dinner yet' look on his face.

"Right," said Michael. "Let's celebrate. We'll drink to Dermot becoming a daddy, maybe, and to the four of us getting out of Belfast for a while. Jimmy, set us up another four pints and four cigars. Turn off the telly and pipe up the music. Danny," Michael called, turning to look back at the big fella, who was still holding a disgruntled look on his face after Michael's betrayal, "should I ask Jimmy for the darts? The four of us could throw some arrows."

"Up yours, Flynn," he replied, returning to his horse-racing page.

"Hang on, Jimmy," shouted Sean from his chair. "Make mine a Pils. I'm on a diet!"

The other three stopped what they were doing, looked at Sean in disbelief and in unison said, "Fuck off."

Chapter Seven

Roisin's House

It was nearly ten o'clock before Roisin managed to drag Michael out of O'Reilly's Bar and away from what ended up as a party to wet the baby's head—a baby that hadn't even arrived, and belonging to a father that hadn't been confirmed yet. Things had really got rocking, though, when they started mixing their Guinness with champagne to make Black Velvets. The expensive tipple was paid for by Danny out of his winnings, after putting his last fifty quid each way on a 33-1 outsider. Danny's excuse for his change in fortune was that he had been studying the form all day of the number six horse in the five thirty at Kempton Park!

7P's

Back at Roisin's house, their evening takeaway had now turned into a supper meal and was being treated to a three-minute zap in the microwave. Michael still hadn't found the right time to break the news about his going away and, when eating his food, came up with a number of ideas as to how to broach the subject, only to then rule them all out as the beer talking. The problem was that the two bottles of wine he and Roisin were enjoying with their meal were only going to keep it talking. Things weren't going as he had intended them to but then again that seemed to be the format of his whole day.

Roisin cleared the food and walked through to the kitchen. Switching on the tap, she filled the sink and began to scrape the plates of the remains of the Chinese takeaway. She could feel in the air that something was on Michael's mind; she had known it since he had visited her shop earlier that morning. Michael entered the kitchen and amorously stood up close behind her at the sink. He pulled the hair from the back of her neck and kissed her skin gently while squeezing her lovingly. The movement in his mind was probably smooth, romantic and loving, but to Roisin, who had barely consumed a quarter of the two bottles of wine, it was clumsy, sloppy and a dead giveaway that he was hiding something.

"Go on then, let's have it," she said, drying her hands on a tea towel and turning to face him.

"Don't you want to go to bed first?"

"Not that," she slapped his chest as a gentle telling-off. "Whatever it is that's been on your mind all day."

"What?" he replied, still undecided as to the best way to broach the subject?

"Come on, Michael. You hardly touched your food. You've spent all night deep in thought, pushing it around your plate, when normally I can't shut you up and you're wanting seconds. And I've never seen you leave a spare rib in my life."

"I just had one too many with the lads, that's all."

"Get away with ye. I've seen you eat five times as much after twenty pints."

Roisin waited for an answer, staring Michael straight in the eyes, looking for a hint of what was wrong. A little bit of paranoia started to creep into her head, wondering if there might be another woman involved, especially with him being out on his own the previous night.

"Look, something's come up," Michael started to explain, unable to dodge the issue any longer. "I have to go away with the lads."

"Is that all? Ye had me going there for a minute." A look of relief came over Roisin's face as this time, she banged both her fists on his chest. "I know ye have to go away when you're told. I've never questioned you on that."

"It's nothing to do with business this time; it's more because of it. I never talk to you about what we do, and I respect you for not asking, but it's these fucking peace talks. They have everybody at each other's throats."

"Are you in trouble?" Roisin lovingly placed her hand on Michael's cheek, fearing for his safety.

"Not yet," he replied while kissing her palm and gently squeezing her fingers. "Well, almost, but it's nothing that can't be solved by putting a bit of distance between Belfast and the lads and me."

"Well, if it has to be done then do it. I'll still be here when you get back."

"You don't mind then."

"No, I don't mind. And there was me thinking you might have another woman." Roisin was concerned at Michael's predicament, but just the same glad to hear that he hadn't strayed.

"Women, is it?" exclaimed Michael in a sarcastic tone. "I've no time for that," he added with a hiccup. "Between you, Ma and Peewee, I've barely time for a cup of tea." Michael kissed her lips and smiled, followed by an expression of remembrance. "Mind you, I was offered a piece just this morning. It's good to know I haven't lost the old Flynn magnetism."

"Magnetism," dismissed Roisin. "I don't see much of that on a Saturday night when you're drunk from the pub with sticky spare-rib juice all over your face. Come on then, who would that be chasing my man?"

Michael, with another smile and a teasing look in his eyes, told her of his exploits in the café.

"It was Mary Deasy from the greasy spoon. I took

old Bobby Tomes in for a feed and there she was, large as you like, flashing her big assets all over the counter."

"And what did you do, Michael Flynn, with your magnetism?"

Michael gave a stupid drunken smile. In his stupor, the term 'Flynn magnetism' sounded good to him.

"I didn't reci… reci… recipocate if that's what you mean."

"The word is 'reciprocate', ye drunken oaf, and ye better bleeding not have done."

"I didn't, I swear it. I came straight to the salon and grabbed a piece of your arse, just to remind me where I belonged." Another hiccup followed his explanation. "What do you think I did, woman?"

"And as well you did. Just wait until I see that old trollop."

"Calm down, woman. You haven't heard the best of it yet. I found out later that she's expecting her seventh child and the lucky father is a very close friend of ours."

"Not Big Danny?"

"Not this time, but almost."

"So he has been there then?" perceived Roisin, unsurprised.

"He's been there all right. He took her out for a test drive about a year ago. He said she handled well and the bodywork was good but there was too much mileage on the clock."

"Too much mileage on the clock?" said Roisin, getting her nails out. "Around the clock more like. And if you're going to relate her to a car, what about all the filler she's had in those false tits of hers? Not to mention the Botox in her face, lips and arse. If she's a car, it's an old banger."

"They don't look false," said Michael, immediately wishing he hadn't, realising it was a stupid drunken thing to say. "Anyway," he quickly continued before Roisin could turn the expression on her face into words, "it's not Danny this time. This time it's our very own little dark horse, Dermot Barry."

"No! So that's what you were celebrating. I wondered why you were all smoking cigars. Why didn't you tell me?"

"Because Dermot wants to keep it quiet and he's sworn us all to secrecy—and you know that once I give my word not to tell a soul, my lips are sealed."

"Until they're opened to fit round another pint," added Roisin. Michael, with a sway, didn't appreciate her comment.

"You've a tongue like an adder, woman. Will you not let me finish?" Roisin smirked sarcastically. "You see, our celebrations may have been a bit premature, because the jury's still out on who the proud father might actually be. So, he's holding back on the announcements until after the birth. And the blood test."

"So, is he happy? Does he want it to be his?"

"I don't think he's bothered either way, so long as it's not Fatty's."

"Sean! What's he got to do with it?"

"Apparently, he was seeing Mary—or 'firing a mix in', as he puts it—around about the same time as Danny."

"You're joking! Well, I don't know why I find that so hard to believe. Nothing about that woman shocks me. She must have a fanny like the top of a wellybob. She should have a turnstile fitted at the top of her legs, she has that many visitors."

Michael couldn't help but laugh at Roisin's descriptions, almost shocked at her cattiness.

"Behave yourself, woman. The lads are as much to blame as she is."

"Don't start sticking up for her, Michael Flynn, just because the old slapper has been flashing you her tits all morning."

"I was only in there trying to make sure old Bobby got a good meal."

"Never mind what you were in there for, what about poor Dermot? She's old enough to be his mother. It reminds me of that film with Dustin Hoffman, the one where he gets seduced by the old tart."

"Dermot looks fuck all like Dustin Hoffman. Mind you, he has got that schoolboy, graduate look. Anyway, getting back to what I was originally trying to tell you, I've convinced him to come away with me and the lads. He took some persuading, though; he was going to stick around out of some sort of sense of duty. I wish I could say she's a changed woman, but by the way she was flaunting herself in the café today, I'd say she's worse than ever."

"Hmm," Roisin agreed with a confirming nod of the head. "Well, the least said about that the better. But why now? What's made your mind up to leave now?" Michael shuffled his position against the kitchen top, straightening himself up for the change in conversation.

"Maguire. He was at the flat this morning."

"What did he want?"

"He came to warn me and the lads off. It seems we've upset a few people. Anyway, we argued and Ma heard most of what was said. I think it shook her up a bit and brought back some bad memories."

"Is she okay?"

"She was fine when I left. She wants us round for dinner tomorrow, but I warn ye, she's brooding for grandkids again." Roisin smiled, not exactly dismissing the idea. "Anyway, it was her idea to go away for a while, and I've given it some thought and I think she's right. I don't like to think of her worrying and that's all she'll be doing if I stick around here."

"Where will you go?"

"Only over to the mainland, possibly London. I've been trying to build up the courage to tell you all day."

"I knew there was something you wanted to say when you came to the salon earlier."

"I think you know me too well, woman."

"And so I should after ten years. A woman doesn't need false tits and Botox to tell when her man's got something on his mind."

Michael gave her a 'that's enough' look to put the subject to bed. Roisin, accepting his flag of truce, put her arms back around his neck as the two of them kissed and cuddled in a warm embrace. Michael wondered why he had ever worried that she might not understand. If there was anything he could be sure of in his life right now besides his mother's love, it was hers.

"Well now, if you're going to be away for a while, I'll need plenty to remember you by," Roisin hinted naughtily, with a twinkle in her eye. This time, it was she who had a piece of his arse in her hand.

"I don't know about that," replied Michael with a

cheeky smile. "Now I have all that off my chest, I'm getting my appetite back. I think I might finish off those ribs after all."

Michael reached for the plate containing the sticky pork pieces, but Roisin was there before him, pushing the leftovers beyond his reach.

"Never mind the food," she said. "It's not you that needs more ribs; it's me that's in need of some bone!" She grabbed a shocked Michael by the crotch. "Come on, Michael Flynn with all your magnetism, maybe your mother's right. After all, if Mary Deasy can do it God knows how many times, why can't we?"

She dragged him towards the stairs in a tight grip so that he couldn't argue or escape. His drunken attempts to explain his going away hadn't exactly gone as he had planned, especially after his slipped comments about Mary Deasy's chest, so he was happy with the result. And the bonus was that he could always have the ribs for breakfast!

Chapter Eight

The Best Yorkshires in Town

"That was great, Ma," complimented Michael, who was the first to empty his plate. He stood up from the table and placed it in the sink before beginning to run the water. "There's nobody can make Yorkshire puddings as good as you."

Catherine, who always welcomed praise of her cooking, revealed some of her secret recipe.

"It's the bulb of spring onion I grate into the mixture and the stalk I chop up finely that gives them their taste—that and an extra couple of eggs. I'll teach Roisin how to make them when you finally make an honest woman of her." Catherine gave Roisin a wink across the table and they shared a smile. Michael ignored the comment, not willing to go over already-trampled ground, and was thankful when young Peter's interruption rescued him from what could become another sticky conversation.

"Paddy Fahy told me that you gave him a bollocking over bringing his horse inside again."

"When did you see young Paddy?" asked Michael, checking up that the pair hadn't been up to any mischief.

"Last night, when our mums went to the bingo. He came down to share his chips and curry sauce with me."

"I wondered why there was no bread for the toast this morning."

"Sorry, Ma," apologised young Peter. "We made butties," he explained while shoving a spud into his already overfilled mouth.

"That reminds me, Ma. If I give you some money, will you pay Mrs Fahy's electricity bill? They've been cut off again."

"You can't keep looking after everyone, Michael. You've enough on your plate with me and your brother. Though I suppose it is cold and the season of goodwill isn't long past, and she has had it hard since her husband was killed."

"He wasn't killed, Ma," corrected Michael. "He drank himself to death, leaving that poor woman by herself with five kids to bring up. The only good thing now is that her eyes aren't blacked up every week. Just pay the bill, please. It's not as though she spends her money on anything other than the rent and her kids. The only time the poor woman gets out is when she goes to chapel."

"Okay, son, I'll do it first thing tomorrow morning."

"If I had a gallower, I wouldn't bring it inside," hinted young Peter, chasing a horse of his own.

"You couldn't even look after that Jack Russell you had when you were younger," replied Michael, dashing his hopes. "The poor thing had to sit cross-legged half the day because you were too lazy to take him out. I'm not surprised he ran away."

"He didn't run off," said Peter, defending himself. "Some bleeder nicked him."

"Watch your mouth," shouted Ma, pulling back her hand in a threatening manner.

"Well, it's not fair," he complained. "Every other kid on the estate has got a horse except me."

"Exactly," answered Michael. "You can't open the windows around here because the house fills up with the sweet smell of manure. A man could make a fortune bagging it all and selling it off as fertiliser. In fact, why don't you do that? Then you can buy your own horse."

At twelve years old, Peter wasn't looking for business advice. He just wanted a horse like all his mates. Roisin, seeing his face, picked up her plate and walked to the sink, passing it to Michael.

"Take it easy on your brother," she whispered. "Remember you're going away this week. Don't leave him upset for your mother to deal with."

Michael dropped her plate into the water and looked over his shoulder at his brother, who was chewing his food angrily. His attitude softened, as it always did when approached by either of the two women in his life.

"I'll do you a deal, Peewee."

Peter looked up to see what his brother was offering.

"What sort of deal?" he asked.

"I'm going away this week for a while." Catherine looked up with a smile, realising her conversation had worked. "If you're good for your mother and do as she says while I'm gone, and that means no blobbing school, going to the shops and taking the rubbish to the shoot when ye told, or even if you're not told, I'll see about getting you one when I get back."

"Brilliant," cried Peter.

"You'll have to look after it, though, because I'm not buying you any smelly cob working horse. I'll get you a three-quarter-bred trotter, a set of harnesses and a sulky from Big Eddie Lowe. If I buy it from him, he won't charge me much each week to stable it on his land and he'll teach you how to tack up and drive. That way, you won't try to get it up the steps like young Fahy. But you'll have to go down there each night after school to feed it and muck the stable out on a weekend."

"I will, Michael, I promise."

"Make sure you do, Peewee, because Big Eddie won't give you a second chance if ye don't."

Young Peter's face shone bright as a star. He was

7P's

like a kid on Christmas morning. Leaping out of his seat, leaving the last of his dinner, he ran over and hugged Michael, saying "Thanks, bro,", followed by promises of fulfilling his duties to the animal, and to his Ma, before shooting out of the door to tell his mate Paddy the good news. Roisin gave Michael a kiss on the cheek and squeezed his hand in the soapy water.

"So, you've decided to go then? I'm glad you made the decision, son." Michael looked at his mother. Once again, and as usual she had got what she wanted. Now, as usual, she would try to make out that it was nothing to do with her.

"Don't act like it was my idea, Ma, and that you had nothing to do with it."

"What do you mean?"

"You know what I mean Ma." Catherine shrugged her shoulders. "Now I've talked it over with Roisin and spoken to the lads. She's okay with it, and the boys are coming with me."

"He talked to the lads before he talked to me, Catherine." Roisin got a little dig in as she sat back down at the table. "That shows you whose opinion your son values the most."

"It's a good thing, though, love, with things being as they are at the moment," added Ma. "Besides, me and you can go out and visit the bingo as much as we want to while he's away."

"So, now I have the real reason you wanted to see me on my travels."

"Well, somebody's going to have to win some money, now you've promised your brother a horse. There won't be much change out of three grand for a decent three-quarter trotter. And that's before you've bought the harness and racing sulky."

"Don't worry about the cost Ma, I have it covered. Suddenly, I've found myself with a spare ten grand, now that you've decided you don't want a bungalow."

Catherine's face dropped like she had found a penny and lost a quid. For what Peter's horse was going to cost, she could have gone to the bingo for the next twenty years. That aside though, she had got what she truly wanted—Michael out of Belfast and out

7P's

of harm's way. All that she needed now to overflow her cup was Roisin down the aisle and a grandchild, and she wasn't bothered, despite her Catholic beliefs, which came first.

Chapter Nine

Notice

Thursday was the day that Michael had chosen for the lads and him to leave Belfast. Today, though, was Wednesday, and today he had chosen as the day to repay Maguire's visit, and inform him of their intended departure.

What Maguire thought or had to say about his travelling plans didn't really interest Michael, but what conclusion the people above him may come to did. You couldn't show them your arse without an explanation, not without sooner or later being shown the end of a gun barrel in return if you did. Okay, he had run off at the mouth a bit when Maguire had come to the flat, but that was to him; the boys at the top, however, were a different matter entirely. They would brush you aside as if you never existed if you caused them any problems, and Michael had caused enough of them already.

Maguire's realm and place of business was a poky little bar on the Falls Road, close to the centre of Belfast. Michael arrived there soon after midday to find the pipe-smoker sat in a corner with his aromatic discharge floating in the air around him. As he crossed the floor, he was confronted by the usual uninviting looks and silence that was the reception given to every stranger upon entering a Belfast bar in the times of the troubles. Ignoring the stares and paying the atmosphere no heed, Michael took the liberty of pulling up a chair and sitting opposite Maguire without invitation. As though a switch had been thrown, the noise of the bar returned, as soon as Maguire gave a look of allowance to the meeting, leant forward and took the pipe from his mouth.

"State your business, mister, and make sure your attitude is a mark better than when we last met." Maguire's words of warning were stern, sterner than they were

Saturday morning. But then he was in Michael's house; now Michael was in his.

Michael took out his cigarettes from the inside pocket of his leather jacket. Maguire waited, not patiently, but more intrigued as to the purpose of the visit. The two locked eyes several times in the moments it took for Michael to light up, until eventually he released a breath of exhaled smoke in Maguire's direction, confirming his already previously stated 'I don't give a fuck' attitude.

"I'm going away and the lads are coming with me. You asked us to stay out of trouble, so this move should suit you fine. 'Out of sight, out of mind,' as they say. Anyway, you can count this as fair notice that we won't be around for a while." Michael took another drag from his cigarette. "I'm telling you this so that there's no misunderstanding, and nobody puts us down as being AWOL."

Maguire, with a dismissive snigger, cast doubt on their plans.

"You lot won't last two minutes away from your mammies. What will you do?"

"We'll be okay. We survived well enough when we

were away doing your bidding. We always have our construction skills to fall back on, don't forget."

"When are you going and where?" asked Maguire, who didn't seem too bothered by Michael's revelation.

"When? Tomorrow. Where's not important. Besides, we haven't really decided yet where our destination will be"

"It's important to me, if I need to get in touch with you."

"Why? You haven't bothered with us for the last two years. We've been sat around like spare pricks at a wedding waiting for work. The only time the organisation has bothered with us lately is when they want their cut out of the robberies we've pulled."

Maguire, replacing his pipe in his mouth, sat back in his seat stewing over the situation in his mind. Again he looked into Michael's eyes, looking for something but finding nothing except a shrug of the shoulders. Michael had made it quite plain in this and their previous meetings that he didn't give a fuck, so why should he now? There again, if he was leaving, why should Maguire?

"As far as I'm concerned, you and your mates can

fuck off to the ends of the earth, or further if ye please. You've been more trouble than you're worth lately and the truth of it is that I'll be glad to see the back of ye. But if anyone asks me where my ASU is, I need to be able to give them a fucking answer."

Michael smiled while extinguishing his cigarette in the ashtray.

"Just lie to them, Maguire. You know how to do that—you've practised on us enough."

"I'M WARNING YOU FLYNN." Maguire's anger boiled over into a raised voice at Michael's return, which in turn returned the silence back to the bar. "You buy a fucking mobile phone and get the number to me. I want to know where you are and what you're fucking doing because if you drop me in the shit one more time, I'll have you nailed to a fucking cross—you and your fucking mates."

Michael, after a brief silence, stood up from his chair, which scraped on the floor loudly in the silence that Maguire's outburst had created. The short and sweet meeting was over and once again it hadn't ended well.

Michael, leaving him with a rebellious smirk, turned and was confronted by several stares from the locals, one in particular from the man who had positioned himself between the door and he.

"Is there something you want to fucking say to me?" Michael snarled at the man through gritted teeth. The man gave no answer, he was probably waiting for instructions from Maguire. "Then fuck off out of my way, ye piece of shite." Michael started to move towards the door but the man in his way was joined by another. Michael, reacting quickly, let go a two-punch combination—a left cross followed by a right upper-cut—flooring the first man after sending him crashing through a table and two chairs. The second man lunged towards Michael, but was halted by the door opening and Dermot appearing.

"Is this a private party or can me and my friend Beretta join in?" Dermot pulled back his coat jacket and looked down at his belt, which held the aforementioned weapon. Its introduction had an immediate calming influence, as the remainder of Maguire's henchmen backed off.

"The boys were wondering what was keeping you," Dermot added, looking at Michael, before extending his stone face to the rest of the punters to show that he meant business, "so I thought I would come and have a look."

Michael smiled at his little mate with the big balls before pushing the second man away and straightening his jacket.

"There's nothing keeping me," Flynn answered, while looking at his floored opponent and then over his shoulder at Maguire. With a further look around the bar revealing no more takers, he began to push his way towards the door and through it. Outside the pair took a much needed breath of fresh air and gave each other a living on the edge smile before both their thoughts turned to getting to another bar and having a much-needed drink. Michael pushed Dermot towards the car where Danny and Sean were waiting.

"You're smiling," said Danny as they climbed in. "Things must have gone okay."

"Things went smooth as silk, big fella. No need to

worry yeself," replied Michael, who never seemed happier than when he was upsetting Maguire. Dermot just shook his head in disbelief, wondering if he would ever see the day when Flynn was bothered by anything.

"So he didn't threaten you then?" Danny was finding it hard to believe that the meeting went so well—not realising, of course, that Dermot's timely intervention had probably stopped things getting very messy.

"Only with crucifixion," joked Michael in response. "Although where he's going to find the nails and timber that will take Fatty's weight, I don't know." Michael, with an even bigger smile, looked across at Sean in the driver's seat, who dismissed the comment with a few puffs of his fag. "Come on," continued Michael, happier now that he had covered all the bases. "Let's go for a drink before we go home and pack our bags. We've got a plane to catch in the morning."

Chapter Ten

Notting Hill

<u>March 1998</u>

Nearly three months had passed since the lads had left Belfast and arrived in London, and although they had not gone there on any illegal business, Michael had thought it still wise to cover their tracks. They had flown into Leeds/Bradford airport in Yorkshire, before going on to spend a few weeks in Leeds with some family and friends and then eventually slipping away by train, making their way to the capital.

Work had come pretty easy to them—it's not what you know, it's who you know, as the old adage goes, and in this case, Dermot's uncle was supplying the scaffold for a large job in Notting Hill. Knowing the agent for the site, he had pulled in a favour and landed Dermot the job as foreman, then he, now being in charge had taken on the other three. Sean was driving the tower crane while Danny and Michael were on the trowel, (bricklaying). They were constructing a supermarket and car park complex and the job was good for about six months, although the plan wasn't actually to stay that long but it was good to know that the work was there if they needed it. The lads, well they all had different views and reasons for being there. Sean was getting a bit homesick for his mum's cooking, but he wasn't complaining—he never did. He had fallen in love for the first time—not with a woman, but with the jerk chicken and the goat, rice and peas you could get in the Jamaican restaurants and takeaways around that area. Big Danny was happy enough. He had got his feet under the table with the landlady of the local, The Rose and Crown. The pub was at the end of the street from the site and had become their regular stop-off after finishing work. Her husband had gone out for a packet of fags about five months previously and had failed to return. He probably couldn't stand the pace—she had Danny at it every chance she got and even the big fella twenty years her junior was finding the going a bit demanding. He would have disappeared himself if the bar had not been so conveniently situated and the Guinness she served as good as it was. She was called Barbara, 'Babs' for short, and she may have been in her middle fifties but she certainly wasn't past it, in looks nor stamina.

Dermot was in his element in his new job. He was in charge of the whole site and, for the first time, he could tell the lads what to do, as well as another twenty workers besides. Belfast could not have been further from his mind. It would suit him if they stayed in London for the whole of Mary's term and then maybe even longer, depending on the results of the blood test. He thanked Michael every day for bringing him to his senses and talking him into coming to London.

Michael, however, knew it was too early to go back. He rang Roisin and his mother every night and although things with them were okay, the same thing could not be said for the rest of Northern Ireland. The situation was still pretty much the same as they had left it. The peace agreement had still not been signed, and although judging by what was being said on the news it wouldn't be long before it was, he still thought it best to stay where they were. His mother's words were beginning to ring true, with tensions not only in Belfast but the whole of the North at their highest. The IRA and INLA were at each other's throats, but it was the RIRA (Real Irish Republican Army), a splinter group from the IRA, that was threatening the worst atrocities if the proposed agreement was signed. Ma was right again—if Michael and the lads had stayed, they would have undoubtedly by now be caught up in the thick of it, Catholic fighting Catholic for that prized seat on the Northern Irish council, no winners and no wages.

As the lads were now looking at the situation in Ireland from the outside through a television screen and the papers, it was very easy to become disillusioned with what was going on. To finally get so close to getting the equal rights that they had fought for all these years, only then to fall out with each other in a quarrel for power, made it look like their reasons for the fight hid an ulterior motive. To imagine that outsiders may think this embarrassed and enraged Michael, who saw it as a slur, not just upon himself but also on the memory of his father, who fought only for the cause and never personal gain. Michael was an Irish man who loved Ireland and what Maguire had said to him back in Belfast troubled him because it was said as though it had already been discussed at higher levels, a foregone conclusion of what the future was going to bring. "There'll be other earners." The other earners could only mean racketeering and drugs, and with drugs came its other two sidekicks, prostitution and robbery, both to fund a habit. It was a vicious circle that formed a dangerous merry-go-round and it was a ride that too many young children were buying tickets for. That wasn't Michael's idea of what Northern Ireland should represent or become. He loved his home and saw no reason once the troubles were over why it could not become as big a tourist attraction as the South, and Belfast another Dublin. He had long had his heart and sights set on buying a bar for himself and the lads, where they could entertain the tourists with live bands playing traditional music, creating an authentic taste of Ireland. Like his father, he didn't hate the English, but he would much rather they were coming to his town as money-spending tourists rather than walking the streets as soldiers.

The problem with Michael's dreams for Ireland was that he knew how easy the transition into drugs would be. The IRA, over the years, had become an immensely organised group, with hundreds of contacts abroad and, between them, thousands of supply lines. Up to this point, those supply lines had been used for the importing of arms and munitions, but it wouldn't take much to change the product being delivered into consignments of illegal drugs. An added scarier thought was also that should this happen, the different organisations that were now arguing for power would all become rival gangs in the drugs trade. And with the amount of weapons available in the province, the war between them could well surpass anything that had been fought with the security forces. If this was to happen, in Michael's mind, Dublin in the South would be the worst to suffer. The tourists, students and hen and stag parties would be targeted, and when too many suppliers go after the same customer, disagreements ultimately ensue; with that much money on offer, those disagreements would get very bloody and very deadly.

On the building site in Notting Hill, Michael and Danny were both enjoying being back at work. They had served their apprenticeships together at brick-laying college in the four years after leaving school and were both skilled with the trowel. The first couple of weeks on-site had been hard on their fingers and backs, as well as their alarm clocks, which often ended up on the other side of the bedroom. Eventually, though, they had got back into the rhythm of things and they, like Dermot, were in their element. They were glad to be back doing some good, honest graft, plus it felt rewarding to go home tired after a hard day's work. It made sleeping easy and the Guinness even tastier, the only thing missing, for Michael anyway, was Roisin.

Today was Friday. The lads would usually finish about four and go for a few pints at The Rose and Crown. They would leave the car on-site and get a taxi home, which would save Sean driving, a good idea considering that by the time they usually left, he could neither walk nor talk. Babs, the landlady, always kept Danny at the pub on Friday nights anyway, so he would bring the car back on Saturday morning to their digs, which were a half an hour's drive back up the M1 in Hemel Hempstead. There were a couple of good reasons for travelling such a distance to and from work each day. Firstly, the digs were cheaper, but also they were being careful to stay clear, not only of London while relaxing at the weekend but also of the usual Irish haunts of Cricklewood and Kilburn, even though Michael's father's old friend and partner Davy Mactazner had a pub there called The Harp of Erin. It was all part of their plan to keep a low profile, while lessening their chances of being recognised, and so far it had worked.

Sean sounded the bell on the crane to attract the attention of Michael and Danny, who were busy walling on the top lift of the scaffolding. They looked over the handrail in the direction of the site to see him hung out of his cab, tapping his wristwatch then holding his hand to his mouth in a drinking motion. It was nearly four o'clock and that meant it was time for the pub. By the time Michael had cleaned his tools, Danny was already down the ladder and heading for the gates, where Dermot and Sean stood waiting. Michael gave his work area one last check, making sure the walk-boards were clear and nothing could blow off down into the road over the weekend. From where he was working, he had a good view of the street below. The Rose and Crown was at the far end and coming back towards the site were a couple of takeaways, a chemist and a video rental, until finally, at this end, almost opposite to where he worked, was a nightclub called The Palm Cove.

"Come on, Michael, will ye?" shouted Sean, mad for the drink.

Michael picked up his bag of tools and started down the ladder, eventually reaching the bottom and putting one foot on the ground. A horn sounded, causing him to quickly jump back on the bottom tread to narrowly avoid being hit by a passing wagon. As the vehicle swerved by, the brakes locked, bringing it skidding to a halt a few feet away. Michael, while clutching for his life to the uprights of the ladder, turned to see a head pop out of the driver's window to deliver an apology in a strong London accent.

"Sorry, guv, I didn't get you, did I? I'm rushing to do the last deliveries before knocking off—you know how it is."

"No harm done," said Michael stepping off the ladder. "I'm still in one piece. Don't worry yourself."

"Cheers, John. That's very good of you. I'll get you a drink some time," replied the cockney. "Be lucky," he shouted as he accelerated away at haste to his next drop. Michael, unscathed by the experience, brushed himself down and joined the other three at the gate.

"Be lucky," said Dermot repeating the driver's words. "We'll need to be, with that mad fucker driving around the site. I'll find out who he is and give him a bollocking on Monday," he added, flexing his managerial muscle. "There's a 5mph speed limit when driving around the site."

"Chill out, fella, and don't be getting anybody the sack," replied Michael. "It's Friday night, so the man is just rushing to get finished, the same as we are. Now, come on, there's a pint in the pub with my name on it." Michael pushed him through the gate and the four of them headed off down the street towards The Rose.

The drink went down well that night and, as the Irish say, "the crack was good". Sean was on form, ripping the arse out of everything that moved, which usually meant Dermot, but the little fella gave as good as he got and had done ever since Sean stopped having the Mary Deasy secret over his head. The rest of the weekend continued in much the same mode, as they carried on

7P's

their drinking in their local pub, The Anchor, close to their digs in Hemel Hempstead. There was also a bookie just round the corner, so it suited their Saturday routine in Danny's eyes to a tee. The landlord was okay to; at any rate, he was happy for their custom. Every Saturday, between them, they would stop at least one barrel of Guinness going sour, and Danny, for once, had picked a few winners so they were all a few quid up, which added to the crack and funded a few more pints of the black stuff. This Saturday was special, though. It was a significant date in the calendar of every Irishman in the world. It was St Patrick's Day, March 17th, and the lads were celebrating it like there was no tomorrow. They were dying to go into Cricklewood and Kilburn, where the partying would have been second to none, but, sensibly, they stuck to their plan and kept their heads low.

Sunday went much the same, picking up where Saturday had left off. What started out as a 'hair of the dog' quickly turned into a full-blown session, accompanied by a drunken singalong, with Sean jigging about the pub, doing his Michael Flatley impersonation.

Fortunately, the rest of the cast from Riverdance didn't end up crashing through two tables and a fruit machine for an encore.

Monday morning and the digs weren't a pretty sight. It was a scene of overflowing ashtrays, half-eaten kebabs and spare ribs picked clean to the bone, as if a pack of vultures had been at them. The four of them got ready for work, coughing and spluttering like geriatrics with a sixty-a-day habit, vowing that they would never drink again.

"We'll have to come straight back here tonight and get a grip on this shithole," said Sean, who was responsible for half of the tabs in the ashtray.

"You're not joking. If mi Ma saw this mess, I'd be getting the thick end of the belt," added Michael, responsible for some of the tabs and most of the rib bones.

Work started off slowly that day, with no sign of Dermot, who was usually a pain in the rear first thing on Mondays, making sure that work got off to a good start. He liked to stamp his authority on the site, letting everyone, especially Sean, know that he was in charge—a bit of payback for all the shit he gave him over the weekend. Not this morning though; even site foremen get hangovers, so he was grabbing a few hours' sleep in the site cabin, one of the perks of being in charge and having an office to hide in. It was mid-morning before Michael had the chance to take the top off his flask for a much-needed cup of tea. He made himself comfortable, sitting on a pile of bricks that he had loaded out ready to be walled, lit a cigarette and sipped at the hot drink.

"Ah, that's good," he said to himself, before repeating the process and looking down onto the street. There wasn't much going on; there never was on Monday mornings, perhaps everyone was at home in bed, nursing hangovers, where he should be. He sat appreciating the rare March sunshine, its briskness visible in his breath and the steam from his cup, which he watched rise into the air until his attention was grabbed by the noise of The Palm Cove club doors banging shut across the road. A Rastafarian-looking man came out and headed off down the street towards the pub. This fella was no stranger to Michael, who saw him every day. "Bang on time," he thought to himself, looking at his watch, and taking another drink and a drag of his fag. The Rasta had a habit of leaving the club every morning just after eleven and Michael knew exactly where he was going—down the street opposite The Rose and Crown, where he would stand in the doorway of the Chinese takeaway and peddle his drugs. Michael had watched him every day for the past two and a half months doing the exact same thing, and when he had sold everything he was carrying, he would return to the club for more supplies. Michael had counted him doing the trip fourteen times one day, with an average of twenty to thirty customers each trip. Now, what Michael knew about drugs you could write on the back of a postage stamp; it was one line of business that he had never showed any interest in. Like most young lads, he had smoked a few joints as a teenager, but after his father's death, he had been landed with far too many responsibilities to entertain it as a regular thing. What Michael did know, though, was his maths, and it was easy to work out that the Rasta was making a lot of money. Not for himself, obviously—who the drugs and the money they created did belong to was behind the safety and security of the club doors. But drugs or not, Michael knew a money-earner when he saw it and this fella was cleaning up.

The sore heads stayed with the four Irishmen until well inside the latter part of Wednesday. All were unable to face another drink; even Sean was off his food. But at least the flat had been cleaned from top to bottom. Michael wasn't bothered; Danny and he were happy about their business, walling away up high on the scaffold. They were both paid for the bricks they laid, not for the time they worked, so when he wanted a break, he would just pour himself a drink from his flask, light a cigarette and chill out, watching the world go by on the street below, and, as always, he could count on being entertained by the movements of the local drug dealer running back and forth between the Chinese and the club.

By now, the Rastafarian's comings and goings had become

second nature to Michael. He couldn't believe how a man in his line of business could afford to be so slack. He begrudged the dealer the amount of space and time he had. If Michael went about his work in Belfast the same way, he would have been dead a long time ago. He was getting more and more intrigued by him and his movements back and forth to the club. A vague idea was forming in his conniving and overactive mind, so vague that he didn't even know himself where it was leading. The more he watched, the more the maths kept multiplying in his head, along with thoughts of wanting to know more—so much so that after several more days witnessing the same routine, he decided that the following Friday, he would go and investigate closer, by having a drink at the club. He didn't mention to the others where he was intending to go or what he was planning. He decided not to before taking a look for himself, just in case nothing came of it, or maybe it was because he thought that something may come of it and the lads would think he was out of his mind, bearing in mind that they had come to London to keep out of trouble and lay low.

"What harm could it do?" he asked himself. He would probably go there and it would all be a waste of time amounting to nothing anyway. Also, he still didn't know exactly what it was he was going to look at, so what could he tell them? "Just go, have a quick look around and set your mind at rest," he continued to think, trying to convince himself that he wasn't doing anything stupid.

When four o'clock came around that Friday, bringing to a close another week, Sean, Danny and Dermot were at the site entrance, waiting as usual for Michael, who was going through his normal safety checks.

"How come you're always last?" Sean complained, as Michael joined them.

"Because, Fatty, I have a work area to check and tools to clean. I can't just switch off an engine and jump out of a cab like you."

"OooH, easy tiger," replied Sean. "I just don't like being on-site any longer than I'm being paid for, that's all," he explained, justifying his eagerness. "And as soon as we get out of those gates, I don't have to listen to any more from that power-wielding little fucker." Sean looked at Dermot, who was definitely going to remember that on Monday morning.

"Well, come on then. It's your round," Michael said, giving Sean a gentle nudge in the back, pushing him in the direction of the pub.

"He's round enough," joked Danny.

Sean smiled at his brother's comment.

"Fuck me, I haven't heard that one before," he replied with two raised fingers. "That joke's about as old as your landlady at the pub." He liked it when any of the others gave him grief. It left the gate open for plenty of verbal retaliation and sitting on his own in the cab of the crane all day gave him plenty of time to think up his lines of attack. "As a matter of fact, I am in a rush to see mi future sister-in-law," he said, following one of those lines. "You know Danny, you and Dermot should get your lovely ladies together one day. They'd have a lot to talk about being of a similar age. They might want to swap knitting patterns or reminisce about the war." Sean laughed at his little dig.

"I noticed you weren't that bothered about old Greasy Deasy's age when you were having a tamper with her yourself," Danny dished back.

"I told you two," Dermot interceded, "I don't want to hear no more about that." Dermot shuddered as the thought of it conjured up terrible images in his head. "I'm definitely getting that blood test," he muttered to himself.

Michael followed behind, listening to his three mates scoring points off one and other like kids. It seemed like nothing had changed between them since they were thirteen and back in the schoolyard, but that's what being life-long mates is all about. A reminiscent smile formed on his face of past memories and, as it did, he couldn't help glancing over his right shoulder back at the club and giving it a 'see you later' look.

Barbara the landlady greeted the four of them as they entered The Rose, but it was probably the sight of Big Danny that put the grin on her face and the twinkle in her eye.

"Four Guinness," ordered Sean, who was first to the bar.

"What happened with your diet?" asked Dermot, who knew it wouldn't last.

"I'm leaving it alone until we get back home. I've put on half a stone since I started drinking those bottles. They're like Thailand hookers."

"Thai hookers?" repeated Dermot, confused as to the similarity.

"They go down too easily." Sean gave him a cheeky wink to go with the punch line. Barbara, who had heard Sean mention going back home, interrupted the pair.

"You're not going back to Belfast, are you?" she asked, fearing she might be losing the big fella.

"Calm yourself, Babs. My brother isn't going anywhere just yet. He's smitten with ye, any idiot can see that. Plus he's had a thing for older ladies this past."

"I'll pay for them," Danny interrupted, while pushing himself between Sean and the bar, deciding that buying the round would be a small price to pay to shut the hole in his brother's face. "Take no notice of him,

Barbara darling. He's been in a piss-taking mood all day. He's lucky I haven't put my club of a fist in his fat gob already."

The landlady smiled at Danny's words, as she passed the drinks over the bar.

"You'll be staying tonight as usual, I hope. I've got a nice ham shank for your supper."

Danny could think of a good answer for that one, but didn't want to talk crudely to the lady. Instead he gave her a confirming wink, then carried the drinks over to where the other three had settled in their usual Friday night corner. Michael grabbed one of the pints, before warning them of his intended later movement.

"I'm only having a few then I'm away back to the digs to get changed. I've somewhere to go tonight."

The other three looked at him, wondering what he was up to and why they hadn't been invited.

"Are you taking a bird out?" asked Sean.

"Does she have a friend?" added Dermot.

"There's no bird, Sean, and no friend, Dermot," Michael replied, answering their questions respectively.

You should have no interest in that, anyway, you nearly being a daddy. What would Mary say?"

Dermot, not liking Michael's return or any other reference to his troubles back home, buried his face in his pint.

"What kind of business? All the banks and post offices are closed by now."

"The kind of business, Fatty, that when I know myself, I'll let you know. So, until then, leave it be."

Michael gave Sean the same treatment, cutting him short in his inquisitive tracks, before sinking his pint like it was a half and standing up.

"Come on, then. I thought you wanted a drink. I'll get the next," he volunteered, while walking to the bar, with Danny following close behind.

"Whatever it is you're doing tonight, I can come with you, if you need me."

"It's okay, big fella. I meant what I said. I'm only after having a look at a bit of business. It may be nothing, but there's something nagging at me. It's like an itch I have to scratch."

"Well, I'll scratch the fucker with you when it's needed, you know that."

"Sure, I always know that, big fella," Michael gave his friend a smile and rested his hand on his shoulder. Danny was like a big security blanket. With him around, Michael's back was always covered. "Besides," he continued, "I think you're going to be a bit busy tonight, judging by the expectant look on Barbara's face."

Michael and Danny both looked at Babs, who was holding onto the beer pump with a smile on her face, as though it was Danny's manhood she had a grip of. Danny took a large gulp from his pint, realising that he was in for another hard night, while thinking that he would rather settle for the 'ham shank'.

Chapter Eleven

The Palm Cove

It was about nine thirty later that evening when the taxi drew alongside The Rose and Crown and Michael stepped out, showered, suited and booted.

"Eight fifty," said the driver, while switching his 'for hire' light back on. Michael passed him a tenner through the window, with instructions to keep the change, then turned his attentions to the pub.

"Cheers, guv," shouted the cabbie, before pulling away and heading down the street towards Michael's eventual intended destination, The Palm Cove. Looking back towards The Rose and Crown, he wondered if the lads were still inside, contemplating another drink before he moved on to the club. He knew Danny would be—there was no way Barbara would let him out of her sight on a Friday night and if Sean and Dermot were still there then they would be well out of it by now. That would mean more of their inquisitive questions about where he was going and what for. He decided to give it a miss and get on with what he had come here to do. Turning to head off up the street, his eye was grabbed by the lights from the window of the Chinese takeaway.

He obviously doesn't work nights, he thought, noticing the absence of the drug dealer in its threshold, but thoughts of the Rasta were quickly quashed when his nose was also grabbed by the aromas of freshly prepared food.

"Mm, spare ribs in honey," he muttered, almost tasting the sticky sweet sauce. A smile broke over his face, thinking of the numerous bollockings he had incurred from Roisin concerning his drunken eating habits. Uplifted, he set off walking towards the nightclub, viewing the street for the first time from this angle and in this light. He looked up to the scaffold where Danny and he worked and beyond, in the background, he could see Sean's crane towering high above the site and everything else on the street. It was difficult to spot in the backdrop of the night sky and as he neared the club, it became almost invisible, blanked out by the glare of the club and street lights.

The club at night presented a whole different face to the one Michael looked at every day from the scaffold. The red neon sign bearing its name, The Palm Cove, was brightly lit and bordered by two green palm trees that flashed from side to side, giving the illusion of movement, as though they were swaying in the wind. If that wasn't tacky enough, the rest of the building was covered in rope lighting and multi-coloured lanterns draped from the plinths of each storey. The whole thing resembled the appearance of an over-trimmed council house at Christmas. Michael smiled at the spectacle, almost having to shield his eyes from the glare while thinking that he now knew the reason why the club owners dealt in drugs—it was probably to help pay their electricity bill.

He joined the queue of about a dozen people and

after a short wait, a good body-search and another tenner from his wallet, he was through the door. Inside, the club's layout was much the same as any other. Square of shape, with a large bar running a good length down the right-hand side. The dance floor took up most space in the room's middle, and surrounding it was cheap button-back seating with dimly lit alcoves and corners. Michael had never seen the club while it was open, let alone been inside, but from what he knew about it so far from the drug dealing and now the décor, he had already drawn his conclusions that this place was a right shithole. He approached the bar, undecided what to drink. He didn't fancy taking a chance with the Guinness. This looked the type of place to churn out beer from dirty lines and cheap spirits passed off as named brands.

"What will it be, babes?" asked the barmaid with a smile.

"Anything you have in a bottle," replied Michael, playing it safe.

"Good choice," she said, confirming his initial worries

and taking the top off a bottle of lager. "That will be three pounds, darling."

"Will you have one yourself?" Michael offered.

"Don't mind if I do. Call it a fiver." Michael passed her the money and asked for directions to the toilet.

"Go to the end of the bar, turn right and right again. If you get lost, just follow your nose and the smell going up it."

Michael smiled at the girl's honesty and, following her directions and sure enough found himself outside the toilets. He also found himself yards from his absent-from-the-doorway friend, the Rastafarian, who was in the process of doing a deal. Michael blanked the proceedings, not wanting to make any eye contact as he passed and entered the toilet door.

Very cute, he thought, admiring the set-up. They search you coming into the club to make sure you don't have any drugs, then once you're inside, they sell you theirs.

The toilets were bog-standard, he thought, grinning at his own joke, and the stench was as pungent as the girl behind the bar said it would be. Michael wondered if Sean had been in the club before him, because going by the stink of the toilets he could have quite easily been the last person to drop his guts in there. There were three cubicles, four urinals, two sinks and a small barred window. Seizing the time while he was alone, Michael stepped up onto one of the toilets to raise himself to the level of the window. It was firmly secured with several screws, but on closer inspection, Ronnie Corbett would have struggled to gain entry through it even if it was open. Climbing back down, he used the toilet he had been standing on for its intended function, then washed his hands, only to find the towel dispensers were empty and the dryers were disconnected. Shaking them vigorously, he left, again keeping his eyes averted, but he could still see the Rasta serving up yet another soon-to-be-happy customer.

He's a busy fucker, I'll give him that, he thought as he made his way back to the bar, where his bottle had disappeared.

"I've got it here, babes," said the barmaid, who had

noticed him searching. She took it from the cooler, where she had put it for safekeeping. Michael leant on the bar above her and as she bent down he noticed the body art that covered her back. A butterfly sat on her right shoulder blade which was partially hidden by her top, and on her lower back, where her top had rode up the words "Carpe Diem" were written, underlined by her baby pink coloured G-string that was visible above her jeans. She was quite a striking girl, enhanced in a sexy way by the sight of her G-string but almost spoilt by the few piercings she had in her face. Michael putting two and two together surmised that she was probably a lesbian.

She placed the bottle back on the bar in front of him. "It's best not to leave your drinks unattended in here," she advised. "They either go missing or some pill-head thinks it's funny to send you on an unexpected trip of the imagination."

Michael looked around at the clientele that were already in the club, most of whom looked like they had already bought a ticket for that same excursion.

"Cheers," he thanked. "It's a classy place you work in. You seem a bit out of place."

"I'm not exactly happy with the situation, but it pays the bills," she shrugged.

"I know what you mean," replied Michael, wiping the bottleneck before taking a drink. "I've seen my fair share of dives in the past." He gave the girl a wink, which got him a smile back. "Carpe Diem," he added, looking for a translation. She smiled, which made Michael a little embarrassed. "Sorry, I couldn't help but look."

"It's ok. I wouldn't have got it if I didn't want people to see it. It's Latin. It means 'Seize the Day,' not that I ever did. I got it after watching that film 'Dead Poets Society,' but soon after that I got caught pregnant and that put an end to my seizing anything. Since then I've been working in shit holes like this to be able to afford to bring my little boy up. Like I said, it pays the bills."

"You seem to have had it a bit rough."

"Things could have been easier, but I don't believe in abortion and I wouldn't change things for no amount of money." Michael looked, thinking something else was out of place. "Ah," said the girl with a smile, noticing the confusion in his eyes. "You thought I was a lesbian." Michael tilted his head and said.

"Sorry."

"Don't worry, it's not the first time. I just like piercings and tatt's that's all." Michael smiled, feeling that he had got off lightly.

"They suit you. The tat's that is, I'm not so sure about the other." Again she smiled, probably appreciating his honesty. Michael changed the subject. "What about the father, doesn't he help."

"Nah, he was gone before I even pissed on the tester." The girl left a look on her face that seemed to condemn all men as selfish pigs.

"You surprise me. You're a good looking woman. It would have been a loss to the men around here if you were gay." She blushed, but took it as a compliment.

"Oh, he wanted me alright, it was the responsibility he didn't fancy. I think it's what's called being a tosser." They both laughed.

"Do you have any pictures of the Wee Fella?" The girl

with a smile appreciating Michael's interest, leant forward over the bar whilst opening the locket that hung around her neck. Michael leant forward meeting her half way.

"He's a cracker, and the double of you." The girl said nothing, she just grinned as though her day had been made. As Michael had already said, she was a good looker, down to earth, easy to talk to and she smelt good which he had noticed when he leant forward, which is why he decided to move away from the bar, and away from temptation. "Take care of yeself, er," he hung on to his words waiting for a name.

"Trudy."

"Trudy, and thanks for looking after the bottle."

"You're welcome." Michael turned. "Just a minute." The girl now turned, to the bar and picked up a pen and paper. "That's my address," she said passing Michael a piece of paper. "I'm not easy, don't think that, nor am I inviting you around. It's just that some thieving prick stone my phone earlier on, which was half the reason I was minding your bottle. Anyway, until I buy another, that's my only way of staying in touch." Michael read the address. "You seem like a nice fella," Trudy continued. "If you ever fancy a drink, in somewhere a lot nicer than this, look me up."

"Thank you-Trudy." He folded it carefully in front of her before placing it in his inside pocket. He had no intention of looking her up, Roisin was his lady but he had no intention of hurting her either. Under different circumstances, though, and without Roisin waiting at home, he would have undoubtedly talked more, but he still didn't know where his inquisitiveness that had brought him there that night was taking him, and he didn't want to leave any lasting impressions, but it may have been too late for that. "I'll be in touch."

"We'll see," she answered, not holding her breath.

"By the way." She turned to look again waiting for his question. "What do they call your little boy?" She smiled, as though for the first time somebody gave a fuck.

"Michael," she replied with a glowing smile.

"It's a good name." The pair turned, going about their business before Trudy turned back.

"What's yours?"

"Michael," Trudy smiled at his coincidental answer. "I told you it was a good name." Now they parted.

After a while and another bottle the club started to get a bit busier, and although it may have been in the running for a rosette in 'London's Biggest Shithole Competition', there was certainly nothing wrong with the atmosphere. Everyone seemed to be in a good mood, probably due to the fact that most of its occupants were stoned on one thing or another supplied by the Rasta, but it definitely had something going for it. Michael stocked up with another drink before moving to a better position at the bottom right end of the club, giving him a good view of the toilets and the dealer outside them. Leaning against a table in one of the dark alcoves, he settled in for the wait, hoping that like during the day, the dealer would eventually need to restock his supply and lead him to the next link in the chain.

The music being played was pretty good and most of it to Michael's taste. A mixture of Aswad, Maxi Priest,

Eddy Grant and the usual Bob Marley hits. The DJ was to Michael's liking also. He wasn't one of those talkers that liked to butt in over every record or, worse, try to sing along with the lyrics as though he was an undiscovered pop star. In fact, the only annoying feature apart from the dirt was the multi-coloured lighting that repeatedly caught him in the eye, blurring his vision. Adding to their intensity, they were enhanced as they bounced off a glitter-ball that must have hung in the centre of the room since the late seventies, a leftover relic of *Saturday Night Fever*, big collars and white suit days; he could almost imagine John Travolta doing the splits in the middle of the dance floor. Michael was starting to enjoy the place, as the bottles he had drank mixed with his earlier Guinness. He tapped his foot to the music and remembered the last time he was in a nightclub. It was on Roisin's twenty-fifth birthday over five years earlier. He regretted now, as he listened to the music, not taking her dancing more, instead of subjecting her to the company of his mates and the sights of O'Reilly's Bar every weekend. To add to his regret, which was now accompanied with a little guilt, he couldn't ever remember hearing her complain.

He was shaken from his thoughts when he clocked the Rasta, who was on the move and heading towards his position. Michael straightened up and took one pace back so that the pillar he had been leaning against was now between himself and his target. Only yards to his front, the Rasta turned left, skirting the dance floor, while walking its full length and several metres more to a single door. Michael watched as he knocked on it and waited for a moment, before it opened and he disappeared through it. This was exactly what he was hoping to see, but he needed to get into a better position. If the dealer's form held true, he would be back out in about five minutes, resupplied to resume his business. He moved across to get closer to the door when it reopened, standing next to some people chilling by the dance floor at the front. Blending in as part of their group, he worked himself a good view and waited for the dealer's return. Moments later, his prediction was confirmed as it opened, revealing the room beyond to Michael's eyes. Immediately inside was a security cage, constructed of thick metal bars, and a monitor hung on the wall to view who was at this side of the door before it was opened. In charge of the gate with the keys in his hand was a mountain of a man who made Big Danny look like a wimp. To the giant's right was a door, which presumably led to the office, and behind him, a flight of stone stairs climbing upwards. The replenished dealer closed the door, ending Michael's window, and took the same route back to his pitch outside the toilets, where punters were already waiting for his return. Michael didn't get much time once the door was open; he would have preferred to change his angle, affording himself a better look inside the office, but what he did see filled in most of the blanks and intrigued him even more. He continued around the other side of the dance floor, completing a circuit of the club while keeping his eyes open for anything else that might be significant. Deciding to have another drink, he joined the queue at the bar, which was now two or three deep of punters waiting to be overcharged. Scanning the room while waiting to be served, a quick headcount brought him to the figure of over three hundred, with still more entering. Once again, the maths started totting up in his head.

"You ready for that drink now, John?" said a man from behind him, while at the same time tapping him on his shoulder. Michael turned, vaguely recognising the voice but knowing the face that went with it; it was the dangerous driver from the site.

"Ah, don't worry about it. You missed me by at least three inches." Michael once again made light of their close encounter.

"Nice one," said the driver. "I like a man that don't hold a grudge, but I said I would stand you a beer, so what will you have?"

"Okay, I'll have another one of these with ye," Michael accepted and held up his bottle so the driver could see the label.

"Lavelly," replied the man, stressing his cockney accent and turning to order the drinks.

Michael checked the time; it was almost eleven thirty. Too late now to get the last pint at The Rose and

Crown, but after what he had seen tonight, he didn't want to stick around too long getting his face known.

"There you go, my old china. Get your north and south around that." Returning from the bar and passing Michael the bottle of beer, the driver at the same time left his hand out for a shake. "Eli's the handle. What about you?"

"Michael," he replied, taking Eli's hand with a slight smile at his quirky name.

"I know," said Eli with a returning grin. "My old man liked to read the Bible in his spare time. It could have been worse, I suppose. He could have named me Abraham or Zachariah." They shared another smile. "Are you staying local?"

"No," Michael answered, "I just came back to pick up some keys I left on-site. I saw this place open and thought I'd give it a try." Michael's answer was cautious—he was always wary of what he let slip.

"I'm surprised you noticed it," commented Eli with a hint of sarcasm. "They could do with a few more lights outside to grab the punters' attention."

Michael agreed with a chuckle.

"I know what you mean. A man could make a few quid outside selling sunglasses."

Eli laughed, as both men took a drink.

"What's your game?"

"My what?" asked Michael, feeling a little paranoid?

"Your game. What's your trade on the site?"

"Oh, right. I'm a brickie, me and my mate are on the front wall, doing the face brickwork."

"Is that the big geezer I saw you with by the ladder?"

"Danny? Yeah, he's a gentle giant. He wouldn't do ye any harm unless provoked, not intentionally anyway, although there are a few fellas who have had a good hiding at the bookies after listening to some of his horse-racing tips."

"I wouldn't fall for any of those," replied Eli. "The dogs are my cup of tea. So are you just on the trowel or are you sticking around to do a bit of the spreading?"

"Nah, plastering's not our game. When the bricklaying's topped out, we'll be on our way."

"The same company's got three other sites on the

go. If you like, I could get you a start on one of them. I deliver to all o' them, so I could put a word in for you. It's the least I can do after nearly killing you last week."

"Thanks," said Michael, clinking his bottle with him to say cheers. "I'll think about it, if we decide to stick around."

Feeling it was time to move on, he knocked back the bottle quickly. Eli seemed okay, he was your typical lairy Cockney, probably a Chelsea fan, but Michael wasn't there to make new friends, especially now.

"Listen, Eli, I'm away. It was nice talking with you and thanks for the drink. Maybe I'll see ye about the site some time."

"No problems, Michael. You carry on, my old china. I'm going to stick around and try my luck with the barmaid. I don't usually go for birds with all that metal in their face. I wouldn't know whether to buy her a drink or weigh her in!" Michael smiled as Eli gave a wink.

"Be nice to her. I was talking to her earlier, she seems like a nice girl. They call her Trudy."

"I will. Anyway, the next time I see you, I'll try

not to run you over. Until then, take care of yourself." The pair shook hands again and Eli repeated the farewell greeting he gave the last time they parted on the site. "Be lucky."

Michael headed for the exit, his mind once again returning back to business. Outside, the queue of people waiting to come in was about fifty-strong, which would easily make the numbers inside exceed four hundred. Between the door, the bar-takings and whatever that busy fucker was earning dealing his shit, there was definitely a lot of money in the office beyond that cage. He began to get that tingly feeling he always got when he was about to plan a job. It wasn't like butterflies in his stomach, more like a warm glow of excitement in his testicles. A feeling that only a good robbery or Roisin could put there. One thing was for sure, though, he wasn't going to gain entry through any routes that he had seen tonight; he would have to find another way if he was going to rob the place. He headed off back down the street in the direction of the Chinese—the smell that had wafted up his nose earlier that evening still lingered, and there was no way he would pass a second time unfed, the pull of spare ribs was just too much.

The next morning at the digs in Hemel Hempstead, Michael was up first. He had heard Dermot and Sean banging about around three thirty when they came in, so it would probably be a while before they saw daylight. He walked into the kitchen with the intention of filling the kettle, but he was stopped when coming up against a sink full of dirty plates and pots.

Scruffy bastards, he muttered to himself, taking everything out of the basin so he could refill it with clean hot water. He washed the first cup and placed it on the side, then threw in a teabag and two sugars.

"I'll have one of them," Sean shouted, alerted by the familiar sound of the rattling spoon while on his way to the bathroom.

"I didn't think you'd be up until later. It was nearly four when the pair of you got in."

Michael washed another cup and poured the tea as

the toilet flushed, followed by Sean walking into the kitchen in his briefs. Stood there rubbing his eyes and scratching his crotch while letting out a large yawn didn't make for the most pleasant of sights and Michael wasn't impressed.

"Fuck me, Fatty. Would you put some clothes on before I bring mi supper back up?"

"What's up with ye," he laughed. "Have you not seen a man with a fuller figure before? Ye know the women go mad for a cuddly shape these days. They don't want no six pack anymore, its beef they want, and lots of it."

"Well, ye have that covered," Michael said sarcastically while shaking his head and dropping to one knee to open the fridge door. "Now I've saved some of my Chinese from last night to have for my breakfast and I don't want to be eating it sat opposite you looking like that, so fuck off and get some clothes on." With his head now in the fridge, he searched for what remained of his takeaway.

"You won't find it," said Sean in a guilty tone. Michael, ceasing his rummaging, looked up for an explanation.

"I was hungry when I came in last night. I couldn't help myself... Dermot had some too."

"You greedy fat fucker," yelled Michael.

"Sorry, fella, I couldn't resist it. But I think I may have done you a favour. I've been up with the shits all morning."

"Good. I hope the piles drop out of your arse, ye fat thieving fucker."

"What's all the shouting about? How's a man supposed to get some sleep?" Dermot complained as he joined them in the kitchen.

"I wouldn't be shouting if you and the fucking Michelin Man here hadn't stolen my food."

"I only had the one rib," declared Dermot, downsizing his part in the great takeaway robbery. "It was lardy arse Keenan here that did all the eating."

"It doesn't matter who ate what. You're nothing but a pair of thieves and, to make amends between ye, you can buy my beer all day."

"Fuck that. There were only three ribs and half a plate of chicken-fried rice. I could buy it ten times over for what it would cost to keep you in beer all afternoon. What sort of a deal is that?"

"The only one you're going to get," replied Michael, pushing past Dermot and taking his tea into the living room.

"I told you not to eat it."

"I told you not to eat it," mimicked Sean, repeating Dermot's words in a soppy voice. "Shut the fuck up, ye little squirt. You played your part in it. Anyway," he continued, raising his voice so Michael could hear. "Where were you last night with your business?"

"I'll talk to you later in the pub when the big fella's with us," answered Michael from the lounge. "Now put the kettle back on and I'll have another cuppa. This one has gone cold while I was searching for my stolen food. That can be the first drink you get me today."

"I'll get that one," said Dermot quickly, knowing it was free.

Chapter Twelve

The Plan

Later that Saturday, the three of them made their way to their usual Saturday pub, The Anchor, just around the corner from their digs. Sean and Dermot had got off pretty lightly so far after taking Michael's food, but only because he had other things on his mind—namely, what he had seen the night before and how he was going to break the news to the lads that he intended to rob the place.

"Do you have any sandwiches?" Michael asked the landlord. "I missed out on my breakfast this morning," he added, passing the other two a sideways glance.

"I can make you some cheese and ham toasties if

that's okay. It's the best I can do at the moment until the kitchen opens at twelve thirty."

"That'll be grand. One of the two thieves at the bar here will be paying." Again, Michael looked at Sean and Dermot, who were each waiting for the other to get their hand in their pocket.

"Don't leave me out," shouted Danny, arriving through the door.

"You're just in time, big fella. Dermot and Fatty have agreed to buy the beer all day. Isn't that nice of them?"

"It is indeed," he agreed. "What did you do wrong this time?" he enquired, suspecting correctly that their generosity was imposed for a reason.

"We ate his leftover Chinese when we came in last night," Sean admitted.

"I only had one rib!" Dermot again declared, as though it made a difference. Danny laughed, knowing the consequences of such an act.

"I'd say it was a wrong move anyway. You know how your man is about his Chinese food, especially spare ribs. You would have been in less trouble if you'd taken a turn around the bedroom with Roisin."

"Yeah, but it's a bit strong to make us buy the beer all day," complained Sean.

"Well then, maybe next time you'll think twice before you go pilfering another man's rations. Don't worry; I'll see if I can pick us out a few winners to ease the cost."

"I can see it being an expensive day!" Dermot sarcastically added, this time receiving one of Danny's dirty looks.

"You're late today, Danny Boy. Did you sleep in?"

"Sleep, is it? It would be nice to get some. I'm not surprised her husband fucked off. Once last night and twice again this morning she had me at it."

"She did well to get a rise out of you last night," Sean remarked. "You could barely stand up yourself, let alone anything else."

"That woman would get sap out of a log. My bollocks are like a couple of garden peas. The old sacks have never been so empty. I'm thinking about kicking her into touch, so I can have a rest. We'll have to find somewhere else to have a drink after work."

"Don't be doing anything hasty, big man. We may need her soon."

Danny looked at Michael, slightly puzzled by his statement.

"Why would we need Babs for anything?" he asked. The corners of Michael's mouth rose before he took a drink from his pint to hide his smile. "What's going on in that devious mind of yours, Flynn? Has this got anything to do with what you were up to last night?"

Michael looked around the room to check no one could hear, before walking over to take a seat in the corner and beckoning the other three to join him.

"Come around the table while I tell you the crack," he whispered, as they formed the usual huddle they always made when business was about to be discussed.

"I went to look at a place last night, not knowing what was on my mind. That's why I went alone. However, now I've had a look, there's no other way to say it, other than I intend to rob the place."

His three friends looked at each other and they couldn't be blamed for thinking 'here we go again'. Although they had never known him to stray from Roisin, they really had thought that when he said he was going out to look at some business, it was just a cover to meet a bird.

"It's not far from The Rose and Crown," Michael continued. "And it's even closer to the site, but to pull it off I think that both of them will be needed."

"What is it?" asked Dermot. "There's nothing worth stealing around there. Not unless we're going rob the takeaways and get Fatty's wages back." He giggled at his own joke, thinking it was nice to get in first for once. Sean said nothing in retaliation and instead filed the comment to be dealt with later.

"I don't want to talk about the job yet or what or where it is. I need to know whether you want to get involved or not."

"Sure we do."

"Not so fast, big fella. I want each of you to speak for yourselves. I nearly got you killed in Belfast, which was the reason we came away. In fact, over the last few years, I've done nothing else but put your lives in danger with one scheme or another, and now here I am at it again."

"Yeah, but we've always made money," remembered Danny, reminding Michael that his previous schemes had not been without reward.

"And we will this time, but what I'm suggesting goes against all my reasoning for leaving home, and it will mean jail if we get caught and plenty of it, because we'll be going in armed and heavy as usual. That is, of course, if we don't get shot ourselves, because I think the men we go up against will definitely be tooled up."

"How much are we looking at?" asked Sean eager to know his cut?

"By my reckoning, there's at least a hundred grand for the taking and from what I saw last night, it's a goer. Now, I wouldn't blame any of you if you didn't want any part of it, but I can't leave it alone. A hundred grand will be a nice lump to take back to Belfast and you know that once I have something in my head, it's as good as done."

Michael knew the lads were interested by the look in their eyes when he mentioned the money, but he thought he owed them more of an explanation before they followed him into yet another of his schemes.

"I know that a hundred grand between us isn't life-changing money, but if we leave it in a pot we can use it for something bigger back home. It could be a nice big deposit on a bar or even give us a good stake in starting up our own building company. We could be doing exactly what we are doing now but for ourselves as equal partners. It's about time we were our own bosses and not having to answer to the likes of Maguire. And there'll be no more kickbacks from the work we do."

"I'll drink to that," agreed Danny, raising his glass.

Dermot tapped Michael on the arm, telling him to be quiet because the landlord was approaching behind him with his food. The two toasties cut into four halves were placed on the table in front of him. Michael looked over his shoulder to thank him and, by the time he looked back, three of them had disappeared. He didn't say anything, just shook his head. Obviously, the bollocking that morning concerning people nicking his food had just gone over their heads, along with his wasted breath. He turned to the landlord, who was making his way back to the bar.

"Do me that again, would ye, fella?" The landlord acknowledged and began to laugh when he saw what had happened to the first lot.

"Well, if it's me you're worried about, don't be," Dermot chirped, while finger-wrestling a piece of melted cheese that was hanging from his mouth. "I might have taken some convincing to leave Belfast, but with that amount of money on the table, I'm up for it. Especially if you say it's a goer." His quick return quashed any of Michael's doubts.

"Fair play to ye, Dermot. Danny Boy, what about you?"

"Do you need to ask?"

"Not really, big fella. Sean, are you in or have ye got something better to do?"

"Sure I'm in," he confirmed, open-mouthed so the rest of them could view how much he was enjoying Michael's sandwich. "Whatever it is you have in mind, I'm up for it. I just don't see why I have to buy the beer all day. It was only a couple of fucking spare ribs!"

Sean's moans were greeted with the shaking of Danny and Michael's heads. Dermot claimed the fifth amendment, trying to distance himself from any mention of Chinese food.

"Right, that's all I wanted to know. Let's say no more about the subject until I have it clear in my head. At the moment, it's all bouncing around in there like a Wimbledon tennis ball, but I'll fill you in on the details on Monday at work."

The four mates raised their glasses, starting what was going to be a long day on the drink and an expensive one for Sean and Dermot.

For the rest of the afternoon, the Guinness flowed steadily, sometimes more steadily than others, while the lads wondered what Michael had in store for them

7P's

this time. Michael just wondered if Big Danny was ever going to pick a winner.

What he had proposed was never mentioned again that day, but the air was electric with anticipation as individually, the other three each conjured up their own ideas about the robbery and what the target could be.

On Sunday, Sean and Dermot went locally for a beer and Big Danny went to see his landlady at The Rose. He was going to give it a miss and catch up on some much-needed rest, but Michael wanted to keep her sweet. He didn't know what part she would play in the plan yet, partly because he didn't even have a plan, but he asked Danny to go there anyway, just in case. Michael spent the day drinking tea and flicking through the television channels, going over in his head the things he had seen at the club. An idea was forming involving Sean's crane, after seeing it from the street on Friday night. A possible solution that he thought may very well solve his entry problems after seeing the stairs behind the security gates. His head was buzzing, but he needed to see the club again to finalise his plans—so much so that he couldn't wait to get to work the next morning to scrutinise the parts of the building that he hadn't taken any notice of in the past. Then, hopefully by the time he had arranged to meet the lads by his workplace at lunchtime, he may have some answers for them and be able to explain just what it was that was making his head buzz.

Unsurprisingly, Danny never made it home on Sunday night, so the lads threw his work gear into a bag on Monday morning and took it with them. He turned up on site about eight thirty, looking like he'd had a hard night in more ways than one. Michael poured him some tea from his flask and lit him a cigarette, while smiling at his exhausted appearance as he struggled to lace up his work boots.

"I hope you were right about that hundred grand, Flynn, because that woman will be the death of me."

"Think of it as being a perk of the job, Danny Boy." Michael, trying not to laugh, passed him the hot drink and a smoke.

"It's no fucking perk, I can tell ye. A man can get tired of something he's getting too much of."

"Well, keep at her, fella. You'll soon wear her down."

"Something's getting worn down, but it's not her." Danny, cupping his groin, hinted at the wear and tear that his tackle was suffering. Michael laughed, thinking there were worse ways to die.

"By the way, I've arranged for the other two to meet us up here for dinner, so I can explain a few things, so don't go wandering off back down the road to see your landlady."

"No chance of that," dismissed Danny, again comforting his crotch.

At lunchtime, as arranged, everybody arrived at Michael's work area. Dermot had got them all fish and chips, and Michael supplied the tea.

"I love takeaways, but you can't beat fish and chips," Sean said, who considered himself the finest connoisseur of fast food this side of the River Shannon. "Mind you, they'd have been a lot better with some mushy farters!" he added, screwing up the newspaper he had just eaten from and throwing it at Dermot's head, who he obviously blamed for the lack of the side order. The crumpled missile bounced off his brow and fell into his tea, splashing the hot beverage onto his hand. Dermot, while shaking the fluid from his digits, did his best not to bite.

"If you had wanted mushy peas, you should have asked for them. I'm no fucking mind reader, ye fat twat. And the last thing you need is anything to aid your flatulence."

Dermot threw back the dripping ball, which Sean dodged, leaving it to go over the scaffold, falling the fifty or so feet to the ground below.

"Will you shut the fuck up, the pair of ye? I bet you didn't argue like that the other night when you were stealing my ribs." Michael's bollocking brought a quick end to the bickering.

"Okay, Flynn, what's the plan? Who's getting it and when?" Danny asked, getting the conversation started, revived after his feed.

"Okay, fellas, come here." Michael went and stood at the scaffolding overlooking the street, with the other three following. With the paper resting in his left hand containing the last of his meal, he began to indicate towards the street, using a large chip held in his right hand as a pointer. "Look down at the doorway of the Chinese opposite the pub. What do you see?" Dermot, Sean and Danny leant on the top rail of the scaffold and looked at the takeaway.

"A black fella with long hair," observed Sean. "I hope he's not hungry; that place doesn't open until six."

"He's called a Rastafarian," corrected Dermot.

"So, you know him then, do ye?" quipped Sean.

"That's not his name, it's his religion, thickhead."

"Well, whatever his name is," interrupted Danny, "if he hasn't got a hundred grand in his back pocket, why the fuck are we looking at him?"

"Come on, lads. Pay attention, will ye?" Michael tried to get their minds back on the job so he could continue to explain things. "I've been watching him now for about ten weeks. At first, I thought he was just another one of the locals, going about his daily chores, until I realised what his game was." At that point, as Michael talked, the Jamaican moved from the doorway and set off back up the street towards them. "Keep your eye on him now he's on the move." Michael bit the chip in half that he had been using as a pointer as the four of them watched the Rasta come all the way back along the street until he disappeared into the club opposite. Michael returned to his pile of bricks and continued eating the last of his lunch from the newspaper in his hand. The other three again followed his lead, still waiting to be fully enlightened.

"I must be getting slower because I haven't got a fucking clue what we were just looking at," said Danny, with Sean and Dermot looking as equally confused. Michael swallowed his food before washing it down with a drink of his tea and continuing.

"I know enough about that fella to tell you that in about ten minutes, he's going to be coming back out of that club he just entered. He'll then walk all the way back down the street and return to his position in the takeaway entrance." Michael paused to wipe the grease from around his mouth with the now empty newspaper. "I watch him do the same trip over a dozen times a day."

"So, what is he? A fucking exercise freak or just the local looney toon?"

"No, Fatty, he's a drug dealer."

"Fuck me, Michael. What do we know about drugs?"

"Dermot, we don't need to know anything. The Rasta converts the drugs into money and we know plenty about that."

"I know, but drugs and all the shite that goes with them have never been our forte. I just don't like being around the stuff."

"Lighten up, Dermot," interrupted Sean. "When we rob the fucker and take all his money, which is what I think Michael's saying, we'll be putting him out of business. Think of it as your good deed to society."

"Cheers, Sean," Michael said, not sure that his input was helping. "Look, to my reckoning, he's earning three and a half to five grand a day and that's every day. Then from Thursday till Sunday when the clubs open, he's at it all night inside as well. I was in there on Friday night myself and there were maybe three to four hundred people, all out of their fucking heads on shit that had been bought from him. All that, along with the door and bar takings, makes me think that there's a minimum of a hundred grand for the taking."

"So, you're planning to rob the club, not the dealer?"

"The club is where the big money is, Danny."

"How do you know that?" questioned Dermot. "There's no way of knowing for sure how much is in there. Do you even know what day they go to the bank?"

"Use your head, Dermot. They're drug dealers. They don't use banks."

"Correct, Danny Boy, and, more to the point, they don't call the police either. Look, Dermot, I don't have all the answers yet, but I do know if we hit that place on a Sunday night, we have a good chance of catching the pot full."

"So, how do we do it?" Danny asked.

"Well, the front way is out of the question—I found that out Friday night—and there's no back door either. I couldn't even see a fire exit. Fuck knows how the place has got a licence."

"So, where does that leave us?" enquired Sean.

"It leaves us in your capable hands, my takeaway-nicking fat friend."

"My hands!" he exclaimed.

"Your hands, Sean. Or, to be more precise, your cement hopper." The three of them looked at each other, baffled at what the cement hopper had to do with it. Michael resumed his explanation of the next part of the plan. "Look over at the club and the building it's in." The other three returned to the scaffold and did as he instructed. Michael remained on his pile of bricks, having a mental picture of what the lads were looking at firmly implanted in his mind. "How many floors do you see?"

"Three, including the club," Dermot replied.

"And what's in the two floors above the club?"

"They're disused by the looks of it. Most of the windows are broken and there are a few pigeons flying around inside."

"And what does that tell you?" Michael got no answer

from his mates. "It tells you that they prefer their privacy because any businessman with any brains would have converted those two floors into flats and be drawing a nice lump each month for rent." They now agreed with a nod. "Anyway, what do you see on the roof?"

"Apart from an access door to a stairwell, nothing at all."

"And that door is in the far left corner of the roof?"

"Yeah. Why? What difference does that make?" Michael didn't answer—he was too busy pouring himself another drink from his flask. The other three waited in anticipation, feeling that they were finally getting to the punch line. After a couple of hasty sips from his steaming brew, Michael continued. "Because that door is obviously the top of some stairs—the same stairs that I think I saw the bottom of on Friday night."

"So how the fuck is it in my hands?"

"Because, Fatty, if your crane will reach far enough over the street to drop us on the roof of the club, then that is how we'll get in!"

"Sure it'll reach. I take deliveries from the street

all the time from wagons that are too big to get on the site and there's at least ten metres of the boom arm left over that I purposely leave retracted so that I don't hit the buildings over there."

Again, the other three looked back at the access door on the club roof and then over their shoulders at the site crane.

"What about alarms?" Dermot asked, as always looking for a downside.

"That's one of the reasons for hitting the club while it's open," answered Michael before listing the advantages. "One—we'll probably catch them with their guard and pants down, because they think they're safe behind their metal gates. All their security measures are designed to fend off an assault from the front, not from above. And two—while the club's open, the alarms will be off. Don't get me wrong, I'm expecting a few circuit breakers on the doors, but nothing that a few lengths of wire and some crocodile clips can't fix. We'll know more on Thursday night when the big fella and me go over for a look."

"Metal gates? What metal gates?" Dermot asked, still looking for that flaw.

"Don't worry about them. The security gates won't be a problem. If those stairs from the roof are connected to the same stairs I saw Friday night, the gates will work for us, not against us."

Danny, Dermot and Sean looked at each other, then the crane and then back at the roof of the club, weighing up Michael's proposed entry route. They were all nodding their heads, as though it just might work. What was more, Dermot had no more queries.

"You seem to have it all worked out pretty good, fella."

"We'll know for sure on Thursday, Danny Boy, but I don't see anything to stop us so far." More agreeing nods followed his words.

The door slammed at the club, grabbing all of their attentions and returning the other three without Michael back to the scaffolding rail. He didn't need to look down onto the street—he knew exactly what it was. It was the Rasta leaving to return to his pitch at the Chinese.

7P's

As usual, and without a care in the world, he casually strolled down the street to resume his business. But, this time another three pairs of Irish eyes logged his every move. Now they were all smiling.

Chapter Thirteen

The Dry Run

Every chance they got over the next couple of days, all the lads would meet at Michael's work area to watch the club and the movements of the dealer. By the time Thursday came around, there were no doubts in any of their minds, and for once they were all in full agreement that the plan thus far was a good one. Sean had prepared the crane a little more each day, slightly oiling and greasing its working parts to make it run as silently and reliably as possible. Dermot had sorted out some overtime for the four of them so that their presence on-site late Thursday night wouldn't draw any unwanted attention and Danny had acquired the equipment that he and Michael would need for their little reconnaissance trip.

Michael was like a cat on a hot tin roof, itching to get started. To him, robbing the club was like a challenge, a gauntlet thrown at his feet by the slackness of the dealer's actions. Planning and pulling a job like this got his adrenaline rushing and his mind ticking. The danger of being caught and the fine line between life and death made his life worth living, but even with his enthusiasm at its highest, he would never jump in feet first or leave anything to chance. His plans were meticulous and precise, another trait passed on from his father. Every detail had to be rehearsed until it became second nature to both him and the lads, and going over there tonight with Danny would finalise those plans and give him the rest of the information he needed to ensure the robbery was a success.

By eight thirty, it was dark, but the moon was full and high, so they couldn't depend on a lack of light to hide their movements. Eleven o'clock was the time they had chosen to start their dry run. It was Michael's thinking that by that time, the club should be up and running and bearing as much resemblance to Sunday evening as possible. Dermot, armed with a walkie-talkie, had positioned himself roughly a hundred yards down the street from the club, making sure that the crane could not be seen or heard by the door staff or any of the queuing punters. Sean was in his cab at the controls of the machine, while Danny and Michael were at the cement hopper, getting ready to climb in. Danny placed a rope and bolt crops inside the vessel, checking that they had brought everything they needed before jumping in.

"Do you have the torch and the radio?" he asked, as Michael climbed in beside him.

Michael pulled back his jacket to reveal a torch tucked in his belt, and took a radio from his inside pocket and placed it to his mouth.

"Dermot, are you in position?"

"I'm tucked inside the doorway of the video rental. I have a good view of everything."

"What about you, Sean? Can you hear me okay?"

"That's a ten four, big buddy. You're coming in loud and clear."

"Sean, that's not a truck you're driving and you're not Rubber Duck. Now stop fucking about for once and concentrate. We're in the hopper, now let's get going." Immediately Michael had finished his bollocking, he and Danny began to rise into the night sky. When they had cleared the obstacles of the site, Sean swung the long arm of the crane in the direction of the club roof. The Meccano-like strip of box metal now spanned the distance between the two buildings, as though somebody had magically constructed a bridge out of thin air.

"Right, Fatty, you're perfect there," Michael relayed. "Now, nice and gently, start sending us across." Sean, as instructed, began to move the hopper and its contents along the long boom arm, which extended towards their objective. As they reached halfway, Michael wanted to know how things were looking from down below. "Dermot, we're moving. Can ye see anything?"

"Not a thing." Dermot took his eyes from the sky above and looked at the queue outside the club to confirm that they hadn't noticed anything either. "And the locals haven't got a clue either."

"Okay, but keep your eyes peeled." After an elbow from Danny, Michael returned his attention to their progress in the hopper. "Sean, slow it down a bit. Another ten feet and we'll be over the club. Five, four, three, two, one, stop." Michael looked over the side of the swaying hopper, judging the distance of their descent. "Now, take us down about twenty."

Sean continued to follow Michael's instructions, tweaking the controls from his blind spot inside the cab. "A little more… more… more… more… slowly does it… stop! That'll do ye fella, we're sweet there."

The hopper hovered inches from the rooftop. Danny jumped out and Michael passed him the tools before climbing out himself. Together, they now headed straight towards the access door to inspect it. With no handle or keyhole visible, it was obviously a fire door operated by a push bar from the inside. They knew that this wasn't going to be their point of entry—not yet, anyway—so they moved to the side of the building in search of an ideal spot. Michael leant over the edge to locate a suitable broken window, as Danny tied the rope around his waist and threw the rest over the side.

"Are you ready?" Michael asked.

"When you are," confirmed Danny, selecting his footing. Michael climbed onto the edge above the chosen entrance, as Danny leant back on the rope to take the strain.

"See you in five minutes, big fella."

Michael, leaving Danny with a wink, disappeared over the edge, lowering himself down to the appropriate window ledge. Resting his toes on the sill, he poked his arm through a broken pane and slid the catch open, before squeezing his fingers underneath to raise the sash window—not the easiest of operations while balancing on a ledge and holding onto a rope fifty feet above the ground. Once the window was open and he had squeezed himself inside, he took the radio out of his pocket to let the others know of his progress.

"I'm inside. Keep off the radio now, unless you hear any alarms or police sirens. Do you hear?"

"I hear you," replied Dermot.

"Okay," answered Sean. It wasn't that Michael didn't trust them both, but he thought it better to turn the volume down anyway, before putting the radio back in his pocket.

"Danny, send down the crops," he said, with his head back out of the window.

The rope disappeared and moments later returned, dangling outside the window with the bolt crops attached. Michael untied them and removed the torch from his belt, before bending down on one knee. The room smelt unpleasant and damp, its odours constantly whipped up by the gentle breeze that blew through the broken panes. He switched on the light, keeping the beam low and away from the windows to the front of the building. The room was dilapidated from its openness to the elements but clear, apart from the odd bit of rubbish and a good covering of pigeon droppings, which obviously accounted for the unpleasant smell. Spotting the door in the corner, he made his way towards it, keeping the light at his feet, unsure of the damp and aged floorboards that were made more treacherous by their shitty coating, which became slippery when trampled underfoot.

Again, he examined the door and its casing. There was no sign of any alarm wires; there wasn't even a lock, it was just a standard internal door. Michael grabbed hold of the handle, turned off the torch and opened it slowly to reveal more darkness and complete silence. Switching the torch back on, he found what he had hoped for—the stairs leading both up to the roof and down, hopefully all the way to the club. The steps were covered in a thick layer of undisturbed dust, which Michael took as a good sign, knowing that nobody had used them in a very long time. Foreseeing he might need to make a quick getaway, he pinned the door open, using the heavy bolt crops as a wedge. Then, using the top step, he scraped the mess he had acquired from the room from the soles of shoes, before starting his descent down the stairs.

Carefully selecting his footing while keeping the light directed at his feet, he also steadied himself by feeling with his hand along the left-hand wall. At the bottom of the first flight, the stairs returned on themselves to the left. Michael turned the corner, where he found another door obviously leading to the second floor, and, in front of him, another flight. Immediately, he became aware of the faint sound of music rising from the darkness. His excitement grew as he thought that surely he was only one flight and one door away from the club. Weighing up the situation, he decided not to go and investigate any further before returning to open the access door to let Danny in. There was safety in numbers should anything go wrong, and remembering the size of the man on the gate, Michael didn't fancy his chances trying to punch above his weight and tackle that situation on his own.

    He retraced his steps, collecting the bolt-crops on his way, and then continued up the extra flight, bringing him to the roof and the access door. It was alarmed and padlocked. Michael reached into his pocket, pulled out the wire and crocodile clips that he had brought, and attached them to either side of the circuit that would be broken when the door was opened. The alarm was probably switched off with the rest of the club because it was open, but if the circuit wasn't complete, it would show up on the zone pad when the alarms were set when closing.

Now it was time to take care of the padlock. He raised up the bolt crops, placing the jaws around the locking bar, and, with a slight struggle, the jaws met and the lock fell to the ground. Michael carefully pushed down on the bar that ran along the back and eased the door open. For a moment, he stood still with his ear in the air, listening for any alarms that may have been triggered. He also turned the radio back up for a second just in case Dermot had heard or seen anything and was trying to get in touch with him. When he was satisfied that his actions had alerted nobody, he called for Danny, who was still standing at his post above the window.

"Psssst, big fella." Danny turned at the words and saw Michael at the door.

He pulled up the rope, removed it from his waist and rushed to join him.

"Be careful of the wire," Michael said, pointing to his handiwork with the alarm and its improvised connection that hung above their heads. Danny acknowledged, then followed Michael back down the stairs to his previous position. When they reached it, Michael placed his fingers over the end of the torch, letting through just enough light so that they could see their footing, before continuing down the final flight to the last door. Quietly and carefully, they approached it until the light that shone from beneath it and through the gaps in the surrounding casing lit their way. This door looked to be made from sterner stuff than the other internals, and looking down the joint, Michael could see that a lock was engaged, backed up by two slide bolts, one ten inches from the top and the other the same distance from its base.

As he pressed his ear against the keyhole, Michael was sure he could hear some voices, but the music from the club made them impossible to distinguish. In his head, he knew that they were in the right place behind the security gates—they had to be, it was the only set of stairs in the place, but he needed confirmation, so they decided to sit down and wait. They made themselves as comfortable as they could on the cold steps, quietly discussing how they would tackle the last door on the night of the robbery. The two bolts and the lock were obviously sturdy fittings, but they were rendered pretty much useless because the casing they were all attached to was not only made from inferior wood but was also shabbily fitted. Danny knew that his weight, combined with a good run down the stairs, would ensure that the whole thing would give way in a second.

Nearly forty-five minutes later, their patience was rewarded when the unmistakeable sound of keys jangling and the banging of a metal gate could be heard over everything else. They could even tell when the dividing door to the club was open, because the music grew louder.

That was all the confirmation they needed. Michael gave Danny the thumbs-up in the torch light and they quietly retreated back up the stairs to the roof. Carefully, they closed the access door so as not to disturb their bypass wire and left a slither of card between the door and the casing so the lock did not fall back into its housing. Michael, now absolutely sure in his mind that the robbery was a goer, began to make plans for their escape.

"At this point, Danny, if we're being followed, we're going to have to rig up some kind of small explosion. If we blow the doorway and the top of the stairs, it should buy us enough time to get clear in the hopper."

"Well, that's Dermot's department. I'm sure he can think of something that will slow them down. Meanwhile, let's get off this roof and discuss it further in a better place, like the pub." Michael nodded in agreement, and while Danny collected the tools he got back on the radio.

"Sean, are you awake?"

"I'm wide awake and gagging for a pint."

"Then stop talking, fat boy, and bring us home." No sooner had Michael requested it than they were on their way, accompanied by more of Sean's radio talk.

"Good evening, gentlemen. This is your captain speaking. We are about to start our descent back into the building site, so could you now please make sure that your seatbelts are properly fastened, your chairs are in the upright position and your tray-tables are securely folded away." Danny and Michael, both listening, couldn't help sharing a smile. "I would like to take this opportunity to thank you for choosing to fly with Keenan Airways and wish you a safe onward journey to the pub, where you are invited to buy your pilot a rake of beer and a kebab for his supper."

"Fatty, will you stop fucking about? And I'd thought you would have learnt your lesson about mentioning suppers!! Dermot, how are things looking from your end?"

"No problems down here. These fuckers haven't got a clue what's going on above their heads."

"Good, then as soon as we've cleared the street take yourself off to The Rose. We'll be with you shortly."

Danny and Michael were soon on the ground, back inside the site, where Sean rushed to join them.

"How was it?"

"No probs, bro. Just one locked door to go through, but by the time we kick that in, we'll be all over the fuckers. They won't know what's hit them." Danny's prediction was voiced with eager excitement.

"Come on, big fella. We can talk later. And you, Fatty—Air Keenan is grounded for the night, so lock the radios and the rest of the stuff inside your cab, then let's get to the pub, where you can fuck about as much as you want."

"I take it you weren't happy with the in-flight service?"

Again, Michael and Danny both smiled. Sean's little joke was funny, but, as usual, his timing sucked.

In the bar, Dermot had already got the drinks in and was waiting for them in their usual corner, where they all settled after Danny prised himself away from the landlady's clutches. They all dived into their Guinness like camels in the Sahara Desert, before Michael started the conversation, going straight for the jugular.

"Right, we go this Sunday!"

"Fuck me, do you not think that's a bit quick?" Dermot blurted.

"No," answered Michael, convinced after what he had just seen that time was of the essence. "The only thing that can stop us is if we can't get the weapons quickly enough. Besides, the way that fucking drug dealer goes about his business, we'll be lucky if he doesn't get himself nicked before then. I don't want to take the chance on leaving it any longer. It would be just our luck for someone to throw a spanner in the works. Someone could even go up those steps and notice our little handiwork with the alarms. It wouldn't matter either if we had removed the bypass wire—they would still see our footprints on the dusty steps."

"I agree with you for getting on with it," said Danny. "But, at such short notice, I can think of only one place where we're going to get the weapons we'll need."

"We have no choice, big fella, unless you have another supplier up your sleeve."

"No, I don't, but if we get caught using Mactazner's

supplies, we may as well have stayed in Belfast because we'll be right back in the shit."

"Well, we either go see Davy for the tools or we end it now, because I'm not walking around the bars of London asking who the local arms dealer is so he can sell us some weapons to rob the local drug dealer. What do you say, Dermot?"

"I told you—I'm in all the way."

"Is that unanimous?" Michael said, wanting confirmation. They all nodded in agreement; they had come too far to back out now and Michael was right, there was nothing stopping them, so long as they could get the weapons to do the job.

"Right, Dermot," Michael said with a beaming smile. "Book me in for a sickie in the morning. I'm going to Kilburn to The Harp of Erin, where hopefully I'll find Davy Mactazner. Now, drink up and we'll have another. I've suddenly developed a hankering for a rake of drink."

Michael was buzzing and Danny wasn't far behind him. From what they had just seen, they knew the robbery was well within their capabilities. In fact, it was beneath them. All they needed now were the tools to carry it out and when you need to obtain specialist equipment without drawing attention to yourself, you need to see the person whose job it is to supply them. That man, in this case, was Michael's father's old friend and partner, Davy Mactazner.

Chapter Fourteen

The Harp of Erin

The next morning, Michael took full advantage of his bogus sick day by enjoying a lie-in, until his eyes opened around ten. The trip to Kilburn would take at least an hour by Tube and it was his intention to arrive at the bar for what he remembered to be Mactazner's opening time of 12 o'clock. In his mind, he knew it was a big ask of Davy to supply the weapons at such short notice, so the more time he gave him the better. That was, of course, if he agreed to supply them at all—it was by no means a foregone conclusion and Michael felt more apprehension about asking his friend this favour than he did about entering the club the previous evening.

Kilburn, besides Cricklewood, is one of the largest Irish areas in London. In fact, there are so many there that it is lovingly known amongst the Irish folk as 'County Kilburn', which was one of the reasons why Michael and the lads had given it a wide berth.

Mactazner had run a pub there called The Harp of Erin for the past thirteen years, but the business was only a front for what really went on behind the scenes. He was a QM for the IRA and it was a quartermaster's job to supply whatever was needed, when it was needed, whether it was tools, weapons or explosives. He had been Michael's and the lads' contact and QM in England for the ten years that they had been together as a unit, but Michael's relationship with him was a lot closer than just business.

Most of Mactazner's time in London had coincided with the peace talks and the Anglo-Irish Agreement, so he hadn't been that busy with the dealings of the IRA, apart from fundraising, of course. But basically these days, for all intent and purposes, he was exactly what he was supposed to look like—a pub landlord.

As Michael approached The Harp of Erin, everything seemed much the same as the last time he was there. Mactazner had given the old place a lick of paint and put some new signs up, but, basically, it was just how he remembered it. He arrived just after opening and, as he had hoped, the bar was empty when he entered, apart from a young woman who was still putting out the beermats and giving the tables a lick of polish.

"I'll be with you in a moment," she said, hearing the door open behind her.

Michael stayed quiet for a spell, admiring the movement of her rear, which swayed with the buffing of the furniture.

"There you go again, Demelza Mactazner, keeping me waiting as usual."

The young woman recognised his voice immediately and turned, showing the shock on her pretty face.

"Michael Flynn, how are ye?"

With her arms outstretched, she ran towards him, while jumping and wrapping her legs around his waist.

"Steady on, girl, you're going to put my back out."

His words of complaint were quickly smothered by the big kiss she planted on his lips. Demelza was a beautiful-looking woman, the flaming hair she inherited from her father blended with the wildness in her eyes, which were now open wide with delight at the sight of Michael.

"It's been three and a half years, Michael Flynn. Where have you been?"

"Just passing the time in Belfast and minding my own business."

"Do you still see that hairdresser girl or do you have time for me now?"

"Me and Roisin are still going strong. Besides, we had our tumble, remember?"

"I remember," she reminisced, with a cheeky smile and a pout of her lips. "But we were only young then. You can't call a bit of a schoolyard fondle behind the bike sheds a fair chance."

"Yeah, but I still have some of the bruises," joked Michael. "Besides, Sean was your biggest admirer then."

"Don't tell lies. It was you and your mate Danny that did all the chasing. I was the only thing I ever saw the two of you fall out over."

"Yeah, but we both stepped aside because we knew it would break little Sean's heart if either one of us took up with ye. The mad deluded fucker was besotted."

"And you weren't, I suppose? You spent enough time at the end of our path, swinging on the gate, waiting for my father to go to the pub with yours, so there must have been something you fancied. Well, I know what you fancied—a grope and a smelly finger."

Michael pulled a face at Demelza's reminiscing of their youth. He was a bit of a prude when it came to women talking smutty, but she was right, he did have a bit of a thing for her—back then, anyway.

"You would have been better off with Sean. You're as crude as he is."

"Calm down. I'm only having the crack. We were only young kids, as curious as each other. How is Sean, anyway? Has he lost any weight or is he still the same old 'pie face'?"

"He's still the same old Fatty, except maybe a bit more obnoxious than when you saw him last. He still speaks of you, though. He'll be glad to know you were asking after him."

"Why don't you ask after me, Michael Flynn? I guarantee you that you will get an answer." Demelza, having a bit more of the crack, carried on flirting.

"Give it a rest, girl. You know why I'm here and who I'm asking after."

With her legs still wrapped tightly around Michael's waist and her arms around his neck, she knew he wasn't going to soften to her advances.

"So, it's my father you're here to see?"

"You know it is, woman. Now behave yourself and fetch him for me, will ye? I'll wait in the kitchen as usual."

Demelza, with a sigh, released her grip from Michael's waist, but not before stealing another kiss and dropping back to her feet. Leaving him with a sultry glance, she disappeared into the back while he made his way to the kitchen.

It had been a while—nearly four years, in fact—since Michael had last stood in the kitchen, waiting for Davy, and this time, like all the others, his thoughts soon began to wander to his father. So many memories and so many regrets.

"Come here, ye wee bollocks." Michael's wait was quickly ended when a larger-than-life Mactazner entered the kitchen, smiling broadly with his arms open wide. "Ah, it's good to see ye, lad," he greeted, throwing his big arms around him and planting a big chinny pie kiss on his cheek.

Mactazner was still the big gentle giant he always was, with a few minor changes that age brings to us all. The thick, curly ginger hair and beard had faded, a little lightened by the grey strands that mingled in its thick mass, while his cheeks and nose were a blend of several different shades of purple and red caused by too much Guinness and too many whiskey chasers. But, to Michael, he was what he always was—as near a man to his father as he could ever get—and it felt good to be in his company once again.

"How are ye, Davy? You look great."

"Bless you, boy, for being a lying fucker. I look like shit, but thanks anyway. Whereas you look more like your father every day and it does my heart good seeing you, lad. How's your mother and that little brother of yours, Peter? He must be nearly in his teens now."

"They're both doing fine, Davy, thanks for asking. I see Demelza hasn't changed much."

"That one will never change; she's too much of her Scottish ancestry in her. Can you not see your way to taking her off my hands?"

"The house would be a little crowded, don't you think, with her and Roisin? Besides, I prefer you as a friend, not as a father-in-law."

"Fair play to ye, son. A man should know his limitations." The two shared a smile, elated at being together again. "So, what's going on? Nobody told me you were coming."

Davy was normally warned of any visits or any impending business.

"That's because nobody knows we're here. We left

Belfast under a bit of a dark cloud two and a half months ago."

"Yeah, I heard about that."

"What did you hear?"

"I heard through the grapevine about your surgical antics in Bangor. I presume it didn't go down with the boys too well. Is that why you left?"

"Partly. Maguire was at the house the next day, laying the law down; it shook Ma up a bit."

"Catherine wouldn't give a fuck about him, sure?"

"No, she didn't, but I think, with these talks putting an end to it all, that she doesn't see the point in arguing."

"I hope he didn't say anything wrong to her, because I'll slap that fucker senseless if he did."

"No, Davy, he didn't say anything wrong, but I did. I gobbed off and said a bit too much."

"Well, you always were well built around the mouth, young Flynn." Michael smiled, obviously knowing that Davy meant well with his description of his tendency to say too much. "So, you came away because your Ma wanted you to, not because of that prick Maguire?"

"Again, partly," answered Michael.

"Good lad." Davy looked proudly at him like he was one of his own. "Here now..." Davy extended his finger to a point. "...go in that cupboard behind you. You'll find a nicely aged bottle of Bushmills Single Malt. We'll crack the seal and have a drink to your father."

Mactazner washed a couple of glasses, while Michael retrieved the bottle of whiskey and two ample-sized tots were poured.

"To your father and your mother, God bless her."

"And to you, Davy," Michael added to the toast. Their glasses were clinked and raised, and, after an appreciative look at the clear dark blend, the contents disappeared smoothly down their throats.

"So where have you been since you left Belfast? You did a good job of dropping off the radar?"

"We were a few weeks up in Leeds, but the past couple of months, we've been working on a site in Notting Hill."

"Notting Hill? You're only away across the city. Why didn't you come and see me before? You missed a great band on St Patrick's Day—Pat Sherry and Scarlet Heights—the place was bouncing and the crack was ninety."

"It would have been grand to come and see you, Davy, and the band, but we've supposedly been keeping our heads down, dropping off the radar, as you put it. We've been doing our drinking after work in a pub called The Rose and Crown next to the site, which is where you will find us if you ever need to. At the weekend, though, we do our boozing at The Anchor, close to our digs in Hemel Hempstead."

"And what is it that's brought you here now?"

Michael didn't answer, while reaching for the bottle and topping up the drinks. Davy could tell there was something on his mind and egged him on a bit.

"Come on, lad. Spit it out. I've got plenty of time, but only the one bottle of the good stuff."

"We're going to pull a job, Davy. Strictly business and non-political. It's just a straightforward money-earner. We don't expect much resistance, but the people we go up against will definitely be armed."

"I'm not sure you know the proper meaning of keeping your head down, young Flynn, but tell me what you need and I'll see what I can do for ye?"

Once again, Michael smiled, but he had to be straight with the facts.

"Before you agree to help us, Davy, you should know that if Maguire finds out, it won't sit too well."

A shudder went down Mactazner's back at the mere mention of his nemesis Maguire's name.

"Michael, I've known Maguire a long time, and I neither like him nor trust him. He's always played his cards too close to his chest for my liking and your father felt the same way about the man." Mactazner gave a small chuckle to go with his remembering smile. "Finbar had him sussed right from the very moment the three of us met. We were only eighteen at the time and the Troubles were just beginning to flare up again back in '69. Your father and I knew of each other's reputations from about the town, but we had never been introduced. We were brought together to form a unit by a fella who was to be our captain, called Ignatius Stanton. You met him once, well I wouldn't say met. You saw him at any rate, stood at the gate the day we buried ye father."

"I remember him. Was he a good captain?"

"He was, and still is. I still answer to him to this day. Anyway, the night we all met, Maguire had one of them ponytails in his hair that hung down to his shoulders. Your father, quick as a flash, picked it up from his back and said, 'You know, whenever you lift a ponytail, you'll always find an arsehole.'"

The two of them laughed out loud. Michael loved to hear the old stories, especially when Maguire was getting a slagging down.

"And there I was thinking that Maguire had always worn that hat and smoked his pipe," commented Michael.

"We were all young once, lad, but it doesn't matter how old he gets, Benny Maguire will always be that same arsehole under that ponytail. That night was also the same night your father nicknamed me Bronx. It made me realise that he knew all about my past, but he had never said a word to anyone. Your father was a tight-lipped man, Michael. That's why they never got anything on him."

"Bronx—I remember him calling you it, Davy."

"Only him mind, and I was the only one allowed to call your father 'Flynny'. To every fucker else, it was Finbar and Davy, or they got a broken jaw. You knew where you stood with your Pa; if you didn't, you were flat on your back."

"I knew you'd come from America, but I didn't realise it was New York and the Bronx where you hailed from. Have you never thought about going back?"

"No, son. That life has passed me by. I left there an orphan without any family at all to speak of and it stayed that way until the day I met your father. When we got together, it was like finding the brother I never had, but, when something good comes along, there's always a bit of shite to balance the equilibrium. I'm talking about Maguire, so I am. For my sins, now I have this pub to run and that daughter of mine to contend with. But I'm not complaining. Each road I elected to walk down in life was of my own choosing. No one forced me, so I have no one else to blame. Not that I have anything to complain about. I've lost enough in life to realise that just waking up each morning is a bonus to be thankful for." Davy sighed and, for a moment, was lost in contemplation.

"Is there no one back there you'd like to see again?"

He gave Michael's question some thought. He was a tight-lipped man himself, but given the company he was sharing the information with, decided to let a bit go.

"There was one fella," he answered with a look of reminiscence on his face. "A young lad I went to school and grew up with. He was the reason I had to leave the States."

"Did you have a fall out?"

"No, precisely the opposite. I took a bullet in the shoulder that was meant for him and then I killed the Italian fella that fired the shot. Well when I say fella I mean kid, because that's all we were, just kids. Sadly, he was connected and my chances of survival, had I stuck around, wouldn't have been great. Ye see, I didn't really grow up in the Bronx—ye father just called me that because he liked the sound of it. I was born on West 39th Street in the tenements of Hell's Kitchen; a rougher place you've never seen, but the Irish community spirit was like no other."

"I never knew you'd been shot, Davy."

"Well, it's not something you talk about, or just drop into a chinwag. Besides, the least said about it the better. Those Italian mobsters have got long memories."

"So, who was the lad?"

"The Italian, ye mean?"

"No, who was the lad you took the bullet for?"

"Oh, he was called James Coonan, Jimmy to his friends."

"Did you never bother calling to see how he was doing?"

"I don't need to call to know that. Ye see, he went on to become a very famous man. That gang we started when we were fourteen ended up taking over the whole of Hell's Kitchen and became known as the 'Westies'. Years later, he ended up sitting down with those same Italian mobsters and making a lot of money controlling the building sites, and the racketeering, of course. He even sat down with John Gotti. A fat lot of good it did him though, because a couple of years back, two of his men gave evidence against him and now he'll never walk the streets of New York again." Davy, still reminiscing, again sighed. "I often wonder if I hadn't have killed that lad that night and we had stayed together, how far we would have gone. If he'd have had an enforcer at his side he could trust."

"A bit like you and my father, you mean?" Davy paused and gave a smile at Michael's surmise.

"That's right, lad, a bit like me and Finbar. Or you could say a bit like you and Big Danny. Everybody needs someone to watch their back while they're busy doin' the thinking." Again, they shared a smile. "Anyway, enough about my life. You tell me what you need and let me worry about how it sits with Maguire and any other fucker, for that matter."

Mactazner poured them both another Bushmills as Michael began to reel off the items he required.

"Three nine-millimetre handguns with full clips,

one piece of C4 plastic explosive—only a small charge with a detonator and a timed power unit – TPU, you know what I mean. Oh, and an FRG with a fifty-grain round."

"A federal riot gun with a fifty-grain?" exclaimed Davy when hearing the size of the round. "What are ye knocking down? A wall?"

"Not a wall. Just a man that's built like one."

"Tell me no more," backtracked Davy. "Just be careful and drop me a nice drink if you make plenty of dough."

"Don't worry about that. It goes without saying."

Michael looked at Davy with admiration. He always had a welcoming smile on his face and would give you the shirt off his back if you needed it. It seemed a shame that he had spent all these years on his own, bringing up Demelza, who at thirty-one, like Michael, didn't look like she was in a hurry to leave home.

"You know, Davy, you should give my mother a call and get together."

Davy sipped at his drink, contemplating Michael's

suggestion, but knew he wasn't referring to a meeting of old friends.

"Are you doing a bit of matchmaking, lad? I'm not sure how I'd feel about that. Your father meant too much to me."

Michael smiled at Mactazner's loyalty, but everyone needed a bit of company and deserved a second chance, including his mother.

"The pair of you are full of life, Davy, and only in your fifties. I just think it's a shame for you both to miss out on a bit of company. You'd have plenty to talk about, you and Ma. Ye may not have lived life together, but ye've lived the same life."

Davy knew that was the truth.

"Maybe I will give her a call, but I've never thought about it, mind. I don't want you thinking that I've had eyes for your mother since Finbar was killed."

"Davy, it was me that suggested it and I don't think I'm disrespecting my father by doing so. I'm just saying that if ever you did have the mind to call on her, I wouldn't object. Peewee will be gone in another couple of years, as will your Demelza, if she ever takes the hint. It would be a shame for the pair of you to be sat on your own on different sides of the water."

"Okay, I thank you for that but let's speak no more about it right now." Davy again filled the glasses. "How quick do you need the stuff?"

"The latest is Sunday afternoon."

Davy looked up with wide eyes, but kept stony quiet about the urgency.

"Okay, I think I can handle that. Are the rest of the motley crew with ye?"

"Danny, Sean and Dermot? Of course they are."

"Is young Sean still a fat wee gobshite?"

"Yeah," confirmed Michael, smiling at Davy's apt description.

"And is he still doing the driving?" Michael nodded, giving confirmation. "Good, then have him at the back gates at two o'clock sharp Sunday to pick up the stuff. If you don't shoot no fucker, I'll have the weapons back. But if you do, away with the lot in the river."

Michael nodded to show he understood the instructions before knocking back his fourth dram.

"Do you mind if I leave through the same gate when I go?"

"No problems. It's probably for the best—there will be a few nosey fuckers in the bar by now." Michael held his hand out for a shake, which Davy took, using it to pull him in for another hug.

"Ah, it does me good to see you, son, but it breaks my heart, because all I can think about is your father, God rest his soul. I miss him so much, it's almost as though my life ended along with his, the day he was taken."

Michael gathered his strength, along with his carefully chosen words.

"I know what you mean, Davy. I see the same look in my mother's eyes every day. I even see it myself when I look at young Peewee. But your life's not over, my old friend."

Michael patted the big man's back, while still locked in their embrace. "Remember, dad went out doing something he believed in, which made it easier for us all to accept. Make sure you do the same, but don't be too hasty to go shuffling off. Demelza needs ye and, for my own selfish reasons, so do I, and I'm not talking about the want of the weapons you're getting for me. It's because I love ye, Davy, and while you still tread your path, I feel as though my father walks right alongside ye."

Davy, almost crying, wiped the makings of a tear away from his eye, before freeing Michael from his caring grip. A joint sigh was released, as they both wished that the space beside them could be filled by the man they missed so much.

The two friends continued their reminiscing about Finbar, both of them with their own thoughts of the same man, but both their memories hugely different of a father and a friend.

"What say we finish off that bottle of malt before you get on your way?" Davy's suggestion was welcomed by Michael, whose eyes were also beginning to well—a point he was often brought to when in Davy's company and they drank and talked of his father.

"Sounds like a plan, Davy. Fill them up."

"Fair play to you, Michael lad. I'll make an Irishman of you yet."

The pair, for another hour or so, talked of days gone by, while polishing off the remainder of the bottle, before Michael left through the back door and grabbed a taxi a few yards down the road. He had decided against using the Tube to get back. The half-bottle of malt was now starting to mingle with last night's Guinness and finding its way to his legs. He was on his way to The Rose to meet the other three for their usual after-work Friday drink and to tell them how the meeting with Mactazner had gone, but could just as well have returned to the digs in Hemel Hempstead and grabbed another few hours' sleep.

The cab dropped him at the side of the pub at quarter past three, so he was a little early, but he had plenty to think about to pass the time. His friend, the dealer, was still in the doorway of the Chinese doing business, but Michael ignored him—he knew all he needed to know about that fella. After last night's visit to the club Michael now regarded him as a small pawn in the proceedings. His thoughts were focused now on the one part of his plan that he may have overlooked. How were four men who had just robbed the club over the road going to walk off a building site with the money and weapons in front of a queue of potential witnesses waiting to enter the same club? To hide on the site overnight and go straight to work in the morning might work, but if for some reason the police did get involved and conducted a follow-up search, the site may be one of the first places they would look. Getting caught with the money would be bad enough, but getting nabbed with the weapons as well would result in a clinking sound as the police threw away the key. He had to come up with some way of putting distance between them, the weapons and the loot.

    Taking a cigarette from the packet, he lit it and stared into the air towards Sean's crane. It was then that he noticed that between the end of the site and the pub was a narrow road, and at the back of the pub was a courtyard that backed onto that same road. Michael walked down it until he was between the wall of the site and the pub's backyard, where two large black wooden gates sealed the entrance. After checking both up and down the road, he placed the cigarette in his mouth before jumping up and grabbing hold of the gates. He pulled himself up so he could see over the top. A few barrels that stood in the corner with some stacked tables and chairs were all it contained, besides the metal doors in the floor that secured the entrance to the beer drop.

Lowering himself back down, he looked behind himself at the half-built wall that bordered the site and then to the rest of the properties to the side of the pub that also backed onto the road. What few windows there were overlooking his position didn't show any signs of being lived in. Most of them were small and frosted, indicating that they belonged to bathrooms at the rear of the properties and the lower windows, like the pub, all had their view obscured by the rear walls. With his mind working overtime, Michael returned to the front of the pub and went inside.

"Hello, Barbara. How are ye, mi darling?" he greeted in a chirpy voice.

"I'm okay, love. You're a bit earlier than usual. Are the rest of them with you?"

"No, I'm on my own. I woke up this morning with terrible back pain, so I threw a sickie and spent the day in bed, dreaming of Ireland and the girl back there that holds my heart." Michael rubbed the lumber region of his back to add weight to his pretence. "I'm okay now, though, now the painkillers have kicked in," he added with a wink. "The drink should numb the rest, so I'll have a pint of the black stuff."

"What do they call your girl back home?" Barbara asked, while putting the glass under the pump. "Danny never tells me anything about any of your families."

"It's pronounced 'Rosheen'," declared Michael proudly, "but in the Irish, it's R-o-I-s-I-n, meaning 'little rose'."

"It's a beautiful name."

Michael walked over to the window that looked over the backyard.

"She's a beautiful girl."

Barbara smiled at Michael's words, wishing if only that a man would talk of her that way.

Michael, looking through the window, could see the reverse side of the gates that he had moments earlier peered over, and beyond it was the wall of the site. It confirmed to him how well it would meet their needs.

"I was just after noticing that you have a yard out the back there? Do you use it for anything?"

"Not for anything special. It's where I take the deliveries from the brewery, and if we get any decent weather in the summer, I throw a few tables and chairs out there and call it a beer garden."

Babs placed the Guinness on the bar and looked at Michael, who was still looking at the view.

"And what day do you get the delivery?" he enquired returning to the bar.

"Fridays. I received it this morning. Why do you ask anyway? What's the sudden interest in my backyard?"

"It's just that the four of us were thinking of having a good drink around this area Sunday night and we were looking for a good place to leave the car. You know what the parking is like around here, plus we'll have to leave it overnight because we will all be too drunk to drive." Michael passed Babs a twenty. "Take for five pints. This one won't last, but a second and the lads will be here soon."

As Barbara turned to the till, Michael resorted to bribery to get what he wanted.

"And take one for yourself, Babs."

"Cheers, darling. I'll have a half of lager."

"A half of lager? That's not a drink. Let your hair down, girl, and get yourself a short."

"I shouldn't, really. Danny doesn't like it when I get on the top shelf."

"Danny's not here, Babs, and I won't be educating the big man when he is, so fill your boots."

"Okay. If you're sure, I'll have a G 'n' T."

"That's the spirit, girl. So, do you think it would be okay to park the car out there Sunday night?"

"What's up with the site? I thought you usually left it there?"

"The site's full, sure; we've taken a rake of deliveries

this week. There's hardly enough room for Sean and his crane."

"Well, you'll have to stack the barrels a bit neater to make room, but I can't see why not, so long as Danny stays with it."

"That might be a problem. We may not be back on time to get in, with it being Sunday and the early closing, that is."

"Don't worry about that. I have a late licence on a Sunday because of the club up the road. I objected to it opening, so they granted me a few extra hours to keep me quiet."

"Well then." Michael beamed as another part of his plan fell into place. "I definitely can't see a problem with the big fella staying. All he talks about all day anyway is finishing work so he can come and see you."

Michael laid it on thick, buttering her up, which put a smile on her face like she had a coat hanger stuck in her mouth. She left him with a few shy giggles, before disappearing into the other room to serve a customer, leaving him propping up the bar at a position where he could see through the window to the yard and beyond to the site wall. Mulling the new part of the plan over in his head, the time soon passed until his conniving was disturbed by the other three arriving from work.

"Babs, pull those other drinks, will ye? The lads are here."

"Give me a minute, Michael, and I'll fetch them out for you."

On hearing Barbara's call, they all took a seat in the corner. Forming their usual treasonous huddle, the other three looked at Michael, eager for news of his trip to Kilburn.

"Before we go any further, Danny Boy, I told Barbara that I was in bed all day with a bad back, just so you don't slip up. Also, in the last half hour, while I've been waiting for you fellas to arrive, I think I may have solved the problem of how we will get off the site once we pull the job."

The huddle grew tighter as Michael went on to describe to the other three the arrangement he had just made with Barbara regarding Sunday and the parking of the car.

"Here you go, lads—four pints," said Babs, breaking up the discussion with her waitress service.

"Barbara, you're one in a million," said Michael, continuing with his buttery bullshit. "I'm not surprised the big fella has fallen madly in love with ye." Barbara smiled, while giving Danny a peck on the cheek, before returning to the bar with yet another coat hanger in her mouth.

"Will you give it a fucking rest? The last thing she needs is encouragement." Danny, while adjusting his crotch, which still hadn't recovered, discouraged Michael from any more egging. "I hope she doesn't start on those gin and tonics again tonight. They make her randy as fuck."

Michael smiled and would have laughed if Sean hadn't interceded with a question, getting them back to business.

"So Davy has no problems with the supplies?"

"None at all. He wants you outside the back gate of

The Harp of Erin at two-sharp on Sunday. He'll throw the bag on the back seat. You don't even have to get out of the car."

"That'll be grand, but can't I just go inside and say hello to Demelza?"

"Of course ye can, if ye want ye teeth knocking down ye throat by her dad." Sean for once was lost for a joke-filled answer. "One last thing," Michael added. "Danny, on your way back to the digs in the morning, stop at a store and pick up a length of climbing rope."

"What's up with the one we used last night?"

"It's not long enough; we need one at least a hundred foot long."

"Fuck me. Are we tying up the whole fucking club?"

"No, Dermot, as much as I know how much you would like to practise your knots from your Boy Scout days, we're not tying no fucker up. Not with a rope, anyway. We'll use cable ties for that—they're quicker and stronger. Put them on your list as well, Danny."

"We have cable ties on site. I can get some from the stores. We may even have some rope."

"No, Dermot. We don't want to use anything that can be traced back to us."

"I'll get everything we need in the morning. Leave it to me," said Danny.

"So, what is the rope for then?"

"Look," said Michael, closing the huddle, before beginning to explain. "After the robbery, when they finally realise just how we got in and out, they're going to go up to the roof and what do you think they're going to wonder?"

"How the fuck we got on and off."

"Correct again, Danny Boy, and unless some fucker tells them that they saw or heard a helicopter about the time we were making our getaway, they're going to look straight across the street at the crane Fatty drives and put two and two together."

"So we throw the rope over the side of the building to make it look like that's how we made our getaway."

"Fuck me, Dermot, you little swot. Go to the top of the class."

Dermot didn't like his geeky looks and disliked it

even more when the lads took the piss. He consoled himself by taking a big drink from his pint, joined by the others.

"All right, Michael, my old china? How's your luck?" The huddle was broken by the interruption of the driver, Eli, from the site. "You just finished?" he asked.

"The lads have," answered Michael turning to face his new acquaintance. "Boys, this is Eli. He drives the delivery truck. Remember? The one that nearly squashed me the other week? I bumped into him in the nightclub on Friday, when I came back for my keys."

The lads cottoned on to Michael's little cover story.

"Good to meet you, Eli," they each greeted, as he shook their hands.

"You know, Eli, Michael comes down that ladder the same time every week if you fancy another go at running him over," joked Sean, extracting a laugh from the group before Michael answered Eli's question.

"I've had the day off. The old back was playing me up. What about you?"

"Just clocked off," answered the Londoner. "I'm

taking the family down to Margate for the weekend—a bit of a treat for the tin pot lids and it keeps the bread knife chipper, if you know what I mean?"

It took the lads a second to work out the rhyming slang, but they got the gist of it eventually.

"Sounds grand. Enjoy yourself."

"I will, cheers. But listen, I only dropped in on the off chance of seeing you, because when I went back to that club the next night I plucked up the courage to try and get into that barmaid's Alan Whickers, after not being able to get a grip of her the night before. Anyway, and you won't believe this. She gave me the old cold shoulder."

"Well, you can't win them all," consoled Michael.

"I know that, but usually when I give them a bit of the old spiel, it knocks the ladies bandy, they're like putty in my hands."

The lads gave Eli a side look. He wasn't an ugly man by any standards, but he was no oil painting either.

"At first," the Londoner continued, "I thought she must be a bit of a Magnus Pike, you know, a carpet-muncher, especially with all that metal shit in her face and the tattoos."

"I thought the same myself," interrupted Michael.

"Yeh, but then I realised that it was you she fancied. She'd seen us talking the night before and started asking after you, can you Adam-n-Eve it." The lads all shook their heads, engrossed in Eli's beliefs of his own womanising capabilities. "Anyway, never to be one to stand in the way of another man going forward, I took her number and promised I would pass it on. She said something about just getting a new phone, and you'd understand." Eli placed the split beermat on which the number was written on the table in front of Michael. "Right, I better get off. I only dropped in for a quick one and to pass you that, so see you later. Good to meet you, lads. Be lucky!"

Giving his usual cockney farewell, he left the lads to continue their conversation. Dermot picked up the beermat and read the name, while showing it to Danny and Sean.

"Trudy," he said in a soppy voice. "Are you sure you

didn't mix a bit of business with pleasure, last Friday night?"

"Of course I did, Dermot," Michael replied in a sarcastic tone, while snatching the number, tearing it up and tossing it in the ashtray. "I went in there to case the joint in a view to robbing it and, while keeping a low profile, decided to try my luck with the barmaid." A soppy look of his own followed, to let Dermot know how he regarded his statement. "But she was a nice girl though, hardworking and struggling to bring up a child on her own so I'll have no derogatory statements said about her."

"It sounds like you had a long and in-depth conversation."

"We did Danny." But that was all it was."

"So, what about this cockney fella, Eli?" asked Sean. "What was he doing there and does anyone else have a problem understanding what he's fucking saying?"

"He's not a bad fella. We had a drink together—his way of apologising for the near miss on the site. He also offered to find us some more work if we need it after the job is finished. But, you're right, he does take some keeping up with."

"Anyway," said Danny, getting the conversation back on track. "It's definite then. We go Sunday."

"It's on. We go Sunday," confirmed Michael. "And there's nothing between us and a hundred grand but a single door and a couple of men, one of which is built like King fucking Kong, but I've ordered just the thing to take care of that fella."

Chapter Fifteen

Fatty's Education

When Big Danny arrived at the flat the next morning, he was met when opening the door by the circulating aroma of crispy bacon and sizzling sausages. Chef Flynn, minus the big hat, was in the kitchen cooking breakfast for the other two, who were still occupying their warm beds. Michael leant back from the cooker to see Danny in the hallway, removing his coat and retrieving the bag from the floor that he had brought with him.

"How ye doing, Danny Boy? Have you eaten yet?"

"No, I'll have a plate of whatever it is you have on the go there, if that's okay."

"No problem, big fella. What do ye have in the bag?"

7P's

As Danny entered the kitchen, he held his nose high, giving Michael's cooking another appreciative sniff, before dropping the holdall he was carrying on the table.

"I stopped off at the street market on the way here; you can buy anything at that place. Anyway, I have the rope you asked for and a few things you didn't."

"And what would that be?" Michael asked while sharing the food between the plates.

"A few ski masks and some black boiler suits. Oh, and your cable ties as well."

Danny pulled the items from the bag and laid them on the table, so Michael could give them the once-over.

"Fuck me, I forgot about masks."

"Well, you can't be expected to think of everything, ye not infallible man." Danny took a seat at the table, eager to tuck into the warm food. Michael had a quick look at the masks and suits before replacing them back inside with the rope, then removed the bag to make room for the breakfasts. "Oh, and by the way. Am I right in thinking that Sean won't be doing anything else on this robbery but driving the crane?"

"That's right," confirmed Michael. "Why do you ask?"

"Because when I said they sell everything, I lied. They don't sell a suit that will fit the fat fucker."

"If they did, the tailor would be getting sacked," quipped Michael, gaining a laugh from Danny. "Here, dive into that." With the plates loaded, he pushed one in front of Danny and placed two more in the oven to keep warm. "Did Babs mention anything about us parking the car in the yard on Sunday night?"

"Barbara said nothing all night. I've told her not to speak with her mouth full!"

"Behave yourself. At least it wasn't for nothing; I said we'd need her. She obviously had you hard at it as usual."

"All night," Danny exclaimed. "Some idiot must have got her on the gin and tonics. They're like fucking oysters to the woman."

Michael stuffed a piece of toast into his mouth to stop himself laughing, knowing he was the idiot in question.

"Well, enjoy it while you can. We won't be around much longer."

"Yeah, but the problem is after all my complaining that I'm beginning to get strong feelings for the woman."

Michael smiled at his big mate, who was hastily replenishing his energy with his breakfast. In all the years he had known Danny, he had never known him to go back to a woman's bed more than a couple of times. Danny may have convinced himself that he was doing it for the sake of the job, but Michael knew that he was an eager visitor to Babs's boudoir long before he had come up with the plan to rob the club.

"There's nothing wrong with that, Danny Boy. She's a fine-looking lady and a hard worker. It can't be easy for her running that big pub all on her own, and we're not disrespecting her by using the yard; you were giving her one long before we decided to rob the club. It's not as though she came afterwards to be used as part of the plan. Besides, hopefully things will go off without a hitch, so there's no reason that she should ever find out."

"Well, we'll see how it goes; everything could change after Sunday night."

At Danny's words, Michael gave two knocks on the wooden table. It was his superstitious way of warding off any ill fate.

"Well, touch wood, Danny Boy, it will all change for the better."

Sean entered the kitchen, woken by the circulating allure of Michael's cooking that had found its way to his bedroom.

"Is there one of them for me?" he asked, stood there in nothing but his boxers.

"You get nothing until you go put some clothes on, ye fat fuck." Michael, with breakfast knife in hand, shielded his eyes from the mountainous mass of cellulite that stood in the doorway. "What is it with this fucking brother of yours? Is he some kind of naturist?"

Danny just smiled. He was sat with his back to the scene and saw no reason to turn around and share the view. Dermot was next on parade, almost squashed by Sean as he pushed his way past in the hallway to go and get dressed.

"Fucking hippo," he muttered under his breath,

about as much of an insult as he could manage in his tired state. "Morning, fellas. That smells good," he enthused, still rubbing the sleep from his eyes.

"Yours is in the oven. You might as well get Sean's out as well—I shouldn't think he'll be long."

Dermot had no sooner put the two meals on the table than Sean had returned in clothes and was sat down, knife and fork primed.

"Do the teas as well, will ye Dermot, and stick a couple of slices in the toaster."

"I'm not your slave. Do your own fucking toast."

"I was only trying to give you a bit of practice. In a few months from now, you may have to run the café when Mary is taking her maternity leave."

"Now you can get your own tea as well," said Dermot, bringing just one pot to the table.

"Okay, fellas, that's enough," interrupted Michael. "Seeing as how we're all here, it's as good a time as any to go over things. Firstly, we definitely do the job tomorrow night, so now would be the time to let me know if there's anything, anything at all, that you can think of that we haven't thought of already. Danny was just after bringing some masks and suits that I'd forgotten about, so there may be other things."

A few seconds passed as Danny and Dermot paused for thought; Sean just put his head down and tucked into his breakfast.

"Can't you leave that for a minute and think about what I said?"

Sean looked up at Michael with a mouth full of sausage and egg.

"I am thinking about what you said," he mumbled as half the egg fell back to the plate. "I do all my best thinking while I'm eating—then or when I'm sat on the bog, squeezing one out. In fact, especially when I'm on the bog, because I have to relax more to open my bowels."

The other three looked at Sean and then down at their breakfasts with a loss of appetite.

"Jesus, bro. You do pick your moments, you disgusting fat fucker."

"What have I said now?"

Sean, oblivious to what they were complaining

about, became victim to his own gluttony as he started to choke on his food. As he struggled with the blockage, he looked at the other three for assistance.

"Don't fucking help then, will ye," he coughed and spluttered, in need of a helpful pat on the back.

"It's your own fault," said Dermot, offering advice as his way of help. "I've told you before, you don't masticate enough."

"You wouldn't say that if you were his brother and you'd had to share the same room with him for fifteen years. He was always giving it the old five-knuckle-shuffle under the bed covers." added Danny.

"Yeah, but it was good practice for when I gave Greasy Deasy the pearl necklace she always wanted," blurted Sean, still choking while delivering the insult.

Dermot enlightened the pair. "I said 'masticate' not 'masturbate'. It means to chew, but go ahead and choke, ye fat fucker."

"Okay then," continued Michael in a 'what's the point' tone. "Sean, you know your job. You're on the crane obviously and without the chit chat this time, please.

That includes any in-flight commentary." Sean gave a cheeky grin but knew enough was enough.

"Dermot, you're the FRG man, but you'll also carry a nine millimetre, just for backup. Stick it in your belt and use it as a last resort. You'll be the second man in line as we go down the stairs, with the big fella leading and me bringing up the rear. Oh, and by the way, before we make our descent you'll also work your magic with the small piece of C4 Davy has supplied along with the weapons. If we're being pursued when we are making our getaway we need you to create something that will buy us a bit of time. A nice surprise at the top of the stairs sort of thing."

"Leave it with me. I'll take care of it."

"Good lad. I know we can count on you to come up with something. Now, staying with you Dermot, when the time comes and Danny kicks the door in, it's your next job to get past him and take out fucking King Kong on the gate. Now I warn you, he is a big fucking fella, so don't fuck about. Let him have it straight in the solar plexus with the fifty-grain round. He'll be out for the count, but if for some reason he isn't, it will be his hard luck because the next hit will be from your nine millimetre. Now I know it would be easier to just shoot the fucker in the first place, but we can't count on the music from the club covering up the noise and we may need as much time as possible once we're inside. Plus, if we do get caught, I'd rather get charged with armed robbery than murder."

The other three, nodding, showed they agreed with Michael and his tactics.

"At this point, it's all about speed," Michael resumed. "Danny, you and I need to be inside the office and in their faces before any fucker has the chance to reach for a weapon—or, worse, an alarm button if they have one. Now, if we've done our job and timed it right, we should have the dealer from the street, the bouncer from the gate and whoever else it is that runs the joint together in the office. Danny, if this is the case, you keep Dermot and me covered while we tie them up. Once we have everything under control and we've checked that all three of us are okay, we then go about our business finding out where all the money is, and once we have it, we get the fuck out of the place. Dermot, you'll carry the cable ties and before we go, you destroy the phone lines and check them for mobiles and pagers. With the keys you find on the big bouncer, first make sure that the outer door to the club is locked, and then second, break the key in the lock of the internal metal gate. That should buy us even more time should we have to have it on our toes. Any questions so far?"

"Cable ties, phones and pagers, keys," repeated Dermot memorising his jobs.

"I've got a question," said a baffled-looking Sean, not even looking up from his plate to ask it. "What the fuck is a solar plexus?"

Michael and Danny looked across the breakfast table at each other shaking their heads yet again—standard practice where Sean was concerned.

"Dermot, do you know what and where a solar plexus is?" Michael asked.

"Of course I do—I'm no eejit like that fucking lard arse."

"Good, that's all that matters, seeing as how you're the one with the FRG, but for the sake of Fatty's education, Danny, show your brother where his solar plexus is."

Sean looked up expecting an explanation but soon wished that he hadn't. WHACK! He and his chair both went backwards, falling to the kitchen floor following Danny's blow to the centre of his chest. Sean winced with pain as he tried to catch his breath with short sharp gasps. The other three watched for a while as he wriggled around like a turtle on its back.

"Fuck me, that hurt. You could have just pointed. I can hardly breathe, ye big heavy-handed fucker." Sean's complaints, while clutching his chest in the area of what he now knew to be his solar plexus, fell on deaf ears.

"That's your solar plexus," explained Michael, still looking down on the floored mass. "Imagine how that feels when you get hit there with a fifty-grain baton round doing a hundred miles an hour from a Federal riot gun. Now are there any more questions or do ye need time to go to the fucking toilet to think about it?"

"No," replied Sean, before giving a last cough, which removed a piece of sausage from his throat, sending it across the kitchen floor.

"You haven't explained what parking the car at the back of the pub has got to do with the getaway part of the plan."

"Thank you, Danny. At least somebody's taking notice. Not like you two, you pair of gloyts."

"What have I done wrong? I'm no gloyt. It was him that didn't know what a solar plexus was," complained a tired and innocent-looking Dermot while pointing a finger, which was slapped away by Sean.

"You stole my fucking takeaway."

Dermot looked at Michael, shocked that he was still holding that against him.

"That was last week, and it was Fatty."

"It was the pair of you and you're not getting away with it that easily. It wouldn't matter if it was last year."

"Well, I'm not buying the beer all day again."

"You didn't buy the beer all last Saturday—I did," interrupted Sean, who had managed to return upright on his chair but was still rubbing his chest. "It was like drinking with Eddie the fucking Eagle last week."

Danny and Michael both joined Dermot, looking confused at Sean's reference to the ski jumper. Seeing their blank faces, Sean explained his comment.

"You couldn't get to the bar for your fucking skis." Only Danny and Michael smiled at that one.

"It's true, Dermot. You are a bit careful with your money," agreed Danny.

"Are you trying to say I'm tight?"

"Tight? You're like a crab's arse at a thousand feet—waterproof."

"Fuck you, Fatty. I pay my way."

"All right, ladies. Give it a rest and I'll do you a deal. If you do your job correctly and we pull it off, I'll forget that you stole my takeaway."

"Two poxy spare ribs and a small portion of fried rice?"

"Don't push it, Fatty. It was chicken fried rice. Now button it or we'll go over the solar plexus part of the plan again." Sean, still rubbing his chest, took his gaze from Michael and looked at his brother, and when seeing a grin that held an eagerness to repeat the punching demonstration, he thought it best to go back to his food. "Right," Michael continued. "When we return to the site, we've got the problem of what to do with hopefully a lot of money and the weapons. Now, we don't want to get caught with either on us, but we can't take the chance of leaving anything on the building site. So, where Barbara's yard comes into it is this—we climb the scaffold at the far end where the Welsh lads work and drop it over the wall."

"But that wall is a gable end; it's nearly a sixty-foot drop."

"We're not going with it, Dermot, just the bags containing the money and the weapons, which Danny will catch. He'll have already slipped out of the site gates and will be at the base of the wall. He'll then throw them over the rear gates of the pub into the yard before walking around to the front and going inside. He'll order the beer for all of us, as though we're lagging behind on our way from the last bar, and then make an excuse to go out to the yard where he'll then throw the bags into the boot of the car and lock them away. And that's where they'll stay until the next evening, when we pick up the car after work. Are there any questions?"

There were none. The other three all sat computing everything that Michael had just said, all of them thinking what a tricky bastard he was and wondering how he came up with it all. "No? Good. Then let's fuck off down the pub and back some more of Danny's losers. Tomorrow we'll have a day in while Sean goes to Kilburn and collects the weapons."

"I've got another question, but I don't want anyone to hit me this time," said Sean, looking at Danny to make sure he understood the terms of the agreement. "What's a gloyt?"

Michael stood up to replenish his mug of tea and leant back down towards Sean's ear.

"On the way to Kilburn tomorrow, go past the library and borrow a dictionary to look the word up."

"Why? What will it say?" he asked.

"Nothing. There'll just be a picture of you there!"

Sean was still none the wiser as to the meaning of the word, and although he guessed it wasn't good, he didn't let it keep him from his food.

They all continued to eat their breakfast, taking the forthcoming events well within their stride. For many people, the thought of robbery, violence and the use of weapons would put them straight on the toilet, but for these four, it was second nature.

Their traditional Saturday afternoon in the pub played out true to form, with the only winner being the bookie around the corner and the landlord of the pub, who'd gone through yet another barrel of Guinness. This week, though, there were no complaints from anyone about Danny's continuing run of bad luck with the nags. The air of excitement and expectation as to what Sunday night might bring was far greater than any disappointments brought by a few losers. Besides, if things went as planned, by Monday morning, money would be the least of their worries. Another reason for their understanding tone, though, was because they were well aware that if things didn't go to plan, this could well be the last drink they would have together. It was a position that the lads had been in many times before. Perhaps it was for this reason that Sean and Dermot decided to chip in and buy Michael a takeaway at the end of the evening—two portions of barbecued spare ribs and chicken fried rice. Debt cleared!!

Chapter Sixteen

The Robbery

Sean set off just after midday, leaving the other three in the flat while he made the solo drive to Kilburn and The Harp of Erin. It was something he had to do alone—being in the car with anyone else if he was pulled over by the police and caught with the weapons he was picking up didn't make sense; besides, it was his job. In the time while he was away, Michael, Dermot and Danny went over and over the plan, leaving nothing to chance until the point when they were satisfied that all the i's had been dotted and the t's crossed. Now, with all that done, there was only one other important thing left for Michael to do—make his usual Sunday call back home to Belfast.

Catherine was in the kitchen, laying the table and preparing the dinner. She shouted through to Peter, who was in the living room with Roisin, to go upstairs and wash his hands, but was almost cut off by the intervention of the telephone ringing.

"Get that would you, Roisin? These pots is on their way to boiling over. It's probably Michael, anyway; he'll be a lot happier hearing your voice."

"Nonsense, Ma," Roisin replied, as she left the living room and entered the hallway where the phone was kept. "If it was me he wanted to speak to, he'd have rung me at home."

"Don't give me that. He knows that you'll be here on a Sunday, having ye dinner."

Roisin answered the call.

"How are ye, Ma?"

"It's me. Ye Ma's busy with the dinner. It's a good job you asked for her, though, because she thinks you only ring on a Sunday because you know that I'll be here." Roisin spoke loudly so that Catherine could hear.

"Pay her no mind; sure, I rang her twice this week already."

"Oh, ye rang her twice already, did ye?" She spoke even louder this time, making sure that Ma could definitely hear. Catherine threw the conversation a deaf one, pretending that she couldn't while banging the potato masher loudly on the side of the pan to back up her pretence. Roisin smiled. She was well versed in Ma's tricks—almost as much as Michael was.

"How are ye, beautiful? Do ye miss me?"

"That's a stupid question, Michael Flynn. You know I do."

"Ah, but which part do you miss the most?"

"Behave, yourself. You know ye Ma can hear."

"Is he talking crude over the phone?"

"No, Ma. I think he was about to propose to me."

"It's about time. Tell him to get on with it."

"Ha. That shut you up, didn't it?" she laughed, returning her three-way conversation back to Michael.

"I might surprise you one day, woman. Maybe even sooner than you think."

"Whatever, Michael Flynn. You'll have to get permission from ye mates first. How are the lads, anyway?"

"We're all grand, but I have something to tell ye that I don't want Ma knowing about." Roisin moved her body, turning just enough so that her back was to the kitchen door.

"Go on," she egged, letting him know the coast was clear.

"We're going to be up to a bit of skullduggery. Nothing much, just a little money-booster. But you know that I always warn ye, just in case things don't go to plan and you get the knock from the police."

In a hushed voice, she replied her concerns.

"Be careful Michael. Don't go getting into any more trouble."

"I won't—leastways, that's not the plan."

Ma, who had heard nothing for the past few seconds, wondered what was going on.

"Has he gone? He didn't even say hello to his own mother."

"He's still here, Ma. He was just telling me that he loves me."

"Huh," Catherine huffed. "Aren't you the lucky one?" Roisin couldn't help but laugh.

"You better talk to your mother; I think she's getting a bit jealous. Now, stay safe and ring me as soon as you're done, so I know everything's fine."

"Done what? What's he up to now?" Catherine had left the kitchen and was stood close enough to catch the end of the conversation.

"He's doing a building course while he's in London." Roisin made the excuse with the phone still near her mouth so that Michael could hear on the other end. "Nothing to worry about, Ma. Anyway," she continued, when returning the phone to her ear, "ring me in the week and let me know how you get on. Love ye." After hearing the words repeated to her from Michael, she passed the phone to his mother.

"What's this course you're going on? You never mentioned anything to me when you rang the other day."

Roisin made her way back to the living room, smiling at the thought of Michael having to think quickly to answer his mother's questions about a non-existent course. She sat down, giving young Peter's head a rub, who, as usual was engrossed in the TV She began to wonder what Michael might really be getting up to, but there was no point in worrying. She'd been through the same thing numerous times before because he always let her know when he was up to something, he had to. That way, she knew to have all the house in order and anything the police might be interested in removed, just in case.

When Sean returned with the goods, the remainder of the afternoon was spent stripping, cleaning and then re-oiling the weapons. Dermot prepared the explosive charge and Michael once again ran them all through the plan, giving them another chance to voice any concerns.

"I've had an idea about how to buy us some time should we need it when making our getaway." The other three looked at Dermot, waiting for enlightenment. "Cement. I'm going to transfer the powder into a holdall so it's easier to carry and bury the explosive inside. We can use the bag as a door stop to hold open the fire-door to the roof, and if we have got company when we are leaving, I will detonate the C4 once we are clear. Anyone behind us will be disorientated by the blast and blinded for a good while by the cement powder. What do you think?"

"It sounds good to me." Danny gave Dermot's suggestion his backing, before giving him a huge pat on the back.

"It sounds fucking brilliant to me," concurred Michael. "What do you think, Fatty?" Sean, with a huff and a puff of his cigarette, didn't seem too over-enthusiastic about the idea.

"It's ok, I suppose. Anyway, it will have to do at such short notice." Sean wasn't happy. He hated the fact that his only part in the robbery would be driving the crane, especially when Dermot was doing so much. He was dying to be in the thick of it with his mates.

"Make it so Dermot, but make sure you remember to bring the bag back if we don't use the explosive. Finding a bag full of cement would definitely have them looking at the building site afterwards."

Before leaving the flat, they cleaned it from top to bottom, making sure that no incriminating evidence had been left behind, just in case the next people through the front door were the police. Michael took his SIM card from his mobile and cut it up before flushing it down the toilet. He then jumped on the phone, smashing it into a hundred pieces in preparation for it to be discarded out of the car window as they made their way to the pub that night. There was only one number on it of any importance—Mactazner's—but Michael didn't want to think of the trouble it would cause if the police were to get that from its memory and go asking questions in Kilburn and The Harp of Erin.

At seven o'clock, they arrived at The Rose and Crown, dressed up to the nines, laying the foundation for their alibi that they were going around the local area for a drink. After parking the car in the backyard, they stayed for a few pints. Or made out that they did—most of their drinks were spilt down the urinal, so they had clear heads for the job before making their way to the site, or as Barbara thought, to the next pub. Once there, Sean checked that all the radios were working and on the same frequency. Danny, Dermot and Michael slipped their black boiler suits on over their clothes and took a ski mask and a pair of gloves each. Sean then checked the weapons, making sure that every inch of them was wiped clean, before removing the rounds from the magazines and giving them the same treatment. After reloading, he cocked the weapons, applied the safety catches and dished them out from, and to, gloved hands. The lads were ready to go. All that was left for them to do now was to wait for the right time to come.

Michael climbed the ladder and sat in darkness, high on the scaffold. It was a cold March evening, but the chill in the air was the last thing on his mind. His excitement was growing as he watched the punters entering the club, counting every penny as if it were already his own. The other three took shelter from the night air in Dermot's office, where Sean was dealing with his pre-robbery nerves in his favourite way, by taking the piss out of Dermot.

"This fucking place is cleaner than our flat," he observed, flicking his ash on the floor in an attempt to get a rise out of Dermot. "Do you do any work or just sit in here all day with your feather duster, polishing?"

"Flick your ash wherever you want, you'll not get a bite out of me tonight. I've got other things on my mind. In case you had forgotten, we're about to pull a robbery."

Dermot's words of wisdom fell on deaf ears as Sean continued his line of wind-up by finishing his cigarette and extinguishing it beneath his boot while giving Danny a cheeky wink. Danny, who seemed to waste half his life listening to the pair bicker, just shook his head and continued to flick through an old copy of *Readers' Wives*. Dermot shifted the conversation by making a statement that also held a bit of a worry.

"I hope when this is all over and we have the money that Michael will calm down and stop thinking of different ways to get us killed."

Danny, turning the magazine sideways to get a complete view of the centrefold wife of the month, shared his thoughts on the matter.

"How long have you known Flynny?" he asked, raising his eyes from the seedy mag and looking at Dermot.

"I've known him for as long as you have—since we were all kids at school."

"And in all that time, did you not realise that money is not the motivation behind the different escapades he drags us on? We'd still be doing this robbery if he had ten million in the bank. It's the planning and the excitement of doing the job that gives him his kicks. If you're asking my opinion, there's only one thing that will calm him down."

"What's that?" Sean interrupted, lighting another tab. "Don't say a bullet in the head because we'll probably get one at the same time."

"Kids," enlightened Danny.

"Kids! I didn't think he was after starting a family?"

"He's not, but Roisin will be, and I know his mother is chasing grandkids. I'm not saying when he'll have them; I'm just saying that when he does, that having kids will be the one thing that finally calms him down."

"Does that mean that when Greasy Deasy calves in a few months, Dermot the office-polisher over here will calm down as well?" Sean added, dragging the conversation back to his favourite subject. "Fuck me, if he slows down any more, he'll end up in a fucking coma."

"What do you mean 'calves'? She's not a fucking heifer." Dermot defended Mary from Sean's description, but he wasn't really sure why. "She's having a baby, possibly my baby, not a calf, ye fat fucker." Sean smiled; he was beginning to get the bite he was chasing so he carried on.

"Well, it will be well fed anyway. She has tits the size of a cow's udders, that girl. The baby will be in no rush to get on the bottle, I can tell ye. And the amount of Guinness Greasy Deasy drinks, the young one won't go short of iron in its milk."

Dermot just sat back in his chair, trying to think of something he disagreed with before Danny found something he did.

"Fuck me, Dermot. Half of these pages are stuck together, you dirty little fucker." Danny threw the magazine back on to the desk, before wiping his fingers on the sides of his chair.

"Dermot wouldn't do that," Sean said jumping to his defence. Dermot thought it unusual but appreciated the backup. "He hasn't got a wank in him," continued Sean, getting back on track.

The door to the cabin opened, breaking the banter before Dermot had time to retaliate. Michael, leaving his feet on the step, leant inside, using the handle for support. He paused before saying anything to look at the other three, as though searching for confirmation that they were ready.

"Right, lads, we're up."

Ten thirty was the time they had agreed to go and it had soon come around to zero hour. When Sean started the engine on the crane, all that could be seen in the darkness was the glow from the end of his cigarette inside the cab. Danny and Dermot climbed into the hopper, followed by Michael, and after a word over the radio, Sean began to hoist them high into the cool night sky until all the surrounding obstacles were cleared. Next, the huge arm twisted on its axis as it turned anti-clockwise, almost to an angle of 90 degrees, until it pointed directly towards their objective. Sean then began to extend the boom arm, giving the crane the extra few metres needed to bridge the gap between the road and the club roof. Michael, as before, was Sean's eyes as he relayed every movement, while judging every distance, allowing him to safely deliver his three-man cargo. Unlike before, once they were out of the hopper, Michael this time—because Dermot wasn't there to keep an eye on things—went to the front of the roof that looked over the main doors. Looking down through the club and street lights, he could see that business was going on as usual, and as before when Dermot was spotting for danger, no one suspected anything. Convinced that their movements thus far were undetected, they moved across to the access door, where they found everything as they had left it. Michael indicated to Dermot the bypass wire, which he acknowledged before placing the holdall containing his makeshift exploding and blinding smoke screen down in front of the door to hold it open. He then loaded the FRG with the fifty-grain baton round that resembled a large torch battery and raised his thumb, indicating his readiness. Danny and Michael checked their weapons before placing them in their belts, where they were easy to get to, and they too gave the same thumbs-up. All three were now ready, and eager.

Danny went first down the steps with the torch, which he shone at their feet. Then Dermot followed, with Michael at the rear. When they reached the bottom, only the one internal door stood between them and their objective. They sat down in the darkness on the steps, waiting patiently for the sound of the security gates opening, which would hopefully mean they had caught the dealer stocking up on more drugs. It wasn't imperative that they did, but it would give them more time for a clean getaway if they managed to get the whole crew in one room. It seemed like only minutes had gone by, but in fact it was nearly twenty when the sound they had been waiting for could be heard through the door.

Big Danny listened carefully, picturing in his head the movements of the dealer as he passed through the security gates. When he judged the time to be right, he pulled down his mask and shone the torch onto his hand so the other two behind him could see. Pointing his finger in the air he indicated that it was one minute until kick-off. Michael and Dermot followed his lead, pulling down their ski masks and disengaging the safety catches on their weapons. Again, Danny raised his hand under the light of the torch, this time with all five fingers splayed. One by one they began to fall, causing Dermot and Michael's adrenaline to rise to almost bursting point and, when the final digit fell, it was almost a relief to see Danny kick open the door with all his force. The door half fell away, but with a follow-through from Danny's shoulder, it smashed against the stairwell, taking the casing with it. Dermot was at his job as quick as a flash, moving past Danny and climbing over the shattered timber towards his objective. Within a second, there were only a few metres that separated him and a startled giant who was moving towards him to investigate the noise. Dermot couldn't help but be surprised by the man's size but keeping his composure he aimed and fired the FRG, scoring a direct hit to the centre of the large man's chest and solar plexus. The giant bouncer fell to his knees, clutching his chest, before falling the rest of the way forward, out for the count. Dermot, with the now empty FRG held above his head in readiness to use as a cosh, breathed a sigh of relief when it wasn't needed.

Danny and Michael now flew past him to get into the office. Inside, the dealer and another man had both started to react to the commotion. The unknown man was pulling a sawn-off shotgun from behind the desk and was swinging it quickly in their direction. Danny, seeing the danger, threw back his left hand, stopping Michael from coming into the line of fire, while at the same time raising his right hand, which contained his weapon. Given no choice, he let go two rounds, hitting the man with both shots and sending him flying backwards into some filing cabinets. Both barrels of the sawn-off were released, as the dying man's twitching finger pressed on the trigger, taking out several ceiling tiles, which fell to the floor, filling the room with dust. Immediately, Danny turned his attentions to the Rasta dealer, who had grabbed hold of a sword that had been leaning against the wall in the corner of the room.

"Not even if you were Zorro himself would you get to me with that before I put two of these nice shiny bullets in your fucking head," Danny warned, leaving the Rasta in no doubt as to his next move, which he made swiftly by dropping the sword. "Good, now move over there next to your very slow, very dead friend."

The Rasta glanced at his dead boss and, in no hurry to join him, did as he was told. Danny gave the man on the floor a hard kick in the ribs, confirming that he was no longer a threat, before removing the shotgun out of the Rasta's way, not knowing in the commotion if both barrels had been fired.

"Are you okay, big man?" Michael asked, while

tucking his weapon in his belt, knowing Danny had everything covered.

"I'm okay. Sorry about the noise," Danny replied, releasing a little cough and wafting the still falling dust away from his eyes. He moved away from the doorway to allow Michael entry. Michael moved in and looked down on the dead man before reaching up and brushing a few pieces of tile debris from the top of Danny's balaclava and shoulders.

"Do you think anybody heard the shots?" Danny asked, while looking back at the metal cage and door to the club, where Dermot stood with the FRG now slung over his shoulder and his handgun drawn in readiness for anybody coming through it.

"I doubt it," reassured Michael. "I can hardly hear you now over the music. I think Bob Marley has us covered."

"Cable ties," shouted Dermot, throwing several towards Michael, who caught most of them and turned to the dealer.

"Lie down on the floor next to your man and kiss the carpet," he ordered.

The dealer did as Michael said, positioning himself next to his boss's corpse. The Rasta's hands were tied behind his back and then his ankles, before both were joined together, leaving him with only his belly on the floor. Dermot, with much more of a struggle, secured the big bouncer in exactly the same way, but doubled up with the ties for extra strength; both of them now lay as though they had just been wrestled into the Boston crab. Michael paused before moving on to the next part of their plan, to reassure himself that the noise of the shots hadn't been heard. He listened to the reggae music, which boomed through the closed door from the club, thinking that surely it would have been turned off if anything was suspected. At the same time, he began to familiarise himself with his new surroundings—a couple of filing cabinets, a desk and, more importantly, an open safe were the main furniture in the room; after that, the dealer and his boss took up most of the floor, leaving not much room for anything else.

"Fella," he said, looking at Dermot but using no names, "get on with your job, take the keys from your man's pocket, and make sure the door and the gate are both locked. Then snap the key off in the lock and take care of the phones. Big fella..." Danny turned. "...when he's done that, give him a hand to drag that lump into the office while I have a word with his friend here."

Danny and Dermot got on with their jobs as Michael moved across to the desk and opened the drawers. The top right contained at least two hundred pre-bagged coke deals and the bottom right held a mixed assortment of different coloured pills. The top left was where the expensive brown gear sat next to boxes of syringes and, below, cannabis resin and green were kept ready to go. It was a regular junkie sweet shop that held no interest for Michael at all; in fact, the sight of the syringes and the damage they caused with their contents made him want to puke. Taking his weapon from his belt, he moved on to the dealer, bending down next to him and pressing the end of the muzzle firmly into his temple, before proceeding with his line of questioning.

"Now, I'm going say this once, and once only. If you

answer my questions correctly, you might live to go to your friend's funeral. If not, then I'll blow your fucking brains all over the carpet and get the answers from Mighty Joe fucking Young over there when he wakes up. Do you understand?" The dealer nodded, rubbing the side of his face on the carpet. "Good. Now, where's the fucking money?" Michael pushed the weapon even harder into the dealer's temple to ensure that he understood what was at stake—his life! The Rasta didn't need to be asked twice.

"In the cabinet, packed in some sports bags. The keys are in his pocket," he said struggling to turn his head to look at his dead boss. "The rest of it is in the safe. It's open."

Michael reached into the dead man's pocket to retrieve the keys and threw them at Danny, who stood panting with Dermot after dragging the unconscious giant into the office. Danny opened the cabinet to find three large holdalls stacked on top of each other. He unzipped the first bag, revealing a large amount of cash, and immediately realised that they had scored a lot more than a hundred grand. He zipped it back up and removed it from the cabinet to check the one underneath, finding a similar amount.

"Fuck me," he said in disbelief.

"Are we happy?" Michael asked, hearing him and looking across while emptying the safe.

"Jack-fucking-pot," replied Danny. "We're Baa Baa Black Sheep happy. Three bags full."

"Good. Throw me the top one for this lot and you take the other two up to the roof."

Danny threw the first bag to Michael then picked up the other two. He was shocked at the weight of the third, which he hadn't opened but with the amount of adrenaline pumping through his body, it wasn't a problem. Michael emptied the contents of the safe into the first bag, which filled it to capacity. He also realised that the score was a big one and immediately multiplied it by three to go with the number of bags, which sent a rush of excitement through his body. Struggling to force the zip shut, he was interrupted by the trussed-up Rasta voicing a few warnings.

"Ya making a big mistake, man. Do you know who you are robbing?"

"Not a fucking clue," replied Michael sarcastically, "but tell him thanks. My Christmas stocking will be full this year."

"Ya crazy, man. The Yardie won't let this go," the dealer continued to warn, as Michael put his head through the strap of the bag before kicking shut the door of the now-empty safe.

"What the fuck's a Yardie?" Michael was unfamiliar with the name but didn't really care who or what it was.

"He's the man that owns all this and a few more clubs besides. He'll hunt you down man. He's one crazy fucker."

"Well, he can keep the clubs, but he doesn't own this little lot anymore." Michael, tapping the bag, which hung heavily around his shoulder, gave the dealer a wink through the slit in his balaclava. "Now, as much as I would like to stay and chat with you, it's time I was going so say goodnight." Michael pistol-whipped the Rasta at the base of the skull, knocking him clean out. "Are you good to go?" he asked, looking at Dermot.

"I'm good," he replied, destroying the last mobile and pulling the phone wire from its connection. Michael surveyed the room one last time before moving his head towards the door, indicating to Dermot that it was time to leave.

The two of them set off back up the stairs. Michael went first with the bulky bag and Dermot followed, closing the office door behind him. Danny, after putting the two bags in the hopper, began to prepare the scene on the roof by securing the rope, before throwing it over the side of the building. The robbery, so far, couldn't have gone any smoother, and with nobody in pursuit they weren't going to need the C4 explosive they had brought to cover their getaway. The three climbed back into the hopper, which was now an even tighter squeeze with the bags, but nobody was complaining. Michael could hardly get the radio from his pocket, but when he did and spoke to Sean, they were on their way back to the safety of the site. As soon as they touched down,

Sean was out of his cab and over to their position, wanting news.

"How did it go?" he asked excitedly, puffing on a tab. "I'm sick I wasn't with ye."

"It's a good job you weren't, brother. We'd have never fit in the fucking hopper coming back."

"Come on, lads," egged Michael. "We're not done yet. Danny, take off your gear and give it to Fatty, along with your weapon, and then set off walking down the street. Take your time and make sure nobody over the road, either queuing or working, notices you. We'll take the bags to the far wall and drop them over when you're there. When the money is in the boot of the car and we're all in the pub with a Guinness in our hands, then we'll relax." Michael wanted to see the job complete and all of them in the safety of The Rose and Crown before counting any chickens.

"How much is there?" Sean asked, seeing the three bags.

"A little bit more than a hundred grand, bro. We hit the jackpot," Danny declared, while passing him his stuff, and after giving him a rare brotherly pat on the shoulder, he turned and headed towards the gates. Opening them to a minimum, he viewed the road outside, took a few deep breaths to compose himself, then slipped quietly and casually into the street. Sean continued collecting the rest of the equipment from Dermot and Michael before securing it all in a smaller holdall, while Dermot recovered the C4 from his bag, then discarded it and its powdery contents. Each of them now grabbed a bag and together they made their way to the wall that bordered the side street and the pub.

"Fuck me. How much is in here? It weighs a fucking ton," Sean happily complained, as he struggled with the heavy bag and the extra one that the weapons and clothes were in.

"You wouldn't have thought so, the way your brother took off up the stairs with one in each hand," replied Dermot.

Michael climbed the ladder first and stepped onto the scaffolding. Carefully in the darkness, he peered over the wall, making sure that Danny was ready below.

Slipping his head from the loop of the holdall strap, he dropped to his knees and manoeuvred the bag forward across the walk boards towards the edge. Dangling it over the side with a tight grip on one of the handles, he waited for Danny's call who, after checking the coast was clear, beckoned for him to let go. He did so and the bag fell safely with a thud to the ground. Danny immediately picked it up, carried it the short distance to the pub gates and launched it over the top. Dermot brought the next up the ladder, which Michael received and sent the same way, but the third he took from Sean was much heavier. Michael commented on the difference in weight, but with neither time nor light to check it, the bag followed the first two. Finally, the small holdall containing the items that Sean had collected was passed forward and that received the same treatment. After that, all that remained was for them to follow Danny's lead and casually make their way to the pub. Michael and Sean went first, leaving Dermot to lock up, and as they walked along, playing the part of two lads out having a Sunday night drink, Michael looked across at the club. The doormen were going about their job, searching the queuing punters as they entered, oblivious to what had occurred. It was obvious that the robbery still remained undiscovered, but it wouldn't be long before the people inside, waiting to get off their heads, would start to wonder what had happened to the dealer. The time now was eleven thirty, which meant the robbery to this point had taken just over an hour. In his mind, Michael gave himself a pat on the back; it was a job well done by him and the lads. He couldn't help thinking, though, that the whole thing had been a bit too easy and gone a little too well, apart from the shooting, of course, which was unfortunate but necessary. But the robbery's simplicity couldn't be put down to any great plan, skill or luck. At the end of the day, it was the Jamaicans and their lackadaisical attitude; they were just too wide open and right for the taking. If it hadn't been Michael and his team, it would have been someone else; it was a robbery waiting to happen.

When they reached the street that ran between the pub and the site, Michael and Sean walked down it, checking the area. They knew Danny would have done the same, but it wouldn't hurt to double-check. After giving it the once-over, they returned to the top of the street to find Dermot had caught up with them and, together, they entered the pub where four pints of Guinness were lined up on the bar.

"Here you go, lads," Barbara shouted as they came through the door. "Danny said you were on your way. He's just gone out back to fetch his spare packet of cigarettes from the car." They all knew exactly what Danny was doing out the back. They each grabbed a pint and raised their glasses to their lips.

"Sean," Barbara added, "your brother said you were paying."

Sean sighed, put down his glass and pulled a twenty-pound note from his pocket. Michael, seeing Sean's face, offered him some advice.

"If you want to get your own back on your brother, buy Babs a G 'n' T."

Sean thought that adding to the cost was an unusual way of getting his brother back for dropping the round on his toes, but went along with it anyway, intrigued by the smile on Michael's face.

"Babs, have a gin and tonic yourself, love."

"Thanks, Sean, I'll do that," she answered reaching up for the optic.

"How is that getting him back, buying his woman drinks?" Sean questioned.

"Gin and tonics make her horny as fuck. He's already struggling to stay the pace—she'll be at him all night."

Sean's face was a picture of enlightenment, as he caught on to Michael's line of thinking.

"Make it a double, Babs, and pay yourself another one on for later. I'm in a generous mood," he added, now with a smile as big as Michael's.

Danny returned from the yard, giving Michael the thumbs up and catching Sean with his Cheshire-cat-like grin.

"What you smiling at?" he asked, suspecting that there was more to his brother's glee than the excitement of the robbery.

"Nothing, bro. I'm just happy to be buying you a drink. Oh, and by the way, I told Barbara that I'll drop your work gear off in the morning. I think she wants you to stay the night."

Danny turned to look at Barbara behind the bar, who was just putting the finishing touches to her drink by adding a nice slice of lemon.

"Fuck me. Not again," sighed a tired Danny, who just wanted to have a few beers and go to bed dreaming of large bags of money. "I'll have to tell her that we're going on somewhere else. You lads will have to back me up."

"We can't do that, Danny Boy," answered Michael, whose refusal seemed to be bringing him a lot of pleasure. "I gave her my word that you would stay with the car if she let us use the backyard, and I don't think that now is the time for breaking promises."

"Fuck me," Danny mumbled as his lips fell to his pint.

Nothing was mentioned in the bar about what they had just done. Instead, they talked a load of nonsense in front of Barbara about a night they hadn't had, still building their alibi. They were all bursting to discuss the robbery and how well they thought it had gone, but each kept their speculations to themselves for a later time. But the rubbish they talked couldn't hide the twinkle in their eyes, which spoke volumes of a good job well done.

Back at The Palm Cove, it was three in the morning before the bar and door staff realised that anything was wrong and another two hours after that, when one of the doorman had gone away and brought back a grinder, that they managed to get through the security gates to untie the dealer and the giant. As Michael suspected, the police were not informed, but a long-distance call was made at six that morning to the owner of the club—the guy that the dealer had spoken of.

It was approaching midnight in Jamaica and the Yardie had enjoyed a heavy night on the rum and girls. He was just about to start on the girls for the second time when the call came through. He reached for his phone, not happy at being disturbed in the middle of things and at such an hour.

"Who the fuck is this?" he bellowed in his groggy state.

"Boss, it's me."

"Who the fuck is 'me'?"

"Winston, boss. I'm calling from The Palm Cove in London."

"Winston? What do you want, man? Where the fuck is Leroy?"

"Leroy is dead, boss."

"Dead. What do you mean Leroy, dead? I spoke to him today, you fool."

"He dead now, boss." A silence followed while the Yardie sat up in his bed, registering what he was being told.

"Leroy is dead? What the fuck?"

"We get robbed, boss, and they shoot Leroy."

"ROBBED! Which rassclat be stupid enough to rob me?"

"I don't know who they were, boss. All I know is

that they spoke with Irish accents and they were professional people. They hit us fast and hard. They took everything, man!"

"What do you mean 'everyting'? I just sent a shipment—twenty-five cars."

Cars was the code word for kilo—a word, along with many others, never used over the phone by drug dealers. Certain words would immediately set off the recording tapes at listening posts such as Gibraltar.

"They take it boss—the twenty-five cars and the money."

"Everyting?"

"Everything, boss," confirmed Winston, while nursing his bloodied head and looking down at the empty safe and locker.

"Fucking Irish bastards."

Again, the phone stayed quiet for a moment, while the Yardie contemplated his next move.

"Winston."

"Ye boss."

"Get rid of Leroy's body, and make arrangements

for me to be picked up at the airport. I'll be there tomorrow."

"Okay, boss." Winston began to put down the phone, glad that the conversation was over but now not looking forward to the next day, and the Yardie's arrival.

"Wait, Winston," the Yardie's voice again came through the phone, which Winston returned to his ear.

"Yeah, boss?"

"Do you have any Irish white boy smackheads buying gear from you?"

"Yeah, man."

"Good, then get me one. And, Winston, I don't want Leroy's body washing up down the river next week. Make sure the brothers bury him deep, man."

"Yeah, boss."

"And Winston..."

"Yeah, boss."

"NO BABYLON." (Police)

"Yeah, boss."

The Yardie put down the phone and reached for the docked reefa from the ashtray that sat beneath the lamp on the cane bedside table. He lit it while doing the maths in his head as to how much the final figure could be that had been stolen. Between the shipment and the money that was part-payment for the previous drugs, the total didn't make him happy. He took a long pull from the massive joint, but its chilling effects definitely weren't working fast enough. Looking at the two naked women at the side of him, he decided to vex his anger on them. One after the other, he placed the sole of his foot in the arch of their backs and kicked them out of the bed.

"Get the fuck out, ya lazy bitches. You," he pointed at the first girl, "make me some food. And you, pack my case. I'm going to London and I'm going to kill me some Irish fuckers."

Chapter Seventeen

The Bubble's Burst

At seven forty-five the next morning, a taxi dropped Michael, Sean and Dermot at the site gates for their usual Monday morning eight o'clock start, as if nothing had happened the previous evening and butter wouldn't melt in their mouths. Danny was already on site, waiting for his work gear to arrive, looking a lot brighter than the lads had expected. Apparently, their plan to ply Babs with G 'n' Ts to give him a hard night had backfired. She passed out before even getting upstairs and Danny had had to carry her to bed. It was the best night's sleep he had had in ages.

With their position on the scaffold overlooking the

crime scene, Danny and Michael spent the morning resisting all urges to stare at the club and attempted to get on with their work like any other day. Michael had brought a wireless with him so they could listen into the local radio station, which he placed between the areas where he and Danny worked. They wanted to keep up with the local news, believing that it would surely report details of the robbery and the killing. The discussion of what they would find the next day had filled Michael, Dermot and Sean's conversation the previous evening, once they had returned to their digs, but when midday came and, along with it, lunchtime, none of them expected what they found—nothing, nothing at all. Not a sign of the dealer or a policeman; the club doors hadn't opened once; there was nothing on the radio about a robbery or a shooting. It was as though it had never happened.

With everything being so quiet at that end, Michael decided to make something happen himself at theirs by seizing the moment and taking the afternoon off work to move the car and get rid of the weapons. Danny took over Michael's workspace on the scaffold, where the view of the club was unhindered, so he could keep a sharp eye on things; it was agreed that they would all meet later, back at the digs. Michael collected the vehicle and drove it to a part of the river that was familiar to him, near Chelsea Harbour. It was a bit of a hike, but he had been there a few years earlier and remembered a secluded spot to dump the bag and check the loot. Driving there, he tried to guess the next move of the club owners, put out by the fact that so far they hadn't made any, which didn't leave him with much to go on. He didn't like it—so much so that he almost wished for some sort of backlash. But that was Michael's way—if he couldn't see it or grab it by the throat, he didn't trust it.

Back on the site, at about three thirty, Danny began to wind things up in anticipation of the four o'clock finish and the meet with Michael. All three of them were eager to find out how successful the robbery had been, especially Danny, who kept having flashbacks to the two bags he had opened, estimating the take to be two or three hundred grand at least. As he began to finish off the work he had done that day by pointing off the freshly laid bricks, a Transit van pulled up outside the club, putting him back in surveillance mode. Two black men got out and went to the club doors, which opened in front of them as though expecting their arrival. They disappeared inside and the doors closed behind them, so Danny made himself comfortable for the wait for their return, only to be interrupted by the sound of Sean tooting the horn on the crane. It was four o'clock and time for the off. From his position, Danny leant over the scaffold to attract Sean's attention, but instead got Dermot's, who had now joined him at the crane. Putting his finger to his eye, he then pointed over the wall towards the club. Dermot gave him the thumbs up, understanding the situation. Danny returned his attention back to the street and the Transit van, but it was a good half-hour before the two men made their reappearance. This time, between them, they were carrying a rolled-up carpet on their shoulders, and following them out of the club to open the rear doors of the van was the Rasta drug dealer, sporting a large plaster on the back of his head.

"I know what ye have in there," Danny muttered to himself, recognising the pattern on the carpet as belonging to the one the Rasta was kissing in the office the night before. The awkward bundle was thrown rather clumsily and, considering what it contained, disrespectfully into the back of the van, before the doors shut firmly behind it. The two men climbed back in the Transit, looking up and down the street as they did to see if their collection had attracted any unwanted attention. The dealer returned to the club, giving the street the once-over himself, before entering and closing the doors behind him. Danny watched as the Transit was driven down towards The Rose and Crown, where it turned the corner out of sight. He had seen what he needed to see. It was obvious that the Jamaicans were doing their own clear-up job and the police were not involved.

His job done, he joined the others, filling them in on what he had just seen while the three of them headed the same way down the street, where, unbelievably, and even though they were all as anxious as each other to meet Michael, the pull of the pub was just too much. Having no transport, they had to phone a taxi anyway, and calling it from the pub would gave them a good excuse to grab a few pints.

It was nearing seven when the three of them got back to the digs to find Michael sitting in the kitchen drinking tea. Danny, while removing his coat, began to tell him of the one and only occurrence at the club.

"Well, two fellas picked up the body this afternoon from the club and unless it was some kind of cut-price Jamaican funeral, I'd say they were definitely not involving the authorities. That is, unless the local funeral parlour is using Transit vans and Axminster coffins."

Big Danny smiled. He didn't make many jokes—that was his brother's department—but he thought his description was worth at least a little laugh. Michael said nothing, just raised his cup to his mouth and sipped at his tea.

"Is there something wrong?" Danny asked at his unusual silence. Michael looked up, broken from his deep thought.

"That depends on how you want to look at it, big fella."

"Well, there was plenty of money. I saw that myself."

"There's plenty of money, all right, but there's plenty of something else, too."

"What do you mean?" asked Sean and Dermot in unison, while taking a chair each at the table.

"The first bag that I emptied the contents of the safe into and carried was full of money, a rake of it—so much that I couldn't be bothered to count it. If we live to spend it, we'll be able to buy ourselves a bar and a building company outright."

"Live to spend it?" repeated Dermot. "What do you mean by that?"

"Never mind what he means," interrupted Sean. "What about the other two bags, the ones Dermot and me carried to the wall?"

"The second bag which Dermot carried was the same," confirmed Michael.

"And the third?" prompted Sean, eager for an estimate of the take. "That was the heaviest of the lot. You said so yourself on the scaffold."

"I remember how heavy it was. That's how I know it was the one you were carrying." He took another drink of his tea, still deep in his thoughts and miles away from the conversation, which was beginning to irritate Sean.

"Well, what was in it?" he urged.

Michael looked up from his cup with a rather deflated look on his face.

"DRUGS!" he revealed in a frustrated and raised voice.

"Drugs?" repeated Dermot.

"You heard me—drugs. A load of the shit. That's why the bag was so heavy."

"Fuck me. What are we going to do?" Dermot jumped straight into his normal worry mode, asking the question that Michael had obviously been contemplating all afternoon since making the discovery.

"Chuck the stuff in the river or smoke it," offered Sean as a solution to their narcotics problem. "At least that way we might chill Dermot out."

"It's not as easy as that," answered Michael.

"Why not? Just chuck the drugs in the river and fuck off back to Belfast with the money."

"Listen to what he's saying, Sean, will ye?" Danny yelled at his brother, knowing by Michael's demeanour that the situation wasn't good.

"It means trouble," Michael continued. "I'm no expert but I'd say the drugs are worth millions. There's no way whoever the stuff belongs to will let it go; they're going to come looking. And this isn't the stuff you roll in a Rizla. It's the heavy gear—twenty-five solid blocks of pure uncut. There's enough sniff in that bag to keep London on its toes for a year."

"Who's going to come looking?" asked Dermot.

"Whoever owns it—maybe the Yardie, the person that the Rasta mentioned before I knocked him out? I should have just killed him. Then there wouldn't be a problem. Fuck me, I only wanted a hundred grand; just twenty-five grand each and I would have been happy."

"Come on, Michael, that's not our way. We don't kill if we don't have to, so you can't have any regrets about that."

"I know, Danny Boy, but my head's so battered from all the thinking I've done this afternoon that I can't separate the good ideas from the bad."

"What difference does it make that you left him alive? You were wearing masks. He didn't see any of your faces, did he?"

"No, Sean, he didn't see any faces. But he heard our voices, so he knows we're Irish. That's why we can't fuck off anywhere."

"Fuck me. What will that matter? There must be two hundred thousand Irishmen in London."

"Probably more, Fatty, but they don't all work across the fucking street, do they? Fuck me, I wish you would put your brain in gear before you engage your gob." Michael raised his voice again and gritted his teeth, becoming a little frustrated with Sean and his lack of speed at grasping how dangerous the situation was. "Like I said to you before, they're going to see the crane, and along with the fact that it's the only place that overlooks the club means they're going to come and check out the site. Even if they believe the old rope trick we played on them, they're still going to come and check it out. And if they find out that four Irishmen left the same week as they were robbed, they're going to put two and two together and come up with us. There will be nowhere to hide because they'll have all our identities and if we do a runner, we'll just be leading them straight back to Belfast and our families. That's why we've got to stick it out here and carry on as normal, and for the first time your size will come in handy."

"How do you mean?" asked Sean, not sure that he was going to like what was coming.

"The Rasta fella we left alive is the only one that saw us—our shapes anyway—and when he sees you getting out of the cab of the crane, he won't be picking you out of any fucking line-up, believe me!"

"What about the big man on the gate?" added Dermot. "He got a look at my shape before I got him with the FRG"

"Don't worry about him," replied Michael. "He'll be telling fisherman's tales."

"Fisherman's tales? What the fuck are they?"

"The one that got away was always the biggest. That man is at least six foot six and twenty-five stone. When asked to describe you, he's going to add at least six stone and six inches. He's not going to admit that he was taken out by a seven-stone dwarf.

"Dwarf!" exclaimed Dermot. "Who's a fucking dwarf?" He wasn't very happy at Michael's description. Out of all the names his mates had tagged him with, he liked that one the least.

"Chill out. I'm only saying it from the big bouncer's point of view," backtracked Michael.

"Don't worry," Sean chipped in, patting Dermot on the back. "You look nothing like any of the six dwarves."

"There were seven, not six," corrected Dermot.

"I know that," laughed Sean. "You're a fucking dead ringer for Dopey."

"Fuck you, lard arse."

"That's for the takeaway jibe the other day," added Sean, keeping score.

Danny gave his brother a slap around the shoulder, wondering if there would ever be a time or situation when he would take anything seriously.

"So what do you want to do?"

"Nothing, Danny, we do nothing except carry on

going to work, looking like four skint Irishmen. It's important that everything on that site stays exactly the same as it was before the robbery. We continue watching the club and wait to see what they bring before we come up with any decisions as to our next move. I always knew that we would have to front it and carry on working as if nothing had happened for a little while; that situation was always going to happen. The only difference then was that, for a hundred grand, it would have gone away. Don't get me wrong, they would have had a little look and asked a few questions, but at the end of the day, they would have just tightened their security and put it down as a loss. Not for this much money and drugs, though. This situation is going fucking nowhere. But we do have one card up our sleeves, don't forget."

"What's that?"

"Dermot."

"Me?"

"Yes, you. If anyone comes on site wanting any information, they'll ask for the man in charge and, the last time I checked, that was you. That means you can tell them everything *we* want them to know." Dermot nodded along with the other two. They hadn't thought of that, but neither had Michael until he'd gone over it in his head all afternoon. "One more thing—you'll have to move me and Danny. Put us around the back some place where we can't be seen. The Rasta got too good a look at the big fella's shape. Put a couple of them Welsh bricklayers on the front wall. That will fuck anybody up trying to get information." Dermot nodded in agreement with the quickly-made plans.

"So where's the money and the drugs now?" asked Danny.

"Both still in the boot of the car. Don't worry—it's parked in a safe place."

"How much was there?"

"You don't want to know, Sean."

"I fucking do."

"Okay, put it this way—it will keep you in takeaways for the rest of your life."

"Fuck me! As much as that!" joked Dermot. "I thought you were just going to say a couple of million!"

Sean gave no comment in retaliation to the insult. The raising of his middle finger from a clenched fist said it all.

Chapter Eighteen

Kingston to London

Heathrow Airport Tuesday morning was a scene of steroid-enhanced gangsters and sweet-smelling tobacco as a ten-man team awaited the arrival of their boss, the Yardie from Jamaica. A black stretch-limo sat between two Range Rovers front and rear, parked as close to the main entrance as the security staff who had formed in numbers would allow. The Yardie soon appeared, looking anything but jet-lagged as he bounced through the doors like a Tasmanian devil on acid after being put through the ringer by customs, who, because he was known to them, had searched everything—he was lucky to get away without grabbing his ankles and spreading his cheeks. Tall and lean, he was filled out by loose-fitting clothes that were embroidered with the Jamaican national colours, while in his hand he carried an ornately hand-carved cane that served no purpose, except maybe as a weapon if needed. His hair was thick with dreadlocks hanging all the way down his back, almost reaching his knees. His whole appearance was clean and tidy, from his manicured nails and gleaming teeth to the designer training shoes on his feet. The only thing that wasn't clean was his language.

"You fuckers—get the bags. Winston—get in the back with me and tell me everything that happened. And where the fuck was Big Robbie when we got robbed? What am I paying that big black fucker for?"

Winston the dealer, who had been dreading this moment since the robbery had happened, climbed in the back of the limo with the Yardie and started to explain everything, starting with how big Robbie had been taken out with a plastic bullet that none of them had ever seen before. He explained how Leroy was shot and what they had done with his body. He explained how the robbers had gained entry and escaped via the roof, and he explained why nobody had heard a thing because the music from the club had drowned out the shots. By the time they reached Notting Hill, Winston had explained it over and over again, but like him, the Yardie still only knew one thing—the men who had robbed him were professional and they spoke with Irish accents.

As the three-car cortège pulled up outside the club, at least another fifteen of the Yardie's men were gathered around the entrance; it was like closing the gate once the horse had bolted. The Yardie got out of the car, followed by Winston, and paused to take in his surroundings, as though admiring everything he owned. It had been over a year since his last visit, which could account for the reason why things had become so slack, but now he was back, that would soon change.

"Winston, did you get what I asked for—the Irish smackhead?"

"I got you two, boss," Winston replied, closing the limo door and following the Yardie into the club.

Inside, Big Robbie stood guard over two petrified young Irish lads who had just been unlucky in their choice of days to go score a fix. Both men fitted the profile exactly of a smack head: two scruffy, scrawny, bags of bones with spotty complexions and sweat leaking profusely from every pore on their body. The Yardie looked at Robbie and sucked his teeth, letting the big man know that he was unhappy with his performance. Robbie rubbed his chest where he had been hit by the projectile, acting like a scolded child, before breaking eye contact with his boss. Turning his attention to the captives, the Yardie walked about the floor, circling the two young men who were sat with their feet bound at the ankles and their hands behind their backs. Putting his cane under each of their chins, he raised their heads and gave them both a wild stare about the eyeballs, before leaving them to go behind the bar, where he took a bottle of fresh orange juice from the cooler. The room now contained at least thirty of the Yardie's gang, who had filtered in from the street, the last man inside slamming the doors shut, making both of the young men jump in their seats. Without anything else happening, this was already the scariest moment the Irish smack-heads had ever experienced in their lives. The Yardie began his interrogation.

"Do you know me?" he asked, walking back towards them. Both shook their heads in response. "I own all this and all the drugs you buy." Both men nodded, not doubting a word he said. "I work hard for years, selling shit on street corners and paying the white man's Babylon to leave me alone, and I did it so that one day I can afford all this." The Yardie raised his cane and turned on the spot, proudly pointing around the club. "And I have two more just like it, plus a nice yard in Kingston, Jamaica, which is where I was yesterday, chilling with my bitches, a big spliff, and a big hard-on." The two men, shaking and confused, looked at each other, wondering why they were there and why they were hearing his life story. "But now I am here in London, and do you know why?" Again, the two men shook their heads. "I'm here because some rassclat robbed my club—this fucking club." The Yardie was now in front of the lads in a crouching position, the three of them separated only by inches. "And you're here because the men that rob me were Irish." Both men again shook their heads in strong denial, declaring their innocence.

"It wasn't us. We don't know anything about no robbery. God's truth we don't."

"Shhhhh." The Yardie put his finger to his lips, making the calming sound. "I know you didn't do it, you don't have the brains." The two men, omitting the insult, almost managed a smile upon hearing the first words of encouragement. "But I think you may know more than you are saying." The smiles dropped from their faces as the Yardie took a drink of the orange juice from the bottle. "You, what's your name?" the Yardie asked, looking at the man on the right, singling him out for the question.

"Declan," he answered, barely able to speak.

"Tell me, Declan, do you like orange juice?" The question was totally out of place and unexpected from the Yardie, who softened his voice while asking it.

"What?"

"Orange juice, Declan," he repeated. "Do you like it? They say it's good for bowels. It helps with the constipation!"

The young man didn't know what to say, just nodded his head to the Yardie, who, seemingly uninterested, was reading the additives from the label.

"Good," the Yardie said, his voice returning to its booming tone as he stood up and drank the remnants from the bottle. He tossed the now empty container at Robbie, who caught it in his right hand and looked around for a bin, presuming it was to be disposed of. But the Yardie had other ideas and hinted at his plans by looking at him and then back at the smackhead.

"What?" asked Robbie, ignorant of his next move as a pearly white smile formed on his boss's face.

"Shove it up his arse."

There was a moment's silence as everybody in the room registered with disbelief the Yardie's order. Robbie looked at the bottle and then the lad, who broke the silence with his protests. Both Irishmen tried in vain to get up and hop away. The Yardie pushed down on the second man's shoulders, forcing him and his chair back to the floor.

"Chill, man," he said showing no emotion, just once again his pearly white teeth. "I'll get to you next."

The largest look of fear and terror filled the lad's face as he wrenched at his bindings in a desperate attempt to break free, but it was hopeless. Alas, his frantic motions soon turned into exhaustion and the realisation that he could do nothing to stop himself from receiving the same treatment. The first man, who had now been lifted from his chair, screamed and kicked, resembling a baby in the giant arms of Robbie, who ripped away at his trousers. The Irish lad did his best to fight back, impaired by his bindings and hugely outweighed by his opponent, but it was no use, his resistance was futile—the outcome was a foregone conclusion. Once the large man used his power and weight advantage to hold him down, the bottle was thrust into the young Irish lad's clenched rear, with every person in the room apart from the Yardie cringing at the thought of it, and the screams. Released from Robbie's grip, the boy now lay sobbing on the floor, unable to remove the foreign object because of his bindings. His torture served only one purpose—to prove to his friend that if he didn't answer the Yardie's questions correctly, he would be receiving the same treatment.

"Take him away," ordered the Yardie, deafened by the cries of pain and turning his attention to the other smackhead, who was now wishing he had never seen a drug in his life. The Yardie walked back in front of him, using his cane once again to lift his chin. The young man, now sat in a pool of his own urine, shook violently with fear.

"Now, tell me what you know or I will tell my men to rape your arse—all of them, one after the other. They will go through your hole like a train through a tunnel."

The young man, through watery eyes, looked at the gang of Jamaicans, who didn't look like they fancied the job, but would do anything they were ordered to do by their crazed boss.

"I don't know who robbed your club," he said fighting back the tears, "but I do know where you might find them—Kilburn. If they were Irish, you'll find them in Kilburn."

"Where in Kilburn?"

The boy took another look at his capturers. He was scared to release the information and scared not to.

"Don't tell anyone that I told you where to go. They'll do a lot worse than this if they find out I said anything." The young Irishman pleaded for the Yardie's silence, thinking it was the IRA he was about to grass on.

"Worse than an ice pick down the end of your cock or lit cigarettes being stubbed out in your eyes? You tell me what you know or the next bottle up *your* arse will have the neck broke off and that's just for starters. Now, where in Kilburn? Give me the address."

The boy's sobbing became intense as the tears rolled down his face, congealing with the snot running from his nose. He had one choice—get himself out of trouble by putting himself in a whole lot more.

"Probably the Harp, The Harp of Erin. It's protected. They'll know who they are in there."

The young man could stand no more and, again

losing control of his bodily functions, followed through with excrement to go with the wet patch already in his trousers and around his feet. The untimely bowel movement, however, probably proved to be his saviour, keeping him from further interrogation because now nobody wanted to go near him.

"Get rid of him."

"Do you want me to kill them?" Robbie asked, dangling the man from his feet at arm's length.

"No, leave them alive, so everybody knows what happens when they steal from me."

The young sobbing man, from his upright position, almost managed a second smile as the light shone from the end of the tunnel, but it was short-lived upon hearing the Yardie's further orders. "But slash the soles of their feet so they can't walk or stand, and their arses so they can't sit down. Let them spend a few weeks on their bellies like the slithering slimy snakes they are." Again, the screams began. The Yardie, shaking his head at the noise, contemplated his next move, but not for long. "Then get two vans ready with ten men packing. In one hour, we go to Kilburn."

"Yeah, boss," replied Robbie, before dragging the young lad to join his friend down the back alley where they were introduced to a sharp blade.

"Now, Winston, show me where they got in and out."

Winston took his boss up to the roof, leaving the rest of his men in the club. If any of them had ever contemplated thoughts of stealing from their boss, their inclinations had just been well and truly quashed.

Explaining how the robbers had bypassed the alarms and gained their entry, Winston led the Yardie to the stairwell and up to the access door. Seeing the lock that lay on the ground had been cut with bolt crops from the inside told him that they had gained entry elsewhere. He pulled the temporary wire that connected the alarm circuit and threw it angrily behind him onto the stairs. He was beginning to realise just how wide open to robbery he was and had been for a long time.

"Two fucking clips and a bit of wire were all it took to fuck me," he muttered angrily. This had been an expensive lesson, showing the chinks in his security, and he wasn't happy.

He wasn't happy on the roof, either, nor convinced about the rope the lads had left as a decoy—not down three floors with all that coke and money. What left the biggest doubt in his mind though was the knot—it was still loose. Bending down to examine it, he could have easily untied it with his fingers. If three men had climbed down it carrying weight, it would have tightened up more around its hitching. He didn't totally dismiss it, but he was no fool; he hadn't got where he was by not doing a bit of thinking. He'd got his education from the 'University of Life', which had taught him always to look before you leap and to trust nothing and no one. Okay, his methods of interrogation and extracting information may have been a bit pagan-like, but he got answers—and answers were what he needed, quickly—as quick as possible because in his mind, somebody, somewhere, was probably already very busy spending his money and snorting his gear or, worse, selling it off to his rivals, in which case he would have no chance of getting it back. Plus if he had no gear to sell to his regular punters, which amounted to half the town, they would go elsewhere to get their fix, and once you lose a customer, it's hard to get them back. The repercussions of this robbery were immense to him—a lot bigger than the money and the shipment he had lost. If he didn't get them back quickly, he would have to arrange for another delivery and that could take weeks to organise—plenty of time for his punters to find another supplier. It really could break up a business that he had spent twenty years building. The final total by the time he got everything back online could be as much as twenty to thirty million, and he wasn't having that.

The Yardie had started out with nothing in a 'dog eat dog' business. He had secured his patch and survived in a vicious underworld where gangland killings were common, and that was only in London. Back in Jamaica, the threats of violence were tenfold, and his main competitors weren't just the other Yardies, there was the police. Over there, you were lucky if the only punishment you received was a foreign object up the rear while being tortured. They preferred to adopt a more permanent solution by sticking old car tyres over your shoulders, adding half a gallon of petrol and setting you alight.

He continued to pace around the roof, looking for further clues and observing the area. The noise and size of the building site opposite obviously drew his attention, and with it, Sean's crane. The Yardie didn't jump to any immediate suspicions, but even at this distance, he could see that the arm would have no problems reaching the roof. Besides, if you're looking for Irishmen in London, a building site was as good a place to start as any.

"Winston. Come here, man."

"Yeah, boss."

Winston joined the Yardie at the front of the roof that looked over the street and across to the site.

"Go over there and have a good look around. Take that big useless fucker Robbie with you. Together you might recognise some rassclat. Find out who works that crane and if he or anyone else was working Sunday night."

It was almost exactly as Michael had predicted, but

it wasn't rocket science. If the robbery had just stayed at a hundred grand, the Yardie would never have left Jamaica. In fact, he probably wouldn't have even found out. The remaining idiots running the place would have got rid of Leroy's body, gone for the rope trick and, as Michael said, wrote the robbery off as bad security. But it was the size of the haul that had changed all that, and the Yardie was here now. And he aimed to get what belonged to him back.

Winston, as ordered, made his way across to the site, taking Big Robbie with him for support and an extra pair of eyes. Entering the gates, they were immediately confronted by Dermot, who had been waiting in the site office for just such a visit after they had seen the spectacle of the Yardie's arrival earlier that morning.

"Oi, you two," came Dermot's shout from the office door, as he set off across the yard to cut them off. "Where are your fucking hard hats?"

The Jamaicans didn't know what to say, but Dermot had done his job—he'd put the pair on their back foot.

"What you say, man?" asked Winston, the two of them eyeing up Dermot to see if his shape jogged any memories.

"Hard hats, he repeated, tapping on his own with his finger. "You can't come on this site without wearing a hard hat. Health and safety will be all over me like a rash. What can I do for you, anyway? We've no vacancies, if it's work you're after."

"Did you work Sunday night?"

"What the fuck has it got to do with you who worked when around here? Who are ye?"

"Just answer the fucking question, man," said the giant, towering over Dermot in a menacing and threatening way.

"All right. Easy, tiger," said Dermot, not giving up the information too easily. "Did I work Sunday night? The answer to that is 'no, did I fuck.' I was seeing double in the bar at the end of the street. No one worked Sunday night, or all weekend for that matter. I know that because I have the only set of keys, besides Sean, that is, who drives the crane. I'll ask him."

7P's

Dermot purposely brought Sean into the conversation, knowing—as Michael said—that they definitely weren't going to recognise him.

"Sean! Sean!" he shouted, beckoning with his arm for Sean to join them.

Sean had been watching the visitors. He climbed out of his cab and made his way over to the group. He eyed up Big Robbie, a tab hanging from the corner of his mouth.

"Fuck me, you're a big fella. Have you come for the hod-carrier's job?"

The giant stared blankly at Sean, not understanding a word he had said, let alone the sarcasm.

"These fellas want to know if anyone was working Sunday night," explained Dermot, starting the pretence.

"Why? What's it got to do with them? Who the fuck are ye?"

Winston, once he had deciphered Sean's twang, came up with a cover story to explain his visit.

"I parked my BMW outside the gates Sunday night and somebody crashed into it."

"Well, I didn't see your car nor was I working. I was in the pub, drunk with him."

"That's right, he was," confirmed Dermot. "Fuck me, I must have been drunk if I couldn't remember being out with this fat twat."

Sean gave Dermot a look that said, 'Don't push it.'

"So you didn't work Sunday night?" asked Winston again, totally confused by the previous conversation.

"No," both Sean and Dermot answered.

Winston looked at Robbie, then the pair stared around the site, looking for anything that might jog a memory. Sean decided to add a bit more confusion to take their minds off the subject in the form of a little piss-take.

"Listen, I'm thinking about getting one of them BMWs. It's not true, is it, that you have to be a black fella to drive one?"

Big Robbie still didn't have a clue what Sean was talking about. In fact, he was more confused than ever, because he knew Winston didn't even own a car. Winston knew two things, though: that Sean was a cheeky fat bastard and that he wasn't part of the team that he had seen committing the robbery on Sunday night.

"Who are the men working on the front wall overlooking the street?" he asked.

"Just a minute there, fellas," intervened Sean. "What are all these fucking questions about?

Again, the giant pushed his big chest out, imposing himself this time on Sean for his reluctance to answer. It was a wrong move by the bouncer, who found exactly the opposite to what he expected.

"Here now, big man, I don't give a fuck about you," Sean retaliated. "Don't think that just because I'm a fat fucker that I won't give you the busiest two minutes of your fucking life."

The situation was heading only one way—towards trouble—and Sean didn't see himself as the underdog.

"It's all right," said Dermot, pulling his vexed friend away from the confrontation. "I'll answer one more question and then you can leave the site." Dermot pushed Sean back, placing himself in a central mediator's position. "A couple of Welsh fellas, Ivor and Dai, are the guys you can see working on the front wall. Now if you're not here in any official capacity and you don't have your hard hats then I'm going to have to ask you to leave."

Winston ignored Dermot. He'd had enough of the two Irishmen's shit. He set off back towards the gates, looking for answers, with Robbie following behind him, diverting slightly on the way to shout up at the two men on the front wall to confirm what he had been told.

"Oi, man, did you work Sunday?" he shouted with his hands cupped around his mouth. One of the Welsh bricklayers looked over the scaffold at the Rasta and his giant sidekick.

"What's that you say, boyo?" he asked with his hand shelled around his ear.

"Did you work Sunday evening?" repeated Winston.

"What's he's saying, Ivor?" asked the other Welshman, joining his friend at the edge of the scaffold.

"I don't really know, Dai. I think he wants to know where we were to, Sunday night."

"Nosey bastard. What's it got to do with him? Mind

what you say, Ivor. They could be from the DHSS, you know."

"They look like a couple of circus performers to me, Dai, or worse, a couple of them poofters. There's a lot of that bare-arse boxing goes on around these parts."

"Get rid of them, Ivor, but be diplomatic like." Ivor nodded and stuck his head back over the scaffold to look at Winston and Robbie, who were still looking up, waiting for an answer.

"Whatever it is you're selling, we're not interested, see. Now fuck off."

"Nice one, Ivor. That will do it," said Dai, both men returning to their work.

Winston, looking stunned, turned and looked at Robbie, who just shrugged his giant shoulders.

"Sheep-shagging rassclats," he muttered, frustrated at the lack of information they were receiving. The two of them carried on looking around the site from the gates, but nobody was ringing any bells. "Fuck this, man. There's nothing here. Let's go back to the club."

Winston decided to call it a day. He looked up at the club roof, where the Yardie still stood, watching everything that had gone on. He beckoned them back, eager to get on his way to Kilburn.

Dermot and Sean's little performance had worked and the Welsh lads had unknowingly put the icing on the cake.

"'Is it true you have to be a black man to drive one?'" said Dermot, repeating the words Sean had said, as they watched Winston and Robbie leave.

"It's true," said Sean with a smile. "That's what BMW stands for—black man's wheels."

For once, the pair shared a laugh, the joke not being directed at either one of them.

"Did you see the look on the big man's face? He didn't have a fucking clue what you were talking about."

"It's a good job he didn't," replied Sean. "I wouldn't want a clout off that big fucker."

"I thought you were going to go for him at one point."

"Nah," dismissed Sean. "That was just my way of bringing the conversation to an end. I might be a fat cunt, but I'm not a stupid fat cunt. I bet you shit yourself Sunday night when he came towards you, though."

"A brick," confirmed Dermot. Again, they laughed together. "Should I tell the others about our visitors?

"No," replied Sean. "They could still be watching. You go back to your cabin and I'll go back to my crane, as if their visit meant nothing. We'll see Danny and Michael after work."

With a confirming nod, Dermot did as Sean suggested. Sean took the time to light a fag before climbing back into his cab, which he did with several huffs 'n' puffs and a straining release of gas from his backside as he squeezed into the tight space.

Chapter Nineteen

Kilburn and the Rat Pack

Outside Mactazner's pub, The Harp of Erin in Kilburn, the normal run-of-the-mill afternoon goings-on were about to be broken, as ten heavily armed black gangsters, Big Robbie, Winston and one pissed-off Yardie climbed out of two Transit vans. The ten men entered the pub in two lines, five men either side, forming a passage for their boss to walk down. Robbie followed behind, towering over everybody in the bar, and Winston followed behind him, still looking for that familiar shape.

It was a busy Tuesday afternoon in The Harp, with not a pinstripe suit in sight. The bar was full of Irish navvies, enjoying a drink after a hard day's work. It was a scene of steel toe-caps and donkey jackets, with a pint of Guinness in every fist. These were hard men, all supporters and most of them members of the IRA, and every one of them now stood in silence, waiting for the trouble that was inevitably going to start at the sight of not one but thirteen black men entering the bar for the first time that anyone could ever remember.

The Yardie walked between his men, defiantly looking back at all the white faces that stared at him. Mactazner's daughter Demelza was behind the bar with a couple of other staff, whom she moved out of the way to handle the situation herself. She turned down the music with the volume switch, quietening Daniel O'Donnell, who didn't quite seem to fit the new mood their visitors had brought with them. The Yardie, with his cane in hand continued his scanning of the room, making his presence felt while looking for signs on any of the faces that his visit was not a surprise.

"Is there something I can do for you, lads?" Demelza asked politely, as three or four of her punters came to the bar as backup. The Yardie paid them no attention, sucking on his teeth dismissively as he turned to answer.

"I want to talk with the man in charge."

"Well, that would be my daddy. He's upstairs having his tea, but I don't think he'll mind if I disturb him. I'll fetch him for you. Would you like a drink while you wait? The Guinness is grand." The Yardie shook his head in response, although he was partial to the odd pint of the black stuff. "Suit yourself," she replied, seemingly unfazed by the visitor's presence, but before leaving to fetch her father, she stopped for one last word with her locals. "Keep it friendly, boys. Ye know mi da wouldn't want any trouble until he has found out what this is all about."

The silence in the bar while she was gone was deafening. The Jamaicans may have been armed, but they were a long way out of their comfort zone. The Yardie was there because he had a point to prove and a reputation that he would protect at any cost. His men, however, were of the opinion that they just weren't getting paid enough to be brandishing weapons around Kilburn in the middle of the afternoon, keeping Irishmen from their drink.

Demelza reached the top of the stairs and shouted to her father that he was needed in the bar. She knew the situation downstairs was a serious one, but couldn't help revealing a slight touch of humour in her call.

"Da, you need to come down. You have visitors."

Davy, with his meal on a tray on his lap, sat in front of the television, trying to relax before his shift that evening.

"You deal with it, girl. I'm having mi tae."

"I can't do that, Da. This one definitely needs your personal attention."

Davy sighed, looking down at the pie, mash and gravy he was enjoying, knowing it would be cold when he returned.

"Ah, fuck me, girl. Can a man not get a minute's peace in this place? Do I always have to take care of everything meself?"

Davy came out of the living room and pushed his way past his daughter, who stood with a 'wait and see' look on her face. Making his way down the stairs, he grumpily repeated his often-voiced moans about being the only one in the pub that did any work.

"What's up with the music?" he bellowed when entering the hallway and hearing nothing. "Haven't I always told you, Demelza, to make sure the jukebox is playing to create a good atmosphere for the punters?"

"Don't worry about that, Da. Believe me, there's plenty of atmosphere in the bar for the customers."

Demelza's sarcastic hint at what was waiting for her father was delivered with a smile behind his back.

"This better be something important," he shouted to his daughter as he made his way along the passage to the front bar, where his complaints were soon silenced when coming face-to-face with the dark visitors in front of him.

"What the fuck?" he exclaimed at the sight.

"I told you this one was one for you, Daddy," added Demelza, while smugly broadening her smile and leaning back against the till, getting comfortable to enjoy the show.

Davy gave his daughter a dirty look. It had been a long time since he had given her a slap round the legs or a clip round her ear for her cheek, but she was very close right now to getting a reminder.

"Go out the back and take the two girls with ye," he ordered, with his thumb pointing the way over his shoulder back down the hallway. Demelza, with her usual rebellion, ignored his request.

"I'll stay, Da."

"Do as I say, girl."

Davy's reply was strong and firm and immediately adhered to by Demelza, who hurried herself and the staff out of harm's way. Davy looked around the pub, weighing up the situation. Of all the problems he had ever taken care of in his life, this one was definitely a new one for the books, which he as much admitted.

"Now here's a situation we never saw together, finbar, my old friend," he muttered to himself, talking as he often did to his deceased mate." He looked upwards for some divine inspiration, but didn't really expect an answer so he returned his gaze to the bar clocking most of the familiar faces, who were all staring back, letting him know that they would pounce as soon as he gave the order. Finally, Davy locked eyes with the Yardie, wondering if this had anything to do with Michael, a big giveaway being the Gulliver-looking Robbie and why Michael said he needed the FRG.

"Now then, what can I do for you, lads?" he asked, respecting the situation at the sight of the weapons, but also knowing that if they had come to shoot up the place that they would have already done it by now. The Yardie took a card from his pocket with a number written on it and slowly, but with some conviction, placed it on the bar in front of Mactazner.

"My club was robbed," he explained, "and the men that robbed it were Irish. I hear they come from around here and they drink in this pub."

Although Davy thought he already had a good idea of who was responsible for the robbery, he played the innocent by once again looking around the bar to see if any of his punters were going to own up. Blank faces stared back, along with shrugged shoulders and shaking heads that went around the room like a Mexican wave. Davy looked back at the Yardie, conveying the response.

"Sorry, I can't help you with that one."

The Yardie pushed his card further across the bar until it was right under Mactazner's nose.

"If what was stolen from me is not returned by the weekend, I'm going to burn down all the bars around Kilburn, starting with this one."

The mass of Irishmen in the room all moved forward at the Yardie's disrespectful words; the raising of Mactazner's hand was the only thing that stopped the tinderbox situation from lighting up. The Yardie continued with his threats, not letting their advances bother, nor ease him from his carefree approach. The rest of his crew, however, weren't feeling quite as secure, as they anxiously took a tighter grip on their weapons.

"Now, you get that number to some Irish white boy who can sort this out, or by the weekend, we go to war." The Yardie really didn't care how far he pushed the situation, but he hadn't gone there to make new friends.

Davy picked up the card and calmly tossed it in a

drawer behind him, out of the way. He turned back, placing his big hands on the bar, leaning against it in front of the Yardie.

"Don't worry about that, sure. With all the grassing fuckers in this bar this afternoon, I shouldn't be surprised if they haven't got your message back in Belfast already. Now, is there anything else I can be doing for you, black boy?"

Davy, not normally a racist talker, repaid the Yardie's 'white boy' comments, letting him know that he didn't give a fuck either. For a moment, the tension in the bar was at its highest, before the Yardie, saying only two words more, "the weekend," turned and walked back down the aisle made by his men and out of the doors. His point well and truly put across, his men followed behind, glad to be getting out of there. All Irish eyes watched the visitors leave before their heads turned back to the bar to see what Davy's next move would be.

"Right," said Mactazner in a raised voice as the door closed behind the last of the Yardie's men. "Now

I'm away back upstairs to finish mi tae, and I don't want disturbing again. I don't care if Sammy Davis Jr himself comes in for a pint, singing Mister fucking Bojangles. Mind you, if he has the rest of the Rat Pack with him, I'll make an exception for Frank and Dean!" Mactazner's words raised a laugh with the customers, but he had no intentions of going back to his meal. "Demelza," he shouted, as he returned back down the hallway, "you and the girls get your arses back behind that bar and get some beer sold, and turn the music up like I told ye."

"Yes, Da."

Davy climbed the stairs and made his way straight to the phone to ring The Rose and bring Michael up to date with what had just happened.

The Rose and Crown was also busy with the workers from the site and the usual locals. Barbara's call from behind the bar and the action of holding her hand to her ear alerted Michael that he was wanted on the phone. An anticipation of woe fell upon him as he crossed the room. Only Mactazner knew to contact him at The Rose and he wouldn't be calling for a chat.

"Michael, it's Davy."

"I guessed as much. Is it bad news, Davy?"

"Bad enough. I've had visitors, son—a black fella whose club was robbed. I presume you know what I'm talking about."

Michael, at the corner of the bar where the phone was located, turned towards the wall to hide his words.

"Yeah, they were on the site today, but I didn't expect them to visit Kilburn. What was the main man like?"

"He's a serious fella, Michael, and he's stirring up shit. He's threatened to burn some bars down if he doesn't get back what you took."

"Would you say he'd be an easy man to take out?"

"I wouldn't have thought so. He's a rake of men around him, all armed to the teeth, and he'll be expecting that now he's made the threats."

"We have no choice then but to ride it out. We got a little bit more than we bargained for," admitted Michael, again wishing the robbery had been less lucrative.

"Well, I didn't think he was that upset because you had stolen his Rizlas. You know they'll be sending someone over. I haven't made any calls yet, apart from this one to you, but the bar was full, someone's bound to have reported what happened back to Belfast."

"Well, take down this mobile number, Davy, then you can reach me any time. Let me know anything that occurs if you can, but don't get yourself in any shit."

"What happened to your old number?"

"I got rid of it before the robbery, just in case things didn't go to plan."

"Sensible thinking," agreed Davy.

"There's only Ma and Roisin have this number, and now you, of course."

"You just stay out of sight, son. I'll let you know if anything happens that I think you should know about, don't worry about that."

"Okay, Davy, but make sure you inform Belfast yourself. That way your back's covered if this goes wrong."

"Nothing will go wrong, lad," Davy reassured. "Not with me helping you to stay one step ahead of the fuckers. Now, keep your head cool and your mind clear. Worrying will only cloud your judgement and cause you to make mistakes. Now, give me that number."

Michael dictated the number to Davy, appreciating his words of wisdom. He hung up and ordered a round, before returning to the lads in the corner to fill them in.

"Well, he's no fool, this man, whoever he is," Michael said, respecting the speed at which the Yardie was working.

"Who are you talking about?" Danny asked.

"The club owner. That was Davy on the phone."

"What did Mactazner say?"

"He's been there, team-handed and tooled up for business, threatening to burn down The Harp."

"Who? Your man from the club?" Dermot jumped in, instinctively knowing when it was time to worry. "How the fuck did he find out about Mactazner?"

"I don't think he knows about Davy. He's obviously hit Kilburn to cause trouble and get his message across because he knows we're Irish. It's common knowledge that The Harp is the main pub. The bad news, though, is that because of his visit, Mactazner said that they'll be sending someone from across the water."

"Fuck me, this gets worse. What will we do?"

Michael, once again showing signs that the weight on his shoulders was starting to bother him, counted to ten before answering.

"We wait, Dermot. Like I said already, we wait to see what they bring. Until then, we go to work as normal. Now, stop fucking worrying until you know what it is you've got to worry about."

Each of them picked up their pints, taking a large drink. They knew Michael was right but they couldn't help wondering what surprises were still to come. They stayed in The Rose for a few more hours and sank a few more while mulling over their options. But, once again, they knew that Michael was right—you can't answer a question that hasn't yet been asked. What bothered Michael now was whether the boys back in Belfast would get involved. This should have been nothing to do with them, so long as they didn't find out about the weapons supplied by Mactazner, and that should never happen because nobody knew it was them that pulled the job. But now the Yardie had made threats against the Kilburn bars, there was no telling where all this would lead. Michael had made some mistakes in the past, but this could turn out to be the biggest can of worms that he had ever opened. One thing was for sure—the boys back in Belfast weren't going to stand for anyone walking into any of their bars and making threats, white or black. So, the Yardie would get exactly what he wanted—they would definitely be sending someone.

Chapter Twenty

Maguire's in Town

Maguire entered the grounds of Murphy's, a farmyard just a few miles from the Southern Irish border near Crossmaglen. It was a secluded place that was shadowed by a large crooked pylon that tilted at a 15-degree angle after the IRA tried to blow it up in an attempt to disrupt the power, for reasons unknown, but presumably there would have been some kind of extortion involved. At any rate, they never tried it again, so a deal must have been struck somewhere along the line.

He climbed out of his car in the fading light and placed his foot in a mixture of rainwater and cow slurry.

"Shit," he said, appropriately, while lifting his foot

back up and tapping it on the sill of the vehicle in an attempt to knock off the offending mess. Taking his hat from the passenger seat, he stretched his arm out of the door and above him, placing it on the roof before stretching his leg out further to stride over the sodden area. He levered himself out of the car, slammed the door shut behind him and then leant back to lock it. Pushing his body back upright, he turned to look at the farmhouse before taking his pipe from his pocket and lighting it. A stride was then taken, before an awareness of the cold caused him to reach up and place his hand on his head, where he felt nothing—no hat, to be precise.

"Where's mi fucking hat?" he said, before turning and looking back through the glass at the passenger seat. "Where the fuck...? Ah," he muttered, raising his eyes towards the roof. Leaning back to the car once more, he collected his lost property, placed it in its rightful place, re-lit his pipe and went towards the farm door.

Inside, the other five captains of the Northern Irish Counties were already gathered around a table. A sixth man, Ignatius Stanton—the former captain of Maguire, Finbar Flynn and Mactazner's ASU—paced about the room impatiently. Stanton was now a major in the organisation and, as such, in charge of the six county captains, and it was through him that they all received their orders. Each month, they would meet at a different and secret location, which was handpicked for its proximity to the border, just in case the illegal gathering was compromised and they had to make a quick getaway to the safety of the South.

"The meeting was for six o'clock, Maguire, not half past. Another five minutes and I would have scattered the men, thinking that you had been picked up on the way here. Where the fuck have you been?"

Stanton wasn't happy with Maguire's late arrival. It was a dangerous time, having all your top men in one location, without prolonging the occasion. Maguire offered no excuse; instead, he simply removed his hat and occupied the one empty chair that remained around the table while puffing on his pipe. Stanton, with a shake of his head letting the other five captains know exactly in what regard he held Maguire, took up position at the head of the table and put the meeting in motion.

"Top of the agenda this month is still the ongoing ceasefire. Your orders remain the same; there are to be no aggressive actions against the security forces or the Prods."

"Never mind the Prods, what about the INLA (Irish National Liberation Army)," said one of the captains. "They're taking us for idiots, while we're standing around doing fuck all. People are beginning to think that we've gone soft. It's not good for business."

"Fuck the INLA," shouted Stanton. "They're just playing up because they've got no say in the peace talks. They're just a bunch of mad dogs, the lot of them, but they will answer later. Now, have any of you got anything else besides your pride being hurt?"

The captains all remained quiet, more interested in smoking their cigarettes and drinking the whiskey that had been passed around while they were waiting for Maguire to arrive.

"Well, I've got one for you," continued Stanton. "A

short while ago, we received a call from London. It seems that some Irish lads over there have been acting up, helping themselves to some money and drugs belonging to a local Jamaican drug dealer. Did any of you give a go-ahead for this or know anything about it?"

Stanton watched as a shake of heads rolled around the table. Maguire's head shook with the rest of them—he didn't know anything about the robbery, but he wasn't admitting that he knew about the Yardie and his visit to the bar. He, too, had received a call, which was the reason why he was late for the meeting that evening. He had no business keeping tabs on what was happening in London, but his hatred for Mactazner was such that years earlier, he had slotted one of his men in as a local to keep an eye on things, waiting for that one slip-up that Mactazner may make.

"Why should we give a fuck if some fucking drug dealer gets robbed in London?" asked one of the captains.

"He turned up at The Harp of Erin in Kilburn earlier today," explained Stanton. "Apparently, he's no pushover, this fella. From what we've been told, he's not your average street corner pedlar, either. He was accompanied by a heavily armed team of men and he's making threats to start a war if he doesn't get his stuff back."

"Bomb the fucker out," said another captain. "We can't have some nigger shouting the odds in any of our bars."

"Didn't I just say your orders were to keep the cease-fire?" reminded Stanton. "That includes the mainland. How would it look if at the same time that Sinn Féin were negotiating the peace agreement that the IRA were running around London, having a pitched battle with a Jamaican drug dealer?"

"Do we know anything about the men that pulled the job? Descriptions or anything?" asked Maguire, eager to fill his inquisitive mind, which had already been activated by his earlier call.

"Nothing," replied Stanton, "only that they were Irish, according to the dealer."

"Why would he go to The Harp of Erin?"

"Again, we don't know," continued Stanton. "But we need someone to go over there and try to sort it out. Amicably," he stressed.

"I'll go," offered Maguire, in an unexpected move.

"You, Maguire?" said Stanton, shocked. "You're the last man I would have expected to volunteer for a trip to the smoke. You do realise who runs The Harp?"

"Mactazner. I know. But we can forget our differences while I sort this out. I'm bored over here at the moment; my unit is inactive since they had their bollocking for fucking up in Bangor, so it will give me something to do."

"Everybody's unit is inactive at the moment," added the captain, who had complained earlier about the INLA taking over while they did nothing. Stanton threw him a dirty look while pausing to consider Maguire's offer. But with none of the other captains stepping up to make the trip, he didn't have a lot of choice.

"Okay," he agreed, killing two birds with one stone. He wasn't a particular fan of Maguire and saw it as a good chance to get rid of him for a while. "You go and speak to this drug dealer, but remember, there's to be no trouble and don't wind up Davy Mactazner—since he's been in charge of the fundraising on the mainland, the charity boxes have never been so full."

Maguire puffed on his pipe. He was a devious bastard who never did anything that he wouldn't be gaining from, so what his motives were for going to London were anybody's guess.

"Right, that's it for tonight. We will reconvene in a month's time at a location which will be given to you on the day, as usual."

Stanton finished the meeting and the members of the gathering dispersed back to their cars and then on to their separate counties. Before Maguire was allowed to leave, however, he was given one last word of warning.

"Whatever your reasons are for making this trip, Maguire, be sure that they don't interfere with business or rub anybody up the wrong way. Do you understand me?"

"I hear you," replied Maguire. "I told you, I'm bored."

"And I'm your Aunt fucking Fanny if you think I believe that. Remember, everybody else is running a tight ship and earning money for the cause, apart from you. So, if it comes down to it, you'll be the one that goes and you won't be needing to pack for that trip."

What Stanton was saying sounded like a threat and probably was, but it was his way of getting Maguire to pull his socks up. Maguire replied the only way he could to make it seem that he had volunteered for the right reasons.

"I'm trying to do something, rather than standing around doing nothing, but if you would rather somebody else went to London, then send them instead."

"No, you go. Just remember what I've said."

Maguire nodded, then returned his pipe to his mouth, before leaving the same way as the others. As usual, he wasn't happy about being told what to do; the words 'wanker' and 'fuck you' fell quietly from his rebellious muttering lips as he crossed the yard towards his car. But Stanton was in charge and not to be argued with, Maguire knew that. He also knew that he had been getting a free ride for a long time, but he didn't like being reminded of the fact. His problem was that he wanted out of his situation, just as much as the people around him wanted to get rid of him. Warnings and a slagging down like the one Stanton had just given him were that numerous in their occurrence that they were becoming like water off a duck's back—in one ear and out the other—and he knew that Stanton was just as tired of giving those bollockings as he was of receiving them. Something had to change, but very carefully, so that any trips he did make were of his choice.

It was the morning of the second day since the Yardie and his men had visited The Harp of Erin and delivered his ultimatum. Now through its doors was about to enter the mediator sent from Belfast, who was going to be a lot less welcome than they were. The doors to The Harp of Erin opened and in walked Maguire. He paused, a few steps inside, to allow himself time to take in the faces around the bar, seeming to give a knowing gesture to one of Mactazner's regulars sitting in the corner. Mactazner stood up from putting some glasses away behind the bar just in time to catch the exchange between the two men, before Maguire continued the rest of the way inside. For a moment, at the sight of his old foe, Mactazner's thoughts were of nothing else but vaulting over the bar and kicking Maguire's teeth down his throat. It would have been good to finally settle his rift. But he resisted the temptation, knowing that he must have been sent because of the recent trouble. Keeping his cool, he lifted the hatch and walked around the bar to front him face-to-face.

"Well, I knew they'd be sending some useless cocksucker, but I didn't expect it to be you, Maguire. What's up? Are all the important wankers in Belfast busy?"

They may not have seen each other for over thirteen years, but Mactazner started the conversation exactly where it had been left, setting the tone for the meeting.

"I'm here because I was ordered. I've no wish to be in this shithole city and no wish to be talking to you, I think we'll both agree on that." If anything, the animosity between the pair had grown over the years. "It came down through the network that you had some visitors, so they sent me across to sort it out."

"Network, my arse. You mean one of your paid lackeys dropped a coin and blabbed his mouth trying to get in your good books." Mactazner raised his voice to cast the aspersion so the punters in the bar could hear, at the same time looking straight at the man who had made eye contact with Maguire as he entered.

"Look, you don't want me here and I don't want to be here, so just tell me the crack and I'll be on my way. I'm getting too long in the tooth to be bothered arguing with you, Mactazner."

Davy gave Maguire a gritted smile. It was a clout he wanted to give him, but he kept his composure, using the action of collecting a few glasses from the tables around the room to calm his temper. Placing the empty vessels on the bar, he took a deep breath.

"Okay, Maguire, your grass probably told you already, but I'll humour you. A black fella came in here team-handed and tooled-up, complaining that some

Irish lads had robbed his club. I think that was the gist of it. Oh, and if whatever they took isn't returned by the weekend, he's going burn down a few of the bars around Kilburn. I think he means to put a bit of a hole in the old IRA fundraising machine. Anyway, nobody in the bar knew anything about it, including myself, so I told him I couldn't help but I would pass his message on. Personally, I hope he carries out his threat. I'm insured and this place could do with a makeover."

"Is that all?" asked Maguire, knowing it wasn't.

"What more do you want? I think he made his intentions pretty clear."

"What about the number he gave you?" added Maguire, slipping up. Mactazner, in his call back to Belfast, had never mentioned that the Yardie had left his card. Davy again returned his gaze to the man in the corner.

"So, your little grass noticed that as well, did he? That's right, Maguire, he gave me a number." Davy walked back behind the bar and took the card the Yardie had left from the drawer beneath the till. "There you go—there's no name, just a number," he said, placing it on the bar. "I think the idea is that you give him a ring."

Maguire picked up the card and studied it briefly before slipping it into the inside pocket of his overcoat. Placing his pipe in his mouth and having no other reason to stick around, he turned and moved towards the door, only to stop a few yards short, as though he had remembered something important he had to say.

"Have you seen anything of young Flynn and his sidekicks?" he asked, turning back to face Mactazner, who was ready for the question and wasn't caught out for a moment.

"Young Michael? Not for a few years now. Why? Did he come over with ye? Now, he would be a welcome sight coming through those doors, unlike yourself."

Maguire paused briefly, studying Davy's expression and words, searching for the truth or lies, one of which was held within them.

"No, he left Belfast a few months ago. I've been wondering where he might turn up. Those lads have a knack of making a noise when they land," Maguire added sarcastically.

"Well, the noise they normally made was under your orders," Davy returned, defending Michael and his mates. "So, if you see the lad, tell him to drop by. He means the world to me, that boy."

Maguire puffed a couple of times on his pipe before turning back for the door, this time stopped by Mactazner, who had remembered something he had to say.

"And Maguire..." Maguire turned. "Don't come in this bar again without an invite, which you know you will never get."

Maguire took the pipe from his mouth and smiled at Davy's words.

"You know, Mactazner, it says 'Oxo' on the side of the buses, but it doesn't mean they'll sell you any gravy. Just like it says your name above the door here, but we all know you don't own fuck all."

Once again, the urge to settle their differences with violence returned to Davy, but he resisted the temptation, settling instead with an insult from the old days.

"You know, Maguire, I always thought that ponytail suited you just right. Maybe you should think about growing it back."

Mactazner's return was delivered with an even bigger smile. Maguire knew exactly what he was getting at.

The two adversaries gave each other a long look, before Maguire turned back to the door and left. Mactazner, still with something else left on his mind to deal with, put his hands on his hips, which broadened his wide shoulders even more. He turned and looked once again at the corner where Maguire's grass was sitting. Nothing was said, but the man knew that Davy had him marked and everybody knew that that wasn't a good place to be. Davy turned back to the bar, where two men loyal to him were stood, and then back towards the grass in the corner. The two men followed Davy's eyes and again, without anything being said, understood what he wanted to be done. The man in the corner took a large gulping drink from his Guinness, knowing it could quite possibly be his last.

Maguire, after finding another pub in Kilburn where he was welcome to have a drink, gathered his thoughts before making the phone call to the number the Yardie had left. He didn't know who he was talking to, so the conversation was kept short and sweet, arranging a meeting that was to be held in an hour's time at The Palm Cove.

Maguire was eager to get to the bottom of things. He was throwing caution to the wind by moving quickly and not knowing what he was walking into, but he was pretty sure that there would be no trouble on the first meeting; the trouble would come later when either side didn't get what they wanted. He had also brought some backup over with him from Ireland in the shape of two heavies, but decided to leave them in the car so as not to antagonise an already volatile situation—he knew he would be outnumbered, anyway, when meeting the Yardie on his own turf, so what was the point?

When he approached the club, Robbie the giant was back at his post on the door. Like everybody else meeting the man for the first time, Maguire was taken aback by his size but paid him about as much respect as Michael and the lads had done—for men that settled arguments with a gun, he was just a bigger target. Robbie showed him through to the main room, where about ten to fifteen of the Yardie's men stood in the area of the bar. He raised his big arm and pointed at his boss with his pork-sausage fingers, as though he was hard to pick out from amongst the mugs and wannabes that stood around him. Maguire approached, removing his hat as always, and slowly placed his pipe in his pocket, being careful not to make any sudden movements that may be misconstrued as aggressive.

"Get rid of your entourage and we'll talk. I left my men outside, so I am alone and unarmed," Maguire said, while unbuttoning and opening his overcoat to show he wasn't carrying any weapons.

The Yardie raised his hand and gestured for his men to disperse to different areas of the club. Now alone,

Maguire and the Yardie took a few moments to weigh each other up and draw a first impression. The Irishman in his fifties was old school and probably looked past his sell-by date to the Yardie. Maguire wouldn't have disagreed; he preferred these days to stay on the thinking, rather than the physical side of things, but then again, he had never been a hands-on type of person either. The Yardie, however, was precisely the opposite—he was a full-on type who stayed on top of everything and enjoyed giving it his personal touch. Maguire already knew that he was a serious and dangerous man. Even with his armed bodyguard, the Yardie had to be respected for the amount of guts it must have taken to walk into The Harp of Erin and pick a fight with the IRA; and if it wasn't guts, it must have been pure psychopathic tendencies, which would make him even more dangerous and unpredictable.

"Now, you and I both know what will happen if you set light to so much as a spliff in Kilburn, let alone any of our bars," pointed out Maguire, instigating the conversation.

The Yardie raised his elbow from the bar, sitting up straight in the stool he was occupying.

"Me not care, man. It's principle. I want my shit back or we go to war, it's as simple as that."

"It's a war you can't win, mister, and a pointless one, considering we had nothing to do with you being robbed."

The Yardie let go a disbelieving sigh, accompanied by one of his dismissive teeth-sucking sounds.

"The men that robbed me were trained, armed professionals, not sneak-thieves. They were Irish—you're Irish and the bars in Kilburn are Irish, so as far as I'm concerned, you did the robbery."

The Yardie shrugged his shoulders after his statement. His reasoning of tarring every Irishman with the same brush didn't make much sense, but it was his line of his thinking and nothing was going to change it.

"We have over three thousand Irishmen in London alone that can all be called upon should they be needed." Maguire looked around the room at the Yardie's men, seeing nothing that impressed him. "What you have here is a handful of dealers and pimps, half of them high on their own shit. You've obviously got balls, but you're no match for what we will send against you. If you touch one bar in Kilburn, Cricklewood or anywhere else for that matter, we will kill every dealer on every street corner. We'll bomb out every club and not just the ones that you own, but every bar and takeaway that runs under a Jamaican banner. Things will be that bad around here that you'll have to go to Birmingham to get a piece of jerk chicken. Your own people will turn against you, because they will know that things will only get back to normal when you are dead. And don't forget, we don't just have the men, we have the explosives and weapons to arm them all as well."

The Yardie, after listening to Maguire lay down the law, obviously thought it was time for a smoke. He took out his spliff-building equipment and began to join a few extra-large Rizlas together. Placing them on the bar, he filled them with the tobacco from three cigarettes and, out of his pocket, he produced a chunk of soft cannabis resin. Tearing off a lump, he began to roll it between his fingers and the palm of his hand into what resembled a six-inch-long shoelace. Maguire, waiting patiently and not to be outdone, decided to help himself to a relaxant of his own—a double whiskey. The Yardie placed the draw in the papers and covered it evenly with the tobacco, before rolling up the family-sized joint, which he held in two hands while running his tongue along the edge to moisten its sticky seal. Lighting it and sucking deep, he savoured its chilling sweet aroma, as Maguire knocked back the far-from-superior blend.

"I've got some weapons of my own," answered the Yardie as he blew the smoke from his mouth across the lit end of his spliff, "but I don't need explosives. I've got Molotov, and when that cocktail come through your window, the result is just the same. As for men, I've got as many as I need because I got the money to buy them. All I have to do is give a smackhead a gun and he'll kill you and any Irishman in his sights for a few wraps. So, you see I don't care how big your organisation be. I told you—it's principle."

Maguire could see his return threats had cut no ice

with the Yardie, who simply didn't give a fuck. If he was going to get anywhere, he was going to have to do what Stanton had said and find an amicable solution. In another lull in the conversation, as the Yardie smoked some more, Maguire helped himself to another double dram while contemplating his approach.

"Okay," he said, while the drink still warmed his throat. "Tell me what happened. We can't account for every Paddy in London, but I'm here now, so I might as well listen and see if we can't stop a blood bath."

The Yardie nodded his head in agreement and looked around for his newly-promoted second in command.

"Winston, come over here and explain to the white man what went on when his Irish friends rob the club."

Maguire took no notice of the Yardie's Irish friends or white man jibe. Instead, he just helped himself to yet another double and pulled up a stool, making himself comfortable. Once again, Winston went on to explain the events of Sunday night to Maguire, even showing him the projectile that had been used to take out Big Robbie.

"It's a baton round," explained Maguire. "It's what the British Army uses to take out protesters in riots. They used to use rubber bullets, but they switched to plastic because it was cheaper and more effective."

Robbie the bouncer, the projectiles victim who was listening like the rest of the men, gave Maguire an agreeing nod as to its effective use; again, he rubbed his chest, looking for sympathy.

"And they obviously knew how big your man was because they used the strongest size you can get; they normally use these for taking down doors."

Now, Robbie began to strut, while looking at the rest of the Yardie's men in the club, feeling that he had been vindicated by Maguire's words.

"Do you have CCTV fitted?" Maguire asked while looking around. "If they were in the club to case it and they saw how big your man was, you may have caught them on tape. I could study it to see if I recognise anyone."

"There are no cameras in the club, only on the door leading to the office," explained Winston. "With the amount of dealing that goes on in here, it would be suicidal to record it. We would be doing the Babylon's job for them."

"Babylon?" repeated Maguire, confused.

"Police," interceded the Yardie with the interpretation of the word.

"Oh, the Police. Maguire nodded, seeing the sense.

Winston continued with his story, remembering every detail he could. As he did, Maguire began to notice some similarities in the way the robbers had worked, but it was when he started to describe the sizes and shapes of the three men that the penny began to drop. He paused before giving his opinion on what had been described, thinking the world surely wasn't that small. It couldn't be his ASU—the coincidence would be too much of a long shot—but the similarities were too close. He needed to keep any suspicions he may have to himself until he had done some more digging.

"The boys that turned you over didn't do it on our orders, I can assure you of that. And from the descriptions your man has just given me, no one jumps to mind. Now I can go away and talk to some people about the town and try to find out who they are. But that's not my job—I was ordered to come over here and warn you off causing any more trouble with us. Not sent here to help you sort out your security problems and get your stuff back. And because we know that the men that robbed you didn't do it on our say so, it doesn't really have anything to do with us."

The Yardie did not look too happy at the way Maguire's excuses were going.

"That being said," he continued, "if you and I can come to some sort of arrangement, then I think that I can help. Off the record, of course."

The Yardie pulled again on his joint, seeing Maguire was hinting at a deal.

"So, what are you saying to me, Irishman?"

"What did you lose?" enquired Maguire.

"I think maybe twenty-five kilo of pure. I'm not sure what was out on bail, but it was a new shipment, so it won't have been much. Also, a good amount of cash went with it."

"Bail? What the fuck is bail?"

Maguire was finding it hard enough to understand the Jamaican's accent, let alone any dealers' slang.

"Bail is what you get when you don't pay for the shit you take until after you have sold it. But I don't know how much was out on bail because they shot Leroy, whose job it was to keep track of it all."

"Why would you let anybody have anything that they haven't paid for?" Maguire was intrigued—in his world, everything was COD.

"Because if you pay upfront or buy in bulk, we have to lower the price, but the price is higher if I give you bail."

Now it made sense to Maguire.

"How much cash are we talking about?"

"Four, five hundred thousand, maybe more. Don't know, don't care. I just want the shit back. Without it, I have nothing for my soldiers to sell and it will take me two to three weeks to get a re-supply. In that time, my punters go elsewhere and I could lose thirty million before I get them all back. See why the money they take means nothing to me?"

Fuck me, Maguire thought to himself. It was obviously a pittance to the Yardie but to him it meant early retirement. His mind schemed. If he could find the people that did the job, that money could be his. Whether the Yardie paid him for the return of his drugs or the robbers did for his silence, the money could be his way of getting out of the organisation and onto Easy Street.

"Okay, here's the deal," offered Maguire. "You get your drugs back, but I keep the money for my services. If I'm going to find these fuckers for you, it's got to be worth it for me. If you refuse, then I've done my job by giving you the warning I was sent here to give. You can go to war with the IRA if you wish. That's your choice—you're obviously up for it. But that won't get you fuck all but dead, because like I said, it's a fight you can't possibly win."

The Yardie took another smoke while he thought about the proposition. For all he knew, Maguire could have been in on it from the start, but if it got him closer to getting his gear back, he might as well go along with it. A war with the IRA wasn't something he wanted, but rather than lose face, he would go ahead with it if he had to. It wouldn't matter to him, anyway—while it was being raged, he would be back in the safety of his Jamaican mansion, surrounded by guards. The only thing was that he would never be able to return to London and he would lose everything he had built there. It would mean losing a whole lot more than he had lost already, but he wasn't an accountant, he was a drug dealer, and drug dealers can't afford to lose face.

"Okay, Irish, but remember this—the deal we make is between me and you, no one else. You've got two days. If I haven't got the drugs back by then, I'll deal with you and your bars in Kilburn."

Maguire said nothing in response. He wasn't fazed by the Yardie's threat; he was too busy thinking about the money. Besides, when the shooting started, like the Yardie he would be well out of the way back in Belfast. He casually nodded in acceptance of the deal, before buttoning his coat back up in preparation to leave.

"Do you mind if I take a bit of that for my pipe?" he asked, pointing at the lump of cannabis resin on the bar.

"You like a smoke?" asked the Yardie.

"I was young once," replied Maguire. "I was smoking joints when you were shitting yellow in ye nappies."

The Yardie smiled and pushed the full block towards him.

"Take it and enjoy, but don't be chilling out too much because you've only got two days."

"Two days it is," Maguire replied, before taking his leave.

Back outside the club, he stopped on the steps to take his pipe from his pocket, while Robbie bolted the door behind him. He nipped a corner off the block of resin and crumbled it into his pipe, mixing it between the layers of shag. He lit it, contemplating the deal he had just struck, while at the same time studying the area and noticing the building site across the road. His eyes followed the line of the scaffolding, which eventually brought him to the tower crane. He turned his head to look behind and above at the roof of the club, remembering what Winston had said about how the robbers had gained their entry. His lips broadened into a smug smile as his teeth clenched on the end of his pipe.

"You sly fuckers," he said to himself, with a giggle respecting the ingenuity and realising that the resin he was smoking was quality stuff. Maguire was doing exactly what the Yardie had done, piecing the robbery together—the difference being that he knew just how significant the building site across the road really was. A flashback to his last meeting with Michael in his Falls Road bar ran through his mind: "Don't forget we have our construction skills to fall back on," Michael said that day.

Leaving the sweet smell of blended tobacco and draw behind him, Maguire returned to the car, where the two men he had brought with him were waiting. Opening the rear door, he stopped to give the street one last look, giving the building site a knowing, contented smile before climbing into the rear and being driven away.

Across the road on the far corner of the scaffolding, Michael was squatted behind some bricks and had seen everything, after receiving a warning phone call from Mactazner. He wondered what the fuck Maguire was doing there. Well, he knew what he was doing there, but why him? He was the last man he had expected them to send over. He hated London and Mactazner, so for him to be here just didn't make any sense. Doubts began to creep into his mind as to the extent of their knowledge. Maybe they did know that Michael and the lads had pulled the job and they had sent Maguire to clear up the mess because he was their captain, but how could they? Mactazner was the only other person outside their circle who knew and he would never talk to anyone, especially Maguire.

Michael was confused and breaking his own rules—he was asking himself questions that at the moment he couldn't answer. He was going to have to stay on the ball and one step ahead in the days to come, the problem being that he didn't know what he was staying ahead of or know how they were going to come at him. One thing was for sure—the job on the site was finished. The Yardie's men had settled their curiosity and Maguire might as well have come over and shook their hands from the way he was looking across. Even at the distance he was, Michael could see him putting two and two together and coming up with them. To anyone else, the building site across the road would have meant nothing, but Maguire knew that the lads always used a building site as their cover for whatever it was they were up to, and although it had not been their intention in the beginning to use it as a cover for the robbery, Michael knew it was a dead giveaway now. Gathering the others together, he explained what he had seen and told them to pack up their stuff. They made their excuses before finishing that day's work and left the site for the last time.

What was Maguire doing there? How much did he know? What should be their next move? These were the repeated questions the lads kept asking themselves and each other in the car on the way home. For once, Dermot was not alone in the worry zone, where the biggest question was not what they should do next but what would Maguire's next move be.

Chapter Twenty-One

Over the Barrel

Roisin lay in her bed, deep in sleep and believing that the knocking she could hear played a part of the dream she was having. Eventually, the continuous noise brought her out of her slumber into the reality that someone was at the front door. Climbing out of her bed, she went to the window and pulled back a portion of the curtain to look outside. An RUC (Royal Ulster Constabulary) Land Rover parked on the street in front of her gate wasn't something she wanted to see—it was a sight that no Catholic in Northern Ireland wanted to wake up to. Her thoughts immediately went to Michael, wondering if he was okay or if it was him they were looking for, especially after his phone call on Sunday. Heading for the bedroom door, she stopped to put on her dressing gown, at the same time checking the time. It was five o'clock. She wondered what could be so important that it couldn't have waited until a reasonable hour, which brought her to the worrying conclusion that it must be something bad. She wanted to pee, the urge intensified by her worries, but the loud knocking hurried her to its source. The knocking, despite her calls, continued as she came down the steps and only stopped when she turned on the hallway light. Opening the door slightly, she peered through the security chain she had left in place.

"Miss Roisin McMahan?" asked the officer on her step.

"That's right. Is something wrong?"

"Miss McMahan, do you own the hairdressers on the high street?"

"Yes. Why? What's wrong?"

"I'm afraid there's been a fire. We need you to come down there and speak to the fire officer."

"A fire? How bad is it?"

"It's not good, Miss McMahan. Your shop has been completely gutted. There's not much left to look at, I'm afraid."

"Shit," Roisin exclaimed, while gathering her thoughts. "I'll get dressed and be there in about twenty minutes."

"Would you like us to wait for you and give you a lift?"

"That's okay, officer. I have a car, but thank you."

Roisin closed the door and rushed back up the stairs to get dressed. Funnily, she was calm now she knew the truth and knowing that the reason for their visit was nothing to do with Michael. Also, she was pretty sure—in fact, positive—she was insured and there was nothing inside the shop that couldn't be replaced. Michael was okay, though, which was her initial worry. Again, she consoled herself that at least the police weren't at her door, bringing her bad news of him.

In a little over twenty minutes, she was standing outside

what once was her salon but what was now a blackened, smoking shell. The efforts of the firemen were still visible by the water that dripped from what was left of the roof and scorched timbers. The officer who had come to inform her of the fire came across to speak.

"The fire officer is looking for any initial signs of what may have caused the fire. As soon as he is finished, he will come and talk to you. In the meantime, can you try and remember your movements last night when you locked up, and I will take a statement from you later."

Roisin once again thanked the officer, who returned towards the smoking shop. As she stood watching and waiting for some answers, she started to question herself and her routine while closing up the previous evening. She remembered turning everything off as she always did, which wasn't really a safety precaution, more a necessity to reduce her electricity bills. The rubbish was also removed, which ruled out the chances of the fire starting in the bin, so she was lost for any immediate cause jumping to mind. She let go a deep sigh as she thought of all the hard work she had put into the salon while building up the business.

"I wish Michael were here," she thought to herself, as the smouldering remains of her shop began to depress and dishearten her. She needed a cuddle, and even though the dawn hadn't broken yet, she could have really done with a drink to help settle her nerves and drown her sorrows. "I'll go to Michael's mum's," she continued to think, trying to lay out some plans in her head. "After I've seen the fire officer and given a statement, I'll go to her place for a cup of tea." She didn't fancy being on her own, and in the past when Michael wasn't around she had always been able to go to Catherine's for company and comfort. The early morning knock and seeing the police had given her the jitters worrying about Michael. At least at his mum's she wouldn't be alone.

"They're funny things, fires. Who knows how they start? Still, I suppose it was a good thing that it occurred at such an early hour; at least there was nobody inside. This time, anyway."

The words came from a man standing behind Roisin at a rather uncomfortably close distance, close enough that she could smell his breath that drifted over her shoulder and it wasn't good. She knew by the tone and the smugness in his voice that it wasn't just a passing observation, more of a hinted warning. She turned, while at the same time stepping forward in order to put some space between herself and the stranger.

"What do you mean?" she asked. "Who are you?"

"Don't worry about that," dismissed the man. "What you should be doing now is making sure that your man Michael rings this number." He produced a piece of paper and thrust it with some force into Roisin's hand. "Maybe then there won't be any more fires."

Roisin looked down at the paper in her hand, and when she looked up, the man had already began to walk away. His words were sinking in—the fire was no accident, which angered and then shocked her. A chill ran down her back, which grew to a slight tremble, revealing itself in her hand as she opened the folded paper and read the number. Again, she looked up at the man, who was almost out of sight down the badly lit street. She turned towards the police for a second, almost calling for their assistance, but then thought better of getting them involved. She turned back towards the man, who was now out of sight. Then back to the police. Then back to her shop. She was confused and disorientated. It was all happening a bit too fast; half an hour ago, she was laid in her warm bed without a care in the world and now with the sleep still crusted in the corner of her eyes, she was involved in something that she knew nothing about.

Composing herself, she tried to think of the best thing to do, which she decided was to ring Michael straight away. The fire inspector was still going about his business, as were the police, so seizing the moment, she slipped away unnoticed from the scene and made her way back home. Sipping on a freshly made cup of tea and steadying her hand, she dialled the number—ironically, not scared for her own safety but more concerned about how Michael would react on hearing the news.

In the digs in Hemel Hempstead it had been a late night

for the lads, who had stayed up for most of it discussing the events of the day. Michael's phone went onto answer machine several times before Roisin's persistence finally woke him up. He looked at his watch through blurry eyes and knew by the early hour that the call wasn't going to be good news. Retrieving the noisy machine from beneath his pillow, he read Roisin's name on the caller ID before answering.

"Michael, Michael, are you there?"

"What's up, girl? Why are you ringing so early? It's only just turned six?"

Michael was almost cut short by the cries of his distressed girlfriend.

"It's the hairdressers, Michael; it's been burned to the ground."

"A fire? Are you hurt?"

"I'm fine. It happened in the early hours, so the shop was empty."

"What happened? Do you know what caused it?"

Michael was now out of his bed and frantically pacing around his bedroom.

"At first, I thought it was an accident, but then a man I haven't seen before passed me a number. He said that I should ring you and that you should ring the number before there were any more fires. Michael, I'm scared. What did he mean? Is this because of what went on a few months ago or what you said you were doing on Sunday?"

Michael paused, as he realised that Maguire obviously knew everything—or at least enough to set the ball rolling. At any rate, his question of how they were going to come at him had now been answered. His heart began to pump and the pit of his stomach felt as empty as one of Sean's dinner plates.

"Listen, Roisin, calm down and give me time to sort this out. You're safe, that's the main thing. The fire was Maguire's way of sending me a message. He wasn't trying to hurt you; he could have done that easily enough if that were his intention. In the meantime, don't say anything to Ma—she'll only be on the phone and I can do without that right now."

"I won't, but it won't take her long to find out. There's

plenty knows about the fire; half the high street was out. Plus the neighbours will have seen the police at my door."

"Okay, but if she asks, just say one of the hairdryers was faulty and if the firemen make it common knowledge that it was arson, just say it was kids. Are you covered with the insurance?"

"I think so. The police got me out of bed and the firemen are still there. I haven't had time to check yet."

"Well, when you fill in the claim form, make sure you tell them that my expensive set of golf clubs were destroyed in the blaze."

"You didn't have any golf clubs; you've never even played the game."

"I know that, sure, but I've been thinking about taking it up for a while now and if I had a new set of clubs, I'd definitely give it a go."

"Don't you think you should be making that call, rather than making jokes and trying to convince me to fiddle the insurance?"

"Take no notice of me, babes; I was only trying to lighten the situation, so you wouldn't be scared."

7P's

Roisin, for the first time that morning, let go a little smile.

"I'm not scared, not now I've spoken to you. Besides, never mind your clubs, I think I'll put myself down for a new coat." Michael smiled, releasing a little laugh down the phone.

"Fair play to you, girl. I taught you well. Look, do as I say and ask no questions. I want you to go stay at Ma's for a few days; Maguire won't dare go near you there. Tell her that while the shop is closed that you're going to have your house redecorated; she won't suspect a thing and she'll be glad of the company. Young Peter has been driving her nuts lately, talking about what he's going to do with his horse."

"Michael, I can't tell your Ma that I'm having the house redecorated—she'll be wanting to take me shopping for wallpaper and paint, and she's never liked the colour of my curtains, so she'll want to change them for a start. That will mean that the carpet won't match, so I'll have to buy a new one. Mind you, that's needed changing for a while, ever since you dropped your spare ribs when you were pissed—that sticky barbecue sauce is a bugger to get out of the shagpile. It will all cost a fortune."

"Roisin, Roisin, calm yourself." Michael cut short his ranting girlfriend, who seemed to be forgetting about her smouldering salon in light of her new decorating plans. "Don't worry about what it will cost. We can definitely afford it right now. I'll get the money to you somehow."

A loud knock came at the front door, startling Roisin which made her jump.

"Michael, somebody is at the door."

"Did you lock it on your way back in."

"Yes, of course I did."

"Good, now go to the kitchen and get the big knife out of the draw. Then don't open it, just shout through it to find out who it is."

Roisin laid down the receiver on the table then did as Michael said.

"Hello, who is it please?"

"Miss McMahan, it's the Police again. I saw you leave and thought you might be a bit distressed. Is everything ok? Is there anyone I can call for you?"

"Thank you officer, that's very kind. I only came home to get a warmer coat, and I'm ringing someone right now."

"Ok, well take your time and I will see you back down at your shop."

"Thank you officer, five minutes and I'll be there."

Roisin went back to the phone, exchanging the knife to the table for the receiver.

"It's ok, it was the Police checking up on me, it was a nice thing for the officer to do. I better get back down there and give them a statement."

"You do that girl, and then go to my house."

"Okay, but watch yourself and remember I love you. It's about time some fucker did for that old bastard Maguire." Roisin's surprising comment slightly shocked Michael. In the past, she had always tried to calm him down when she would listen to his complaints about Maguire's treatment of him and the lads. But this was the straw that broke the camel's back; this was one push too many and she had had enough.

"Funny, I was just thinking the same thing," Michael concurred. "Now, give me the number then hang up."

Michael grabbed a pen from the table at the side of his bed and, having no paper, tore the lid from his cigarette packet then flattened it out to accommodate the number. "Okay, love, I've got that. Now, hang up and get yourself to Ma's."

"Okay. Love you."

While talking, Michael had done well to keep his tone and make light of the situation. But now, with time to think, his blood began to boil. He was furious with Maguire and himself. "How the fuck did doing a straightforward robbery in London end up getting my girlfriend's shop burnt out in Belfast?" he thought, beating himself up in his head, but still not knowing where he went wrong.

"Get up," he shouted, rousing the troops as he left his bedroom, banging on the doors on his way to the kitchen. The other three were with him in a flash; flash being the appropriate word, with Sean once again in his shift.

"What is it? What's wrong?" the three asked between them.

"It's Maguire—he's had Roisin's salon burnt out."

"How do you know?" asked Sean.

"I'm tele-fucking-pathic. How do you think?" Michael replied sarcastically. "Roisin was just after telling me on the phone."

"I meant, how do you know it was Maguire?"

"Yeah, sorry Sean. I'm just a bit vexed."

"That's understandable."

"One of his goons, probably the one that started the fire, passed her a number."

"We need to end it for Maguire and fuck the consequences."

"Well, that seems to be a unanimous thought for the day, Danny Boy. Even Roisin wants the fucker dead. I should have seen it coming, but with Maguire being in town, my mind had slipped from any warnings coming via Belfast."

"But Roisin's? Why?" queried Dermot, again.

"He's letting us know that he knows. He obviously can't be bothered looking for us around London, so he's bringing us out of hiding. I'm surprised he didn't save himself all the trouble and just walk onto the building site yesterday."

"But how did he find out it was us? You don't think Mactazner threw us in, do ye?"

"Don't be so fucking stupid, Dermot. I don't know how he found out, the same as I don't know how the black fella ended up in Kilburn either. I thought I'd covered everything, but obviously I didn't. What I do know, though, is that Davy would never do us any harm, so get that out of your fucking head."

Michael's anger after Roisin's call was channelled through his words to Dermot.

"Calm down, Michael," said Danny. "Dermot wasn't accusing Mactazner; he's just searching for answers, the same as the rest of us."

Michael, releasing the last of his anger, punched one of the cupboard doors.

"I know," he said, showing his remorse. "Sorry, Dermot. I'm just mad because I fucked up and landed the three of you in the shit again. But take it from me, Davy would never sell us out."

"I know that," replied Dermot, regretting his insinuation. "But you didn't fuck up either," he reassured.

"There was nothing wrong with the plan. For every action, there's a reaction: we started the action and this is all part of the reaction. Now, get that famous Flynny thinking head of yours on and come up with a plan to get us out of this shit."

Michael was flattered by Dermot's confidence in his mental abilities, but he couldn't help feeling a little bit under pressure.

"To be fair, though," added Sean, with a joke for every situation, "there's only Michael that could have us pulling a robbery in London, while supposedly keeping a low profile, resulting in his girlfriend's business being burned out in Belfast. And, at the same time, have half the Jamaican drug-dealing world, not to mention our former employers the IRA, chasing us around the town, wanting our guts for garters. It's not easy being your mate, Flynny, but you're good for my diet. I hate to think how much fatter I would be if I was sat at home safe with no worries."

"Thanks for that input, Sean," Michael said sarcastically, but he couldn't complain, having had the same thought earlier himself.

"Any time," answered Sean, still smiling. "But seriously, what now?"

"Now," Michael paused, "now I ring the number Roisin had passed to her, firstly to confirm that it is Maguire and nobody else and secondly to find out what the fuck he wants, as if we don't already know."

"Maybe you're right. We can't be sure it was Maguire," said Danny. "We've upset a lot of people in our time; it could have been any one of them. And there's no name with the number."

"No, big fella, it was Maguire—I'll have money on it. Even the Protestants and the INLA don't go after your women. There's only Maguire with enough disrespect to break the rules and do that. But I'll play it dumb and cautious."

Michael took a seat at the kitchen table then dialled the number with the other three watching. The phone was answered after a few rings; the call was anticipated, even at this early hour.

"Is that you, Flynn?" asked Maguire.

"Maguire? Is that you? What the fuck's your game?"

Michael resisted the temptation to scream threats down the phone until he found out how much Maguire really knew.

"I had to find some way of getting your attention, mister. Don't worry, we knew the place was empty. Your woman was never in any danger, and my man made it look like an electrical fault so the insurance shouldn't have any problem paying her out. Besides, if your friend Mactazner had been more helpful, it need not have happened." Maguire was fishing for information.

"Davy? What the fuck has he got to do with anything?"

"You mean to tell me that you haven't seen him and that he didn't supply you with the weapons?"

"Weapons. What fucking weapons, and for what? We castrated the fucker with a broken bottle."

Michael tried to make out that he thought Maguire's arson attack was a delayed reaction to their last confrontation.

"Don't take me for a fucking idiot, mister. I'm not talking about your fucking games in Bangor. I'm referring to the robbery that you and your mates pulled in London with weapons supplied by Mactazner."

"I haven't seen Mactazner. Why don't you go and ask him? We're not even in London."

Maguire realised that Michael wasn't going to slip up and give anything away.

"Look, Michael, I'll not play games. The black fella whose club you robbed wants the stuff back. If you don't return the money and the drugs, he's going to start a war, and we don't need it right now. Now, I don't know 100% that it was you, I'll admit that, but with the descriptions that I've been given and everything else, I'll be reporting back to Belfast that you and your mates are my best guess as being the perpetrators we're after because I'm not letting you drop me in anymore shit. After that and my back is covered, it won't be nothing more to do with me and the fire at the salon will only be the start of it because the good old boys back home won't give you any more chances. I told you that back at your flat but you wouldn't fucking listen. But if you come clean now and stop fucking around, I'll keep it between me, you and the black fella, and try to sort this mess out. But if I do I want to see some appreciation and a mark more respect paid to me."

The game was up. Michael knew it was pointless to deny their involvement any longer.

"And what happens when we give the stuff back?"

"Well, I'm glad you're starting to see sense and not going to continue to waste my time."

"What's the point? You seem to know most things but you're wrong about Mactazner—he knows nothing. We haven't set foot in Kilburn; your grasses there must have told you that."

"We're not interested in whether he helped you or not. I can read between the lines and tell that this was just a straight robbery that was made outside the IRA's jurisdiction so it doesn't matter where you acquired the weapons to pull it off. And for all we know, even though you didn't have to, you could have been fully intending to kick back a portion of the loot to the cause so if it had gone off without a hitch you would have got a pat on the back. But it didn't, it blew up in your faces, and all we want now is for you to give the money and the drugs back, so the black fella doesn't go through with his threat."

Again, Maguire was lying through his pipe-gripping teeth. If he ended up with the money, dropping Mactazner in it would be a welcome bonus.

"Don't tell me that the IRA is scared of a wee black club owner?"

"Again, lad, it's like I told you that morning after you caused trouble in Bangor, we don't want anything rocking the boat right now. The INLA are already doing enough of that."

"And if we don't, I suppose you'll be starting more fires?"

"We'll not go near your mother out of respect for your father, but your mates have families, too."

"And what's to stop you doing for us after we hand the shit over?"

"He just wants it returned and that's the end of it. He's not bothered about the man you killed and I told him that if he goes to war with us, it's one he can't win.

We're not about to let no black fucking drug dealer kill any of our own. If anyone finds out that you were involved then it's in Belfast where you'll answer, mister. It's not as though you meant to cause all this shit, so it won't be with your life or your knees, but there will be a price to pay, you know that. But if I can sort this out amicably and make this situation disappear, then maybe no one need ever know it was you. Whereas if you don't follow orders and fail to bring the stuff back..." Maguire paused before delivering the final ultimatum. "Well, I don't need to say it, do I? You understand the consequences."

"Well, I suppose we have no choice then. How do we get it to you?"

"Ring this number again at six. I'll tell you where the drop is."

Michael ended the call and paused to collate what had just been said. He knew Maguire was lying somewhere, but the threat to their families was clouding his judgement.

"What did he say?"

"Hang on, Dermot. I'll answer your questions in a

minute. Just let me make another call first." Michael did so immediately, this time to Mactazner.

"Hello," answered a groggy voice on the other end.

"Davy, it's Michael. Sorry to get you up, but this is important."

"Don't be worrying yourself, lad. What's wrong?"

"Maguire burnt down Roisin's place back in Belfast."

"That cowardly fucker! Is she hurt?"

"Don't worry. She's okay. It was his little way of getting me to call him, which I just did."

"He obviously knows you did it then."

"He wasn't sure, but we were his prime suspects. Anyway, he knows now."

"What did he have to say?"

"He was handing out ultimatums. If we return the stuff back, he may be able to get us off the hook; if not, they'll start on our families back home."

"Sounds plausible, but do you trust the fucker?"

"Of course not. That's why I need another favour."

"Name it, lad."

"Could you ring back home to your old mates and

find out the crack on the quiet, around the houses, so to speak? They all know that you don't like Maguire so they will just think that you're asking because you're pissed off with him being at your bar."

"And they wouldn't be wrong. Consider it done, lad. I'll be the soul of discretion. Just give me a few hours."

"Cheers, Davy. I'll wait for your call."

Michael again hung up the phone and checked the time; it was six thirty. His only consolation at the moment was that he had all day to prepare and try to second guess what Maguire may have in store for them.

"Fatty, put some fucking clothes on and make the tea," Michael said, walking off to get dressed himself but stopped by another question.

"What did Maguire say about families? I heard what you said to Mactazner."

"Don't worry, Dermot. Our families won't be touched, I promise you that, but I can't make the same promise about ourselves."

Dermot was uneasy with this answer, but no more than Michael was giving it.

"Danny, I need yourself and Dermot to go back to the site and watch the club. I'm expecting Maguire to visit there today. You might want to say goodbye to your lady friend as well. We'll either be gone for a while or for good. Either way, she deserves telling; she's been a fine lady."

Danny gave Michael a wink in agreement. He knew he was right, but he also knew he was covering everything for the worst scenario.

"What's your plan?" asked Dermot.

"I'm going to get the stuff and do a lot of thinking. You asked me to get my Flynny mind working, so that's what I'm going to do. We'll meet back here at five thirty on the dot."

"What do I do?" asked Sean.

"I told you—put some clothes on and then the kettle."

Everybody disappeared to their rooms to get dressed, with an air of urgency now filling the flat. Sean finally made the tea in his clothes and the four of them sat around the kitchen table for the next hour or so, with surprisingly little mention of food or anything else. Eventually, Michael finally stood up and put his pot in the sink.

"Let's get on with it," he said. "Fatty, lock the door behind us and don't leave the flat. Keep your eye on the street and if anybody knocks before five thirty, it won't be none of us, so let them have it."

"What the fuck with? You threw the weapons in the river."

"Use your loaf. Keep the kettle hot all day and a couple of pans boiling on the stove. Any unwanted visitors, give 'em the boiling water in the face then smash their fucking heads in with the empty pans. If that doesn't work, you could always try sitting on the fuckers."

Sean said nothing about Michael's instructions even after he caught Dermot laughing at the remark on the end.

Michael, Danny and Dermot left the flat, and Sean locked the door behind them before beginning to search the cupboards for some large pots.

Michael had no other reason for leaving Sean in the digs than security. When you think you know where your enemies are, it's an oversight and a mistake to think that they know nothing about you and your whereabouts, and today wasn't the day for coming home to any surprises. They didn't really need to watch the club, either; he just wanted to keep everybody busy, especially Dermot, plus it was only right for Danny to say his goodbyes to Barbara while they were in the area. The woman thought a lot about him and, by his own admission, Danny was starting to feel the same way about her. Michael's main reason, though, for giving them something to do was that he needed some time on his own to pick up the drugs and money and think things through. With the threat to their families, they had no choice but to return the Yardie's stuff; but maybe he could fix it so that the day wasn't a total loss and they didn't all end up dead.

It was now two thirty and Michael was leaning into the boot of the car, zipping up one of the bags, when his phone rang. He stood up and took it from his inside jacket pocket, while in the background the boats and yachts of Chelsea Harbour bobbed about in the water.

It was Davy's name on the caller ID. A small prayer fell from Michael's lips in the hope that he might know something that could help.

"I couldn't find out much for you, lad, but what is strange is that Maguire volunteered to come over—he wasn't ordered. Plus, at the moment, the black fella's threats aren't being taken too seriously. Everybody's too busy back there; it seems there's something big going to happen at Easter."

"Maguire volunteered to come?" repeated Michael. "Why would he do that? I don't know which he hates the most: you or London."

"Well, whatever his reasons, there has to be something in it for him or else why would he bother? You know how that bastard loves to feather his own nest. I smell a rat, especially because he hasn't reported back yet, so nobody else knows that it was you that pulled the robbery. Plus, I've had no calls. He's keeping an awful lot of information to himself."

"I've smelt that same rat all day, Davy, but he has

me over a barrel. Although he did say that if we played ball, he would try to keep our names out of it, so that could account for the reason why he hasn't reported our involvement back. Listen, can I ask you one last favour? Well, two actually?"

"Ask away. If I can do it, lad, I will. You know that."

"If me and the boys don't make it tonight, kill Maguire and make that call to my mother."

"I was going to do that anyway—kill Maguire, that is, not ringing your mother, although if I have your blessing, I'll do that as well. Not that she'll have me and if she does, it will be the end of my drinking days. I won't live any longer, but it will feel like it."

"Don't worry, Davy. Just do her a deal that when she goes to the bingo that you go for a drink. You will be out three times a week at least."

"I'll remember that," answered Mactazner with a laugh.

"Listen, Davy—I've fixed it so the families will be looked after and left something for Demelza and yourself. Now, I've denied that you've had any involvement all along, so don't go admitting anything, and thanks for being a friend to me and my father."

Michael rang off before Davy could say anything more; he wouldn't be able to handle any sentiment right now, and there were preparations to complete—preparations for what, though, was the question on his mind.

When he made the phone call at six to Maguire, he knew if the drop was local in town, they might have a chance of coming out of it alive, whereas if the rendezvous was secluded, chances are they wouldn't be coming back at all. But he wouldn't know any of this until after the call, which wouldn't leave him much time to prepare for anything.

Leaning back on the boot of the car, he took a deep breath of the fresh salty air that flowed into the harbour from the Thames estuary. In the background, the faint ringing of the bells that hung from the masts of the yachts could be heard as the vessels swayed from side to side in the rising swell. When Michael had returned to the harbour a few days earlier, he had been surprised at the transformation it had gone through since he was last there, many years earlier. Then, it was just a jetty surrounded by old fishing boats and crab and lobster pots, which is why he thought it would be a good place to dump the weapons. He decided to take a walk along the quayside to do a bit more thinking, while admiring the yachts and dreaming of how close he had come to being able to afford to buy one.

Danny and Sean would have loved one of these, he thought, thinking back to their Wicklow youth and the tales they told of their father and the boats he built.

After an hour's more contemplation and fresh air, he drove back to the digs, arriving there just after five thirty. He took one large holdall from the boot and entered the flat to find Danny and Dermot already there.

"Did you sort everything?" Danny asked.

"Yeah, the drugs are in the boot with another bag filled with money and there's more money in the third bag I have here."

Michael threw the bag he was carrying onto the floor near the table.

"Did you see anything at the club?" he asked Danny.

"Maguire came about three o'clock. He was there for maybe half an hour. He also had two fellas in tow, but I didn't recognise either of them."

"I did," said Dermot. "They were two of his men from the bar in the Falls Road; one of them was the fella you gave the clout to."

"You never mentioned you knew one of them," said Danny, looking at Dermot. "And you never said you had trouble that day when you went to see Maguire," he added turning to Michael.

"I wouldn't call it trouble," he answered. "Just a little tiff between Maguire, and me. Besides, Dermot had my back that day." Michael gave Dermot a wink, who smiled appreciatively for the recognition.

"Just the same, if there's any slaps to be dished out or backs to be watched, that's my job. I don't go fucking around with Dermot's explosives, now do I?" Danny jokingly gave Dermot a little tilt of the head, as though warning him off his territory.

"What's the crack, Michael? What are the chances of coming through this one?"

"Well, Sean," he replied with a sigh. "We'll know more when I make the phone call, but we have no choice than to do as he says. If we don't, it's our families for sure."

Michael could tell his words had fallen heavily on his friend's shoulders and felt he needed to say something for getting them, once again, neck-deep in trouble.

"Look lads, I..."

"Don't start apologising, Michael, thinking that it's your entire fault that we're in this mess." Danny cut his friend short, knowing what was about to come out of his mouth. "You gave us a choice and we all went for it, as we always do, as a team. Now, let's see it through as a team."

"Yeah, Michael, none of us blame you. We wanted the money—just not that much," confirmed Dermot with a smile.

"We stick together until the end," added Sean, making the vote of confidence unanimous. "Just like the musketeers." Although in a slightly deluded way as only he could do. "All for one and one for all," he shouted, raising his hand aloft with an invisible sword, mimicking their call of solidarity. "I can be d'Artagnan, the good-looking one that always gets the birds."

"Make the call, buddy," Danny said, while shaking his head at his brother's last comments, wondering what planet he was on. "Let's see what they've got for us."

Michael gave an appreciative nod at Danny's and all the lads' words, before pressing call on his phone. Maguire answered.

"There's an industrial estate out past Heathrow—Ten Yards Lane, off Victoria Road. Get a map and be there for nine, all of you, with the stuff."

Maguire was precise and to the point with his instructions, which came across more like orders.

"Why don't you just pick the stuff up and save us the drive?" Michael answered, trying to avoid any secluded meetings.

"You stole the shit, you bring it back. I'm not moving drugs around London to save your arses. I'm already going out on a limb trying to keep your names out of it," ranted Maguire.

"Okay then, I'll bring the stuff myself; it doesn't need the four of us."

"I said the four of you, with the shit and the money," reiterated Maguire. "That's the deal. The black fella doesn't trust you or me, and wants us all in one place so there are no tricks. I'll be armed and there are two fellas with me to make sure everything goes smooth. We sort this tonight and that's the end of it. Those are my orders, direct from Belfast, and I'm not going to disobey them to suit you fuckers."

With that, Maguire ended the call. It wasn't exactly what Michael had hoped for—he was really hoping to swing it so he could take the stuff himself.

"We're not letting you go alone," Sean said forcefully, having picked up on that part of the call.

"Don't worry—that's not an option," said Danny, agreeing with his brother. "I'm not so sure about being musketeers, but either the four of us go together or we don't go at all."

"They didn't go for it, anyway," said Michael. "Maguire reckons the Yardie doesn't trust us and wants all of us in one place to make sure there are no tricks."

"I don't suppose you can blame him for that," said Danny. "It sounds like something we would want if the places were reversed."

"What about just chucking the stuff in a couple of lockers at the station and telling Maguire where to find the key?" added Dermot, offering an alternative to the secluded meeting.

"I've already thought about that, but I'd rather be dead than unable to hold my head up back in Belfast because people were thinking that we bottled it."

Michael's words were concurred, with an agreeing nod from the other three.

"So, what do you think?" Danny asked.

"Like you said, I can believe the Yardie would want us all there. I know I would, even if it was just to get a look at the fuckers that had robbed me. But whatever his reasons, I think we have no choice. Maguire reckons that he'll be armed and he admitted to having the two men in tow so he can secure our safety, but I still don't trust him. Mactazner rang me back earlier—he couldn't find out much except that Maguire had volunteered to come over here and that he hasn't reported anything back yet."

"So nobody back in Belfast knows that it was us that pulled the job?"

"That's what I'm thinking, Danny. Something just isn't sitting quite right."

"That pipe-sucking bastard never volunteered for fuck all in his life," ranted Sean, in between puffs. "He's been a dab hand at volunteering us for every unpaid dangerous job over the past ten years, but I can't believe he'd come over here without some sort of hidden agenda."

"That's what's been nagging at me all afternoon since receiving Davy's call."

"Something tells me that you managed to come up with a plan," Danny said, knowing Michael was seldom without one.

"Not much of one, big fella. Maybe Maguire is being straight, but if he's not, then we need to be ready. Grab the bag there and put it on the table."

Danny did as Michael asked and unzipped the bag to

reveal the money. Danny, Dermot and Sean, seeing it for the first time, took a deep breath, thinking "so near but so far." Michael stepped forward and dug his hand inside, pulling out the C4 plastic explosive that was left over from the robbery, with the detonator and the time power unit. He then put his hands behind his back, lifted his jacket and pulled out two weapons that had been tucked inside his belt.

"I thought you had got rid of that stuff," said Sean, who could have done with one of the weapons earlier, instead of potentially defending himself with a pan of boiling water.

"I got rid of the Glock Danny used to kill your man at the club and the FRG, along with the masks and gloves, but I kept everything else after seeing what was in the bags. Like I said, I knew somebody would come looking for us."

"What do you want to do with the C4?" asked Dermot, explosives being his forte.

"The time of the meet is nine. Set the TPU for nine fifty. By that time, we'll either be walking away or dead.

If they keep their side of the bargain and let us go free in return for the stuff, then we'll tell them about the explosive. If they double-cross us and we're dead, then hopefully Maguire or the Yardie won't be far behind us. It won't help us, but it will make getting killed a little easier."

The four of them smiled at the thought of a little retribution.

"Maybe if they're in it together, we might get both the bastards."

"Exactly, Danny. That's my line of thinking."

"We aren't giving ourselves much of a chance, are we?" said Sean. "Even Danny could put a bet on this one and come out with a winner."

"Hold those horses, Fatty. I do have a couple of outs. The odds aren't entirely stacked against us."

"Yes, brother. Shut your gob before I remind you of where your solar plexus is again." Danny held his giant fist up to Sean's face, obviously getting a bit touchy with jokes about his bad gambling.

"Dermot, what sort of blast area can we expect from that size of charge?" asked Michael.

Dermot picked up the piece of C4 explosive and examined its weight and size.

"It's not a large amount of explosive—remember, we only wanted to cause confusion on the roof to cover our getaway. But I'd say if this was to go off, you wouldn't want to be stood out in the open within fifty yards— you'd be dead for sure, or minus a few important bits, if you were still alive."

"Right then, here's the first of our outs." Michael again reached into the holdall and removed a plastic bag containing four cheap digital watches. "Take one of these each," he said, passing them out. "We'll set the time to coincide with the detonation of the plastic explosive, only our alarms will go off six seconds before the bomb does."

"Why six seconds?" asked Sean, thinking he could do with about six minutes to reach a safe distance.

"Because the sixth of December was my father's birthday and it's my lucky number, and because if we give it any longer, it will give the people pointing their weapons at us too much time to react and fire. If that happens you won't have to worry about the explosion because you'll be dead anyway. Now don't wait for your alarms going off before you start picking a spot to hide. As soon as we get to the meeting, pick out something that you can use to take cover from the blast. If there is nothing, then the only option is to run for four seconds, but make sure you're on the ground before the time of the explosion."

Michael stopped talking and looked at the faces of the other three, looking for any disagreeable frowns. If there had been any, it wouldn't have made a difference—he'd worked on the first part of the plan all day and it was the only thing he had come up with.

"And what's the second out? Tell me it involves the bomb not going off."

"Funny you should ask that, Sean, because it involves you."

"It figures," he replied with a 'why is it always me' look on his face. "Every time you say that lately, my being a fat bastard has usually got something to do with it."

Michael smiled, thinking this time was no different.

"You're going to hide the two weapons down your trousers, strapped to the inside of your thighs, either side of your knackers. Don't wear anything tight. Put on your tracksuit bottoms and make sure that both weapons are cocked and ready for firing. When we get there, they are bound to search us, but I doubt if any fucker will be patting you down, especially down there. You should have no problem hiding two small handguns in between all them rolls of fat."

Sean looked disgruntled. Although his weight this time could be a life-saver, he still couldn't help feeling a little insulted.

"If it looks like it's on top before our alarms go off," continued Michael, "me and the big fella will have a go at them while you and Dermot make a grab for the weapons and try to back us up."

Dermot's face formed into a look of disgust at Michael's plan.

"What's up with you now?" Danny asked, noticing his grimace.

"I don't fancy that."

"What?"

"That. Having to put my hand down that fat fucker's trousers and go searching around his knackers."

"Fucking hell, Dermot. It'll be a matter of life or death."

"I think I'd rather have the death," he added.

"Ah, fuck him," said Sean. "He's just scared that he'll grab a hold of the wrong weapon and realise why Mary Deasy will never forget the nights she spent with me."

"Or I might grab the right weapon and fire a shot before I even get it out of your trousers." Dermot smiled, while delivering the threat. "At least make him have a shower," he added.

"I had a wash today," rebutted Sean, in his own defence. "I realised late on that I wouldn't be needing all the water that I was boiling, so rather than waste it, I had a bath."

"Look, lads," continued Michael with a shake of his head, "I know it's not much of a plan, but let's hope the man doing the searching feels the same way about touching Fatty down there as you do, Dermot. Now, we have to get a move on, so if there's anything you want to add then say it now."

Nobody said anything, except for Sean, who couldn't resist one last joke.

"If we get away with this, you'll have to call me Sean 'the weapon' Keenan. That will impress all the ladies."

Danny put his big arm around Sean's shoulder, pulling him in close with a tight squeeze for a word in his ear.

"Between Dermot's explosives and your weapons, if we get away with this, I'll call you what the fuck you want," he said, showing a bit of very rarely seen brotherly love. "Anything but fucking d'Artagnan."

The situation was grim and their chances of surviving the night slim, but Danny's words managed to lift their spirits with a little laughter.

Back across the water in a smoke-filled Belfast bar, the phone in the corner could be heard ringing over the noisy chatter of its boozy customers. The barman made his apologies to the punter he was serving before moving across to answer it. After listening for only a second, he looked up to the other end of the bar, catching the attention of a man stood there. It was Stanton, who acknowledged and moved towards the phone.

"Who's this?" he asked with the receiver to one ear and a finger in the other.

"It's Maguire," said the voice on the other end. "I've visited Kilburn and I've talked to the black fella that was robbed. He realises that he was a bit hasty with his threats and understands that he is out of his depth. He tried to offer me a deal to help him recover his money but I told him we weren't interested."

"Good. We've no time to be bailing out drug dealers. You've done your job so get yourself back here. There's something big going down next week, so there's going to be another meeting. Did you happen to find out who the Irish lads were that robbed him?"

"No, I couldn't find out anything. No one knows anything and Mactazner wasn't very helpful."

"Okay. Report back here within two days."

"My dealings here are done—I'll be out of this shithole by tomorrow"

Maguire, with a devious grin, put the phone down in the public call box and stepped outside. Taking a deep breath of satisfaction from the cool night air, he couldn't help but feel that he had pulled the master stroke. Looking like the cat that got the cream, he climbed in the back of the car containing his two henchmen and ordered them on their way to Heathrow and the warehouse.

Back in the Belfast bar, Stanton called to one of his men.

"Murphy…" A man turned. "Bring yer ear over here." The man immediately joined him at his side. "Has big Davy Mactazner been on the phone asking any questions about Maguire's visit?" The man paused. "Come on, Murphy. I know he's an old pal of yours. I'm not asking you to drop him in it; I only want to know what he said about Maguire."

"He said that Maguire had been to The Harp, which Davy obviously wasn't happy about. He also said that

Maguire was strutting around like he owned the place and gobbing off about being ordered to go over there and take care of the business with the black fella, because nobody else could handle the situation." Davy's friend laid it on thick—obviously he didn't care much for Maguire either. "He also asked if Maguire had been reporting back and trying to drop him in any shit."

"And what did you tell Mactazner?"

"The truth. I told him that we hadn't heard from Maguire since he left."

"So, Maguire's telling people that he was ordered to go, is he?" Stanton stroked his chin, wondering what the slippery bastard was up to this time. He didn't read too much into it; he put most of it down to Maguire trying to rub Mactazner up the wrong way in his own bar.

"Okay, Murphy. I just wanted the full picture."

"I didn't mention Davy's call because I didn't think it was important. There was nothing official talked about. It was just a bit of' banter between two old pals. That's all."

"It's okay; you did nothing wrong. Now, grab yourself a pint and I'll have one with ye."

Stanton was another man who liked to stay on top of things, especially when it involved anyone he didn't trust, and Maguire was right at the top of that list in his book.

The call Maguire had made was solely to cover his back—a little bit of security, just in case things didn't go to plan that evening and the Yardie made good his threat to reveal their dealings. His line of thinking was that if he had already revealed to Stanton that a deal had been put on the table, he could argue later that the Yardie was trying it on because of his refusal to help. Plus, he couldn't help getting in a little dig at Mactazner.

Either way, from the lies he had just told, it didn't look too good for the lads. If they didn't return the Yardie's property, Maguire would make sure it was revealed that they were the robbers, so they were dead men for starting a war, especially after their previous warnings; and if they did return the stuff then they were dead men also, because Maguire couldn't afford to leave them alive to reveal the deal he had done for the money, especially after just telling Stanton that he knew nothing of their involvement. For an added bonus to Maguire's little plan, if The Harp of Erin was the first bar attacked, Mactazner could well be one of the first casualties. That would mean that without really knowing the truth, he could report back to Belfast that Mactazner had supplied the lads with the weapons they used to commit the robbery and start the war in the first place. Believing he had all bases covered, he sat in the back of the car on the way to the meeting at the warehouse, wearing a broad smile around his pipe-gripping teeth, enjoying the moment with a little bit of help from the Yardie's cannabis resin.

Chapter Twenty-Two

The Warehouse

Getting into the car that evening was probably the hardest thing that any of them had ever done, and was only accomplished through the strength the four friends drew from each other. Sean's jokes and usual 'couldn't give a fuck' attitude kept all their minds on something other than the fact and reality that this could quite possibly be the last journey they would ever make together. Sean drove the car, as always, with his usual tab hanging from his mouth, while frequently shifting in his seat, trying to find a position that didn't squash his testicles between the two weapons hidden in his trousers. The warehouse by Heathrow was quite a distance, but the road signs soon became a more frequent occurrence directing them ever closer to their meeting.

Michael took two cigarettes from his packet and put one in his mouth, before passing one across to Sean, who was still smoking. Noticing his mistake, he stretched down to the ashtray between them and placed the cigarette inside for later. As he did, his hand shook slightly, showing signs of the pressure that he was under. He pulled it back quickly, a little embarrassed knowing Sean had seen his hand tremble.

"No, thanks. This is my last," Sean said, taking the tab from his mouth. "I promised the doctor that I would give up one day and I'd hate for him to be calling me a liar at my funeral next week. Mind you, I will be proving him wrong in one way because he always said it would be the smoking and the drink that killed me, not a bullet in the head. You know, if I had a pound for every time that fella has mentioned cholesterol or blood pressure to me, the money in those bags in the boot would be fuck all."

Michael smiled, knowing Sean was saying it for his

benefit—confirmed as Sean gave him a wink out of his left eye. Michael lifted his lighter to his cigarette then paused to study his hand, which was now steady as a rock after Sean's words. He began to relax a little, enjoying his smoke, and as the cat's eyes in the road passed quickly by, shining back their mesmerising light, he began to think back to the last time he'd had the shakes—a time he didn't like to think of too often. It was the night the police came to the flat, bringing the news to his mother that her husband, Finbar, had been killed. Michael was seventeen at the time and that evening he'd been up to no good with his mates. They had stolen a car to use as a barricade and then set fire to it, while throwing stones at the soldiers, so he believed they were there to arrest him. From his hiding place beneath the stairs, he heard the police giving the news to his mother and, before his mind had even registered the grim reality of it, his body had already broken into a cold and sweaty shake. But it was his mother's never-to-be-forgotten shrill cries that put the shudder in his spine.

As so many times before that day, guilt once again fell upon him, as he realised that he was probably going to put his mother through that whole horrible situation all over again. He felt even more guilt, because he had only thought of her feelings now, as they were nearing their destination. Feelings of selfishness now joined his guilt as he became his own worst critic. All his mother had asked was for him to get away for a while out of harm's way. Now, if he was killed, she would undoubtedly blame herself, because she would see it as being her idea. "Selfish, selfish, selfish," he thought to himself, regretting the choices he had made, not only in the past couple of weeks but as far back as the night in Bangor that had set the ball rolling. As he rested the side his head against the cold door window, his thoughts became deeper, as the stark realisation of the sorrow his actions would cause ran frantically through his mind. He started to make promises to himself about the things he would do and put right in his life if he was lucky enough to survive this evening. Marrying Roisin and giving his mother some grandchildren being top of the list, then getting a steady nine-to-five job and giving up his criminal ways were there, too, but basically, they were repentant promises from a Catholic boy who believed that before too long, he would be in front of his God, accounting for his sins.

His thoughts began to switch to the different events that had shaped his life. He drifted back to his sixteenth birthday and his first pint of Guinness in O'Reilly's Bar. He remembered watching Davy Mactazner and his father, dressed smartly in their suits for Sunday Mass, and after, watching them slip away quietly from his mother in the direction of the same bar. To Milltown Cemetery, where he had stood with his mother at his father's grave; he could feel the shots that were fired that day as though they were still vibrating through his body. He smiled at the memory of kissing his mother goodbye as she tested her bingo daubers and dabbers, and cheered with young Peewee when he took him to the football, as his father was never able to do. He thought of the nights out to the pub with the lads and remembered the first day they had all met at school.

There were a few kids who got a good hiding that day after taking the piss out of Sean's weight, not realising that Danny was his brother. Finally, he found himself looking through the window of the hairdresser's and watching Roisin move about her shop. His thoughts weren't of her shape or their times together; they were simply of her smile and her lips when she said his name—he could almost smell her hair as he closed his eyes and held her close.

"What's the name of that road we're looking for?"

Michael's dreams were ended by Sean's words. It took a little time for his question to register before he reached into his pocket and pulled out a slip of paper on which he had scribbled the directions.

"Victoria Road, and then we want Ten Yards Lane."

"Well, here's Victoria Road," said Sean, taking the left turn.

Dermot and Danny, who had sat quietly in the back with their own thoughts, sat up, realising they were nearing the warehouse. Michael looked at his watch—it was eight forty-five. He questioned his plans one more time in his head, searching for mistakes.

"Does anybody want to go over anything again?"

Danny and Sean both shook their heads and Dermot answered, "No," in a strong voice. But he did have another slight worry. "I just hope that Maguire doesn't search the bags, suspecting that we may have left him a little surprise. He knows how we think."

"He won't," reassured Michael. "He's confident that he caught us on the hop this morning and that he's had us running around like headless chickens all day. He knows we can only go to Mactazner for supplies and he knows we haven't set foot in Kilburn today because he will have had every inch of it watched. What he doesn't know is that we already had some plastic explosive, so the most he's going to think we have in our arsenal are the weapons we used to rob the club, and once we've been searched and they don't find them, he'll think we're clean."

"I hope you're right," replied Dermot.

"So do I," Michael muttered to himself under his breath in a half-hearted reply. "So do I." In the distance, he caught sight of a white flash, as a sign was partially caught in the headlights. "Slow down a little, Sean. There's a sign coming up on your right."

Sean slowed the vehicle and switched on the full beam, making the sign visible.

"Ten Yards Lane," he said, reading the name out loud before taking the right turn.

The lane was dark and a lot longer than ten yards, but after a while the red and white stripes of a barrier could be seen and, beyond it, the silhouetted shapes of some warehouses became noticeable in front of them. Sean stopped the car at the barrier that blocked the entrance. Robbie the giant approached and shone a torch through Michael's open window. The four sat in silence as one by one he pointed the light in each of their faces. He paused for a moment at Dermot, maybe for a second recognising him as the FRG shooter or maybe just remembering him from his visit to the site. He moved the beam across to the driver's seat, finding a not-in-the-mood Sean.

"Get that fucking torch out of my eyes or I'll shove it up your arse, ye big ugly shithouse."

7P's

Robbie didn't move. In fact, he grinned and intensified the light by searching for Sean's pupils. Sean reached over and took Michael's cigarette from his hand. He sucked hard on the tab, making sure it was well lit, before flicking it back across his chest and out of his window, scoring a direct hit in the face of the annoying giant. The sparks flew as it bounced off his cheekbone and onto the floor, making the big man jump backwards with the shock. He wasn't happy and set off around the front of the car, obviously intending to seek retribution on his projectile attacker, but he was stopped in his tracks by the back door opening and Danny stepping out.

"I think you'll find that I'm more your size big man, not my wee brother. Now, if it's trouble you're looking for, then I'll be the member of the family that accommodates ye."

Robbie stopped at the bonnet and shone the torch back at Danny, who was out of the car and ready for action. He hesitated at the sight of the Irishman who was stood with his shoulders back and fists clenched ready for action. He obviously wasn't used to going up against men of his own size, although he still had at least three inches and five stone on his more-than-willing opponent.

"Come forward," said Danny, beckoning the bouncer away from his brother. "You'll make no name for yourself over there." Danny with his finger, tapped himself on the chest. "Here's where your destiny lies."

Robbie, still hesitant, was then caught off guard by Sean's interruption.

"Let him come," he in turn beckoned, now halfway out of the car himself. "I'm more than willing to do the accommodating, if he pleases."

Big Robbie, now over faced with offers of a good tear-up, was almost happy to see Michael be third man out of the car, trying to bring an end to the stand-off.

"Big fella," he said looking at the giant. "You're making us late for our appointment. Now, do you want to fuck about with that torch all night or do you want to do your job and lift the fucking barrier so we can continue?"

Robbie still said nothing. He passed a few more dark menacing looks between the brothers before returning to raise the barrier, while indicating with a raised arm the furthest warehouse on the left. Sean left him with a parting gesture of a clenched fist and a raised finger.

"Talkative fella," remarked Michael when they were all back in the car and finally on their way.

"Come to think of it," said Dermot, "he didn't say much that night we met at the club, either."

The four of them joined in a laugh, which took a little edge off the nervous tension, before Sean added a comment.

"For a minute there, I thought he'd recognised the dwarf that shot him."

"Just drive, fat boy," returned Dermot, not biting.

"Listen, lads, whatever is waiting for us inside this place, don't let the fuckers faze you. Just remember you're with your mates and there's no better place to be."

"Don't worry, Michael," interrupted Dermot, suddenly becoming the bravest of them all in the face of adversity. "It was on the cards that this day would come eventually, and considering the way we've carried on over the years, I'm surprised it didn't arrive sooner. So, now it's here, let's go front the bastards."

Nobody could argue with Dermot's line of thinking, and as Sean pulled up the car in front of the warehouse, they gave each other a reassuring nod before climbing out and taking the bags from the boot.

Lined up four abreast in front of the large warehouse doors, they were confronted by Winston the dealer, with instructions to raise their arms and spread their legs so he could search them. Sean was the last in the row, and when it came to his turn, the dealer started at his shoulders and began to work his way down his bulky body. Reaching his waist, Sean had some advice for him before he went any further.

"Mind what you grab a hold of down there, fella. If you feel the size of my weapon, you'll have an inferiority complex for the rest of your life."

The other three looked at Sean and then each other, unable to believe how close to the wind he was sailing, but it didn't have the effect he hoped it would, because Winston continued with his search. As he neared the concealed items, Sean went to the next part of his plan by turning his body as though trying to help the dealer in his rummaging, but really it was to get his big backside facing the right way before playing his trump card—trump being an apt description, as he let go one of his famous ripper farts that he had been saving for that precise moment. The propelled gases ripped through his underpants and tracksuit bottoms, as though they weren't there, scoring a direct hit in the dealer's face, who was crouched at the perfect level. He fell backwards away from Sean's rear, gagging from his throat, while trying to eject the foul, almost sticky stench from his mouth. He looked up at Sean in disgust, while wafting his hand in front of his face, as the burning tears that formed in his eyes began to run down his cheeks.

"What's up," said Sean with an accomplished grin. "Do you not like biryani? Next time, I'll make it goat, rice and peas. That should be more to your taste."

The other three couldn't help but laugh, and Michael used the moment to steer his way past the grounded dealer, who looked like he was going to spew his guts.

"I think I may have followed through with that one," said Sean.

"Great," replied Dermot sarcastically, really not looking forward to sticking his hand down his trousers.

Michael walked through the double doors of the warehouse first, followed by Danny with a holdall and, behind him, Sean and Dermot with the other two bags. The four of them immediately began to scan the inside of the building, looking for cover should it come to getting out of the way of the bomb blast. Finding suitable objects to take cover behind wasn't going to be a problem—the place was full of crates and pallets stacked high to the rafters. Four shipping containers were lined up on the left, while to the right, two wagons with continental trailers were parked. Further back, there were more rows of shipping crates; this was obviously where the Yardie landed most of his drug deliveries. In the centre of the room stood Maguire, puffing on his pipe, with his two men off either shoulder behind him. To Maguire's left, with about four metres between them, stood the Yardie; he had three men behind him, all armed to the teeth with automatic weapons. The Irish team approached beyond the point of no return.

7P's

"Are you boys expecting trouble?" remarked Michael, looking at the overkill of weapons in their hands.

"That's far enough," said the Yardie, in no mood to share pleasantries as he eyed up the lads when coming face-to-face with them for the first time. There was a pause before he spoke again with some orders. "You. Big man. Danny was singled out first. "Put all the bags in the middle, then open them up so I can see what you've got."

"Just a minute," interrupted Maguire as he put his hand into his right overcoat pocket, as though reaching for a weapon. "What did you do with the weapons you used on the robbery?"

"We threw them in the river the same night," answered Michael. "They were too warm to keep hold of after the unfortunate accident with your man in the office." Michael looked at the Yardie, hoping that his lessening of the slaying of his man in the robbery would cut some ice. "We were searched already outside, but if you want to do it again then be my guest."

Michael raised his arms out by his side, followed in

his move by the other three. Maguire removed his hand from his pocket.

"That's okay. Just don't try anything stupid," he warned, before indicating to Danny to do as the Yardie had said. Danny walked forward and dropped his bag on the floor in the middle of the circle that was now formed by the three parties, before turning and taking the other two from first Dermot then Sean, and placing them alongside. Dropping down on to one knee, he unzipped the first then lifted one end and tilted it towards the Yardie so he could see inside. The bag contained the drugs, which Danny now tilted to the left so Maguire could also see.

"How many?" asked the Yardie.

"Twenty-five," answered Michael quickly. "It's all there, just like the money."

The Yardie looked at Michael, realising that he was obviously the leader of the gang that robbed him. With nothing to lose, Michael defiantly returned the stare, only drawing away when Danny unzipped the second and third bags, revealing their contents as he had done the first. They were full to the brim with money—ten-grand bundles all tied round with an elastic band, fifty of them to be exact. Maguire's eyes opened wide with delight, seeing that there was easily the four or five hundred grand inside them that the Yardie had estimated.

"There, we've done as you asked," said Michael, getting in first to test the water. "That's everything we took returned. Now do we leave the same way we came or is there something else on your mind?"

He received no answer to his question from Maguire or the Yardie, both with other things on their minds.

"The two bags with the cash inside—zip them back up and throw them over here," Maguire said while looking at Danny, eager to get his hands on the loot. From his words, Michael immediately knew that, as they had suspected, Maguire had done a deal.

"Easy man," said the Yardie, raising his hand. His three goons immediately raised their weapons. Maguire's men reacted, going for theirs, but the Jamaicans had them covered.

"Leave it," said Maguire, knowing that his men would be dead before their weapons were out of their belts.

"Yeah, man. Now, put them on the floor," ordered the Yardie. The two men paused, waiting for confirmation from their own boss.

"Do as he says," said Maguire taking his pipe from his mouth, after further assessing the situation and realising that they had no choice. Maguire's men did just that, but it was a wrong move. No sooner had they complied than on the Yardie's nod, two bursts of gunfire rang out, killing them both. Maguire looked at the fallen men and then back at the Yardie.

"You double-crossing black bastard! We had a deal—you get your drugs back and I take the money," he shouted.

The Yardie sucked his teeth, then revealed a big pearly smug smile.

"You think me a fool, Irishman. I'm not paying you for getting my own shit back. For all I know, you were all in on it together from the start."

With Maguire's deceit unravelling in front of them,

Michael gently gestured with his hand for Dermot and Sean to close in behind him. By the looks of what was going on, they were going to have to put their weak plan into action, because things were definitely going from bad to worse. When they walked into the warehouse, Michael gave them a fifty-fifty chance of survival, but right now, they seemed odds-on for a bullet in the head. There was no way Maguire would leave them alive, not if he wanted to keep the money for himself, and not now they knew he had done a deal with the Yardie. But, in the same instance, Maguire's future wasn't looking too bright at this point, either, which he obviously realised as he began to talk.

"You might double-cross me in the deal, but if you kill me, what I told you *would* happen to your clubs *will* happen. And all the money in the world won't stop it, because I'm not that stupid that I came here tonight without somebody knowing where I was going and who I was meeting."

Maguire quickly laid out the flaws if the Yardie's plans were to send him the same way as his two henchmen.

The Yardie paused before answering, using the time to further impose himself on the lads with vengeful looks.

"Okay, Irish, chill your white arse. I've got my shit back, so I'll leave you alive, but I'm paying you nothing. The trouble between us is finished. I'll not touch Kilburn, but if any fucker comes near me, I'll make sure that your people know what deal you struck."

Maguire could do nothing about the Yardie's double-cross. He was carrying a weapon, but was too well covered and outnumbered to make a move. The Yardie continued to smile and laughed at Maguire, knowing he had him by the balls, but it was Michael and the lads that he wanted to reap retribution upon. A silence fell on the room that the word 'uncomfortable' didn't do justice to in its description.

"Winston, move the bags to the vehicle," ordered the Yardie, while looking deep into Michael's eyes with a lust for blood.

Maguire took one last look at the money as Winston took the bags from Danny and zipped them back up. Danny took five paces backwards to re-join his mates in their line-up. Michael knew it was now or never. He and Danny were almost certain to get shot, but the commotion they caused might give Sean and Dermot the vital seconds they would need to retrieve the weapons and save themselves. Again, the Yardie gave his order to his dealer to move the bags, wanting him out of the line of fire between his men and the Irish boys.

"Winston, move the bags."

Michael and Danny didn't need another warning and after a shared glance were about to pounce when...

"I WOULDN'T DO THAT IF I WAS YOU, WINSTON. Just leave the bags where they are."

Everybody in the gathering was startled as a raised voice came from the shadows between the containers to the right of the group.

"Who's there?" shouted the Yardie, while his men reacted by pointing their weapons in the direction of the uninvited stranger's voice. "Clive, Vernon," he continued to call, trying to raise two more of his men that he had left on guard outside.

For a few seconds, another silence fell over the warehouse, as the clicking sound of a pair of brogue shoes was all that could be heard coming out of the darkness. The stranger was walking forward with his hands held wide from his side, his fingers splayed showing that he was holding no weapons.

"If you shoot me, you'll be dead before I hit the floor," said the stranger, still emerging from the half-light.

The Yardie's three men looked at their boss for orders. The Yardie gave none—he knew whoever the person was that he must have had some help to get past the rest of his posse.

As the stranger drew closer and entered the light, the Yardie stared intensely at him, quickly trying to gather his thoughts as to who he might be. But it was Michael who showed the biggest reaction, his jaw nearly hitting the floor. Now, mouth wide open with a dumbfounded look, his head buzzed as though it was under an acid attack as his brain registered what his eyes were seeing.

"No, no, no, no, no," was the first thought through

his head. "How the fuck could I have been so stupid," was his second, with others following, all calling into question his recent actions. An unwilling smile formed on his lips, as memories flashed back in his mind. As he sifted through them, ironically he almost admired the ingenuity and smoothness in which he had been infiltrated. For the first time in his adult life he had let his guard down and been taken in. If they had come to the mainland on IRA business, there was no way anyone would have been able to get so close to him, no way that he would have relaxed and allowed himself to be sucked in. He had been that busy with his personal plans to rob the club and then its ensuing problems that he had well and truly been caught napping.

The stranger was Eli, the driver from the site.

The cockney accent had been dropped for a more sophisticated London tone and the work gear swapped for a tailored suit, underneath a stylish, velvet-collared, brown camel-hair Crombie, and polished brogues.

"Lower your weapons," ordered Eli, looking at the Yardie's men as he continued to approach the group.

"Who the fuck are you? How did you get past my men?"

The Yardie, in a defensive move, took hold of both ends of the carved cane he carried and pulled on the handle to reveal a gleaming sword hidden inside. His men, seeing his action, began moving towards Eli, backing up their boss in his aggressive show.

"This is the last time I'm going to fucking say it," reiterated Eli. "Put your weapons down. Your men outside are still alive but, obviously, as my presence here proves, they've been taken care off. Now my men inside have got you covered, so lower your weapons while you've still got a choice. This is my final warning. If you don't comply immediately, my men will shoot you without hesitation or further orders."

The Yardie and his men slowly turned around, as from the shadows, three armed men converged on their position. They were dressed in British Army-issue camouflage uniforms and balaclavas. To the Yardie they were just armed men in uniform, but for Michael and the lads, it was their worst nightmare. They were SAS troopers, given away to the Irish lads by their sub-machine guns weapons fitted with suppressors, a form of silencer, and Eli, Michael's new drinking partner, was obviously in charge. The Yardie and his men, seeing they had no choice, reluctantly complied, while Danny turned to Michael with an indescribable look of foreboding on his face.

"Well, there's a turn-up for the books. We never saw that one coming," he said, wondering if the night could get any worse. "I'd say if we weren't dead already, we fucking are now."

Michael shook his head in disbelief at his own stupidity. The overwhelming feeling of guilt that had visited him so many times already that day was back again. There was no getting out of this one. Their plan for Danny and him to create a diversion while Sean and Dermot made a play for the weapons may have worked with the Yardie's men, but not with SAS troopers—they would all be dead as soon as they made a move. The bomb hidden in the money was their only way out now and their chances of surviving that were slim.

Eli, now in the centre of the gathering, turned and looked at the Irish.

"Fuck me, Michael, I haven't seen a look on a man's face like that since I came home early from work and caught the milkman stuck up to the nuts in the wife," he said, enjoying the moment.

"So, I guess when your wife's not fucking the milkman, she's taking the kids to Margate on her own," returned Michael.

Eli smiled at his answer. "Nice one," he said, as he pulled a cigar from his pocket, lit it and blew out a long puff of smoke while deciding on his next move. He continued to smile as he turned around to address the Yardie.

"So, what do I call you then, my old china? Mr Yardie, Mr Drug Baron or do you have a first name?"

"What the fuck are you saying to me, man?" he replied, unwilling to play Eli's mind games.

"I just figure that if we're going to be partners, we should at least be on first-name terms."

"Partners?" The Yardie was put back for a second,

wondering where his new nemesis was going with his thinking. "I don't need no white-boy, two-bob partner, you ras'."

Eli made a tutting noise, condemning the Yardie's words of reluctance.

"You know, if we're going to be working together, you're going to have to drop that racist attitude. Now, tell me your name or I'll shove that sword up your 'arris and make your fucking eyes water."

The tone of Eli's voice changed dramatically, causing the Yardie to rethink his attitude. He looked down at his sword, which lay on the floor next to his men's weapons, then returned his stare to Eli and revealed his name.

"My men just call me Boss."

Eli smiled.

"Well the only person I call Boss is the wife, now give me your name."

The Yardie paused.

"Allan. Allan Mabenga."

"'Allan'?" Eli exclaimed with a laugh. "Fucking 'Allan'?

What sort of a name is that for a big Jamaican drug baron? Aren't you supposed to have a proper name that strikes fear into your enemy's hearts, like Escobar or Capone, not fucking Allan? Fuck me, I bet you're not even a Yardie. You were probably born in Brixton, you cunt."

"Fuck you, man," ranted the Yardie at Eli's piss-taking. "I don't give a fuck about you or your men."

Eli respected the retaliations of the Yardie and believed him when he said he didn't give a fuck. The smile stayed on his face, as he switched his attention to Winston and the bags in front of him.

"Open them back up," he instructed, looking down at the dealer, who hadn't moved since Eli had entered the room and was still crouched over the bags, with the zip of the first one in his right hand. "Let's have a look at what you could have won," he continued, doing his Jim Bowen impersonation, while looking at Maguire. Winston did as he was told, starting with the one containing the drugs. "Fuck me, Allan. How much is that lot worth?" he sarcastically enquired when seeing the coke. The Yardie said nothing, except to give one of his dismissive teeth-sucking insults.

"Now the other two." Eli kicked one of the other bags with the toe of his brogue while looking around at the faces that surrounded him. Winston opened them both and pulled the zips wide apart, revealing the money. Eli stood over them, puffing on his cigar, before looking up and staring directly at Maguire.

"Thirty pieces of silver," he said, comparing Maguire to Judas for his betrayal. "Okay, zip them back up and then join your mates." Winston did as instructed, but was a bit reluctant to move, thinking, as Danny had done minutes earlier, that the line-up he would be joining would soon be facing a firing squad. "On the double, lad," hastened Eli. "There's a good little drug dealer." Winston, still in no hurry, finally joined his boss. Eli now turned to the others, who had been able to do nothing else but watch and contemplate in what form their demise would be dealt to them.

"I want you Irish lads to feel free to talk amongst yourselves for a moment while Allan and I have a little discussion about future business. But don't do anything stupid because my three lads there don't miss." Eli, turning back, looked beyond the Yardie at the three SAS troopers that occupied raised positions behind them.

Michael and the lads again looked at each other, wondering why they weren't already dead. Maguire was surprisingly quiet, still stood between the bodies of his two henchmen, whose blood was now starting to pool around his feet.

"Right then Allan. From what I've seen of you these last few days and our meeting thus far tonight, I know you're a serious man, so I'm not going to fuck about by going around the houses."

The Yardie shrugged his shoulders, as if to say is there any other way.

"Okay, what's on your mind?" he added. He realised that he was going to have to play ball, but he also knew that he wasn't going to like it.

"What's on my mind, Allan my old china, is this—five weeks ago, we didn't even know you existed, until the good old boys from the Belfast Brigade here decided to turn you over. Then, because they were watching you and we were watching them watching you, we now know everything about you and your business. Are you following me so far, Allan?" Eli puffed on his cigar, still walking around the bags, while occasionally keeping his eye on the four Irish lads.

"So, you've been watching me? So what?"

"You've got a nice set-up, Allan, that's what. You've got the product and the transport." Eli pointed to the Yardie's numerous wagons and trailers that were parked up inside the warehouse. "You've even got the customers coming to your own clubs to buy the shit. I've got to hand it to you, Allan—you certainly know how to corner a market. You're a logistics genius, my old son."

The Yardie gave a little tilt of his head, acknowledging the praise of his business acumen.

"So, here's what I've got in mind, Allan. In short, my Caribbean drug-pushing friend, here's the fucking deal." Eli looked him in his eyes as if to say, are you ready. The Yardie looked back as if to say, let's have it. "At the end of every month, from now until the day you die, my mate Errol is going to come to your club and collect one hundred grand. Errol, come here and introduce yourself to our new partner, Allan."

One of the SAS troopers broke away from the other two and walked in front of the Yardie and his men.

"And take that fucking silly mask off, so Allan can see who he's dealing with."

The trooper did as instructed and removed his ski mask, to reveal a face blacker than the Yardie's. Eli again grinned, enjoying the moment.

"You see, Allan, we're not all white boys in the British Army. That's why you've got to ease up on all that racist talk." Eli then changed his voice into a soppy sounding piss-take. "It's politically incorrect, you know," he continued while giving the Yardie a cheeky smile and a wink before taking another puff on his cigar. The Yardie still remained silent, waiting for the rest of the offer. Eli turned back to Errol.

"Leave the drugs, but pick up the two bags of money, then take them outside and throw them in the Rover," he ordered, now that the introductions had been made. Errol removed the bags and walked off through the double doors into the darkness with all four sets of Irish eyes following him, as they watched their only remaining chance of survival leaving with the trooper. "Now, Allan, don't go moaning about the amount. We know you can afford it." The Yardie didn't disagree, but he was no pushover.

"Why should I pay you? What do I get for a hundred grand?"

"Fuck me, Allan. Are you sure you're not Jewish? You haggle like you were circumcised at birth." Another smile followed his little joke and another puff of his cigar. "For this," he continued, "you get to pick up the other bag full of the old hooter gear and you and your men get to leave here alive and go on about your business." The Yardie stood silent, his mind working overtime as he computed the offer. "Now I know what you're thinking, Allan. You're thinking say yes now to the deal, so you can walk out of here with your life and your drugs, and then fuck the silly white soldier boy off later." Still the Yardie said nothing, because Eli had taken the thoughts straight out of his head. "You see the problem with that idea, Allan, is that we don't own any bars in Kilburn where you can come and find us. There are no home addresses and no families you can threaten, unless you want to pick a fight with the British Army, of course, but that would be a bigger mistake than picking one with the IRA. But look at my boat race, Allan, and mark my words well." Eli pointed his finger at his chin and gave the Yardie a solemn look. "If anything, anything at all, ever happens to Errol—any mysterious muggings while he's leaving the club with our money each month, or if anyone so much as talks to him—we'll come to Jamaica, where you'll probably be hiding, thinking you're safe, and you will find out that jungle fucking warfare is our speciality, my son. So, if you accept this deal, make no mistake that it is well and truly binding because there's nowhere for you to go. No little corner of this Earth where you would be safe, should you double-cross us." Eli gave the Yardie a deep look, letting him know that the ultimatum was final and non-negotiable. "And remember this, Allan—we know everything about you, more than you think we know. We even know that you really are circumcised because Errol was stood next to you in The Palm Cove bogs Thursday night. Now, the next and final words to come out of your north and south, Allan, want to be, 'Yeah, man,' because if not, you're going straight in the river with those two cunts you shot earlier, saving us the trouble."

The Yardie looked Eli in the eyes, contemplating his options, which didn't take long because he knew he had none. Basically, he was fucked, but took great comfort from the fact that he only wanted one hundred grand a month, which was nothing to him. He would have stood for a lot more, if it meant getting out of there alive. In any case, he was getting his drugs back, which had a street value of about ten million, but more to the point gave him back his product that he needed to keep his customers happy and his business turning over, so the result as it stood was a good one, and only the same as the one he had struck earlier with Maguire. Plus, he had killed two of theirs for his one, so his reputation, which was important to him, was intact.

"Yeah, man," he said before gesturing to Winston to pick up the bag containing the drugs.

"Leave anytime you want, Allan," said Eli, pointing the way towards the warehouse doors. "You'll find that big doorstop of a bouncer of yours and those other two mugs having a nap next to the barrier on your way out."

The Yardie paused before leaving, just to give Michael and the boys one last look. If things had gone his way, they would have all been joining the other two Irish lads at Maguire's feet.

He reached slowly into his pocket and pulled out another one of his family-sized spliffs, which he placed in his mouth, before holding out his hand in a gesture to borrow Eli's lighter. Eli again admired the Yardie's balls and coolness. Placing his own cigar in his mouth, he pulled out his Zippo and, in a well-rehearsed move, flicked open the lid then ran his thumb down the striker. Cupping his hands around the flame, he offered it to the Yardie, who ignited his potent weed while never breaking eye contact.

The two men shared a moment of mutual respect, as the white smoke from both their hand-rolled preferences climbed high into the rafters of the warehouse roof. Eli bent down in front of the Yardie and picked up the sword and its sheath. After admiring the long shiny blade and saying the word 'nice', he slid it inside, joining the two together, before offering it to the Yardie. The Yardie, with an appreciative look, took it, then with his head held high, headed off through the double doors, satisfied that everybody knew that he was a man that could not be fucked about or messed around with.

"See you at the end of the month, Allan," Eli shouted as the Yardie and his crew disappeared in to the darkness. "Be lucky."

Eli now turned back to face the lads with a big grin on his face.

"He's a nice chap, that Allan. I'm going to enjoy working with him," he joked, taking another puff on his cigar and giving a broad smile to Michael.

"Get the fuck on with it," Michael said defiantly, bringing yet another grin to his capture's face.

"Don't be in such a rush, Flynn. There's questions to be answered and knowledge to be shared."

"You'll get no answers from us," replied Michael, continuing his defiance.

"You misunderstand me, lad. I'm the one who will be educating you, not the other way around."

Michael looked puzzled at his return, while Eli again turned to look at Maguire, then back at him and the lads.

"Young Michael Flynn, Big Danny Boy Keenan, Sean Fatty Keenan and Dermot the Worrier Barry."

Eli listed them as though he had known then all his life, while slowly walking down the line.

"How long is it now until old Greasy Deasy drops the kid, Dermot? You want to watch her, son—she's a proper handful, that girl. I think Errol was giving her one the last time we were in Belfast." Eli's joking manner continued, along with his enjoyment of the moment and his cigar.

"Stop fucking around," Michael interrupted. "You obviously know as much about us as you do the

Yardie, if not more. How long have you had us under surveillance?"

Eli lifted his head, looking into the air while doing his calculations. He jokingly began to count using his fingers like a five-digit abacus.

"Let me see, how long would it be? One... two... three..." He looked at the two balaclavaed troopers as though they were going to help him with his maths. "Nah, longer than that. Since you were seventeen, I think, so that would make it about fourteen years."

His reply shocked Michael, who expected an answer of about three months.

"Well, I wouldn't exactly call it surveillance," he continued. "Your father's funeral was what we were really watching, but I couldn't help noticing how well you supported your mother that day. Since then, it's been my job to know all your business. In fact, it's fair to say that if the lads and I were to go on *Mastermind* with old Magnus Magnusson that you four could be our specialist subject."

The four Irishmen almost felt violated at the thought of being under the microscope for so long.

"I notice you boys have gone into business for yourselves," Michael said, looking behind Eli at the doors where the trooper had taken the bags. "There's a nice few quid in those holdalls."

"You should know—you nicked it," replied Eli with a pointed finger. "All this is down to you, young Flynn. You simply can't resist having a bite, can you, lad?"

Michael released a sigh because he couldn't disagree.

"You know, when 14 INT told me to keep an eye on you lot while you were in London, I never expected, three months later, to be holding bags full of a drug dealer's money and having shares in three nightclubs; it's funny how these things turn out, ain't it?" Eli again gave the lads a cheesy grin. "We were getting bored shitless watching you and the big man laying bricks on that site. In fact, we were going to call it a day until you went for a drink in that club. Then we knew you were up to something—why else would you be there? It was obvious from the start that your reasons were non-political, so we reported back that you were of no risk. After that, the lads and I kept tabs in our own time, just to see if there was anything in it for us. And guess what—there was."

The Irish lads shared a look, realising that they had been used for the donkey work—just another downer to add to an ever-increasing list of that day's setbacks.

"You see, the peace talks in Ireland don't just affect you," Eli continued. "It's the end of our jobs as well. Our government won't keep us around once there's peace in Northern Ireland. We're D-Squad you see, the old men of the regiment—most of our lads have already been given their cards and the rest of us won't be far behind. Give it two months and we'll all be unemployed, unless the Argies have another go at the Falklands, that is."

Eli stopped talking for a moment and looked across at Maguire, who made eye contact then looked away, but the look was enough to put Eli on his case.

"How will you go on, Benny? I can't see the government paying you any more if there's peace. You'll have to finally start pulling your weight and earning a proper living."

Maguire lifted his head quickly, shocked at what Eli

was saying. His words also caused confusion amongst Michael and the lads.

"What the fuck's he talking about, Maguire?" asked Michael.

"He's talking rubbish," dismissed Maguire. "Don't listen to him—he's trying to stir up shit. He wants to drive a wedge between us, so he can gather information."

The lads all looked back at Eli, whose continuing smug smile seemed to be hiding a lot more information, which he was intent on sharing.

"Stirring up shit, Benny? Why should I do that? And, as for information, I already know all there is to know about you chaps. For instance, I know that I'm not the one who's been lying to these four all these years."

Again, the Irish lads looked at Maguire, with Michael again looking for answers.

"Maguire, what's he fucking talking about?"

Maguire this time gave no answer, as the blood rushed into his cheeks and face, showing his discomfort. But things were about to get a lot worse for him, because Eli wasn't stopping there.

"I'm talking, young Michael Flynn, about one of the biggest informants that the British Government has ever had on the inside of the IRA."

"Ah, that's bullshit," said Dermot in disbelief. "Maguire working for the Brits? I don't believe it."

"I fucking do," said Sean. "I can believe anything of that fucker."

"What's wrong, Dermot?" asked Eli. "Does it twist your guts to think that the man who's been giving you your orders all these years is a paid tout for the British?"

"Shut the fuck up," Maguire ranted at Eli, his shout revealing the desperation in his voice. A silence fell on the group as they tried to come to terms with what was being said. None of them wanted to believe it, but why would Maguire be telling an SAS soldier to shut up?

"He was nearly caught once in the past," Eli continued as though on a roll. "One of your own got close to him."

"What the fuck are you saying?" Maguire again ranted. "You're ruining everything." Frantically, he looked at Michael and then back at Eli, still in disbelief that he was being outed. "You've gone too far, you stupid bastard. Now we have no choice but to kill them."

All the lads turned their heads at Maguire's words, especially the word 'we', which implied that he and the soldiers were pissing in the same pot. And the part about killing them seemed suddenly to be imminent, as Eli pulled a 9mm Browning handgun from his overcoat pocket. Maguire, at the same time, moved his hand towards the pocket where he had earlier reached for his weapon, as though he was going to join in with what was coming next.

"Ah ah," said Eli, shaking his head. "I'll take that." Walking over to Maguire, he stopped short of the pool of blood and retrieved the weapon, before reversing back to his position and turning to face Michael to deliver the killer revelation.

"You see, you've been vexing your anger in the wrong direction all these years, young Flynn." He paused for a moment after his words, which added even more tension to the situation, but it wasn't Eli's intention to do so. He had paused, because he knew that what he was about to say was going to rip Michael's heart right out of his chest.

"It wasn't our lot that did for your father all those years ago. There was no SAS ambush. There wasn't even a soldier in Drumintee that day, just your father and Maguire. We only came in later to provide the cover story."

A moment passed, before Michael's eyes pierced Maguire's, who lowered his gaze and hung his head in shame.

"Say something, Maguire," Michael shouted, almost pleading for him to prove Eli wrong. "Tell me that this cunt is a lying British bastard. MAGUIRE, SAY SOMETHING!"

Maguire was startled by Michael shouting his demand. His eyes began to pool, as his lower lip began to quiver at the realisation that the revelation of his past had been revealed.

"Go on, Benny. Tell them," Eli continued, goading Maguire almost as though he had a deep hatred for him himself. "Tell them what a great servant you've been to the cause. Tell young Flynn that when you shot his father that you did it for the greater good of the Irish people and not to save your own skin."

Maguire stared back at Eli with his own hatred in his eyes, as if he were the one being betrayed. He moved his look to Michael, but immediately wished he hadn't.

"You shot my father."

Michael's quiet words fell from his lips with such gentle disbelief that if he were to say them softly enough, the situation may simply disappear. Maguire attempted to respond but nothing emerged from his mouth. Anything he said he knew would be received as futile and inadequate. He raised his hand to his brow, wiping away the perspiration that was forming as quickly as his discomfort grew. His finger and thumb crossed his eyes, while dragging their lids to the bridge of his nose, before releasing a sigh of admittance.

"I'm sorry, lad," he said in a sobbing voice. "They had things on me. I was a young man when I first got caught. I couldn't get out and I just got deeper and deeper into their grip. They threatened me with twenty years or worse, they were going to out me to the organisation."

Maguire, against his better judgement, was trying to offer some kind of excuse, as though it would make a difference to what he had done.

"You shot my father," Michael repeated, more sterner this time, forcing the veins in his neck to protrude, while stiffening his stance. Eli, seeing his eagerness to confront, interceded with more information.

"You see, Maguire wasn't caught doing IRA business—precisely the opposite in fact. No, he was caught running drugs and they didn't take kindly to any of that shit in those days."

Michael stood deflated and drained by what he was hearing. A tear ran down his right cheek into the corner of his mouth, which he collected with his tongue. He savoured the taste, as though it was flavoured with all his heartaches and anger. A rush of experiences and memories exploded in his mind, too numerous to contemplate, combined with a gut-wrenching and leg-weakening realisation that the man who had killed his father had been within his grasp for the past fourteen years. Big Danny's hand fell on his shoulder with a comforting and steadying grip, bringing Michael back to his senses with a vengeance.

"And my father got too close to you, so you shot him. You fucking informing, collaborating bastard, Maguire."

"Your father didn't know everything," interrupted Eli, knowing Michael was understandably about to snap. "If he had, Maguire would never have got the drop on him that day. The problem was that he knew Maguire was dealing in drugs, but he had no idea that we had already caught him and that he was one of our touts, feeding us information. He arranged for it to be just them two in the car that morning, so that he could confront Maguire and give him the opportunity to turn over a new leaf before Stanton, their captain at the time, found out. That's also the reason why your father didn't pick up Mactazner that day for their trip to Drumintee. Your father knew that Big Davy would blow the whistle if he found out. Davy Mactazner's not exactly a fan of yours, is he, Benny?"

Eli looked back at Maguire, whose silence said it all.

"But how do you know all this? How do you know my father wasn't going to turn him in?"

Michael needed to know the truth—to find out after all these years that his father's life was taken by one of their own wasn't an easy thing to accept and, to understand it, he needed all the answers.

"We know all this because Maguire told us. You see, your father didn't know he was armed. In those days, none of the IRA players carried weapons until they were doing a job because we had the power to stop and search them any time we wanted. The difference was that every time we searched Maguire, we overlooked the weapon we knew he was carrying. You see, all our touts carried weapons, just in case they were sussed. Why should your father worry, anyway? After all, he was doing Maguire a favour. He didn't expect to get shot in the back for trying to give a man a second chance."

Michael's eye's flicked across to Maguire when hearing his father was shot in the back. Eli continued his story, bringing the young man's attention back to him.

"He offered to stand by Maguire, so long as he cleaned up his act and stayed away from the drugs but Maguire here, with his habit, didn't fancy that and, thinking that the rest of his secrets may come out, panicked and shot Finbar in the back. He didn't even have the balls to look your father in the eyes." Eli now returned his gaze towards Maguire, showing his own disapproval of the man. "And what did you get for it, Benny? What did you get for betraying and killing a man whose boots you couldn't fill or lace?"

Maguire again raised his head, his face showing the extent of his shame.

"To this day," Eli continued, "nobody likes you. You've still got the same old habit and the drugs you took made your hair fall out."

Tears rolled down Michael's face, as Eli's portrayal of his father's death cut to his heart like a knife. But still Eli hadn't finished.

"After he had killed your father, he hid his body in the bushes then drove to a phone box to call us. He explained what had happened and we came up with the cover story of your father being shot in an ambush. The sad part was that we had to shoot your father twice more with a rifle to make it look like he had been shot by us and not once with a small calibre handgun. After that, we simply held back the body for a couple of weeks, to make it impossible for the civilian coroner, who we knew Sinn Féin would employ, to tell the difference. All we had to do then was make sure the press releases confirmed Maguire's story and we kept our man on the inside."

Michael, wiping his cheek, was almost numbed by the information being revealed. Words weren't easy to muster, but he had to know the whole of it, no matter how painful it was.

"You said it was a sad thing to shoot my father. Why would it be sad for you?"

Eli sighed, knowing that what he was about to say would hurt Michael even more.

"Because Finbar Flynn didn't deserve to have his body mutilated like that, especially to cover up for a mug like Maguire. Your father was intelligent and he played by the rules. He would have made a brilliant soldier."

"There are those that would say he *was* a brilliant soldier," Michael replied proudly, with a choky voice.

"And I wouldn't disagree with them if they did, but if it hadn't have been Maguire that killed him, it would have been us eventually."

"How do you know you would have got to him? You said yourself he was good at his job."

"Because we would have had no choice—your father was that much of a threat. While other members of the IRA and the INLA were all running around disorganised, kneecapping and shooting who they wanted, your father was picking targets that would do the most damage to the security forces. And, worse than that, he wasn't telling anybody what his plans were, which made our job very difficult. He was a maverick, but an organised one—your father was no loose cannon. The tactics he was employing, if taken on by the rest of the organisation, had the potential to change the troubles in Northern Ireland in the IRA's favour. Luckily, though, we had another man on the inside whose information put an end to some of his more sophisticated plans but he wasn't one of our touts, so the intelligence was fed to us internally. But believe me when I tell you, young Flynn, that your father had ideas well above the IRA's punching weight at that time, ideas that weren't ambitions—they were feasible and achievable targets that he had the knowledge to turn into reality. We knew he was destined for the top and we could never have allowed him to get there. We prefer the idiots to get the top jobs, people we have something on, like Maguire over there. But the problem with him was that nobody liked him—it wasn't just Mactazner. His face didn't fit wherever they placed him. That's why he was left as a captain all these years, looking after your ASU. Imagine if he had been any good—we could have had a top man in the ranks of Sinn Féin by now."

Michael again turned his hate-filled stare at Maguire, who was still trying to snivel his way out by offering feeble excuses.

"It wasn't like that, Michael. I never meant for it to happen. It was those Brit bastards; they had me jumping through hoops. Your dad was no fool. He knew something wasn't right, so they ordered me to do it."

As usual, Maguire's words and pleadings amounted to nothing more than lies and thoughts of himself. Even the crocodile tears that ran down his face couldn't go in a straight line. His crooked life and dealings were all returning to haunt him in one fell swoop and there was nothing he could do to prevent it. Michael could look at him no longer for the fear of what he might do. The soldiers had him covered and although the thought of getting his hands around his throat just once before he died was enough, he still had to think that the burst of fire that killed him could also do for his friends.

"Why, why would you tell me all this now?" Michael looked at Eli with anger, frustration and gritted teeth. "You're obviously going to kill us so why would you put me through it, you sick fucker. You must be the biggest bastard in the British Army." Michael turned back to Maguire, unable to hide his tears. Tears that were not for himself but for his mother and a younger brother who had been denied the chance to ever meet his father. He searched for the strong words he needed to smite Maguire for what he had done.

"You took my father from me and my mother, who was carrying his unborn child, and all because you couldn't do a bit of time in jail for some drugs. And your way of showing remorse these past fourteen years was to put me and my mates through as much shit as you could."

Michael couldn't keep his restraint any longer. *Fuck it. They're going to kill us all anyway,* he thought to himself as he started to lunge for Maguire, thinking exactly that. That this would be his last chance before Eli ended it for all of them.

BANG!

A shot rang out from Eli's weapon, stopping Michael in mid-flight from his intended assault. The deafening echoes of the fired gun bounced around the warehouse, repeating several times before fading to nothing. Michael, disorientated by the noise, looked down at his body. He knew he hadn't been hit, so he immediately turned to his friends to check on them. Seeing all were okay, he followed the stare from their shock-filled faces in the direction of Maguire, who was rolling about the floor, screaming and clutching a fresh gaping wound. The round from Eli's weapon had entered his leg, shattering his kneecap, and exited downwards, taking off his shoe and with it his toe. Michael looked at the gun in Eli's hand and then back at Maguire and his bloodied patella and mangled foot.

The situation was now about as confusing as it could ever possibly get. He believed it was him and the lads that were going to get the bullet, not the collaborator. Maguire's screams and curses directed at Eli were like music to the ears of the four Irish lads. Broad smiles beamed across their faces as they watched him squirm in agony, almost forgetting in their glee that they were next—an ending that seemed to be once again imminent, as Eli turned and pointed his weapon in their direction. The smiles fell from their faces, expecting the worse, but Eli's next move was something none of them could have foreseen. He removed the magazine from its housing, sending the evening into the Twilight Zone, as he offered the Browning to Michael.

"There's one in the chamber," he said with his hand outstretched. Michael couldn't believe what he was seeing or hearing and looked behind him at the other three for support. With the only advice being offered coming from a shrug of their shoulders, he turned back to Eli, who only had one thing to say.

"Shoot him," he said, looking down at the weapon.

"Fuck you," refused Michael. "Is this some sort of sick SAS joke? Watching Paddies kill each other?"

Eli, stern in his stance, outstretched his arm further.

"I'm offering you the chance before you die to avenge your father. I'm not playing games and this is no joke."

Michael looked at Eli's face and saw no sign of jest. Once again, he looked back at his three mates, searching for a little more guidance than he had previously received.

"SHOOT THE BASTARD!" yelled Sean, wishing the gun had been offered to him.

"Go on, Michael. He deserves it," seconded Dermot. Lastly, he looked at Big Danny, his friend and confidant, who simply nodded, sealing Maguire's fate.

"And another thing," added Eli, with the final piece to the jigsaw. "It was us that ordered Maguire to come to London. Well, when I say 'us', I mean British Intelligence, but it was on my advice. We knew all about the Yardie's visit to Kilburn because we were watching and we knew that the Belfast boys were planning to send somebody over, so we told Maguire to volunteer if he got the chance. He thinks it was all part of a plan to get him over here, so he could keep us informed with what Sinn Féin and the IRA will be up to this Easter, which he has already done. But *I* had another reason for wanting him close.

"You dirty bastard," yelled Maguire from his squirming position on the floor.

"Well, seeing as how you all think that I'm a bastard, I might as well be one."

BANG!! Another shot was fired from Eli's weapon, the round this time entering Maguire's right arm.

"AARGH," he cried. "You fucking double-crossing British bastard."

"Yeah, yeah, Maguire, I'm a bastard, it's unanimous. Now shut the fuck up or I'll put the next one

7P's

in your fucking Jacobs." Eli replaced the magazine in the weapon then cocked it to reload before pointing it towards Maguire's balls, or his cream crackers, as he would call them in his rhyming slang. The movement had the desired effect, because the rest of his cursing was done through tightened lips.

"What we didn't bring him over here for, however," Eli continued "was for him to do a deal with our drug-dealing friend Allan and try to have you four topped while lining his own pockets. And he had no intentions of keeping you alive—dead men tell no tales. He would have probably killed those other two mugs as well, if the Yardie hadn't done it for him. He would have had a nice life, old Benny, with all that money in some far-off sunny place, while you four were feeding the fishes down the estuary."

Eli's confirmation of what the lads already suspected truly was the final piece in the puzzle. Once again, he released the magazine from its housing, leaving a single shot in the chamber, and outstretched his hand.

"Do him, and then we'll talk about who's a bastard,"

Eli's voice once again changed into a sterner, more order-like tone as his eyes fell to the weapon in his hand. Michael slowly, but showing no sign of nerves, took the Browning, watched by the two remaining troopers, who raised their weapons just in case he decided to send the shot their boss's way and not Maguire's. He turned towards his target and aimed the gun at his head. Maguire, in his last pitched attempt for sympathy, looked past the muzzle and down the length of the weapon into Michael's eyes, searching for a glimpse of forgiveness that he knew he wouldn't find. His whole body trembled as he realised he was about to pay the ultimate price for his betrayal of a comrade and friend. Michael could have said a thousand things. A million thoughts were running through his head, but none of them would have brought his father back. He thought about using the weapon as a club and beating him to death to vent his anger in a more satisfactory manner, but in the end he simply squeezed the trigger, firing the shot into Maguire's face, which sent the back of his head skidding along the concrete floor of the warehouse.

Michael paused in his position for a moment, arm outstretched with weapon in hand, viewing the body, which lay lifeless between the two others, Maguire's blood now mixing with theirs on the floor, forming one large pool of retribution. The echoes of the shot bounced off the walls of the warehouse, followed by absolute silence as Michael's thoughts now turned to his father and his graveside memories.

"Is there another one for you?" he asked, turning to Eli. "You were there. Did you fire any of those shots into my dead father's back?"

"No, lad. I had no part in that, but if I had been ordered to, I would. It was—and for the moment still is—my job."

Michael accepted Eli's frank words and returned the now-empty Browning to its owner. Eli paused for a moment, in which time he gave all the Irish lads a look in the eyes, as though contemplating a move.

"What was the other reason?" asked Michael, still wanting information before he met his own end.

"The reason for what?"

"The other reason you wanted Maguire over here, besides the information he was supplying."

"Oh, that," remembered Eli, as though it was something he had missed from his shopping list. "That's simple. I brought him over here to kill him." With a smile of accomplishment, he turned his head and looked down at Maguire and the rest of the trio of bodies. "Errol, what are you doing out there?" he shouted, as he replaced the magazine in his weapon, cocked it and applied the safety catch before putting it in his pocket. The SAS trooper ran at the double, back into the warehouse from the outside. He looked at Maguire's semi-headless body, before turning to Eli with some words of warning.

"I hope they sign that agreement next week, because we are going to struggle for information now if they don't."

"Never mind that, you soppy mug. Where's the fucking Range Rover?" Eli looked towards the doors as though the vehicle was going to drive itself inside.

"You never told me to bring the motor in," replied Errol with a shrug of his shoulders.

7P's

"Well, I didn't expect you to leave it outside with all that fucking money in it, so some fucking twocking teenager can 'ave it away."

Eli shook his head and Errol shook his back, each blaming the other for the break in communication. Eli turned his attention to his two other men, who were still standing guard.

"You two, get those fucking balaclavas off and put those bodies in the back of the van. The SBS boys can get rid of them later. Well, come on then. Move it. Chop fucking chop—you're not civilians yet."

The troopers jumped into action, carrying out Eli's orders. Eli himself was now looking back at Errol, wondering what he was still doing in front of him.

"Well, go on then. You as well. Go get the Range Rover. I don't know where your head is today, Errol, I really don't."

The four Irishmen looked at each other, wondering what the fuck was going on. The mood had changed, almost relaxed, and no one was covering them with any weapons. No one was even watching them. Sean began to slide his left hand down the front of his tracksuit bottoms in search of one of the weapons.

"Do we go for it now?" he whispered from the corner of his mouth.

Michael tilted his wrist and slowly lowered his gaze to look at his watch. It was nine thirty. In twenty minutes, their little surprise in the money bag was going to make an appearance with a bang, and after watching Errol walk out with it ten minutes earlier, he was now on his way to bring it back.

"Wait. Don't do anything yet," Michael answered, when hearing the returning vehicle behind them. He knew that to give themselves and their plan any chance of success that they needed all the soldiers in one place, and in view. He watched as Errol parked the vehicle alongside them before climbing out and walking to their front to help the other two soldiers with the bodies. "Good, now where's their boss," he thought to himself. Eli was now at the vehicle, opening the rear door, and when he stuck his head inside, the perfect opportunity had arrived. Michael knew that this was the best chance they were going to get, confirmed as Eli leant further inside, reaching for the zipper on one of the bags.

"Now, Sean. Slowly," Michael gave the go-ahead. It was now or never. Sean got his hand around the pistol grip of one of the weapons and began to make his move.

"SEAN KEENAN," Eli shouted with his back to the lads and his head still inside the Range Rover. "STAND FUCKING STILL." Sean froze, wondering how the fuck he knew. Eli pulled himself out and faced the lads with four bundles of money in his hands.

"That's exactly where I would have hidden them," he said with his cigar between his teeth. "Don't worry, I'm not psychic. We've had your flat bugged for months. I was listening to you earlier, preparing for the meeting. Mind you, we did struggle a bit to keep tabs on you when you were outside the flat making arrangements by phone. That was Flynn's fault, though, for being so in love with his lady Roisin and not ringing that Trudy bird from the club. Obviously, the number didn't belong to her—it was one of ours. You would have just got an answer machine and we would have got your number. Then we could have listened in any time we wanted." Again, the lads felt out of their depth, realising how far they had dropped their guard.

"That Trudy bird from the club," Michael asked, wondering if he had been taken in there also. "Does she work for you?"

"Nah," replied Eli. "What I told you in the Rose that night was the truth, apart from me trying it on with her. I'm a happily married man. Anyway, the night after I saw you, I went back in trying to suss things out and she gave me her number to give to you after seeing us talking the night before. You must have left a right impression on her. Anyway, I decided to use this to our advantage and switched the numbers, but you never rang her, you love sick mug." Michael smiled, glad that the girl was genuine, and glad that he had stayed faithful to Roisin.

"Catch," said Eli, throwing the bundles of money at them, one each. Again, they looked at each other, gobsmacked. Now it was really getting weird.

"What the fuck is your game? What are you up to?" Michael asked, staring at the wad in his hand.

"Why? Would you rather be with Maguire and his two goons in the back of the van?" Michael didn't have to answer that one. That was definitely a rhetorical question. But he was confused after Eli's earlier comment.

"A moment ago, you offered me the chance to avenge my father before I died."

"And die you shall, as we all will. Death and taxes, as they say—the only two things in life you can be sure of. But not today, young Flynn. Today's not the day for any of you to depart this mortal coil."

The lads once again couldn't believe what they were hearing. Blank stares and open mouths filled their faces as they each looked at each other as though looking in a mirror.

"Look," said Eli, taking the cigar from his mouth and leaning on the back of the Rover. "You heard what Errol said. Next week, on the ninth of April, they're going to sign that treaty they've been talking about for the last twenty years. They're going to call it 'The Good Friday Agreement'."

"So, after all the ceasefires, peace talks and voting, it's finally going to happen," said Danny, with slight disbelief.

"It's finally happening," confirmed Eli. "Even President Clinton is getting involved, to make sure nothing fucks up. It's all been sorted out."

"So, where does that leave us, Eli, if that is your real name, and why the money?"

"Eli is my real name, young Michael. I don't hide behind pseudonyms or soubriquets, and where it leaves us, gentlemen, is finished. It's over. After next week, there is no more *me* and *you*. If we're not at war, then there is no war, conflict or Troubles—it's over. I'm a soldier, not a murderer. We're not going to kill you for the sake of a week. You lads have never killed any of our lot anyway. Well, apart from Maguire now. But as far as I'm concerned, there's no score there to settle. Sure, you did plenty of sabotage work, but you were only following orders as soldiers, just the same as us, so we won't hold that against you."

It had been a day for looking at each other in search of answers and, once again, the Irish lads repeated the movement, unable to believe that they were going to walk away from this situation alive.

"So, do you still think I'm a bastard?" Eli had to get that one in. Which pleased him greatly as he let go another smile and had another puff.

"You killed Maguire," added Danny. "Why not us?"

"That wanker needed killing. He was a grass. I couldn't leave him alive—he would have opened his gob about me doing the deal with the Yardie."

"We know about your deal with the Yardie."

Eli grinned at Danny's words.

"Yeah, Danny, I know you do, but you're not grasses, are ya?" Eli smiled and so did Danny. "Anyway, as I said, it was Flynn that blew his fucking brains out, not me. I only gave him a limp." Eli once again gave them all a cheesy grin. "Listen, lads, a good soldier knows when to kill and when not to kill. Besides, I have need of you in the future. Somewhere down the line, I've got some work for you lot. A bit of private enterprise."

"Fuck me," muttered Sean under his breath. "He wants us to boldly go where no man has gone before."

"I said PRIVATE enterprise, Fatty, not starship. Now, wind your fucking neck in." Sean received an elbow in the ribs from his big brother, to go with the bollocking from Eli. "It means doing a bit for ourselves. We might as well—we're all being laid out to pasture by our old employers. You see that's what we've all been getting up to these last few weeks, and that's what's needed in the future—a bit of private enterprise. Look, the way you lads knocked over that nightclub was sweet as a nut. My lads and I couldn't have done it any better. Ok, you were a bit sloppy with the one fatality, but you've got to expect the odd casualty now and then."

"So, you're going to let us go with ten grand each and, in the near future, you're going to be calling on us to do a bit of work for you?"

"That's right. But if you've got a problem with that then the van is still outside. I think there's still room left next to Maguire for four more."

"I've got no problem with it," announced Sean, not

fancying the alternative. "But could you possibly see your way to making it twenty grand each?"

Eli tilted his head with a 'don't push it' look, as Sean got another elbow from his brother.

"Well, if you don't ask..." said Sean with a shrug of his shoulders.

The Irish lads were in no position to refuse. In fact, they were beginning to admire Eli for his outlook. But the four of them couldn't help thinking that Jeremy Beadle would show up at any moment. Eli could see they still needed more convincing, so he gave them a bit more of an explanation.

"Come on, lads. Think about it," he said closing the rear doors of the motor. "The Yardie's got his gear and he's off your case. You didn't want the stuff anyway and neither do we—none of us are fucking drug dealers. Plus the lads and I get a hundred grand tickle every month for as long as our new Caribbean friend lives—and believe me, that fucker will get a telegram from the Queen if I've got anything to do with it. Also, my lads and I have got a bag full of dosh to split and you four are walking out of here, *alive* and with your bus fare home." Eli was obviously a *Bullseye* fan. "And the beauty of it all is that the only grassing fucker that can connect all this together is lying in the back of the van with a 9mm lodged between his mince pies. Now, fuck off and go see your families, and Dermot, I was only joking about Greasy Deasy. She seems like a nice girl, but I would still get that blood test if I was you—she has been known to put it about a bit!"

"What's the point?" Dermot thought to himself. He might as well just accept that his life was an open book.

Errol came back into the room, giving his report on their progress.

"The lads have loaded the bodies and they are on their way. It's time we were making tracks, too."

He climbed into the driver's seat of the Range Rover and started the engine ready to move. Eli nodded and extinguished his cigar butt under his foot, before picking it up and placing it in his pocket.

"DNA—it's the future," he said, explaining his actions before climbing into the passenger seat. "I'll see you soon then, chaps. Don't be hanging around here too long. You never know if the local plod might come moseying after all that gunfire. You don't want to be getting caught around here with all that claret and brains on the ground, especially with what Fatty's carrying down his trousers."

Eli gave them all a smile before putting a fresh cigar in his mouth and instructing Errol to drive off. The lads all looked at each other, trying to make a quick decision, but it was Big Danny who gave Michael the push to stop the vehicle.

"ELI! STOP!" shouted Michael, chasing the Rover and banging on its rear.

Errol hit his brakes and stopped the car. Michael opened the rear door, unzipped one of the bags and dug his hand deep inside. From underneath the money he pulled out the block of C4 with a detonator attached. He approached Eli's window and eased the detonator out of the explosive, disconnecting the TPU.

Eli looked across at Errol and then back at Michael.

"How long did we have?" he quizzed.

"About three and a half minutes," replied Michael, looking at the clock on the TPU.

"I hope my new partner Allan's not got the same surprise?"

"No, we only had the one piece of C4. We figured Maguire had done the deal for the money, so we thought it only right that he should have it."

"You're a slippery bastard, young Flynn," Eli said meaning it as a compliment. "There you go, Errol, a man that uses his 'seven Ps', not like you, ya gormless git. You can't even check a fucking bag!"

"You didn't tell me to check the bag. Just like you didn't tell me earlier to fetch the Rover inside."

"You just can't get the staff," Eli complained, while smiling and giving Michael a wink.

"What the fuck are the seven Ps?" Michael asked curiously.

Again, Eli smiled, this time reminiscing on the many hundreds of times he had screamed them at the soldiers under his command.

"What are the seven Ps? The soldier's bible, my son, after his marksmanship principles, that is: Prior Preparation and Planning Prevents a Piss Poor Performance."

Michael laughed at the phrase, and as he repeated it in his head, he could see the sense in it.

"So how does it feel?" asked Eli.

"How does what feel?" replied Michael.

"How does it feel to have avenged the death of your father?"

Michael paused to think about the question, but he had no idea. Nothing about tonight had sunk in yet, but he still answered.

"It feels good, Thanks."

"It was my pleasure. But why did you stop us from driving away? Notching up a couple of regiment boys would have been a nice feather in your cap."

Michael had never even thought about that and was actually glad that he hadn't.

"Like you said, it's over. I didn't think it was possible, but in the last twenty minutes, you've obviously convinced me and the lads of that."

Eli smiled at Michael's answer and, without talking, gave each of the Irish lads a look of approval, knowing that his decision to leave them alive had been the right one. Michael joined him, thinking the same, as Eli enlightened him a little more.

"You might not realise it, but by doing what you just did, you just saved your own lives."

"How so?" asked Michael.

"Because, like I said, your flat's wired for sound. I heard all the plans you made earlier. I knew all about the bomb. If you had let us leave this warehouse without saying anything, I would have defused it and returned to put you lot in Maguire's taxi."

"You were testing us."

"Seven Ps, young Flynn. Learn them, digest them and don't forget them. You can never be caught off your guard if you are prepared for what's coming." Eli tilted his head, waiting for Michael to acknowledge that he understood what he was saying before adding a few more words of wisdom. "Most men have the luxury of being able to walk around each day with their head in the clouds. But men like you and I, young Flynn, we don't. We can never be caught off guard or unprepared. 7P's." Michael nodded in response. "Right then, I think I better take that." Eli took the explosive and placed the detonator in his pocket, before chucking the now-dormant C4 over his shoulder onto the back seat and rubbing his hands to remove the specs of cement dust that had transferred on to them. He turned again to look at Dermot while still rubbing a few particles between his finger and thumb. "That was a nice sneaky little trick you had worked out with the C4 and the cement. I might use that one myself in the future." Dermot smiled in acknowledgment of the praise of his idea. "Right," continued Eli. "I'll see you sometime in O'Reilly's Bar. Fatty, it'll be your round—BE LUCKY!"

Errol and Eli disappeared through the double doors, with Eli's usual goodbye leaving the four Irish lads alone.

Call it being put back, gobsmacked, shocked or just in contemplation, but the lads were experiencing it all as they watched them leave in an air of wonder.

"Does anybody have a fucking clue about what just went on?" asked Dermot, who looked around the now-empty warehouse, which showed no signs of the night's events, apart from a very large pool of blood that contained at least three types of DNA.

Michael and Danny weren't offering any explanations, but Sean was never lost for a smart answer.

"I do," he declared. "We came here to get done in by a Caribbean drug dealer and a collaborating Irish bastard who turned out to be the fucker that murdered Michael's father fourteen years ago. Our lives were saved by a truck-driving SAS man who talks in rhyming slang and will soon be leaving the army to go into the nightclub business, God help Peter fucking Stringfellow. Then, sometime in the future—when, we don't know—he will be calling on us to do something involving Captain Kirk! We're walking away with ten grand each, Greasy Deasy's baby could turn out to be that Errol fella's and I'm fucking starving. Now, shut the fuck up and let's take ye man Eli's advice and get the fuck out of here."

Sean's summing up of the situation as usual was crude, but swift and accurate.

"Sean's right," said Danny. "Let's put some distance between this place and the four of us."

They exited through the same double doors, cautiously and slightly paranoid, still looking around themselves for any more surprises that the night might yet bring. Sean removed the two handguns from his Y-fronts before they all climbed into the car. He put the key in the ignition, but didn't turn it, still in the paranoid zone.

"Just start the car, Fatty," said Dermot finally sick of worrying. "They would have shot us if they had wanted us dead, not gone to all the trouble of putting a bomb under the car, and it would be a silly waste of the forty grand that they just gave us."

Sean turned the key with his eyes shut tight, then opened them with a smile at the sound of the engine and not an explosion, despite Dermot's words of wisdom, though they must have all been a little nervous because together they all jumped when the alarms on their watches sounded. Simultaneously and quickly, they reached for the off-buttons and breathed a sigh of relief. If things had gone differently, it could easily have been the time of their own deaths, give or take six seconds.

"I've had enough of this night," said Dermot, with his hand on his chest, feeling his palpitations. "Let's go somewhere where there are no Jamaican drug dealers, no IRA grasses and definitely no undercover SAS wagon-driving, sneaky-beaky bastards."

"Where *are* we going, by the way?" asked Sean, through his giggles. "All our gear's in the boot and we posted the keys for the digs back through the letterbox."

"Don't worry about that," Big Danny said, throwing his ten-grand bundle into the air before catching in again. "We can afford a decent hotel tonight. At least we got away with nearly half the money we went after in the first place."

"Chelsea Harbour," declared Michael out of the blue.

"Chelsea fucking Harbour? What the fu...?"

"Don't ask, Fatty," said Michael cutting him short. "Just take us to Chelsea Harbour and all will be revealed."

Chapter Twenty-Three

Chelsea Harbour

The road to Chelsea Harbour was a journey filled with giggles and laughter. Their spirits were high and why not? They had just looked death in the face and walked away. They say life begins at forty, but for these four, it began an hour previously when they walked out of that warehouse. Everything from that point on was now a bonus. They were proud of each other and themselves. None of them had bottled it. They had stuck together as they always did and come through the other side, but while the other three joked and patted each other on the back, Michael just sat quietly in the passenger seat, listening to his friends' jokes with an unusual, smug, contented look on his face.

"I hope there's a bar in this place. I'm fucking parched."

"Don't worry, Danny Boy. There's a cold Guinness in the fridge," informed Michael.

"It must be a posh hotel, if there are fridges in the rooms. I'm going to get rat-arsed on the miniatures."

"There's no hotel room and no miniatures. Just drive the car, Fatty." Michael was playing his cards very close to his chest as to what the lads would find at Chelsea Harbour.

"Where the fuck are we going, Michael? What's the big secret? Haven't we had enough surprises already this evening?"

"Just another five minutes, Danny Boy. Then, as I said, all will be revealed."

"Well, I hope there's some food in that fridge, because I'm fucking starving."

"Like I said, Fatty, just a few more minutes. Less, in fact, because here we are." Michael, noticing the signs for the harbour entrance, pointed it out to Sean. "Pull in here and drive down to the end of the car park. I'll tell you where to stop."

Sean did as instructed and they were soon parked up in a space at the far end of the marina. They all exited the vehicle, each taking an appreciative breath of fresh air as they surveyed their surroundings in the cool evening breeze.

"Okay, fellas. Take everything you need from the car because we won't be coming back."

"What do you mean we won't be coming back? What about the car?" asked Sean. "Just because we have ten grand each, it doesn't mean we can go chucking good cars away. I bet I could get at least fifteen hundred quid for it at the auctions."

"Sean, just leave the car where it is. The brakes don't work, anyway. It's lucky we haven't killed anyone."

"It's okay, now, I've sorted that out."

"You mean you've had them fixed."

"No, I've made the horn louder."

Sean gave Michael a wink to go with yet another

punchline. Michael agreed it was funny, but the car was staying put.

"If it makes you feel any better, we'll post the keys to Davy, so he can use it after he's had the brakes fixed. Anyway, I have something else for you to drive."

"Fuck this, Michael. Can you not just tell us what is going on?"

"Bear with me, Dermot. Have I ever put you wrong?"

The other three all looked at Michael in disbelief at his words after what they had just gone through. Michael, who had already started walking, stopped when noticing the silence and absence of the others behind him. He turned to see the looks upon their faces.

"Okay, forget I said that. But I promise you, this time the surprise is a good one. Now, just bring your stuff and follow me down the quay."

What did they have to lose? The night couldn't get any freakier, but with Michael, you never could tell. They followed him as he had asked, walking along the marina and the water's edge until he stopped at the foot of a gangplank.

"Here we are," he said, raising his arm and supporting a large smile.

"Where, what?" asked Sean. "We're stood in the middle of a freezing cold marina and I'm fucking hungry."

"Here," Michael repeated. This time he pointed at a boat that was moored in front of them.

"It's a boat," blurted Dermot, pointing out the obvious.

"No, Dermot. It's our boat," Michael corrected, before setting off walking up the gangplank with a spring in his step.

"Fuck me. You're joking!" Sean shouted, following, with Dermot and Danny close behind, both of them lost for words and now sporting smiles of their own.

The three of them watched as Michael walked to the front of the vessel and bent down to where, hidden on the bottom rail, barely visible, a piece of fishing line was tied. Michael pulled the wire from the water, eventually revealing a set of keys attached to the end. He held them up in front of himself with a big grin on his face as the drops of water fell to the floor. Snapping them from the line, he walked over to the cabin door. With the first key, he removed a security bar, and with another he opened the door. Sean rushed in all excited, immediately making for the wheel.

"This is the fucking dog's bollocks!" he said.

"The thing is, my fat pie-eating friend, can you drive it?" asked Michael.

"You don't drive it, you steer it," Sean corrected, "and of course I fucking can. Danny and me were brought up on the old fella's shrimper when we lived in Wicklow."

"I didn't know that," said Michael, while giving Dermot a sarcastic look, both having been put through numerous fishermen's tales by the brothers since they were teenagers.

"Michael, just stop a moment, will you, and tell us what the fuck is going on. How much was the boat for a start? We've only got forty grand between us."

"Don't worry, Danny Boy. We can afford it. In fact, we already own it."

"But how?" asked Dermot, joining the cross-examination. "We gave all the money back. All we have is the ten grand Eli gave us and fuck knows what he'll have us doing for that."

"No, Dermot. We gave half of it back."

"But I saw the bags myself when I put in the C4. They were full to the top."

"And that's exactly how they were supposed to look. What do you think I was doing all day while you and Danny were watching the club? I knew if it looked that way and it was all in bundles that they wouldn't bother unwrapping it all to count it. So, I rewrapped all the money loosely in ten-grand rolls. Ye see, it was nagging at me all day after the phone call with Davy that Maguire might have done a deal with the Yardie for the money, which was confirmed later when he made us bring the bags to the warehouse so he could have us killed. Otherwise, he'd just have taken the bags when he first caught up with us."

"Why didn't you tell us?"

"I couldn't, Danny. It wasn't that I thought you may

not go through with the meeting if you knew Maguire was definitely going to try to kill us; it was because if you had known there was only half of the money there when it came to opening the bags, one of you may have given it away with the look on your faces."

"What about you? You knew."

"I just kept thinking of our families being looked after with a few quid. You see, once the bomb had gone off and blown Maguire and the other half of the money to smithereens, no one would have been any the wiser."

"Fuck me. That Eli was right—you are a slippery bastard," Danny remarked.

"So, how much was in the bags we took to the warehouse?" Sean asked, climbing down from the wheel.

"Half a million."

Three shocked faces stared back in amazement.

"So, if that was half the money, that means we've still got five hundred thousand ourselves." Dermot winced, almost scared to say it in case it wasn't true.

"Well, give or take a few quid," confirmed Michael. "The boat was fifty grand and there's fifty grand for

Davy Mactazner for a drink. Then there's a few other little bits plus the Guinness I bought to fill up the fridge. Oh, and I sent that Trudy bird fifty grand."

"Who," said the other three?

"The girl I met when casing the club." Michael looked at his mates, who seemed a little lost.

"Why," asked Dermot.

"I don't know. I didn't fall soft, or do it for any ulterior motive. It just seemed that the girl needed a leg up in life and I suddenly found myself in a position to help." Michael sighed with his arms open wide showing he was being genuine.

"That's good enough for me," said Danny, followed by an accepting nod from the other two.

"But how," again Dermot quizzed. "You tore her number up when Eli gave you it and threw it in the ashtray."

"She gave me her address on the night we talked because she didn't have a phone. Then, when I came here to collect the money I had the same jacket on and found it in my pocket. It made me think about how hard life was for her and that I could do a bit of good with the money before Maguire had us killed. The next thing I knew I was helping her out, looking after our families and coming up with a back-up plan.

"She must have left a good impression on you."

"She did Dermot. In a single mum, struggling to bring up a kid on her own way, nothing else."

"I hope you sent her a note. Fifty grand is a lot of money to fall through the letter box without an explanation of where it came from, and a lot of money to be caught with soon after the place where you work has been robbed.

"I sent a note," confirmed Michael, with a smile and a sigh. As usual, he could always depend on Dermot to point out the flaws. "It simply said. Don't let anyone know about this money. I will never contact you again. Thank you for taking care of my bottle. Have a nice life, and take care of your son Michael."

"You signed the letter."

"No Dermot, I didn't sign the letter. Her young son is called Michael. On the bottom I wrote, Carpe Diem."

"Carp."

"Stop Dermot. Don't ask, it's not fucking important. It was just something between me, and her that she will understand." Michael was tired of the questions and was happy when Sean butted in.

"Well if it felt like the right thing to do, then it was the right thing. Fair play to ye. And, because of her you came up with a plan and here we are stood on our own boat."

"Cheers Sean. I'm just glad she wasn't part of Eli's team though, because if she had of been then he would have known that I had this money hidden."

"Well she wasn't, and he doesn't," remarked Danny rubbing his hands. Now how much have we got."

"Well it works out, with the ten grand you have already, at about a hundred thousand each," Michael paused before his last thought. "Worth sticking your hand down Fatty's knackers for, eh Dermot?"

"You've got some fucking balls."

"Thanks," said Sean.

"Not you, ye fat fuck. Michael."

"Not really, Danny Boy. When Maguire went on about the money and the drugs, he never once mentioned the exact amount, so the Yardie obviously hadn't mentioned it to him. It was then that I thought: 'What if the only man who actually knew how much money there was in the office that night was dead, because you shot the fucker during the robbery?'"

"Good shooting, brother," Sean said, proudly patting Danny on the back.

"I mean, it didn't take a lot of figuring out," Michael continued to explain. "We knew the Rasta was the dealer and that the big man was the bouncer, so the other fella had to be in charge of the accounting."

The other three agreed with his reasoning.

"Okay, so where's the money now?" asked Dermot, immediately catching the keys that Michael threw at him, foreseeing the question coming.

"It's in the cupboard, under the fridge. Throw me a Guinness while you're there."

Michael pointed to the fridge in the corner and to the cupboard beneath it.

Dermot threw each of them a can from the fridge and placed his own on top, before going below, into the cupboard, and pulling out a padlocked box, which he dragged across the floor to their feet. The lock was soon off, using the third key on the bunch, and the lid flipped open to reveal the money. Four big smiles beamed across their faces, as from inside the box, the Queen smiled right back at them, over four hundred thousand times.

'Pssst, pssst, pssst, pssst' was the sound that filled the cabin, as the ring pulls were lifted from the top of their cans, followed by gulping noises. Standing there refreshed on their own boat, staring into the box of money, the lads couldn't help but savour the moment. Apart from Dermot, who had one last worry to get off his chest.

"But how would our families have known about all this if things had gone wrong?"

"I wrote Ma a letter and posted it this morning. It explained everything, where the boat was, the keys on the fishing line and what to do with the money. That reminds me—make sure I ring Roisin later and tell her to intercept the letter. I don't want Ma opening that. I'd never hear the last of it."

"Did you tell her anything about what we had been up to?" asked Dermot.

"No, I just told Roisin to mourn me for a year and then find herself another fella, and I told my mother I loved her and to buy young Peter a horse."

"And the SAS fella thought he was smart, being one step ahead," observed Dermot admiringly. "Fuck me," he added in a startled manner, as he remembered something. "Eli knew about the weapons in Fatty's trousers and he knew about the bomb because he had the flat bugged. What if he knows about the boat?"

Danny and Sean also looked at Michael, realising that Dermot could be right.

"Chill out. I never mentioned the boat in the flat or anywhere else for that matter. You've only just found out about it yourselves and I wasn't followed when I came here to get rid of the weapons. Believe me, I was paranoid as fuck that day. My eyes were never off the rear-view mirror. I got a shock, though, when I turned up here and saw this large marina. They've spent some money on it since I was last here. When I came back the second time, I walked around doing a bit of thinking, while I waited for Davy's call. That's when I saw the 'for sale' sign on this boat. Before I knew it, I was buying it for us and coming up with a damage-limitation plan, to try and get something out of it for our families."

"You did well, Flynn," praised Danny. "It was a good plan and a good buy; she's a beautiful vessel." Michael nodded, appreciating his friends' words of approval.

"Right, Fatty. Start her up. She's fuelled and ready to go. We'll put a few miles under us and park up further down the Thames, where we can get a proper drink and a takeaway. I'm dying for some spare ribs."

"Moor."

"What?"

"You don't park a vessel, you moor it."

"Sean, moor it, park it or shove it up your fucking fat arse. Just let's get out of here."

"I'm just saying. If we're going to be spending time

on a boat, you and Dermot are going to have to learn the correct seafaring terminology. Now, the front is forward, the rear is astern and that side is port..."

"SHUT, THE FUCK, UP!"

The lads pulled away in their new boat from its *mooring* in Chelsea Harbour, heading off towards the estuary in search of a good pub and a Chinese takeaway. The noise of laughter and ring pulls faded, along with the noise of the engine. The wake left behind them calmed and the tranquillity returned to the harbour, as they sailed further and further away.

In the empty berth they had just left, a frogman broke the surface of the water. The diver raised his mask and removed his flippers, before throwing them onto the side of the quay and climbing out.

"Cold enough for you, Harry?" a man said, emerging from the shadows, puffing on a cigar. It was Eli.

"Cold enough. I'm supposed to be down the British Legion tonight, playing darts with the lads."

"Don't worry, Harry. They won't miss you—I've seen you play!" Harry, picking up his flippers, swung them in the air to get rid of the excess water, sending it Eli's way in retaliation at his statement. "You looked like a West Ham fan coming out of that water, blowing bubbles," he added, while dodging the spray with a side step.

"You should try a bit of diving yourself, Eli. Mind you, you'd struggle smoking them cigars down there."

"Ducking and diving, maybe, but that type's not for me, Harry. My feet belong firmly on terra firma."

"That's a right statement for somebody in the Special Air Service to make."

"I jumped out of a plane once—once, and that was enough. I'm better doing my thinking with my feet on the ground, watching other people fall from the sky or getting wet."

"Watching other people doing the hard work, you mean."

"Harry, don't be like that. You could hurt my feelings. Anyway, what have you got for me?"

"I've fitted a standard tracking device upgraded with

a GPS It's attached with a normal limpet clamp, so it should be good for a few months."

"That's cushdy, Harry. What are you doing tomorrow?"

"Why?" Harry asked cautiously.

"I'm just asking, that's all. I was just interested how you and the lads down Pool were getting on."

"I'm taking some marines out for a training dive off the West Coast." Eli smiled, causing Harry to revert back to his cautious mode. "Why, what you after, Moon?"

"Just a favour, that's all."

"I knew it." The word 'favour' turned Harry's head in Eli's direction with a 'you'll be lucky' look on his face.

"Don't look like that, Harry. Wait until you've heard what I have to offer." Harry, not expecting much, gave him a 'go on then' rise of his head.

"Take my van and get rid of the contents on your training dive tomorrow and there'll be a nice drink in it for you."

"Never mind a drink. I've just swallowed half the fucking Thames. Now how much are you offering?"

"A monkey," bid Eli.

"Huh," dismissed Harry. "Five hundred quid? You're having a giraffe. Make it two grand and you've got a deal."

Harry upped the wages, knowing that whatever was in the back of the van wasn't just a few bags of rubbish.

"Laavly," said Eli, throwing him the keys to the van.

Harry didn't like it. Eli had agreed far too quickly.

"And a grand for my time here tonight. Those trackers don't grow on trees—they're an expensive bit of kit.

"You probably nicked it out of the QM's stores, but all right." Again, Eli agreed but with an extra clause. "But I want the van back, cleaned inside and out."

Harry still didn't know what he was getting rid of, but he accepted the terms, coerced by the three-grand wages.

Errol pulled alongside in the Range Rover, with the other two SAS troopers in the back. Eli climbed in, still smiling at the deal he had just struck with Harry. Errol, seeing his glee, knew exactly what it meant.

"So, I presume Harry Cawood is getting rid of the bodies?"

"Yeah," Eli replied, smiling even more.

"How much is he charging?"

"Not enough," was declared with a giggle.

"So why did we let the Irish lads get away with so much?"

Eli paused, taking a smoke, while asking himself the same question.

"Because, my friend, there's a bigger picture. What they've got is fuck all compared with what we're going after next and we need those lads to pull it off. All we've done is make sure that they've got a bit of cash on the hip so they'll stay out of trouble until we call on their services. Besides, I like them, and they did tell us about the bomb, which proved their character. They're professional, they've got balls and they fucking stick together. It must be nice to have mates like that."

Eli, pushing his point, looked across at Errol with a smile and then over his shoulder at the other two troopers, nicknamed One-Way and Ringer. He did have friends like that and these were them. Like the Irish lads, they had been through thick and thin together. Maybe it was because of these similarities between his crew and Michael's that he had spared them, but you never knew with Eli. You never knew his reasons for any of the decisions he made.

"Right, come on then, me old china plates. Let's go down the pub and get pissed. One-Way, it's your round!"

The Range Rover pulled away, leaving SBS Harry still taking off his wetsuit at the rear of the Transit. With the keys Eli had just thrown at him, he opened the rear doors and looked inside to satisfy his curiosity. It was dark, but even with the only light coming from the mooring lamps of the yachts around him, he could still make out the shapes of the three bloodied bodies in the back. His head shook slowly side to side, accompanied with a deep sigh.

"Eli Moon, you fucker. I knew I should have asked for five grand," he muttered to himself, knowing he'd been kippered on the deal.

"Be lucky, Harry," came Eli's fading goodbye, as the Range Rover disappeared from sight.

TO BE CONTINUED?

AND FINALLY,
BUT MOST APPRECIATIVELY

I WOULD LIKE TO THANK THE MEMBERS OF MY FAMILY, FRIENDS AND PEOPLE I RESPECT, WHO ALLOWED ME TO USE THEIR NAMES AND WAYS. IT WAS ANOTHER AID THAT MADE WRITING MY NOVEL MUCH EASIER BY BEING ABLE TO VISUALISE YOUR FEATURES, MANNERISMS AND QUIRKS WHILST APPLYING THEM TO MY CHARACTERS.

ESPECIALLY YOU, "MISTER," BENNY MAGUIRE. A TRUE IRISHMAN AND FRIEND TO MYSELF AND MANY MORE. LIKE THE OTHERS PORTRAYED YOU BARE NO RESEMBLANCE IN LIFE TO THE CHARACTER I MOULDED IN YOUR AURA, APART FROM YOUR CANTANKEROUS WAYS AND PIPE.

ZANI on Social Media

If you love this book and ZANI, please follow us on Social Media.

ZANI is a passionate and quirky entertaining online magazine covering contemporary, counter and popular culture. A full spectrum of modern life regardless of gender, religion, race, age and lifestyle.

Follow us on Twitter
https://twitter.com/ZANIEzine

Follow us on Facebook
https://www.facebook.com/zanionline?fref=ts

Follow us on Instagram
https://www.instagram.com/zanionline/

More Books from
ZANI – Available on Amazon

Feltham Made Me: Foreword by Mark Savage – Paolo Sedazzari

ISBN-10: 152721060X
ISBN-13: 978-1527210608

The poet Richard F. Burton likened the truth to a large mirror, shattered into millions upon millions of pieces. Each of us owns a piece of that mirror, believing our one piece to be the whole truth. But you only get to see the whole truth when we put all the pieces together.

**A Crafty Cigarette – Tales of a Teenage Mod:
Foreword by John Cooper Clarke – Matteo Sedazzari**

ISBN-10: 1526203561
ISBN-13: 978-1526203564

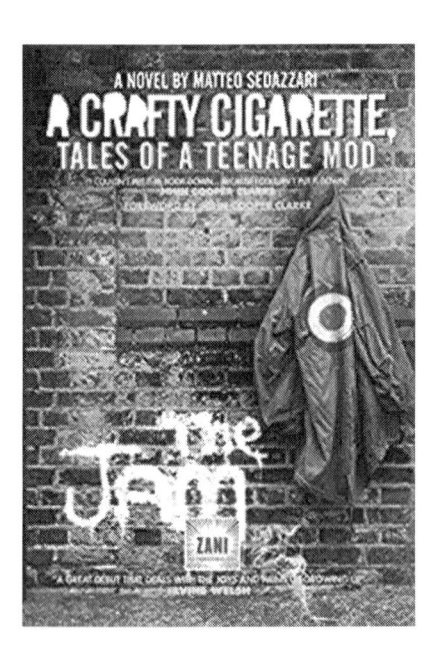

A mischievous youth prone to naughtiness, he takes to mod like a moth to a flame, which in turn gives him a voice, confidence and a fresh new outlook towards life, his family, his school friends, girls and the world in general. Growing up in Sunbury –on-Thames where he finds life rather dull and hard to make friends, he moves across the river with his family to Walton –on –Thames in 1979, the year of the Mod Revival, where to his delight he finds many other Mods his age and older, and slowly but surely he starts to become accepted...."

The Secret Life Of The Novel – Dean Cavanagh

ISBN-10: 1527201538
ISBN-13: 978-1527201538

THE SECRET LIFE OF THE

NOVEL

a unique metaphysical noir that reads like a map to the subconscious
- Irvine Welsh (Trainspotting)

DEAN CAVANAGH

"A unique metaphysical noir that reads like a map to the subconscious." Irvine Welsh.

A militant atheist Scientist working at the CERN laboratory in Switzerland tries to make the flmesh into Word whilst a Scotland Yard Detective is sent to Ibiza to investigate a ritual mass murder that never took place. Time is shown to be fragmenting before our very eyes as Unreliable Narrators, Homicidal Wannabe Authors, Metaphysical Tricksters & Lost Souls haunt the near life experiences of an Ampersand who is trying to collect memories to finish a novel nobody will ever read.

Tales of Aggro – Matteo Sedazzari

ISBN-10: 1527235823
ISBN-13: 978-1527235823

Meet Oscar De Paul, Eddie the Casual, Dino, Quicksilver, Jamie Joe and Honest Ron, collectively known around the streets of West London as The Magnificent Six. This gang of working-class lovable rogues have claimed Shepherds Bush and White City as their playground and are not going to let anyone spoil the fun.

Printed in Poland
by Amazon Fulfillment
Poland Sp. z o.o., Wrocław